BLACK CRO CARDINALS

Ian Robert Bell

Published by New Generation Publishing in 2023, Copyright ©
IAN ROBERT BELL 2023

First Edition

All characters and events in this story are the product of the author's imagination and have no connection with actual persons living or dead.

The author asserts the moral right under the Copyright, Designs and Patents Act 1988 to be identified as the author of this work.

All Rights reserved. No part of this publication may be reproduced, stored in a retrieval system or transmitted, in any form or by any means without the prior consent of the author, nor be otherwise circulated in any form of binding or cover other than that which it is published and without a similar condition being imposed on the subsequent purchaser.

ISBN
    Paperback 978-1-80369-864-9
    eBook 978-1-80369-865-6

www.newgeneration-publishing.com

New Generation Publishing

Contents

Acknowledgements 1
Prologue 2
1 4
2 16
3 18
4 40
5 51
6 53
7 74
8 83
9 91
10 96
11 99
12 105
13 110
14 124
15 136
16 147
17 172
18 175
19 185
20 197
21 210
22 258
Epilogue 269
About The Author 272

ACKNOWLEDGEMENTS

The author wishes to thank the poet Anne Micklethwaite for all her help and encouragement over the years. I also wish to thank my friends Deepa Shetty and David Doncaster for having been such good neighbors and for helping me to sort out all the minor computer glitches that writers are prone to.

PROLOGUE

The Reverend David Saunders was in a happy mood as he sped along the country lanes of rural Oxfordshire on his brand new mountain bike. Three weeks ago he'd been appointed senior lecturer in theology at London University and was now considered a rising star in the faculty of Religious Studies where he worked. It only remained for him to enjoy the rest of his impromptu vacation, pedaling his bike across the Oxfordshire countryside before returning to college to take up his newly acquired position. Truly he didn't have a care in the world as he traveled down the winding lane that led to the village of Buckwell which had been his home and place of residence for the last five years.

Turning a bend in the road, he adjusted his speed and listened out for traffic. Apart from the shriek of a fox and the twittering of a few birds in the leafy hedgerows that lined either side of the lane, everything was quiet, indicating he had a clear run through for the final leg of his journey to the cottage where a welcoming breakfast of grilled bacon, button mushrooms and tomatoes would be waiting for him, expertly cooked by his wife Gail who was herself a deacon in their local parish church.

Picking up speed, he pushed down on the pedals and headed for home, already savouring the taste and smell of the freshly brewed tea and sizzling bacon he would enjoy once he got there. So absorbed was he in the anticipation of his feast, that he utterly failed to notice a sinister cloaked and hooded figure emerge from the shadows of a steeply wooded hedge to his right and step lightly across a drainage ditch into the centre of the road. Nor did he hear the hiss of steel as the figure drew out a long Japanese sword from the rather arcane and ornamental scabbard that hung from a belt around his waist.

It was over in less than a second. The speed and velocity of the bike, combined with the expert sweep of the blade in the stranger's hands had taken the Reverend Saunders head clean off his shoulders without so much as a gasp of surprise from the recipient of the blow. As David's decapitated head bounced off down the road, his bicycle, together with his headless body spouting fountains of blood, continued on for several seconds before finally keeling over into a ditch with both its wheels still spinning furiously and nothing more to mark the occasion other than the sound of a solitary owl calling out to its mate in the branches of the trees above. Of the mysterious cloaked and hooded figure there was no sign, for he – if indeed it was a man – had vanished from the scene almost as suddenly as he had appeared, leaving the narrow country lane free once more to return to its sweet and tranquil sleep.

1

Cardinal Foscari was a man in turmoil. Barely fifteen minutes ago he'd been sleeping peacefully in his bed when the phone had rung. Now he was hurrying through the darkened cloisters of the Vatican towards the bedroom of a dying Pope.

Foscari was praying as he ran, but his words were not the customary prayers of a senior member of the Catholic Church. Indeed, they were far more urgent and demanding:

'*Do not take him yet. Spare his life I beg you. Without him I am lost*'.

In spite of his age – he was seventy-three next birthday- Paolo Foscari toiled up the stairs of the papal apartments two at a time and managed to reach the second floor landing almost as quickly as the elevator which was coming up fast behind him from the floor below. On his way up he almost collided with a nun of the Order of Maria Bambina who was making her way downstairs at a brisk pace. Thinking nothing of it, the cardinal simply nodded an apology then continued on his way, all his attention now focused on the grim task that lay ahead of him.

Hesitating at the top of the staircase, he adjusted the bright red cardinal's cap on his head and began walking towards the group of people who were gathering outside the door of the papal suite. As he did so, he noticed an elderly priest who he recognized at once as Father Michael Donnelly standing alone beside the elevator door immediately to his left. The priest was trying to attract his attention with a wave, but the depth of the crowd and the unique gravity of the situation would not allow the cardinal to respond, so instead Foscari simply turned to the priest and raised his hand in benediction before proceeding on towards the closed doors of the papal private rooms.

As he drew closer, the cardinal lifted his chin and gave a sharp nod of his head. The doors opened and a thick curtain of security guards parted to let him through. He heard one agent mutter words into a device beneath the lapel of his jacket: 'The dean has arrived.' Then he went in.

Maybe it was a trick of the light, but the sitting room which formed the ante chamber of the pope's private apartment seemed smaller than he remembered. What surprised him even more were the number of people actually present in the room. There were at least two doctors, a nurse, two secretaries, Archbishop Meyer the Prefect of the Papal Household, four members of the Order of Saint Francis and five nuns, of which three were standing huddled together in a corner sobbing. Evidently he was too late. The Pope was already dead.

It was Archbishop Meyer who came forward to meet him. The seventy-year old German prelate was on the verge of a nervous collapse, prompting Foscari to take him gently by the arm and say: 'Leopold. You did your best for him while he was alive. Now we must attend to the practicalities of the succession.' These words seemed to have a calming effect on the old man who quickly regained his composure and began leading the cardinal forward into the dimly lit interior of the papal bedchamber beyond.

Entering the bedroom, Foscari was filled with a sense of foreboding. Directly in front of him was the huge Renaissance bed on which the body of Pope Gregory had been laid out in preparation for the ceremony that was about to commence. The bed took up much of the space in the otherwise bland and featureless room.

Around the bed, three senior cardinals were gathered, soon to be joined by Foscari himself in his capacity as Dean of the College of Cardinals. On the right side of the bed, Cardinal Alfredo Riboldi, the Secretary of State, and Cardinal Ottavio Martinelli, the Chief Confessor were already on their knees engaged in silent prayer, causing Foscari to have to edge his way round them to get to where the body of Pope Gregory lay beneath a plain white coverlet with the head slightly raised on a flat cushion, both hands neatly folded on his chest.

As he bent over to kiss the Pope's forehead, Foscari noticed a faint smear of what looked like vomit at the corner of the Holy Father's mouth and caught the unmistakable scent of almonds in the air intermixed with a hint of perfumed soap. Glancing up in the realization of all this might imply, he looked across the thin body of the dead Pope straight into the piercing gaze of Cardinal Lorenzo Spada, the Chamberlain of the Holy See and former Patriarch of Venice.

Foscari's blood suddenly ran cold in his veins. The man was not praying. He was waiting. Simply going through the motions of prayer and biding his time until the voting began for the election of a new Pope. More to the point, what was Spada doing in Rome at such short notice? As far as Foscari knew, Spada had been away in Venice on some business or other, though it was far more likely he'd simply taken a brief vacation to remove himself from the oppressive heat of the Roman summer. Perhaps because it was fairly late in the year and Rome was not so hot now that explained his timely return to the Holy City. Or perhaps, like some hungry vulture, he had already scented blood and was now circling in for the electoral feast that would surely follow on the news of Pope Gregory's death.

How would Spada do it, he wondered? Would he simply stand for the job of Pope himself, or would he put up a stooge to fill the vacancy – someone tame enough to carry out his orders without thinking? Gregory had been a capable administrator, neither too conservative not too liberal in his religious beliefs. Spada on the other hand was an unknown quantity. A casual opportunist with no particular axe to grind, nobody knew what he was thinking or where his true interests lay. He could be in league with the Devil for all anyone cared. There simply weren't enough cardinals around who were sufficiently capable of filling the role of Supreme Pontiff and Spada knew it. All those that mattered had simply shied away from the poisoned chalice that was the job of leading the Church, and of the others, there were few who had not committed some major misdemeanor over the years sufficiently grave enough for them to be ruled unfit for holding office as the Vicar of Christ. Such a situation left only five cardinals remaining who stood any chance of being elected: Martinelli the Chief Confessor; Alfredo Riboldi the Secretary of State; Bartolemeo Boschi, the Prefect of Ecclesiastical Affairs; Lorezo Spada, the Chamberlain, and, of course, *himself*...

He shuddered at the thought of becoming Pope, but even more worrying was the realization that now, as Dean of the

College of Cardinals, it would become incumbent upon him to manage the papal election.

He'd never have believed it possible. He'd always assumed that he would die before Pope Gregory who was only sixty-nine years of age and in reasonably good health for a man of his years. Now it seemed Foscari would be responsible for the organization of the electoral conclave under the most difficult of circumstances. A true poisoned chalice if ever there was one.

As Cardinal Riboldi began intoning the liturgy, Foscari realized the others were waiting for him. Lowering himself carefully to his knees, he cupped both hands together in prayer and rested his elbows on the side of the bed. Closing his eyes, he listened to Riboldi's sonorous voice reverberating inside the tiny room:

'*Receive his soul and present it in the presence of the Most High...*'

The words fluttered around inside his head without any meaning. When the liturgy ended, Foscari remained kneeling where he was with the other three cardinals in silent prayer. However, it was not a prayer for the soul of the dead Pope that he recited in his mind, but an altogether different and far more urgent prayer. He was now desperately praying that he might perform his duties as Dean of the Electoral College in the days that lay ahead so that a new Pope might be elected with the minimum of damage to the Church. And he prayed that it would not be Spada.

His thoughts were interrupted by the sound of a police helicopter clattering across the sky above the Piazza Santa Marta outside; a salutary reminder of the ever present threat of terrorism that had dogged the footsteps of the papacy ever since the resurgence of militant Islam and which threatened to impinge itself on the dead Pope's funeral and the election that would follow.

As the sound of the helicopter receded, Foscari returned to his thoughts. Still kneeling by the bed, he recalled his final meeting with Pope Gregory when he had requested permission to leave Rome and retire to a monastic order, effectively giving up his duties as Dean. But the Holy Father had only scolded him for his false humility before saying: 'Foscari. Yours is not the spiritual path nor ever will be. You are what we term one of the guardians of the Church. Without the wise stewardship of men like yourself there would only be chaos and...' The Pope had stopped in mid-sentence. It was almost as if he had some great secret to impart but couldn't bring himself to do so. Not even to the Dean of the College. That was the last time Foscari ever saw him alive.

With the liturgy over, the four cardinals remained where they were for a while. What terrible secret had stilled the Pope's words that day, Foscari wondered. What awesome power was it that he feared. Yes, it was fear that he had witnessed in the Holy Father's eyes during that final conversation. A very deep and sacred fear that was beyond human comprehension.

The room was utterly still. Hardly daring to move, Foscari turned his head a fraction and half-opened his eyes. Behind him was the sitting room where everyone was on their knees with their heads bowed. He sensed a movement and turned back. As he did so, something caught his attention. There was another man standing in the shadows immediately behind the kneeling figure of Cardinal Spada. He could make out the man's face very clearly but noticed that whoever it was, he appeared to be wearing the full regalia of a cardinal just like himself.

Such a thing was in complete contravention of the rules, thought Foscari peering into the gloom to get a better view of the shadowy figure standing partially concealed behind the hanging drapes that surrounded the bed. In what little light there was, he imagined he saw in the man's face the unmistakable features of Umberto Lomellini the Vatican Librarian, but he couldn't be sure. What was even more irritating was the fact that he would just have to bide his time and wait for the ceremony to end before he could question the man. Returning to his prayers, Foscari pressed his face back into his hands and closed his eyes. When he opened them again, the man had gone.

The silent vigil completed, Foscari rose to his feet and allowed the Prefect of the Papal Household to edge past him. The papal ring had to be removed and it took some time for

Archbishop Meyer to work it off the dead Pope's finger before it came free. Then, carrying the ring over to Martinelli, he offered it to the cardinal who took a pair of metal shears from a silver box and inserted the seal of the ring between the blades. There was a sharp snap and the seal depicting Saint Peter was severed. Then Foscari helped Martinelli place a thin white veil over the Pope's face. The throne of the Holy Father was now vacant.

* * *

In the sitting room, the crowd had broken up into several small whispering groups. Only Archbishop Meyer chose to stand alone by the sofa with his back to the others. He was staring down at a chessboard laid out with a set of pieces on a small table next to the sofa. A telephone was close by.

'They say it was a heart attack that finished him.'

'Oh really,' Foscari replied placing a comforting hand on the Archbishop's shoulder. 'But I thought he'd been given a clean bill of health from the doctors.'

'Not entirely,' continued Meyer turning round. 'There were signs.'

'Signs… What sort of signs?'

'The Holy Father had been unwell for several weeks. He was quite lethargic at times and complained of stomach pains accompanied by nausea and vomiting. Headaches as well.'

Foscari blinked in surprise. 'He said nothing to me.'

'He wouldn't. He told me to keep quiet about it. He said the moment the news got out there would be a scramble for his job. He had enemies.'

Enemies…? It was a strange word to use thought the Dean. All living Popes had rivals to power. Those who held different views to their own… issues about abortion, women in the church; that sort of thing – but never *enemies.* It was the sort of term a medieval Pope might have used but certainly not an expression in keeping with the twenty-first century.

'Who found him?' inquired Foscari, regarding the Archbishop firmly. 'I know this is difficult for you Leopold but we need to prepare a detailed press release. Who found the Holy Father's body?'

'I did, Your Eminence. As Prefect of the Household I am usually the one who is closest to the Pope on a daily basis apart from those nuns of the Order of Maria Bambina who prepare his food and old Father Donnelly who lives in the attic upstairs.'

'And what did you do?'

'I called the Holy Father's doctor,' Meyer replied nodding in the direction of a youngish-looking man with dark hair and spectacles who was standing in a corner talking with Cardinal Spada.

Foscari thought for a moment then turned back to the Archbishop. 'You discovered the Pope dead in his bed?'

'Not exactly. The Holy Father was still alive, but only just. He managed to utter a few words before his soul left him, then he turned his head onto the side of his pillow and died. He vomited as well... only a little at the corner of his mouth. Doctor Casella wiped it off with a damp flannel. I think he was going to attempt mouth-to-mouth resuscitation but...well, it was too late anyway.'

'What time was it when you found him?'

'Around five thirty, Your Eminence. The Holy Father was in the habit of waking up around four in the morning when one of the nuns serve him a pot of coffee and some buttered toast. I usually tap on his door at half past five when we have our first meeting of the day.'

'Why wasn't I informed sooner of his death?'

'I would have called you, Eminence, but Cardinal Spada took charge of the situation first. He is the Chamberlain after all.'

Spada turned his head at the mention of his name. It was quite a small room and the sound carried easily. Pretending not to notice, Foscari continued with his gentle interrogation of Meyer.

'I believe you told me that the preparation of the Pope's food and drink were solely the duty of the nuns of the Order of Maria Bambina. The only nuns I see present in this room are the five standing over there by the door, and they belong the

Daughters of Charity. Who was it who served the Holy Father's breakfast this morning?'

'It was Sister Veronica, Your Eminence. She is of the Order of Maria Bambina. It was she who served the Pope his coffee and toast at around the usual time.'

'And where is she now?'

'On her way back to the Naples region I expect. That's where she comes from. She'd requested two weeks leave to visit some relatives and I signed her off after a brief discussion with the Pope. He said it was okay and that Sister Catherine could take over her duties for the time being. Sister Veronica left to catch the morning train after serving the Holy Father his breakfast.'

Foscari nodded. That would explain the presence of the nun he'd almost collided with coming up the stairs earlier on. She was from the Order of Maria Bambina and she'd been carrying a suitcase. Even so, he thought it prudent to ask a further question.

'How long has Sister Veronica been with us Archbishop?'

'Not long, Your Eminence. In fact she only arrived last week. She came on Cardinal Spada's personal recommendation.'

Meyer's words confirmed the Dean's worst fears. The old fool had allowed Spada to get a foot in the door. Sister Veronica – whoever she was – had been planted in the papal household right under his very nose.

'The cup, Archbishop— Where is it? Fetch me the cup Pope Gregory drank his coffee from.'

'It's on his bedside table, Eminence. I'll go and get it right away.'

As Meyer left the room, Cardinal Spada broke off his conversation with the doctor and came over to where Foscari was standing by the sofa. In spite of the gravity of the occasion, his appearance was remarkably fresh and youthful. Exactly how old he was, it was impossible to guess. He seemed to be a man in his late forties or early fifties, yet according to the register of cardinals he would be celebrating his seventieth birthday next spring. Foscari made a mental note to check the records. Spada looked way too young to be a cardinal…

The man came up beside him and spoke in a measured Venetian accent: 'I'm sorry, Dean if you were offended by the delay in informing you of Pope Gregory's death, but I felt that as Chamberlain it was my duty to protect the integrity of the Church. Whenever a Pope dies as suddenly as our dear Gregory did, it is important to ascertain the facts. You only have to remember all those malicious rumours surrounding the death of Pope John Paul the First – all the media and press speculation that he'd been poisoned. This time there must be no doubt that the Supreme Pontiff died of natural causes.'

The power of Spada's physical presence was almost too much for him, causing Foscari to back away a little before replying: 'My dear Lorenzo, my sole concern has always been for the well-being of our Holy Mother Church. I really should have been informed sooner. I am after all the Dean of the College of Cardinals.'

The Venetian edged closer once more and presented Foscari with a sheaf of papers which he hastily withdrew from beneath the folds of his cassock. His breath was cold and smelled like a graveyard.

'What's all this?'

'Pope Gregory's medical records. I requested them from Doctor Casella over there. These are the results of an angiogram that was carried out only last month. As you can see, there was clear evidence of a problem with the Holy Father's heart.'

Foscari ran his finger down the column of print. Signs of a blockage together with an enlarged aortal valve. The records could easily have been faked, but either way Spada had him in a trap. The public had to be informed and the faithful had to be reassured that Pope Gregory had died by the will of God and not by the hand of man. An autopsy was out of the question.

'Very well Lorenzo. Release the data to the press if you must, though I'm not entirely convinced that the Pope died of natural causes.'

'I agree Dean, but what choice do we have.' It was Cardinal Lomellini the Vatican Librarian who spoke. He'd just entered the room and was reading the report over Foscari's shoulder. Foscari turned, and as he did so he noticed

Archbishop Meyer returning from the bedroom empty-handed and with an expression on his face like someone who had just boarded an airliner then realized they'd left the gas on at home.

'It's gone, Your Eminence—'

Foscari excused himself from the conversation and both Spada and Lomellini returned to talk with the doctor.

'*What do you mean, Archbishop?*' inquired the Dean quietly.

'The cup the Holy Father drank his coffee out of— It's no longer there!'

The Dean furrowed his brow; 'And what about the coffee pot?'

'It was a cafetiere, Your Eminence; and yes – that's gone too.'

For the second time that morning Foscari's blood ran cold. There were simply too many coincidences. But who would be stupid enough to poison the Holy Father, especially after the scandal surrounding the death of Pope John Paul the First. It would mean the end of the papacy surely...

'… And what in the name of God is that!?' exclaimed the Dean pointing to a small paper bag which Meyer had just retrieved from beneath his robe.

'It's a bag of sweets, Your Eminence. I found them on the Pope's bedside table.'

'A bag of sweets?'

'Yes. They're sugared almonds. They were the Holy Father's only vice. Care to try one?'

Almonds… That would explain the peculiar scent hovering around the Pope's mouth. He'd been eating sugared almonds shortly before he died. So it wasn't cyanide the assassin had used… assuming the Pope had actually been murdered. Perhaps he really had just died of a heart attack after all. But that didn't explain the missing cup and cafetiere, nor did it account for the presence of the man standing immediately behind Cardinal Spada in the Pope's bedroom. The one who disappeared so mysteriously…

Archbishop Meyer was staring down at the chessboard by the sofa lost in his thoughts. 'Those chess pieces are in the

English style,' he remarked. 'They were a present to the Holy Father from his friend Cardinal de Valois.'

'Who?' replied Foscari only half-interested.

'Edward de Valois, Your Eminence. Both he and the Pope used to play chess together whenever the cardinal visited Rome. They'd been friends for years apparently. That old-fashioned telephone sitting there next to the board is what the Holy Father used to call him on. He wouldn't use any other phone when he was talking to Cardinal de Valois. Strange thing that when you come to think of it.'

Cardinal de Valois... The name sounded familiar but for some reason Foscari couldn't recall ever having seen it in the register of active cardinals and made a mental note to check it out just as soon as the meeting in the sitting room was over. He would also have a word with Father Donnelly as well. He recalled how Donnelly had tried to catch his attention out on the landing shortly before he'd entered the Pope's apartment. Maybe the old Irish priest knew something?

'Leopold—'

'Yes, Eminence?' replied the Archbishop looking up.

'Leopold... You said that the Holy Father managed to utter a few words shortly before he expired. You don't happen to remember what they were by any chance?'

'Indeed I do, Your Eminence.'

'Oh really. And what did the Holy Father say?'

'Well most of it was pretty much garbled, but I distinctly remember him saying something like: *"Silver did this... It was Jimmy Silver... He has powerful clans backing him... The Camorra... He means to claim the Vatican for his own and take control of the Bene Noctu."*'

Foscari became silent for a moment. Nothing of what the dying Pope had said made very much sense apart from the word *Camorra;* the name of a notorious criminal organization based around the city of Naples which controlled much of the surrounding region including parts of central Italy and the north. Was it possible that the Camorra were in some way implicated in the poisoning of Pope Gregory and that the murder was carried out on behalf of a criminal mastermind called Jimmy Silver who appeared to have plans to take control of the Vatican using men like Spada to front the operation? It all seemed too far-fetched to be true, but wait a minute - didn't the Archbishop say that it had been Sister Veronica who had served the Holy Father his coffee that morning. She was from the Naples area wasn't she? Maybe she'd been planted in the papal household by the Camorra acting on the instructions of this guy called Jimmy Silver? Here was a connection at least.

'Leopold—!'

'What, Your Eminence?'

'Get these people out of the sitting room immediately and seal off the papal apartment. No one is to go in or out of this room without my express permission, is that understood.'

'But…'

'No buts, Archbishop. Do it now! That's an order.'

'Yes, Eminence.'

'Oh, and before I forget; did the Holy Father manage to say anything else before he died?'

'No. Not very much. There was one thing though…'

'And what was that?'

'He said: *"Warn them… Warn them in England… The war has started… A blood sacrifice… Tell Cardinal de Valois to summon his exorcists… Tell him to warn Sterling and the others… Tell Sterling to watch her back… She's the only one who can end this… Sterling is our only hope—"*'

The Dean raised an eyebrow. 'And that was all he said?'

'Yes, Your Eminence. That was all, apart from some gibberish about a winged lion or some such nonsense. Shall I order the people out of the room now?'

Foscari was only half-listening. He was deep in thought, tapping a curled forefinger against pensive lips. 'Uh… yes, I think you should do that Archbishop. Do it immediately. I'm going to have a quiet word with Father Donnelly. I have a feeling he may be able to cast some light on the situation.'

2

Thames Valley Police HQ
Oxfordshire, England.

'That's the strangest thing of all.' remarked DC Paul Conran answering his colleague, Detective Inspector Martin Welbeck. 'The victim's helmet camera was switched on at the time of the incident but doesn't actually show what caused the reverend Saunders to lose his head.'

'There's no explanation for the decapitation then?'

'None that I can see inspector, and I've watched the recording more times than I care to remember. Want to see it again?'

'Okay. Run it through one more time just to be sure.'

Up until half an hour ago, the major incident room of the Oxfordshire police station had been a hive of activity, with cops meeting up for their briefing on the murder of David Saunders and what each member of the investigation team was to do next. Now the room was practically deserted except for the presence of DC Conran and DI Welbeck who had stayed behind to discuss the significant details of the case. Unfortunately there weren't any. All the helmet camera had shown was the image of a country lane. Tall hedgerows and trees seen from the vantage point of a moving cyclist at dusk. Then:

'There—Look! Saunders has glanced to his right. He's seen something in the bushes.'

'Yes, inspector. Then his head came off along with his cycling helmet and the camera attached to it and started bouncing off down the road.'

'No. Look closer. There's a shadow in the bushes. It's moving...'

Conran peered at the monitor screen for a moment then shook his head. 'It's nothing. Just a bit of pixel distortion, that's all.'

'Run it again.'

DC Conran obliged, and the sequence started up once more with Inspector Welbeck drawing closer to the screen until his nose was almost touching it.

'Those aren't pixel distortions Paul. It's the image of a man stepping out into the road in front of the oncoming cyclist. It's not very distinct but you can just about make out the head and shoulders… It's like he's wearing a hooded cloak or something.'

Conran followed DI Welbeck's pointing finger and drew in a sharp breath. The image of the man in the road was wavering like a poorly engineered hologram – three-dimensional and yet without any real substance to it. And there was something even stranger about the cloaked and hooded figure who was brandishing something that looked like a machete or Japanese sword. He didn't appear to have any legs.

'He… He's got no legs, inspector. The man's body stops at his waist.'

'Well that explains a lot, Conran.'

'How do you mean, sir?'

'The lack of footprints for one thing. According to the Crime Scene Manager, there were no footprints in the bushes where the incident occurred.'

'What… Nothing?'

'No. Not so much as a snapped twig or a blade of compressed grass. It's just as if nobody had been there at all.'

'That doesn't make any sense, sir.'

'I agree. Either our killer's been exceptionally clever in covering up his tracks or…'

'Or what, inspector…?'

'…Or we're dealing with a bloody ghost!'

3

Father Donnelly's apartment was quite small in comparison to all the other rooms in the building. There was nothing personal in it. Just pale yellow walls and plain curtains. A standard issue desk plus a sofa and two armchairs completed the picture along with the obligatory crucifix on the wall near the entrance to the kitchen. On the coffee table in front of him, Foscari noticed a tiny traveling chess set, its miniscule red and white pieces all huddled together in the centre of the board, locked in some deadly endgame that seemed destined never to be resolved.

'We used to play chess together,' declared Donnelly emerging from the kitchen carrying a tray. 'His usual partner was Cardinal De Valois, but I stood in for him whenever the cardinal was away.'

'You played chess with the Holy Father?' said Foscari, barely able to conceal his surprise.

'And why ever not?' the old priest replied. 'The Pope was a good player and he said it helped him relax in the evenings.'

'Who usually won?'

'He did, Your Eminence… More often than not.'

Foscari glanced around as Father Donnelly poured out the coffee and offered him a biscuit. Snapping the biscuit in half, the Dean took a bite followed by a sip of coffee.

'Don't worry,' observed the old priest wryly. 'It's not poisoned.'

'Why do you say that?' Foscari responded, taken aback by Donnelly's inappropriate sense of humour.'

'Because I can tell what you're thinking, Your Eminence. I used to be a Benedictine monk in my younger days. A vow of silence teaches a man to be observant.'

Silence…Yes, that was it, thought the Dean. Father Donnelly had been silent for almost the whole time he'd been in the room. That was well over twenty minutes ago and apart from the current conversation, Donnelly had barely uttered a single word… *until now.*

'The medical records say he died of a heart attack,' the Dean continued, taking another sip of coffee.

'And you believe it?' Donnelly replied taking a seat.

Cardinal Foscari could tell the bearded old Irishman was in no way intimidated by his presence in the room. If anything, it was almost as if the priest had assumed control of the meeting from the outset. Benedictine monks had a notorious reputation for doing that sort of thing ever since the time of the Spanish Inquisition and clearly Father Donnelly was no exception.

'I'm not sure,' said the Dean, beginning to feel increasingly uneasy beneath the priest's steady gaze. 'I mean, it could just be a coincidence. The Pope had been ill for quite some time apparently.'

'*Apparently...?*' echoed Donnelly, his gaze not wavering for a second. It was almost as if the old man was peering into his soul.

Was that how the Inquisition did it all those years ago, thought Foscari. Getting those accused of heresy to talk their way into a trap? For an instant, the Dean felt himself transported back in time to a more harsh and brutal age. Tapering wax candles and barred windows. The silence of the condemned cell. The inevitable confession under torture and the final walk to the execution ground...

'Yes. Apparently the Holy Father had been suffering from a chronic heart condition. His medical records confirmed it.'

'Pope Gregory had the constitution of an ox,' exclaimed Donnelly cutting in. 'Why the sudden decline? It makes no sense.'

Foscari was becoming increasingly irritated and decided to put the impudent old priest in his place:

'Were you by any chance a doctor before you became a priest, Father Donnelly?'

'No, I was not, Your Eminence, but I've had some training as a male nurse. The Pope was in reasonably good health for a man of his years.'

'Then how do you explain all the symptoms, Donnelly?' According to Archbishop Meyer, the Pope was suffering from chronic lethargy in the weeks before he died. He was also experiencing some abdominal pains, nausea and vomiting.

Headaches as well. What more proof do you need? At first I thought he may have been poisoned when I smelled the scent of almonds on his lips – usually clear evidence of cyanide toxicity. But then Meyer showed me the sugared almond sweets the Pope had been eating shortly before he died. He even offered me one from the bag the Holy Father kept on his bedside table. So you see, the Pope couldn't have been poisoned with cyanide.'

'I never said he was,' replied the priest lowering his gaze for a moment as he reached into the folds of his cassock and withdrew a small shiny object made entirely out of glass.

'What's that?' inquired Foscari looking down at Father Donnelly's outstretched palm.

'It's an empty poison vial, Your Eminence. The same one that was used to deliver the poison that killed the Holy Father.'

The cardinal blinked in surprise. 'You did it—!'

Father Donnelly shook his head. 'No, it wasn't me. I didn't kill Pope Gregory. I found this vial on the secret staircase that leads down into the Pope's bedchamber. His assassin must have got careless and dropped it there.'

'Secret staircase…?'

'But of course, Dean. What did you expect? This is the Vatican after all. Our ancestors were a cunning load of bastards, I'll give them that!'

Foscari reached across the table to take the vial out of Donnelly's hand only to have it snatched away with a firm reprimand.

'No you don't— We need to keep this for evidence.'

'But I'm the Dean,' protested Foscari. 'I outrank you by at least five levels of seniority within the Church. That vial is my responsibility.'

The old priest only sighed and put the vial back inside his robe: 'On the contrary Dean Foscari. It is I who now outrank you. The vial is mine to keep until I am instructed otherwise. Rest assured that it will be handed over to Inspector Moro of the Vatican police in due course should the need arise.'

'What—? I don't believe I'm hearing this!'

'You'd better believe it cos it's happening. The Pope was poisoned and now I'm in sole charge of this vial until Cardinal de Valois arrives in Rome and decides what best to do with it.'

De Valois... There was that name again, thought Foscari. The man who was the personal friend of the Holy Father. What in God's name was going on?

'But Pope Gregory died from natural causes. His medical records confirm as much.'

'Medical records be blowed. Gregory was poisoned with digitalis. They'd probably been feeding him with it for several months before he died to fake the symptoms of an illness. What killed him was a final massive dose poured into his coffee from the vial.'

'Digitalis you say?'

'Yes, Your Eminence. More commonly know as foxglove. It's a bit old-fashioned I'll admit, but then that's the kind of people we're dealing with. Folk who are a bit *old fashioned,* if you know what I mean. It's just the sort of poison they would use'

'They...? And who exactly are *they,* Father Donnelly?' inquired Foscari growing increasingly tired of the charade.

'Mother of God! Next you'll be asking me how much I know and what an old Irish priest like myself is doing living directly upstairs from the Pope.'

'The thought had crossed my mind, Donnelly. What exactly *are* you doing here?'

'Simple. I'm the Holy Father's spiritual guardian, Your Eminence. Have been ever since he was elected. All Pope's have them'

'*Spiritual guardian...* Appointed by whom might I ask?'

The priest said nothing in response to Foscari's question but merely gave a beatific smile and glanced upwards towards heaven. Obviously the old man was stark raving mad, prompting Foscari to ignore his lunacy and continue delivering the protocols of the situation: 'The only people responsible for the well-being of the Holy Father are Archbishop Meyer, Cardinal Martinelli his confessor, and of course, Lorenzo Spada, the Chamberlain of the Holy See...'

Foscari stopped in mid-flow as the realization of what he'd just said sank in. Now all his suspicions were confirmed. 'Cardinal Spada is implicated in the poisoning of Pope Gregory. It was him...'

'Aye, him and a few others, Your Eminence. But you mustn't blame yourself. We've all fucked up on this one. Taken our eyes off the ball so to speak.'

The Dean became silent for a moment. His thoughts were racing around inside his head like a pack of greyhounds on dog-track.

Spada means to become Pope and implement a more conservative regime in the Vatican. But who's behind him? He couldn't have planned this all by himself. He needed to have accomplices.

'Accomplices...' The voice belonged to the priest but for some reason it seemed to come from somewhere else deep inside Foscari's brain.

'What...? But I didn't say anything, Father Donnelly.'

'Yes, but you thought it, Your Eminence.'

The priest was smiling again, but this time it was an all-knowing self-satisfied kind of a smile. He could tell that he'd startled the Dean and sat back waiting for the reaction.

'You know what I'm thinking?'

'Thinking, Your Eminence? There's some like myself who can see into your very soul. And you do have such a beautiful soul, Paolo Foscari. A very beautiful soul indeed. A soul that has a great deal to accomplish in the days that lie ahead.'

Foscari dismissed the priest's words as being nothing more than the ramblings of someone in the first stages of senility. Not an uncommon state of affairs in an organization filled with so many old men. But then Donnelly suddenly changed tack:

'You're probably wondering what I was doing on the secret stairwell when I found the empty vial.'

'I was as a matter of fact,' answered Foscari, growing more and more bewildered at the priest's apparent ability to read his mind.

'Well, I thought I heard a noise and came downstairs to check it out. The secret staircase begins in my apartment and leads off down to the level of the papal suite before tapering off into the rest of the Vatican.'

'Mmm… But you found your way to the Pope's apartment did you not, Father Donnelly?'

'Indeed I did, Your Eminence. When I reached the level of the staircase immediately outside the papal bedchamber, I found the empty vial on the floor and heard a sound coming from inside the bedroom. It must have been Archbishop Meyer finding the Pope's body, because a couple of minutes after that I heard the doctor arrive along with someone I took to be a nurse. With all the commotion going on, I made myself scarce and went back upstairs to my room. Here, I'll show you where my section of the secret staircase begins if you don't believe me.'

It was true. There really was a concealed stairway running through the building. It began in the priest's own bedroom hidden behind a stand of hinged bookshelves and wound its way downwards like a snake into the darkness below. 'There's another hinged panel in the wall to the left side of the Pope's bed downstairs where a person can enter and have a private meeting with the Holy Father without anyone being any the wiser. It's most likely been there for centuries, Your Eminence.'

'*So the Holy Father wasn't poisoned by Sister Veronica,*' muttered Foscari thinking aloud.

'Oh yes he was,' answered Donnelly, 'but Sister Veronica didn't drop the empty vial, nor did she enter the Holy Father's bedchamber by the secret way. She came in through the sitting room and delivered the Pope's breakfast to him in the usual manner. Someone else then entered via the hinged panel and emptied the poison out of the vial into the Pope's coffee cup when he was lying in bed listening to the radio. All Sister Veronica had to do was collect the coffee cup and cafetiere later to remove the evidence, but for some reason she didn't. The vial itself must have been dropped by the same person who put the poison in the Pope's coffee, and it was dropped on the secret staircase. An easy mistake to make.'

'Lomellini—!' exclaimed the Dean forgetting himself for an instant. 'He must have returned to pick up the coffee cup and search for the vial.'

'I don't understand, Your Eminence.'

'Let me explain,' said Foscari making his way back to the priest's living room. 'When I was kneeling in prayer by the Pope's bedside, I thought I saw a shadowy figure standing directly behind Cardinal Spada. At first I couldn't make him out, but then I thought he bore a distinct resemblance to Umberto Lomellini the Vatican Librarian.'

'Hmm, it would make sense,' observed the priest. 'Cardinal Lomellini is Spada's right-hand man. He has connections with the Naples region like Sister Veronica.'

'He has?'

'Yes. It's where he was born— Didn't you know?'

'Er... well, no I didn't as a matter of fact. I know I'm Dean of the College of Cardinals but I can't remember every single detail about them all. Whatever the case, it looks like Sister Veronica and Lomellini were both working together as part of an assassination team, don't you think?'

'It certainly looks that way, Eminence.'

Foscari halted for a moment, regarding the priest intently. 'Father Donnelly,' he said. 'Do you think Spada has his eyes on the Holy See?'

'Spada has had his eyes on the throne of St Peter's for years, Paolo. He means to become Pope, of that I am certain.'

'My reasoning exactly, Donnelly. How many votes do you think he can muster in the forthcoming election?'

'Off-hand I couldn't say, but he's a popular candidate among the more conservative members of the Church. He also enjoys considerable support with large sections of the general public.'

Foscari's eyes darkened. 'Who's behind him, that's what I want to know. Do you think we have another Sindona on our hands?' he added, referring to one of the main players in the notorious Vatican banking scandal of the 1970s.

The priest looked away for a moment, then sat himself down again in his armchair studying the endgame on the chessboard in front of him.

'It's more serious than that,' he murmured, idly moving one of the chess pieces then putting it back into the same position on the board. 'All the pieces that can be taken have already been taken. Now both sides prepare for the final conflict out of which there can only emerge one winner.'

'What do you mean, Father?' said the Dean, now in the full realization that Michael Donnelly knew an awful lot more than he was letting on.

The old priest let out a sigh. 'This may come as a bit of a shock to you Cardinal, but there's a great deal more at stake here than the future of the Papacy.'

'Such as what?'

'Ha! Now there speaks a man who's been thoroughly institutionalized by the Church. I was of course referring to the future of humanity as a whole.'

Sitting down in the chair opposite, Foscari narrowed his gaze and addressed the priest directly: 'What are you trying to tell me, Donnelly? Speak freely, for I can assure you that your words shall not pass beyond these four walls.'

The bearded cleric smiled. 'Cardinal Foscari, he said. 'Are you in any way familiar with an organization known as the Minor Order of Exorcist?'

The Dean frowned. 'No I am not. Is that a Benedictine group?'

Donnelly threw back his head and roared with laughter. 'No, Your Eminence. The Office of Exorcist was never part of the sacrament of Holy Orders as such, but as a sacrament it was first confirmed on those who had the special charisma to perform its duties.'

Foscari cut in. 'All priest are trained in exorcism these days, Donnelly. It's been that way for a long time. I repeat, I have never heard of the Minor Order of Exorcist. Where is it based?'

'Right under your very nose, Cardinal Foscari,' replied the priest leaning forward in his chair. 'Right under your very nose…'

'Pardon me—?'

'It's based in Rome, Your Eminence. Has been ever since the Council of Carthage back in 398 AD. That was well over one thousand six hundred years ago in case you didn't know.'

'What? You mean to say there's an entire department of the Church that I'm not even aware of?'

'Yes, but I wouldn't go beating yourself up over it. Very few people actually know of its existence, and why should they. It's not as if they have any reason to.'

'Who heads it? Somebody must be in charge of it?'

'The man currently responsible for it is Cardinal deValois who performs the role of Chief Exorcist for the Vatican. The organization currently has around two hundred and fifty priests under its command; a higher number than usual on account of the upsurge in demonic possession in recent years – and of course because of the increase in the number of vampires.'

'Vampires…?'

'Yes, them; and quite a lot of other stuff as well - but mainly them. Their numbers have been growing recently to the extent that they have even begun to infiltrate the Church and threaten the very foundations of society.'

More lunacy, thought Foscari. *Priests like Donnelly should have been retired years ago. It just isn't fair keeping them on beyond their time.*

'And then there's the problem of the Camorra and organized crime to consider,' Donnelly went on, seemingly oblivious to Foscari's look of pity and derision.

'What about it?' queried the Dean, suddenly becoming interested once more. Vampires were one thing, but Donnelly's reference to the Camorra was more than topical given the connection with Sister Veronica. Now *that* actually made sense.

'They mean to take over the reins of government, Your Eminence. It used to be that they only concerned themselves with feeding like vultures on the remains of the banking system, a few lucrative building projects plus a bit of fraud and such like. Now they've got their eyes on the main prize – complete control of the Italian state and most of Europe with it.'

'So what's the Church got to do with it, Father Donnelly?'

He shouldn't have said it, should he? The most obvious thing in the world and he'd totally missed the point. The Church actually *had* got something to do with it and a whole lot more. If the Church wasn't prepared to step in and halt the tide of decadence and corruption that was currently sweeping the world, then who was: *'In nomine Patris et Filii et Spiritus Sancti...'*

'Amen,' said the priest, concluding Foscari's quiet prayer.

'How?' was all the Dean said in response.

'Ah now, there you've put your finger on it, Eminence. How indeed. Men like Jimmy Silver have had an awfully long time to build up their criminal empire on Italian soil. Whole centuries in fact, along with others like themselves who shun the light of day. Years of spiritual neglect has rendered the Church practically in capable of doing anything about it but stand on the sidelines and watch as whole sections of—'

'Stop!' exclaimed the Dean raising his hand. 'What did you say just then?'

'I said, years of spiritual neglect had rendered the Church practically useless in the face of the rising tide of—'

'No. Before that. You mentioned a name. What was it?'

'Jimmy Silver?'

'Yes, that was the name—Jimmy Silver. I've heard that name mentioned before.'

'Oh really,' exclaimed the priest, somewhat surprised. 'And where exactly did you hear it?'

'The Holy Father uttered it in his final words shortly before he died. Archbishop Meyer told me.'

Donnelly looked concerned. 'Did the Holy Father say anything else?'

'Yes. Rather a lot, but most of it didn't make much sense.'

'Go on... Tell me.' The priest said quietly.

Foscari glanced to one side, thinking. 'Well, according to Meyer, the Pope said something like: *"Silver did this... It was Jimmy Silver... He has powerful clans behind him... Camorra... He means to claim the Vatican for his own and take control of... of the..."* - 'Oh, I can't remember his words exactly.'

'The *Bene Noctu?*' said Donnelly, finishing Foscari's sentence for him.

'Yes. That was it. The Bene Noctu— You've heard of it?'

The priest said nothing in reply but simply continued with his interrogation of the Dean, only this time his questions were more urgent and demanding.

'And what else did Pope Gregory say?'

'He said; *"Warn them in England... The war has started... A blood sacrifice... Tell Cardinal de Valois to summon his exorcists... Tell him to warn Sterling and the others... Tell Sterling to watch her back... She's the only one who can end this—"* 'What does it all mean, Father Donnelly? I need to know.'

Again the priest said nothing. Rising slowly out of his chair he stood up and regarded the Dean kindly. 'Would you like another coffee Cardinal Foscari, or maybe something a little stronger? A brandy perhaps…?'

'Urm… Well it's a bit early in the day for me and I don't usually drink brandy, but…'

'Good. I'll make it a double then. Just a moment.'

From where he was seated, Foscari watched as the elderly priest wandered into the kitchen. In a short while, Donnelly returned with a bottle and two medium-sized glass tumblers. 'Here,' he said; 'get this brandy inside of you Dean. You're going to need it. And would you care for a cigarette as well?'

'Smoking isn't permitted in the Vatican, Father.'

'It is up here, Your Eminence,' the priest continued, sliding a pack of cigarettes across the table towards the Dean. 'These are Chesterfield Blues. I have them specially imported. Care to try one?'

Cardinal Foscari shook his head. 'No thanks, Father, but you go ahead anyway. I'll make an exception in this case.'

* * *

It was getting on for about three in the afternoon and Foscari had been talking with the priest for well over two hours. He had also drank more than his fair share of the priest's brandy and was beginning to feel ever so slightly intoxicated.

'Yes, Silver is the man behind Spada', replied the priest lighting up his fourth cigarette of the afternoon. 'He also has connections with the Neapolitan Camorra crime-gangs. Reports coming our way suggest a major build up in their activities in that region lately. Silver controls a lot of what goes on but lets the Camorra have a bit of leeway on their own turf.'

'And what part of Italy does Jimmy Silver come from, Father?'

'He's not Italian. He's an English aristocrat by birth, though that was all a long time ago. He visits Italy occasionally to attend to his business interests but tends to spend much of his time on the south coast of England and in France. His criminal empire is growing and now covers a considerable part of Europe including Italian soil.'

'But how has he managed to do that in so short a space of time Donnelly? Such an undertaking should have taken him years to accomplish. It doesn't make any sense.'

'Well lets just say that Jimmy Silver, or Sir James Blackthorne as he was once known, has been at it for quite some time and leave it there shall we. His plan is to get Lorenzo Spada elected as the new Pope. Once he has accomplished this he will have gained political control over the whole of the Italian peninsula and most of continental Europe.'

'I don't understand,' said Foscari. 'How would taking control of the Vatican possibly guarantee Silver any political influence in Europe? It might have worked in the Middle Ages perhaps, but not in this day and age surely.'

'What makes you think I'm talking about temporal power, Your Eminence? Jimmy Silver is strictly old-school. He means to take control of the Vatican for spiritual reasons – which is of course where the only real power in this world of ours actually resides.'

'Oh... erm, yes, yes of course, Father Donnelly. Spiritual power is what it's all about in the final analysis. I dare say it would give him control over much of the Catholic population I'm sure, but what about all the rest?'

'I wasn't referring to people or any specific belief system, Dean.'

'Then what?' continued Foscari who was now gazing with covetous eyes at the cigarette packet which lay half open beside the priest's brandy glass. Donnelly obliged by sliding the packet across the table to him once again. Go on, Your Eminence— Take one. You know you want to.'

The Dean hadn't smoked in a long while and feared he might be sick, but then he quickly relaxed when he rediscovered the feeling that smoking a cigarette was the most satisfying thing in the world. It was then that another thought occurred to him:

'You mentioned that Jimmy Silver used to be known as Sir James Blackthorne, Father. When was that?'

The priest raised a bushy eyebrow. 'Ah, now that would be asking a lot, Your Eminence.'

He was playing with his mind again, thought Foscari taking another draw on his cigarette.

'You haven't answered all my questions about the Pope's final words, Donnelly. As well as mentioning Silver, the Holy Father also said that Silver had powerful clans backing him up. I'm assuming he was referring to the Camorra and other criminal organizations; but who exactly are the Bene Noctu? You didn't say…'

The priest cleared his throat and thought for a moment. 'The Bene Noctu are a group of loosely connected clans ranged against Jimmy Silver and those who support him. Silver means to take over the Vatican first then deal with the Bene Noctu later.'

Donnelly had chosen his words carefully. Too carefully in fact. A rudimentary study of his body language said it all. The priest was concealing something – something very arcane and strange, or so it seemed to Cardinal Foscari now sitting forward in his chair ready with another question.

'And who heads this organization?'

'What organization?'

'The Bene Noctu, Father. I thought I made myself clear on that point.'

'Oh, that— Yes, yes you did, Your Eminence. Loud and clear in fact.'

'And…?'

'Well, the Bene Noctu aren't exactly a criminal organization as such. They're more of a council really... A bit like the College of Cardinals if you like, only they don't exactly represent what you would call *Christian interests* if you get my meaning.'

'They're criminals then?'

'Not in the usual sense of the word, Eminence, but I dare say all of them have done some pretty bad things in their time. They're headed by Count Francesco Grimaldi. He's a former Italian aristocrat who used to be Lord of Milan when titles like that still mattered in the world.'

'And when might that have been, Father Donnelly?'

'I can't remember off-hand, Your Eminence. Oh, ever such a long time ago it was. Ever such a long time ago...'

'What's a *long time,* Donnelly? How long ago?'

'Oh, maybe a couple of centuries or more, give or take a few decades. Count Grimaldi was a product of the eighteenth century - and not one of its better products either.'

The priest was being evasive again. Foscari realized that he would have to become a lot more astute in his questioning if he wanted to catch the Irishman off his guard.

What exactly was it that he was concealing, the Dean wondered? Considering everything he'd learned so far, it appeared that he'd stumbled across a conspiracy so labyrinthine and arcane that it rendered any storyline invented by a contemporary thriller writer practically amateurish in comparison. No, he had merely scratched the surface of things, hadn't he. Aristocracy was involved in the plot too, and it was an aristocracy that went back a long way. Whatever this thing was, and whatever its origins, it had its roots so deeply embedded in the past that it made his flesh crawl.

'Cardinal de Valois—!' exclaimed Foscari, banging his fist down hard on the table. 'What's his part in all of this?'

To his surprise, the elderly priest hardly stirred in his seat, his gaze remaining as steady as a candle flame during High Mass.

'Dean Foscari,' he said in his soft Galway accent; 'Edward de Valois is beyond reproach in these matters I can assure you. Indeed, you would not have been so accusatory in your tone if

you had not realized that Cardinal de Valois has only recently been bereaved of a very close friend.'
'Oh... I'm sorry...'
'No matter. You weren't to know,' continued Donnelly offering Foscari another brandy. 'It happened a couple of days ago. The reverend David Saunders – an Anglican vicar – was killed while out riding his bicycle in the Oxfordshire countryside when some bastard stepped out from behind some bushes and decapitated him with a Japanese sword.'
'They what—?!'
'They cut off his head with a Japanese sword... One of the bigger ones at that.'
'Spare me the details, Donnelly... Why for heaven's sake?'
'We don't rightly know, Your Eminence, but we suspect it may have had something to do with the reverend Saunders being a practicing exorcist and with him living in England, which is also Jimmy Silver's country of origin among other things.'
England... There it was again thought Foscari, recalling the Pope's final words: *"Warn them in England..."* Was there a connection between the reverend Saunders's death and the poisoning of Pope Gregory he wondered?
'But why would anyone do such a thing, Donnelly?' Were they insane?'
'Not in so many words perhaps, but I know what you mean. There are plenty of loons out there with a grudge against the Church, but this particular killing was quite specifically targeted.'
'By whom?'
'Jimmy Silver and the rival clans more than likely. David Saunders wasn't a member of the Catholic Church as such, but he had been trained as an exorcist in Rome and was a personal friend of Cardinal de Valois. It was Silver's way of softening us up for his main assault on the Vatican.'
'A declaration of war in other words?'
'Yes Dean. You could put it that way I suppose. We think the assassin may have been a Frenchman by the name of Charles Martel – also known as the Executioner of Paris. He's

a freelance hitman by the way who has occasionally worked for the Church – but not recently.'

'He's what—?!'

'There- I thought that would shock you, Dean. Never mind. Have another cigarette. It'll calm your nerves.'

Determined to get to the bottom of things, Foscari renewed his interrogation of the Irishman with increased vigour, this time focusing his attention on Pope Gregory's last words.

'Tell me Father Donnelly, exactly what did the Holy Father mean when he said, *"Warn them in England... The war has started... A blood sacrifice..."* What did he mean by the term *"blood sacrifice"?* Was he referring to the death of the reverend Saunders perhaps?'

The priest sighed, realizing he would now have to divulge more than he should. 'The war the Pope was referring to has been coming on for a long while. It's a grudge match between all the vampire clans of Europe with control of the Vatican thrown in as the final prize.'

'Uh-huh,' Foscari nodded. 'Go on...' He didn't believe a word of what the priest was saying but for some reason he kept on fingering the pectoral crucifix he wore around his neck just to be on the safe side.

Father Donnelly shifted his position in his chair and continued: 'Jimmy Silver is what you might call an *alpha vampire* – a top apex predator who has somehow survived long enough to establish control over a large number of the Undead. He is also a criminal mastermind with an underworld empire that covers most of Europe, including the criminal gangs of southern England and the Italian mainland.'

'I see. Hence the Camorra's involvement and the killing in Oxfordshire?'

'Exactly. You got it in one, Foscari. Silver is a powerful clan-master in all senses of the word, and as such he is a danger to the Church and society as a whole. Ranged against him are the Bene Noctu and a number of other loosely knit vampire clans and criminal organizations who would stand to lose out big time if he ever took over, not to mention the effect it would have on the Church and whatever else remained of human civilization in the aftermath of such an event.'

Foscari looked down at the chessboard on the coffee table. He still didn't believe a word of Father Donnelly's story but there it was all laid out on the board in front of him. The red pieces held all the power in the game, threatening checkmate in less than three moves. There wasn't much time.

'The papacy is a huge burden, Cardinal Foscari. People need to be reminded of that fact.'

The old priest was looking directly at him this time, almost accusatory in his gaze. What did he mean? More to the point, Donnelly still hadn't said anything about the use of the term "blood sacrifice" and its connection with David Saunders.

Donnelly shook his head. 'No, Your Eminence. It wasn't Mr. Saunders. It was someone else. Someone who we must protect at all costs; or at least until the papal election is over and Cardinal Spada is eliminated.'

Foscari didn't understand. Either he was way out of his depth or the priest was indeed suffering from senile decay. But whatever the case, there was still a number of other questions the Dean required answers for and for which Father Donnelly might provide a more rational response.

'In his final words, the Pope made reference to a "winged lion." Have you any idea as to what he may have been referring to?'

'I don't know off-hand, Your Eminence. The only winged lion I can think of is the Lion of St Mark the Evangelist which is also the symbol of the city of Venice. It might be a reference to Spada who was the Patriarch of Venice before he became Chamberlain to the Pope. Other than that I truly cannot say.'

Well at least the priest was making some sense at last, thought Foscari preparing himself for the final inquisition. Somehow he fancied his next line of inquiry might prove to be the most important one of all.

'Pope Gregory said something else before he died, Father Donnelly. I believe I mentioned it to you before, but you failed to give me a satisfactory answer...'

'Mmm... What was it, cardinal? I don't remember things too well these days.'

'Gregory distinctly said: *"Tell Cardinal de Valois to summon his exorcists... Tell him to warn Sterling and the others... Tell Sterling to watch her back... She's the only one who can end this."* What does it mean, Father?'

The priest narrowed his eyes. 'Don't issue me with ultimatums, Cardinal Foscari. When I said that the papacy was a huge burden I meant it! The Holy Father had been under a considerable amount of strain shortly before he died, which is the main reason why I was sent here in the first place. To protect the Pope!'

'Sent here—? Who by? I certainly didn't send for you, and, as far as I am aware, neither did Archbishop Meyer or the Secretary of State!'

Father Donnelly simply smiled. 'There are those in authority with far greater power than you or I, Dean. A man like yourself should know that by now.'

Now Foscari grew desperate. 'I need answers Donnelly and I need them fast. Soon there will be cardinals traveling into Rome from all over the world for the election of the new Pope. I will be forced to summon the Conclave and then there will be no time for an inquest into Gregory's death.'

'That won't be a problem, Dean.'

'Oh... And why not may I ask?'

'Because there isn't going to be an inquest or even an autopsy for that matter. The Holy Father's medical records were clear enough. He died of natural causes. In fact, as far as I know, Pope Gregory's body has already been embalmed so there's no point anyone looking for traces of poison. They probably won't find any.'

'What—?'

'I'm afraid it's true, Cardinal Foscari. Now you see what we're up against.'

'But I didn't order any embalming to be done.'

'You've been overruled, Dean. It was most likely Spada who gave the order, and he's a bit difficult to reach at the moment on account of him having to travel to Venice on urgent business. He won't be back until next Wednesday, or so I've been informed. That's when he will return for the election.'

'How convenient for him.'

'How convenient indeed – and it would be a damn sight more convenient for us all if you would cease this fruitless interrogation of me and just listen to everything I have to say. What Pope Gregory said to Archbishop Meyer in his final words was important. Cardinal de Valois is in England at the moment attending to some urgent matters at his end of the problem. He will be alerting all the exorcists under his command to be on their guard for when Jimmy Silver launches his main assault. They will be armed and under strict instructions to show no mercy.'

'Armed? I wasn't aware that our exorcists were armed, Father Donnelly. What sort of weapons will they be carrying if you don't mind me asking?'

'Each will be issued with a 9mm automatic pistol and one hundred rounds of ammunition. They're special bullets made in Rome and blessed with holy water from St Peter's basilica.'

'For what purpose exactly?'

'Killing vampires of course! What on earth did you think—!?'

Foscari said nothing in reply. There was simply nothing more he could say other than to express his thanks to Father Donnelly and apologize for having wasted his time. The old priest was clearly stark raving mad.

'That's perfectly alright, Your Eminence,' replied Donnelly showing him to the door. 'I expect you'll be wanting to get a bit of rest before your trip to London.'

'Pardon me?' replied Foscari with a flicker of his eyelids.

'Your flight to London. It's been booked for the day after tomorrow. It's a specially chartered flight by the way. Only the very best for a cardinal of the Roman Church.'

'But I don't recall having ordered any flight to be booked in my name.'

'You didn't. It was booked in advance. I had Sister Bernadette purchase your ticket shortly before you arrived here. You'll find it posted through your letter box when you arrive back at your apartment. It's outbound only on account of the fact you'll be traveling back on the Vatican jet with your cargo, assuming everything goes according to plan.'

'Cargo?'

'Yes, you'll be returning with a passenger more than likely.'

'Who?'

'A young English lady if you must know. Her name is Rachel Morrison and she's a student of theology at London University. She's been placed under the protection of the Church until further notice. Any more than this I cannot say until I receive further instructions from my superiors.'

'But I can't go to London, Father Donnelly. I have to make preparations for the election of a new Pope.'

'Ah now, don't you go worrying yourself about a little thing like that, Dean. It's all been taken care of until your return. There'll be plenty of time for the election once we've neutralized Cardinal Spada and his supporters. It's what Jimmy Silver's up to that should be our main concern for the moment. He's the prime-mover in all of this.'

'But this is all highly irregular, Donnelly. You can't just interfere with a papal election like that... it's... it's tantamount to interfering with the Will of God!'

The priest smiled benignly and gazed directly into Foscari's eyes. For a moment, the Dean could have sworn he heard the sound of heavenly voices. There was also the distinct smell of almonds in the air which at first reminded him of the peculiar odour hanging around the Pope's deathbed until he recalled that the scent of almonds was also a sign of great sanctity and spiritual presence. Clearly something else had taken over the proceedings and he wasn't altogether sure as to what that particular *something* might be...

'Following your arrival in London, Cardinal Foscari, you will be met at the airport by several of our operatives and taken to a safe house. There you will wait until your contact arrives. Assuming our people in England have done their job and everything has gone according to plan, Rachel Morrison will be delivered into your hands and then you are both to return to Rome and the relative safety of the Vatican City.'

'Who is this person called Rachel Morrison? Why is she so important?'

'Rachel is the weakest link in our chain, Your Eminence. She is what the ancient Hebrews used to call a sacrificial lamb. She is Jimmy Silver's principal asset without which his plans will surely fail.'

'How come?'

'That is a very good question. From the intelligence reports we have received from Cardinal de Valois, it would seem that Rachel Morrison has been specially selected to be sacrificed to the infernal powers of Hell in return for control of the Vatican. Once Jimmy Silver has the person of Rachel Morrison in his possession and her ritual sacrifice has been accomplished, then his path towards the complete and total domination of the Western world will be a foregone conclusion.'

'The election of an Anti-Pope in the form of Lorenzo Spada...?'

'Precisely, Your Eminence. So you can see how important it is for you to travel to England without delay.'

'But why me?'

'Because the burden of the papacy is a hard one to bear, Cardinal Foscari, and because you are the Dean of the current administration. It now falls to you to ensure that the forthcoming election of the new pope goes according to God's Will and that Lorenzo Spada is eliminated from the contest in the first or second ballot. *It's your job.*'

'It is?'

'I'm afraid so, Dean. Oh, and talking of elimination, you may be interested to know that Sister Veronica was killed shortly after her arrival in her home town. She was gunned down in the street by someone riding on the back of a motor scooter. Needless to say, her assassins have yet to be found.'

'She was murdered?'

'Yes. It looks like the Camorra are busy covering up their tracks, most likely at the behest of Cardinal Spada I shouldn't wonder. Anyway, we've drifted off the subject of our conversation. The house you'll be staying in during your time in London belongs to the Church. It's a Catholic seminary called St Jude's and has largely been evacuated of its present incumbents for the duration of the hostilities.'

'Hostilities—?'

'Yes. You may encounter some resistance from Silver and his associates during your time in England. I shouldn't worry though. You'll most likely have plenty of protection – Cardinal de Valois will have seen to that. The only other problem you may experience would be the presence of Cardinal Patrick Streffan. He's a personal friend of Lomellini and we think of Jimmy Silver also. Leastways, that's what de Valois and Sterling believe.'

'Sterling…? I've heard that name mentioned before. Pope Gregory alluded to it on his deathbed. He said something like: "…*Tell Sterling to watch her back… She's the only one who can end this…*" What exactly did he mean, Father Donnelly? Who is Sterling? What is her part in all of this?'

'You'll find out soon enough once your plane lands on British soil. No doubt someone will put you in the picture on your arrival in London. Now, if you've no further questions, I will bid you farewell and wish you a pleasant journey.'

With that, the priest made to open the door and show Foscari out, but the Dean stayed his hand: 'Wouldn't you like to ask me for my blessing Father Donnelly? I believe it is the custom on occasions such as these.'

'*Your blessing—?*' exclaimed the old Irishman, somewhat taken aback. 'It's my fucking blessing you'll be wanting if you're on your way to meet Sterling and her crew! Take my advice and get a good night's rest, Believe you me, you're going to need it—!!'

4

The Admiral Rodney Public House
North London

Late evening. A sleek, low-rider motorcycle with raised handlebars and twin exhausts pulls up outside a rundown pub in north London. The engine is switched off and its female rider swings a leg across the saddle before heeling down the kickstand with her other foot. Standing in the road for a moment, she glances round to make sure she isn't being followed, then strolls over to the pub and pushes open the door.

Heads turn as she walks into the bar with a slow and purposeful stride. She is a young, sharp-featured white woman with long black hair the color of midnight and wearing mirrored sunglasses that totally conceal her eyes. A few people glance up from their drinks. Those who don't know her simply return to their newspapers, mobile phones and conversation without giving the matter a second thought. The few who do just get up and leave. It's safer that way.

As a pub, the Admiral Rodney had seen better days. A conventional sort of place, its last makeover had been in 1998 when the landlord had sold it off shortly before topping himself following a row with his girlfriend. Since then, it had been downhill all the way until the old redbrick building had ended up as little more than a drinking den for terminal alcoholics, petty thieves, prostitutes and those members of the student population who couldn't afford to drink anywhere else. It was also where the local branch of the British Far Right were rumored to hold their council meetings, but the woman who had just wandered in through the door wasn't any of these people. Her name was Sterling and she was ten times worse.

Now she moved closer to the bar counter, glancing all the while to her left and right. It didn't pay to drop your guard in a dive like the Rodney. The tables and benches scattered throughout the room boasted several professional pickpockets, two hookers well past their sell-by date, their pimp, a crack dealer and an old bag lady forever locked in deep conversation with her imaginary friend. Up at the far end of the room were two glowering skinheads from the Far Right performing a slow ritual movement around the pool table. Otherwise the place looked fairly secure.

However, experience had taught her that appearances in a venue such as this could prove dangerously deceptive, so she scanned the room once again just to make sure. No, there weren't any of her kind in here. Just the ghostly, spectral form of the pub's former landlord who was sitting by the window staring down at the floor in despair. The fate of all suicides who spit in the face of God and decide take their own lives.

Walking up to the counter, she was able to get a closer look at the current bartender. He was a youngish-looking man with light-brown hair, a sallow complexion and the sort of face that is forever helping police with their inquiries.

'Hello,' she said.

'Yeah?' answered the man. His way of asking a potential customer what kind of drink they wanted.

'I'd like a whiskey,' she answered back firmly.

'What sort of *whiskey?*' the bartender inquired, adding bad breath and three days growth of chin-stubble to his reply.

'Jack Daniel's—and make it a double.'

The young man reached down and withdrew a small tumbler glass from beneath the counter before turning on his heels and filling it from one of the reversed servitor bottles that hung upside down on a rack behind the bar.

'Cheers,' the woman exclaimed, taking a swig from the glass. 'Having one for yourself?'

'No thanks,' replied the bartender eyeing her suspiciously. He'd never seen her in the pub before and there was something about her that made him feel distinctly uneasy. She telegraphed him the flicker of a smile and he felt all the hairs on the back of his neck slowly begin to rise.

'No worries,' she answered, casually looking around. Then she turned to the barman once again: 'Say squire, I was wondering if you could help me?'

'What makes you think I can?' the man responded, standing his ground even though his knees had started to tremble violently and his bowels had begun to loosen.

The woman smiled again, this time pulling down the metal zip of her black leather jacket ever so slightly. 'Well I've often found that if I really need something, then there's usually a bloke on your side of the bar who can give it to me. I'm looking for a young lady called Rachel Morrison. Y'know her-?'

The man blinked then glanced over to the two skinheads standing beside the pool table. They'd stopped their game and were now gazing apprehensively at the scene now being played out at the bar.

'- And do I know you?' said the bartender staring straight into the face of the mysterious woman with the sunglasses, black hair, biker jacket and jeans.

'No – you – don't,' she answered back without shifting her stance.

'I see... Billy! I think we've got trouble—'

At this, a third man appeared from the back room adjacent to the pool table and strolled across the floor of the bar followed by the two skinheads, each of them brandishing their pool cues menacingly in their hands. Silence descended on the lounge bar of the Admiral Rodney as the woman turned to face them. A couple of people got up and left the room.

'You've got a bleedin' nerve coming in here Sterling,' said the third man who was much older and more powerfully built than the other two. 'If Shaun Tulloch ever finds out you're on his turf there'll be hell to pay. He still hasn't forgiven you for causing the death of his brother. You know that—'

'It was all a long time ago, Billy. His brother just got caught up in the crossfire, that's all. Let it go.'

'Is that a warning, Sterl?'

'No. Just good advice, Billy.'

The man, who's full name was Billy Taylor and who stood a full nine inches taller and wider than the woman he was talking to, signaled the two shaven-headed thugs at his side to stand down and relax. 'Everything's cool,' he murmured softly to his chums. 'She's just here for some information, that's all.'

'She was asking after Rachel,' the bartender put in, his hand slowly reaching under the counter once again. The man called Billy made eyes at him and the bartenders hand reappeared above the counter, empty.

'What you looking for Rachel for?' inquired Taylor, squaring up to the woman, desperate not to lose face in a place as public as the Admiral Rodney.

'Because I'm on a mission from God,' she replied with a thin, wry smile.

Hearing this, the giant troglodyte with the cropped ginger hair and facial tattoo's suddenly burst out laughing: 'You—on a mission from God!? That'll be the day, Sterling. Hey, you hear that boys. Sterling's says she's on a mission from God. Anyone here believe her?'

The two skinheads shook their heads but didn't share in their master's joke, preferring instead to flank him like a pair of minders even though he was probably the last person on earth who needed their protection.

Billy Taylor was over six foot nine inches tall and weighed in at three hundred and fifty pounds. Judging by the shape of his head and the row of enormous incisor teeth in his upper jaw, Sterling could tell that Taylor wasn't fully human, being most likely descended from a mountain Troll way back in his remote ancestral past when the world was a far darker place. She also noticed another member of the Rodney's regular clientele get up and leave. This time it was Jenny Hancock, one of the district's more notorious pickpockets. She'd obviously decided to vacate the place before a fight broke out and take her trade elsewhere, as had her accomplice who'd been sitting next to her. As they both left, Sterling considered reaching for the small semi-automatic pistol she kept concealed in her inside jacket pocket, but then thought better of it. Opening up so early in the game wasn't a mistake she could afford to make. Besides which, it would have alerted Jimmy Silver to exactly where she was and what she was up to, and that was another mistake she couldn't afford to make.

'So you're on a mission from God then are you, Sterling?'
'That's what I said, Billy.'
'Well you don't look like no *Angel* to me.'

'I guess that puts us both on the same page then, Bill.'

'Yeah. I guess it does. So, what do you want to know?'

'The precise whereabouts of Rachel Morrison. I've heard she sometimes comes in here with a few friends. You happen to know where I might find them?'

She could tell from the deeply entrenched furrows in his brow that the process of thought was an alien concept to a man like Billy Taylor. As the seconds ticked by, Sterling became aware that she was fast running out of time. If Jimmy Silver had truly planned to snatch Rachel Morrison from the streets of London, then he would most likely have done it by now and there wasn't a damn thing that she or any of her associates could do about it. Somewhere deep inside her guts, she already knew that Rachel was gone, and, that if Silver had truly killed her, where her body was most likely to be found. It was a foregone conclusion.

Memories... A body washed up on the south coast of England. The place – somewhere near the town of Rye. The time – 1977. Back then, the body had been her own – or rather, it had been the body of a young woman called Julie Kent – the person Sterling used to be but somehow wasn't anymore.

Images... The British movie actor Christopher Lee starring as Count Dracula in a 1960s horror movie. Fangs extended, he moves towards the camera and hisses out his challenge to the world. Well that much was true, but the scriptwriters had left out all the rest: The grim metamorphosis. The first realization of precisely what it was that you were turning into. The loss of your reflection in mirrors, and, finally, the loss of your soul. No. The scriptwriters hadn't mentioned that bit... What it actually meant to be a member of the Undead. And yet, in some perverse kind of way, Sterling had survived her ordeal at the hands of Silver and his friends. Survived to become the creature she was today – a walking nightmare straight out of the tales of myth and legend, forever doomed to wander the earth until some chancer got lucky and put an end to her when her back was turned. But at least she was still "alive" in a certain sense, even if she cast no reflection in mirrors and left no shadow on the ground. Somehow she knew the same could not be said for poor Rachel Morrison. No, Rachel was going to be used by Jimmy Silver for a much different purpose entirely. Had not Cardinal de Valois told her as much.

Taylor had stopped thinking now and was regarding her with a strange look. 'No,' he said. 'I don't know where Rachel or any of her friends are, and even if I did, I doubt very much if I would tell you. I wouldn't know what I was letting myself in for.'

'Oh, and what do you mean by that, Billy?' she inquired softly.

'You know exactly what I mean. The last time any of the north London firms got caught up on a ruck between you and Silver, two of my crew were found dead in a back alley missing at least five pints of regular 'O' type from a hole in the side of their necks, while a third ended his days banged up in a loony bin complaining of voices inside his head and a pair of red eyes that kept staring out at him from the walls of his padded cell— That's what I mean!'

'But this time it's different, Billy. I work for different masters now. You know that.'

'It still doesn't make it any better though, does it? Even with the Church on your side, you'd be hard put to offer us any protection if Silver and his cronies ever got to know we'd helped you out.'

'What— Not even if the future of democracy and the fate of mankind as a whole were at stake?' she replied, drawing herself closer to Taylor's ear so the others couldn't listen in on what she was saying.

Again Taylor laughed: 'Since when has that ever bothered a creature like you, Sterling? You're just another bloodsucker like all the rest of them. There's no real difference between you and Jimmy Silver when all said and done. Now just piss off and leave us alone. You know the rules—'

The rules… Yeah, she knew the rules alright. But the rules went so far back in time that nobody followed them anymore. From what she'd been told, the laws that governed the interaction of the realm of the Undead with that of the criminal underworld were all written down in a book called the Incunabulum – a book of such enormous power that only two copies of it were known to be in existence. One was held in the

Vatican Library in Rome under the jurisdiction of the Pope. The other was kept safely under lock and key by an alpha-vampire know as Count Francesco Grimaldi, the current secretary of the Bene Noctu who also happened to reside in the Holy City. But Grimaldi's hold on power among the vampire clans was waning, a situation that was equally matched by the Pope's inability to regulate the warring factions within the Catholic Church. Try as they might, each of the two leaders had very little influence over events within their respective organizations. Basically, no one gave a shit anymore. Human or vampire.

'Okay Billy. Suit yourself then. But don't expect any help from me or Jerry Skinner next time the police come knocking on your door. You're on your own this time.'

Taylor frowned. 'I'm sorry, Sterling. Really sorry. It's just that I can't afford to lose any more men. Not like the last time.'

'Yeah. We've got a thing about outsiders,' added one of the minders flanking Taylor.

'Meaning what exactly?' said Sterling, turning to look at the youth.

'Meaning, we don't trust them.'

'You shouldn't,' she replied with a thin, wry smile.

Scanning the boy's mind, she caught the shock-wave of suppressed rage and hatred that surged within his soul. Already a killer at the age of thirteen, he had gone on to commit a whole series of other violent offences including at least three rapes and a particularly nasty mugging. The darkness that was beginning to eat away at his aura said as much. He was a piece of work.

Turning towards the door, she made her way out of the pub and onto the darkened streets outside. A strong breeze was picking up leaves from the pavement, causing them to dance before her eyes like so many carefree spirits of the night, but there was nothing carefree about Sterling's mood as she strode purposefully towards her motorcycle. She was just about to heel the kickstart down and ride off in the direction of Tower Bridge when she heard a voice from behind. It was Billy.

'Alright,' he said walking up to her, 'I'm sorry about what happened back there. I'll tell you what I know, but you must promise me never to reveal the source of your information, is that clear?'

'Okay, Billy— It's a deal. Tell me.'

Satisfying himself they couldn't be overheard, Taylor drew closer. 'It looks like Silver is involved with whatever it is that's going on around here. I got to know about it from Jenny Hancock just before you walked in – her what's friends with that mate of yours... Oh, I forget her name...'

'Debbie?'

'Yeah, that's right. Debbie Stephenson the shoplifter... Anyway, to cut a long story short, it seems like young Rachel went and got herself involved with the wrong crowd, if you know what I mean.'

'Who? People like you Billy?' Sterling replied with a mischievous grin.

'What— No, listen - I'm being serious here. Like I said, Rachel started associating with the wrong crowd of people. She was heavily into the Goth scene you see and had recently taken to dying her hair black and hanging out at that weird nightclub up in Kilburn.'

'The Jabberwock?'

'Yes. That club. It used to be run by a woman called Linda Bailey – the one who got her head cut off in France a couple of years back. Odd thing that. I never liked the cow myself. The one time she came in here she was bang out of order, throwing her weight around like she owned the place.'

'A bit like me then, eh Billy?'

'Oh, I wasn't meaning no offence, Sterling; honestly I wasn't.'

'None taken William. Anyway, do carry on. You're beginning to sound interesting.'

'Right. Well like I said, Rachel took to hanging around with this crowd from the Jabberwock. Most of them were students like herself. The Jabberwock is an easy place to get in, the booze is cheap and nobody asks any question.'

'But *I am* asking questions, Taylor, and I want some answers fast! Stop pussyfooting around and get to the point. I've a feeling we haven't got much time.'

'Okay, Sterling. So it's like this. Rachel was last seen in the Admiral Rodney on Saturday evening, which was about three days ago.'

'Was she on her own?'

'No, she was with a bloke.'

'Boyfriend?'

'No. At least, I don't think so.'

'Must have been her dealer then. What did he look like?'

'Fairly young. In his mid-twenties I'd say, with light brown hair and wearing an expensive-looking Hawaiian shirt and fawn-colored chinos. A regular little nonce if you ask me.'

'Did you happen to catch his name?'

'Yeah. Johnny I think he was called, but I didn't get his surname. They didn't stay long and both left the pub around nine o'clock. Rachel told one of the regulars they were going up Kilburn way to the Jabberwock but it seems like they never arrived.'

'How do you know?'

'One of Rachel's friends came into the Rodney around half-past ten asking where they both were. Apparently, neither of them arrived at the Jabberwock and they haven't been seen since Saturday night, though I've heard tell that this bloke called Johnny was spotted pissing it up something awesome at the Rose and Crown late on Tuesday afternoon like he'd just won the lottery or something.'

'That's interesting Billy. I think I know who this young man might be.'

'You do?'

'Yes. From your description of him, he sounds like a guy called Johnny Nolan – one of Linda Bailey's old firm from Maida Vale. And he's not a drug dealer neither.'

'What is he then?'

'He's a pimp, though I dare say he peddles a bit of dope on the side.'

'And you reckon he's done her in?'

'No I don't, Billy. Personally I think she was kidnapped by Nolan and then handed on to someone else.'

'People trafficking you mean?'

No, Bill. It's probably a lot more serious than that. Nolan had connections with Linda Bailey remember. Before she was killed, Linda was one of Silver's top agents in London, responsible for controlling much of the street crime and extortion rackets that go on north of the river. Looks like your hunch about Silver being involved in all of this was a correct one.'

'Oh…'

Taylor lapsed into silence as the precise nature of what he might be dealing with gradually sank in. The very mention of the name Jimmy Silver was usually enough to scare the shit out of most members of London's criminal underworld, and Billy Taylor was no exception. Even so, his natural curiosity and an overwhelming desire to always be in the know finally got the better of him.

'Linda got her head cut off, didn't she?'

'Yes, William, she did. What of it?'

'Nothing really, it's just that I heard in the news recently about this vicar who got himself killed while out riding his bike in the Oxfordshire countryside. Apparently, some nutter stepped out of the bushes and took his head clean off with a Japanese sword. Happened a couple of days ago.'

'Really—' exclaimed Sterling, suddenly growing interested. 'A vicar you say. What was his name?'

'I…erm… I'm not really sure.'

'His name, Billy! What was his name dammit?!'

'Er… Saunders I think it was. Yes, the Reverend David Saunders. Young bloke he was. Married an' all.'

'And his killer— You mentioned a weapon. It was definitely a Japanese sword his killer used, wasn't it?'

'Yes it was. Why do you ask, Sterling?'

The woman made no reply. She was too busy thinking. *He's killed a priest. Silver's hired the Executioner to kill a priest – an exorcist too. There'll be Hell to pay for this…*

'You okay, Sterling?' inquired Taylor with a look of concern.

'Uh… What? Oh, yes I'm fine. I was just thinking, that's all.'

'I see. So this David Saunders was someone you knew then?'

'You could say that our paths have crossed, William. I knew him through a friend of mine.'

Taylor knew when to leave it alone with her and promptly dropped the subject, only to resurface once more with another revelation.

'There was something else, Sterling. I was meaning to tell you earlier but I got sidetracked.'

The woman did not smile. In fact she seemed unusually tense. 'What was it?' she said urgently.

It's about Rachel. According to one of the regulars at the pub, young Rachel was up the duff.'

'She's pregnant—?'

'Yeah. Three months gone apparently. One of the students told me. Anyway, I'd best be getting back inside. There's a pint of Carling waiting for me at the bar and it's getting a bit chilly standing out here. Be seeing you. Bye—'

Sterling watched as Taylor departed. He glanced back only once then pushed open the door of the pub and went inside leaving her alone with her thoughts.

So Rachel's pregnant. But who by, that's the question? Eve was tempted by Satan and in that first act of sin the race of Vampires was born. Perhaps the seed of Satan has already been planted...?

She had to phone Cardinal de Valois and break the news to him as soon as possible, but just as she was about to reach for her mobile, she heard its unmistakable ring tone.

The cardinal had rung her.

5

It was getting on for eleven o'clock at night when a tall, smartly dressed elderly looking gentleman made his way across London in the direction of Oxford Street. He walked with a steady, measured pace and had about him such an air of confidence and arrogant superiority that it caused all who crossed his path to move out of his way and let him pass without so much as a word of complaint. Everyone that was except for Jenny Hancock.

Jenny was a dip – and expert pickpocket and one of the best on the streets of London. Moving like a symphony of stealth, she drew closer to her target until she was almost within striking distance. Then something made her pull back. He was a strange sort of a chap; well turned out but dressed in a manner which she found somehow oddly repellant. The fashion of a bygone age – almost Victorian in fact and definitely not the England of today.

No matter. That just made him an easier target as far as Jenny was concerned. With a secret gesture, she beckoned another young woman across the street to walk over and ask the man for a light of her cigarette. That was the distraction.

Now Jenny went straight for his wallet pocket with her nimble fingers and lifted out the contents in one swift movement. He never noticed a thing.

'Thanks mister. You're a toff!' said the distracter, taking a draw from her freshly lit cigarette before she and Jenny wandered off down the street as if nothing out of the ordinary had happened. Turning a corner, they heard the sound of a police mobile unit approaching and froze in their tracks. Had they been spotted on street-cam they wondered?

No. The police vehicle just sped on down the road, presumably on its way to attend to another incident. Good. Now was the time to see what they'd got. A fine leather wallet containing a thick swatch of high denomination banknotes. Real money in age of digital currency. Quite a haul.

'There's well over two grand in here,' exclaimed Jenny's accomplice. She couldn't have been much more than sixteen years of age but looked a lot older. Life on the streets had seen to that.

'And what's this?' she went on, running her fingers over a small black notebook with a red spine.

'Looks like the old geezer's diary,' observed Jenny. 'Pass it here. There might be stuff inside.'

Opening the book, she flicked through its pages, her rapidly knotting brow indicating complete mystification at its contents. 'I can't make no sense of it,' she said turning over the pages. 'Most of it is printed in Latin with Gothic lettering and looks quite old. There's some weird diagrams included as well and someone's written something in blue biro on the front flyleaf. It looks like a coat-of-arms showing three wolf heads on a shield with the name *"Blackthorne"* written beneath it. On the other side of the flyleaf also written in biro is what appears to be a list of numbers and letters all jumbled up. Probably some kind of a code I shouldn't wonder along with the names of two cities in Switzerland – Zurich and Lugano – both with arrows drawn pointing to the letter "V". The leather cover of the book has been embossed with the symbol of two old-fashioned keys crossed over one another beneath what looks like a broad-brimmed hat. Makes no sense at all.'

'Should we chuck it then?' said her friend glancing over her shoulder in case the police returned.

'Hmm… Maybe not,' replied Jenny closing the book and tapping it gently on her lips. 'I've got no use for it, but I've a feeling I know someone who might.'

6

An executive decision had been made to locate Operation Clergyman's Major Incident Room at West End Central police station – one of London's main police headquarters where there was still enough space available to accommodate the influx of personnel necessary to deal with the case. The incident room itself was situated on the third floor of the building where a number of senior police officer were now gathered to discuss the strategy for dealing with a series of horrific murders which had taken place over the previous few days, including one apparently committed in broad daylight in a popular London park, right slap-bang in the middle of a sleepy Sunday afternoon.

West End Central was an old nick recently scheduled for closure under the government's latest round of spending cuts until it was pointed out that it was one of the only police stations left in the capital large enough to host a venue for the type of incidents that occasionally happen in cities the size of London. *Just as well,* thought Detective Superintendent Sally Reid looking round the office. *There's enough senior coppers in here to police Wembley Stadium on cup final day. Somebody's really pulled out the stops on this one.*

The whole thing would be a home-from-home for Sally who had worked out of West End Central for the last five years. According to the spam circulated by email, the rest of the senior supervision would comprise Detective Chief Superintendent Colin Mathews from the Serious Crimes Division and Detective Chief Inspector Jim Carter, who was acting as the Office Manager for the duration of the investigation. Both these men were know to Sally, so it was fairly easy to guess what their management style would be, but there were several other men in the room who she wasn't familiar with, including a young Detective Inspector from Oxford CID called Martin Welbeck and another man from North Wales constabulary who went by the name of Owen Jones. Finally, sitting at the back of the room, was an elderly police officer who she recognized immediately as Inspector George Lefarge – or "Hooky" Lefarge of the Metropolitan Police. At this, Sally drew in a breath. *Lefarge*— What was an old dinosaur like George Lefarge doing at a meeting like this she wondered? And he was in uniform too—

'Morning everyone,' said DI Trevor Rodgers speaking from the front. 'I'm very pleased to see you all here... especially those of you brought in from outside and at such short notice. My apologies if I keep this introduction brief. We've got a lot of work ahead of us over the next few hours so I'd like to get down to business straight away.'

Rodgers was another Serious Crimes Division man, but to Sally's eyes he looked more like someone who'd just wandered into the room by accident from the police civilian branch. Did he really know what he was doing here she wondered? Pretty soon she found out.

'You all know why we're here and the precise nature of the task that lies ahead of us,' Rodgers said scrutinizing his audience carefully. 'So I don't want to waste any more of our valuable time with the usual formalities. You'll obviously get to know each other better on your first coffee break. We're all wearing name-tags anyway and there's a chart on the wall showing all our mugshots.'

Sally glanced up. Among the maps and diagrams ranged on either side of a large, widescreen VDU, was one showing blown-up photographs of each detective present along with their names, rank, collar numbers and police force of origin listed beneath.

Rodgers gaze scanned the room. His delivery was slow, tight and monotone.

'There's really no other way of saying this, but the particular case we're dealing with is a very strange one and may well constitute the latest in a series of bizarre and gruesome murders which have taken place over the past few days and in different part of the country. In all cases, the victims were members of the clergy, and in every incident bar one, the perpetrator of the crime seems to have first decapitated their victim and then mutilated the body in what appears to have been a very precise and ritualistic manner. The first set of photographs you will see are those of the London vicar killed while out for a stroll in Regent's Park last Sunday afternoon plus a few of the others.'

A ripple of shock ran through the audience as the first of a series of images appeared on the VDU screen. As to be expected, the crime scene photos were all pretty gory, and yet from a criminologist's point of view, there were striking similarities between them all. The most recent victim – the Reverend Mark Hitchins – lay on his back with a pool of blood where his head used to be. His chest cavity had been ripped open, exposing what remained of its contents to the sky.

DI Rodgers waited as the assembled team took in the full enormity of what lay before them; then he continued with his narrative: 'And if that hasn't scared the shit out of you, wait until you see the next set of photographs—'

He called up various images on the VDU and outlined the progress of all the inquires thus far in the Greater London Area. Then he moved on to discuss the fate of the Reverend Hitchins in more detail.

'Like all the other victims, Mark Hitchins was a clergyman and his murder was not the random act of some nutcase out for an afternoon jolly in Regent's Park. Whoever killed him seems to have had a precise knowledge of his whereabouts on the day of the murder and no scruples whatever in the way they went about it. Medical examiners now feel certain that his head was taken clean off with a single blow delivered by someone with an expert knowledge of ancient weaponry – specifically someone who knew how to use a Japanese sword. Once the killer had done their work, they then proceeded to dissect the Reverend Hitchins torso and remove his liver. This the medical examiners say was done with a thick serrated blade of the sort a butcher might use to saw through bone and gristle. Clearly it was done by someone who went prepared to do what they did. As I have said, the attack was not a random one, and it matches several others all carried out over the previous two weeks. The first of these was the killing of an elderly Cistercian monk in Wales. According to the Welsh police, the body of Brother Mathew Green was found lying in the vegetable plot of his monastery garden in Snowdonia last Tuesday. Like the

Reverend Hitchins, he'd been struck with a single blow to the neck, though in this case the monk's hood he was wearing interfered with the path of the blade, forcing his assailant to finish him off with a sword thrust to the abdomen. On this occasion, the killer removed the victim's genitals.'

Another gasp of shock rose up from the audience as the photograph was displayed on the VDU.

'Investigating officers are now firmly convinced that the type of person we are dealing with clearly has a pathological hatred of the church and will in all likelihood carry on killing until he is stopped.'

A hand went up in the middle of the room.

'What about terrorism, sir? It could be the work of Islamic fundamentalists.'

'Good point,' replied DI Rodgers, privately grudging the interruption. He'd specifically requested that no questions be asked until the end of the talk but now endeavored to deal with the young policeman who'd raised the issue as diplomatically as possible.

'The internal security services are currently engaged in the process of searching through a list of their chief suspects, but so far they've drawn a blank. The lack of any genuine internet activity from known terrorist cells has largely ruled out the possibility of terrorism as having been the prime motive of our killer.'

Three more photographs appeared on the screen.

'These are the bodies of Father Luke Barrymore and the Reverend John Slater, both from the city of Bristol. The third photograph is that of Sister Mary Kelly, a Roman Catholic nun from a small Carmelite convent on the outskirts of Rochdale.'

At this, one of the female officers got up and had to be helped out of the room by a colleague as DI Rodgers looked on with some sympathy before continuing with his narrative.

'It's not a pretty sight, is it? Evidently the killer reserved his greatest atrocity for the young nun. In Sister Mary's case, her abdomen was ripped open and the uterus removed. You will also notice from the crime scene photograph that most of her face has been rendered unrecognizable; a particular feature also associated with one of the most famous murder cases in

British criminal history – the Jack the Ripper murders of 1888. And as a matter of interest, do any of you present here know the name of Jack the Ripper's last victim by any chance?'

The audience shook their heads, forcing Rodgers to answer his own question.

'Her name was Mary Kelly also; though in the original Ripper murders, all of the victims were women and none of them were what you might call particularly religious. Of course it could all just be a coincidence, but I've got a gut feeling that our own killer not only holds a grudge against the church, but also against the police as well, and that
in his choice of the young Sister Mary, he is taunting us with a chilling reminder of past misdeeds that went unpunished.

Or he's throwing us a massive red herring, thought Sally Reid sitting uncomfortably on a blue plastic chair between two burly officers from CID. *Our killer is a lot more cunning and sophisticated than any two-bit chancer from Queen Victoria's time. He's also working a much wider geographical area as well and striking at the exact moment when his victims are at their most vulnerable and off their guard. Not only that, but according to the medical examiner's estimated time of death, two of the murders appear to have happened almost simultaneously – one of the killings in Bristol and the other of Brother Mathew in Wales. How come the killer was in two places at once?*

DI Rodgers paused in his delivery long enough for Sally to become aware of the sound of movement behind her. It was the uniformed Inspector Lefarge sitting by the door shuffling some papers on his lap. For a moment their eyes met, then Lefarge looked away and returned to his notes. What on earth was he doing here she wondered? Men like Lefarge should have been retired years ago, not invited to a top-level briefing like the one she was attending. It just didn't make sense.

Of all the coppers she knew, George Lefarge was perhaps the scariest. Well into his late fifties, he seemed to spend most of his time locked away in his own private office, or else wandering the corridors of West End Central like some residential ghost. Other than that, you'd hardly ever be aware of his presence, except perhaps on the odd day or so when he received an official visit from two men in plain clothes who would just stroll into the building like they owned the place. The "men in black" they were called – the sort of characters who would have kicked you to death if you ever said a word out of place. At least that's what most of the people at West End Central thought, including DI Rodgers who was just about to call up another series of images on the VDU.

'And now for a bit of intel on the sort of person you're likely to be dealing with in your inquiries,' said Rodgers looking at the screen. 'I doubt if you'll encounter any of these characters personally but you'll need to be on your guard if you ever get anywhere near them.'

Three new faces came up on the VDU.

'Any of you know who these three charmers are?'

'The one on the left is Micky Thatcher,' spoke up one of the women in the front row of seats.

'Correct—!' Rodgers replied with a gleam. 'And for any of you who've spent the last ten years of your police career directing traffic, Micky Thatcher – or Hatchet Mike to his friends – is thought to have been responsible for at least twenty murders over the past fifteen years or so. Most were contract killings, but a few of them appear to have been of his own volition. His favourite method of dispatching his victims is with a long machete of a type that may have been used to kill the Reverend Hitchins in Regents Park last Sunday afternoon as well as all the others, though it is possible that a Japanese sword may have been the weapon used, the reasons for which will become clearer once I have finished with these three suspects. Given Hatchet Mike's history, it will come as no surprise for you to learn that he was recently sentenced to a period of indefinite detention at Broadmoor high security hospital from which he absconded about three months ago sending a shock wave through the political establishment from which it has yet to recover.'

Sally looked on in fascination at the image of Michael Thatcher. His face was lean and hard-edged. Very few psychotics were plump. He also wore a pair of steel-rimmed spectacles with rectangular frames. Odd thing that in an underworld hitman.

DI Rodgers cleared his throat and took a sip of water before continuing with his talk.

'Our next candidate is Robert Elliot, alias "Scotch Bob" on account of his activities north of the border. Elliot began his career as a small-time money lender on the council estates of Glasgow and Lanarkshire. His trademark was extreme terror. He would punish people who refused to pay up by cutting them with a sword – in his case it was a replica Roman gladius with a live blade. It wasn't long before he branched out into the more lucrative field of contract killings in which role he employed a semi automatic pistol, occasionally returning to his sword if he felt the occasion demanded it. It's reckoned he must have earned the better part of three quarters of a million pounds for some of his hits.'

Rodgers paused to take another sip of water and smiled for the first time. It was a rather tired smile, Sally thought. The smile of a man all too used to thinking how unfair it was that some of these criminals were multi-millionaires while the average copper spent much of their free time worrying about their mortgage and the cost of living.

'As I said, you're unlikely to meet up with either of these two individuals,' Rodgers went on. 'They're operating so high up the food chain they'll most likely have plenty of padding between themselves and the law on account of the sort of people they work for. All of which brings us to the third and final member of our trio, and this particular chappie is someone Interpol have been wanting to collar for a good many years.'

He indicated the right-hand photograph, and this time Sally's blood ran cold. The image portrayed a much younger man, perhaps only in his mid-thirties, but possessed of a lean, hard face with a vaguely insane grin. Sally got the impression that if some computer whiz-kid had added a goatee beard and a pair of horns, it would be a perfect match for the Devil, right down to his narrow, piercing eyes.

'*Oh fucking hell,*' she heard Inspector Lefarge mutter softly behind her, and she immediately knew that the person in the photograph was the man she was after. She could almost feel those same piercing eyes peering into her soul the way they just stared out at her from the image on the VDU screen. It was almost as if the creature portrayed on the screen was looking directly at her, sizing her up in fact. And even though she knew such a thing to be quite impossible, somehow she knew it to be true.

'Who is he, guv'nor?' inquired one of the male detectives seated in the front row.

'Your guess is as good as mine,' replied DI Rodgers. 'This is one of the few actual mugshots we've got of this chap courtesy of the French police. He's thought to be of Algerian extraction, though obviously Caucasian judging by his looks. This shot was taken about ten years ago when he was picked up as a suspect in a murder case following a particularly nasty killing in Paris. The French authorities had to let him go due to lack of evidence, but they knew it was him alright. He gave a false name and was subsequently deported back to Algeria – not that it did any good though. Whoever he is, he seems to have a gift for traveling quite freely wherever he chooses without any apparent concern for border police or customs officials. There have been a fair number of sightings of him in recent years from street cameras all across Europe and the United Kingdom but so far none of the CCTV images have come out particularly well. It's almost as if the guy is somehow resistant to having a clear picture taken of him, the way his image seems to flicker in and out of focus each time a camera zooms in on him.'

'Just like that alien creature in the film Predator,' observed the detective half-jokingly.

The young DC's comments drew a ripple of laughter from the audience but Sally Reid didn't join in. Nor did Inspector Lefarge, and when she turned round to look at him again, their eyes met for an instant before he turned to look away. *He know something*, thought Sally making a mental note to speak to the old inspector during the coffee break before turning her attention back to DI Rodgers who was about to make another announcement.

'Before we adjourn for coffee,' said Rodgers addressing the audience, 'there is one more item of information I would like to share with you courtesy of Detective Inspector Martin Welbeck and the Thames Valley Police. The following piece of video footage was recovered from a cyclist's helmet camera and shows the last few seconds of the Reverend David Saunders life shortly before he was decapitated while out riding his bicycle in the Oxfordshire countryside. It actually shows the killer in action, though once again I must warn you all that most of the footage is quite gruesome in the extreme, so be prepared.'

Sally looked on as the image of a tree-lined country lane came into view on the screen. The picture swayed from side to side a little as the Reverend Saunders cycled his way down the road, occasionally taking glances to either side of him as he went.

'Here comes our chappie now,' put in DI Rodgers. 'He's stepping out of that clump of bushes over to the right. Anyone see him?'

A murmur rose up from the audience as a heavily cloaked and hooded figure seemed to emerge from the foliage wielding what looked like a huge Japanese sword.

'The next bit you're not going to like,' exclaimed Rodgers pointing with his cursor at the screen. 'According to some martial arts experts we have since interviewed, our killer has taken up the classic posture required to deliver a sweeping blow to the victim's head just before Saunders comes within striking distance. Then he makes his move—'

The picture on the screen became chaotic. A tumbling series of images of sky and treetops followed by a swirl of heavily pixilated vignettes of roadside shrubbery and hedgerows before eventually coming to a halt beside the rather unsettling portrait of a toxic wild mushroom framed by wild grass and fallen leaves.

'These final few seconds of the video represent David Saunders's head becoming separated from his body and bouncing off down the road before coming to rest on a grass verge where it was subsequently found by officers of the Thames Valley Police.'

Rodgers paused to take in the reactions of his audience. Everyone was maintaining a suitably professional attitude, but quite a few of the younger ones had noticeably paled.

'I'd imagine none of you are feeling any the less nervous after what you've just seen. Well I'm sorry about that, but the next bit of the video isn't any less chilling, in fact it's just plane weird. I'm going to play the video through once more, only this time it's going to be running at half-speed. Tell me what you see when our culprit first steps out of the bushes with his sword. Those of you who are into Harry Potter novels may very well find this version of events rather interesting...'

Once again the image came onto the screen, and the masked and hooded figure was seen to emerge from the bushes brandishing his sword, only this time he didn't so much step out from behind the dense clump of foliage like any normal human being would have done. Instead he simply appeared out of nowhere, the top half of his body shimmering and flickering in the early morning sunlight before it finally materialized by the side of the road hovering in mid-air.

'*Thought so,*' muttered Lefarge almost despairingly. Sally turned and caught a glimpse of the ancient inspector sitting alone by the door. *That old guy definitely knows something,* she thought once more. *I'll have a word with him later on even if it costs me the price of a coffee. There's something very strange going on here.*

The video was shown another couple of times until Rodgers was satisfied that he'd got his point across. 'That my friends, is the only evidence we have of the attack on David Saunders. The faceless culprit left no shoe marks on the ground, not even so much as a heel print. In fact, it was almost as if he'd never been there at all – well, the bottom half of him at any rate. Anyone got any ideas, because I'm damn sure I haven't.'

* * *

They broke for coffee around eleven. As the group made their way down to the canteen, Sally pulled up alongside Lefarge.

'Inspector Lefarge, isn't it?' she asked.

Lefarge waited to let the others pass. 'That's right. And who might you be?'

'Sally. It's Sally Reid,' she answered hoping he might remember her.

The inspector blinked. 'Ah yes. You were the one involved in the acid throwing investigation a few years back. The one that went pear-shaped and got chucked by the courts.'

Sally's heart sank. No matter how well a person did in the police force, no one ever let you forget your first mistake.

'Yes, inspector. That was me,' she replied trying to brazen things out. Lefarge for his part merely regarded her with an odd kind of indifference which Sally found quite unnerving.

'So you just admit it then?' he said. 'No excuses?'

'None whatsoever. I just fucked up, that's all, and now I'm trying to make up for it with this case.'

Lefarge adjusted the sheaf of papers under his arm. 'I worked with Jenny Hancock for over five years. You blew her cover and she paid for it with her looks.'

Sally's cheeks reddened. 'I'm just glad she's alive, inspector.'

'If you could call it living.' He yanked at his tie to loosen it. 'She's running with someone from Sterling's old crew now, or so I've been told.'

Sally thought she'd somehow misheard. 'Who's Sterling?'

'Sterling…? Don't tell me you haven't heard of Sterling?'

'No, I haven't. Who is he?'

'She… Sterling's a woman… or what passes for a woman. She was a notorious female criminal who ran one of the big firms south of the river back in my time.'

'Oh yes. I seem to recall someone of that name but I never knew she was real.'

'Yes, well she was, though she works for different masters now.'

'Like who?'

'The Catholic Church if you must know.'

'I see, inspector. Got religion while she was in the nick, did she?'

He shrugged. 'Who knows. You could never tell with Sterling. She was a law unto herself that one. They all are…'

Assuming Lefarge was referring to criminals, Sally suggested they both take coffee together in the canteen and offered to pay. The inspector accepted her suggestion and they went inside.

The canteen was already noisy and crowded, mainly with plain clothes and civilian staff from the incident room, though uniformed police officers and traffic wardens also occupied some of the tables. 'You'd best grab us a seat while I order the coffee,' said Sally as they threaded their way through to the counter. This place is heaving.'

Ten minutes later she returned with her tray to where Lefarge was seated at a table immediately opposite to that occupied by three traffic wardens. In spite of the proximity of the other table, neither Sally nor the inspector could be overheard talking on account of the general background noise caused by the others present in the canteen.

'So what's Jenny up to these days,' inquired Sally, depositing a steaming hot mug of coffee in front of the inspector.

'She's a pickpocket most of the time,' replied Lefarge emptying two full sachets of sugar into his mug before stirring them in with the wooden stick provided. 'She's a friend of Debbie the shoplifter, hence the connection with Sterling.'

'Oh... I see,' answered Sally meekly before getting to the point.

'George,' she said calling him by his first name.

'Yes?' the inspector replied with a smile, anticipating her next question.

'What's your view on this case? I mean, you've been in the force for a long time. Surely you must have some idea of what we're dealing with?'

To her surprise, Lefarge got to the point immediately.

'We're dealing with someone who's deadly serious about what he's doing,' the inspector said glancing over his shoulder. 'You can tell that much by the score-card he's racking up.'

'Someone with a grudge against religion?'

'Not necessarily.'

'What do you mean, inspector? So far all his victims have been clergymen apart from Sister Mary, and she was a nun.'

'That's not my point, Sally,' replied Lefarge taking a sip of coffee. 'Yes, you're right. All of the victims were either

Anglican vicars or Catholic priests but that wasn't the only thing they had in common.'

'It wasn't?'

'No, it most definitely wasn't,' continued the inspector adopting an almost conspiratorial look.

'I see. So, what was it that all the male victims had in common then?'

Lefarge leaned forward in his chair. 'All the men had some association with a religious organization known as the Order of Exorcist.'

'The what—?'

'The Order of Exorcist, or Minor Order of Exorcists to give them their proper title. It's a little know department of the Catholic Church based in Rome. It's where certain hand-picked priests are sent for specialist training in the art of casting out demons and such like.'

'I didn't know you were a religious man, inspector.'

'I'm not. At least I wasn't until I met Sterling and her kind. Everything changed after that.'

'Oh really. Why?'

Lefarge looked away. 'It's not something I'm prepared to discuss, okay. Let's just say that there's a whole lot more to this case than meets the eye and leave it there, shall we.'

Sally noticed the strained expression on the inspector's face. Was it fear she detected in those hard, grey eyes of his she wondered?

'So, do you think our culprit is mentally deranged or not, inspector?'

'A lunatic? No, I don't think so, Sally,' replied Lefarge sitting back in his seat. 'The man we're looking for is most likely to be a hitman.'

'A what—?'

'A hitman. And what's more, I think I know who he might be working for.'

Sally's mind was racing now. What possible motive could anyone have for hiring a professional killer to knock off a group of highly specialized priests and vicars in such a gruesome manner other than if they were completely of their rocker? It wasn't long before Lefarge answered her question, albeit with one of her own.

'Tell me, Sally,' he said looking her straight in the eye, 'did you notice any connection between the victims first names and the Holy Bible? I am referring to the New Testament in particular.'

She thought for a moment, giving a curt nod to someone across the room who she recognized before replying; 'No inspector. I didn't. Kindly enlighten me.'

Lefarge gazed upward for a moment as if imploring heaven for guidance. 'Okay,' he said, 'let's take a look at four of our killer's male victims shall we.'

'Uh-huh. Go on,' replied Sally somewhat perplexed. This just wasn't how the modern police worked and it made her feel uneasy.

'Right,' continued the inspector, 'first there was the Reverend Mark Hitchins killed while out for a stroll in Regent's Park. Then there was Father Luke Barrymore, the Reverend John Slater and Brother Mathew Green. Can you spot the connection?'

Sally thought hard. 'Not really, apart from the fact they were all men of the cloth so to speak.'

Lefarge was patient. 'Would it help if I put their names into some kind of recognizable order, Sally?'

'I don't know, but go on. You might as well.'

'Very well then – here goes: Mathew Green, Mark Hitchins, Luke Barrymore and John Slater. Does that order of their names ring any bells with you?'

Sally shook her head, prompting the inspector to offer the solution to his conundrum.

'Mathew, Mark, Luke and John… They were the names of the Four Evangelists who were responsible for the four main gospels of the Christian Church. It all fits together rather well, wouldn't you agree. In ending the lives of those four men, our killer was not only committing murder, he was also perpetrating a blasphemy of the worst kind.'

'Well, I suppose there is a connection, inspector, but what about the Reverend Saunders? I don't recall there being a

Gospel according to David Saunders. Your theory breaks down there.'

'Yes, but Saunders was an exorcist, Sally. Not only that, but he was a personal friend of someone very high up in the Catholic hierarchy.'

'Who?'

'A cardinal. His name is Edward de Valois and he's staying in England at the moment, though not for very much longer on account of the death of the Pope. He'll be recalled to Rome soon to attend the Conclave. That's significant, don't you think?'

Sally wasn't a practicing Catholic. In fact, religion wasn't something she was remotely interested in and she couldn't for the life of her work out why it so fascinated Inspector Lefarge. More to the point, what exactly was it that he was afraid of? She could see it in his eyes.

'What are you driving at, George? What part does a cardinal of the Catholic Church have to play in all of this?'

Lefarge frowned. 'The murder of David Saunders was the most significant of all the killings, Sally. Not only was the Reverend Saunders a friend of Cardinal de Valois but he was also an exorcist.'

'So? - I don't see the connection.'

'Well, in case you didn't already know, Cardinal de Valois is a leading member of the Order of Exorcist. In fact, he's the acting head of it. In attacking Saunders, the killer was sending a chilling message to the heart of the Curia.'

'The what?'

'The Curia. It's the governmental department of the Vatican. The papal court in other words.'

Far-fetched was the phrase that entered Sally's mind on hearing the inspector's latest revelation. Of course, there were plenty of connections if you wanted to see them, but nothing of any substance. More to the point, she was beginning to find Lefarge's new-found interest in the politics of the Catholic Church somewhat unsettling to say the least.

'You mentioned the Pope, inspector. What's he got to do with it?'

'I'm not altogether sure, Sally, but most of the killings began shortly after the Pope died and there'll be a papal election coming up soon to choose the new pontiff. It's almost as if someone's already put their hat in the ring in a very big way and wants the whole world to know about it.'

'Well it's not our killer, George, that's for sure. He's a bloody loony so I can't see him standing for Pope. Oh, and talking of lunatics, which of the three suspects DI Rodgers showed us on the screen do you think fits the profile?'

She knew what the inspector was going to say even before he opened his mouth. It had been his reaction in the incident room when Rodgers had shown the photograph of the third suspect with the thin face and piercing eyes that had clinched it in her mind, but she just wanted to be certain.

'Me?' replied Lefarge finishing his coffee with a single gulp. 'Well if the case were mine, I'd go for the third member of the trio. He's our man I'm sure of it. And I'll tell you something else as well. He's the same man who stepped out of the bushes in that video and cut off David Saunders head.'

The old inspector was holding a lot back, she knew, but just before she could ask another question, Lefarge picked up his sheaf of papers and placed them on the table in front of her.

'These are some of the photographs from the medical examiner's report. Notice anything strange about them?'

Sally looked at the colour photocopies and was horrified at what she saw. It wasn't as if she'd never seen pictures of the dead before. Indeed, several of the images had already been shown by DI Rodgers during his briefing so she was more than familiar with some of them. The new photographs, however, were all close up shots of the victim's bodies, including that of Sister Mary Kelly who's image was one of the worst of the mutilated corpses on display.

'Look at the upper left section of Sister Mary's torso,' Lefarge exclaimed, pointing at the photo with his stirring stick. 'Tell me what you see.'

The images were very feint, but on close inspection, Sally noticed what she took to be two birthmarks situated to the right of the dead nun's shoulder just below where she guessed the collar bone might be.

'It's a birthmark, inspector. What's so special about it?'

'Nothing, Sally, except that it's present on all the other bodies too and in exactly the same place as well. Look...'

The inspector was right. There were two identical patches of raised, pigmented flesh on each of the victim's bodies, and each in precisely the same position. They reminded her of the hoof prints of a small deer she'd once seen while out walking with a friend one afternoon in the New Forest.

'How peculiar,' Sally exclaimed. 'What did the medical examiner have to say about them?'

'She didn't. At least, there's nothing mentioned in the reports other than the usual medical jargon and other clinical details. In any case, they're quite difficult to spot – unless you're looking for them of course.'

'And you *were,* inspector?'

Lefarge ignored her comment. 'Do you know what these marks represent, Sally?' he said placing both his elbows on the table and folding his arms across the papers.

'Haven't got a clue, George. Tell me.'

'They're cloven hooves, that's what they are. They most likely appeared a couple of days after the victims bodies had been brought into the mortuary, which is probably why they were never noticed in the first place. They're very feint – so feint in fact that it's a miracle the camera picked them up at all.'

'So what are you saying, inspector? That they're the mark of the Devil or something?'

Lefarge removed his elbows from the table and sat back in his seat.

'Do you have a better explanation, Sally; because if you do I would certainly like to hear it.'

She looked down at the photocopies and shook her head. 'No I don't, George, but I wouldn't go so far as to suggest a supernatural explanation for the deaths. I mean, the culprit may just have used a chemical marker that only revealed itself after a few hours. Maybe you should go and have a chat with some of the boffins from forensics. I'm sure they'll come up with something.'

'Hmm... So you're still going down the scientific route are you?'

'Well this is the twenty-first century, inspector.'

'Quite so, but not for some...'

Sally blinked: 'I'm sorry—?'

'I said, *not for some*. Would it surprise you to learn that there are still forces active in this country of ours who are hellbent on bringing back an aristocratic government of a type last seen in these islands well over two hundred years ago?'

'I don't follow you...'

The inspector lowered his gaze. 'Let's just say that I'm privy to certain information which, if it were to become public knowledge, would cause a full-scale riot on the streets of London, not to mention the rest of the country and much of Europe as well.'

That clinched it, thought Sally. Lefarge really was a spook after all. It would certainly explain why he'd had access to the medical examiner's reports even though he wasn't officially on the case. But who was he working for – the Home Office or MI5? She would have to tread very carefully.

'How's the Rachel Morrison case going, George? I hear you've had some involvement with it.'

'Why do you ask?'

'Oh, I just thought I would change the subject, that's all. So what's the score with Rachel then?'

The inspector frowned. 'Not good, though I've heard from a reliable source that Rachel was pregnant at the time of her disappearance. It seems likely she's been kidnapped then handed on.'

'Who was your informant?'

'I can't tell you that, but what I will say is that it's possible Rachel's disappearance is linked to the killing of those priests and Sister Mary as well...Especially Sister Mary.'

'So that's why you're here, George...?'

'In a manner of speaking, yes it is. Rachel was a student of theology at London University and her course tutor just so happens to have been David Saunders. It's more than likely he got her pregnant as well, but whatever the case, the mere fact that she's carrying a baby is significant given what happened to Sister Mary.'

'Why do you say that?'

'Why, Sally? Because I happen to know how those bastards work, that's why. The people who arranged Rachel's kidnapping are part of a highly sophisticated cosmopolitan elite and they've been around for a bloody long time. The killing and mutilation of Sister Mary was a clear message to the Vatican that war has been declared and the forces of darkness unleashed upon the world.'

'War? I don't get it George. What war? What are you talking about?'

'It's simple. Sister Mary was a nun and her name was Mary. Does that make any sense to you?'

'No it doesn't. Is there a connection?'

'Yes. Mary was the name of the Holy Virgin and Mother of Christ. In mutilating Sister Mary's body in the way that he did, our killer was committing the ultimate blasphemy against the Church. After that, the only thing left for him to do would be to kill a woman made pregnant by someone in holy orders, and that woman could be none other than Rachel Morrison, don't you see?'

'But our killer is just a lone nutter, George. He's clever I'll give you that, but in reality he's nothing more than a serial killer with a grudge against organized religion.'

'No he isn't, Sally. He's definitely not insane and he most certainly isn't working on his own, that much I know for a fact.'

Sally Reid glanced round the canteen. The crowd was thinning out now with people leaving to go back on duty or returning to the meeting upstairs. She didn't have much time.

'George?'

'Yes, Sally?'

'Who's the killer? I promise I won't reveal my source of information.'

'I know you won't.'

'Okay. So who is he then?'

'It's the third man in that line up of police mugshots we saw. His name is Charles Martel, though in the criminal world he's normally referred to as the Executioner of Paris. He usually works for anyone who can afford his fees.'

'Who told you this, George?'

'One of my contacts in the Criminal Intelligence unit. They've been searching for this guy for years but so far he's proved to be extremely elusive. Plans his hits so well you'd hardly think he'd been there – well, up until now that is.'

'What's his background? He must have a history surely? Anyone know?

'There's not much to go on. The French authorities reckon he used to be a Catholic priest.'

'A priest?'

'Yes. He was ordained at some obscure seminary in the north of France. An exemplary student apparently, although he doesn't appear to have been seconded to any diocese by the Church for some reason.'

'Probably because they knew he was a loony.'

'No, I don't think so, Sally. In fact, he was last reported having been summoned to Rome about ten years ago and that was when his trail ran cold.'

'Why was he sent to Rome?'

'It looks like he'd been selected for training as an exorcist.'

'To banish demons?'

'Something along those lines, but I've a feeling his brief was probably a good deal more specific than that.'

'Such as…?'

'Do you really want to know?'

'Yes, George. It may have some bearing on this case. What was he being trained to do?'

'Kill vampires, that's what—'

Sally's jaw dropped in surprise. 'Vampires?' she echoed, trying hard not to burst out laughing.

'Yes, Sally. Charles Martel was being trained to hunt down and destroy the Undead. For some reason he took a dislike to his superiors and turned against the Church. Then he turned into a hired killer.'

'And the French authorities told you this?'

'No. I got to know from someone with inside knowledge of the Vatican.'

'Who?'

'Cardinal de Valois if you must know. I was introduced to him some time ago by Sterling. She's his contact in England – along with a few other people.'

'Sterling? But I thought you said she was a criminal.'

'She's a lot more than that, Sally. She's a...' Lefarge hesitated. He realized he'd already said enough, besides which, the canteen was almost empty now and the meeting upstairs had most likely already been resumed.

'Come along, Sally. We'd best be getting back to the incident room.'

'Wait a minute, George. You didn't tell me about Sterling or why Cardinal de Valois is so important?'

'I... I really don't know. It might have something to do with the forthcoming papal election and the choice of the new Pope, but other than that I can't really say. Take my advice and just let the matter drop. You might also consider a request for a transfer to another job. This thing goes all the way to Hell.'

7

Cardinal Foscari opened the window of his apartment. The morning air was cold. Across the piazza, the great bell of St Peter's tolled eleven, almost drowning out the sound of the helicopter above. No doubt it belonged to the security forces detailed to protect the Vatican for the duration of the election. The threat of terrorism was now considered imminent and police snipers had already been stationed on the roofs of the buildings even though the holding of the Conclave was still three weeks away.

Three weeks. Was that all the time he had? Given all that Father Donnelly had said, would that be enough time to accomplish all that was expected of him? Somehow he doubted it, but what choice did he have? He had to get over to England and back within a couple of days, and all with a full papal election on his hands as well. Not only that, but he still didn't know what it was that he had to do once he got there other than what Donnelly had already told him.

It was a matter of some regret to Foscari that he would not be present at Pope Gregory's funeral. Archbishop Meyer had taken charge of the arrangements in place of Cardinal Spada who was distracted by some urgent business up in Venice. Obviously it was a matter of considerable importance to him whatever it was, but what could be so pressing at a time like this and for a man like Spada who was officially the Chamberlain of the Holy See? Surely the pope's funeral took precedence over anything else?

The body of Pope Gregory had already been embalmed and was now awaiting its lying in state before burial. It had all been done with undue haste and without an autopsy, but better that the body had been embalmed if only to avoid the embarrassment of it falling in to corruption and decay before it had actually been laid to rest. Such a thing had once happened before and could not be allowed to happen again.

Spada…

What was the former patriarch of Venice up to, Foscari wondered? It was almost as if the wily old Chamberlain were acting as the new Pope already, so confident did he seem of being elected to the post of Supreme Pontiff. Umberto Lomellini had been keeping a low profile too, and according to what Father Donnelly had said, Lomellini was Spada's right-hand man with connections in the Naples region which was where the unfortunate Sister Veronica had come from and also the home of the notorious Camorra crime gangs, supposedly under the control of a former British aristocrat called Jimmy Silver who was rumoured to be a high-ranking member of the Undead. However unlikely it all seemed, Foscari sensed a plot was being hatched to turn the papal election in Spada's favour once the Conclave was underway. So what on earth was Father Donnelly doing sending him on a wild goose chase all the way to England and for reasons which frankly bordered on the fantastic and insane? Things just didn't add up.

And yet for some reason he actually believed the creepy old priest who lived in the attic room above the pope's apartment. Believed it with all his heart and soul. There was something distinctly malignant and arcane about Lorenzo Spada that set his nerves on edge and forced him to accept the idea that there might just be some grain of truth in everything Father Donnelly had told him – everything that was except for the bit about vampires.

Making to close the window, Foscari happened to glance down into the street below. Two Italian priests, young men, were crossing the square and walking slowly in the direction of the Vatican gardens. They were both locked in conversation, presumably discussing the latest developments within the Curia and the pope's impending funeral. With their neatly styled hair and designer sunglasses, they more resembled a pair of male fashion models than any devout, hard-working member of the Roman clergy. There were a lot like that, thought Foscari. Had been for quite some time. Some of them even held down lucrative part-time jobs out in the secular world to supplement their meagre incomes. Well, who could blame them. The world had changed a lot since Foscari had been their age.

Shutting the window, the Dean wandered into the kitchen to pour out his third coffee of the morning. It was an Italian blend specially made up for him just the way he liked it. Allowing it to settle, he went back into his study and opened up his laptop. With less than a day to go before his trip to England, there was still a bit of time left to do some research into all the things Father Donnelly had told him.

First he would begin with the man called Edward de Valois. That was easy enough. Foscari's position as Dean gave him access to all the files held on senior members of the Church, and pretty soon Edward's name came up on the screen together with a list of the man's personal credentials, educational background and current posts held.

So it was true. Edward de Valois really was a cardinal. Not only that, but he'd also been presiding head of the Minor Order of Exorcist for the past seven years. Born in Louvain, he'd attended Oxford University before converting to Catholicism at the age of twenty-four. After that, he'd held several positions ranging from lowly parish priest to Archbishop before finally being awarded his red hat by Pope Gregory at the age of fifty-five in an act of defiance against the more conservative Cardinal Spada and his rapidly growing circle of right-wing supporters in the Vatican, who were hell-bent on hijacking all of the perfectly splendid liberal reforms of the previous five decades.

Well that explained a lot, thought Foscari pottering back into his kitchen to fetch his cafetiere. Archbishop Meyer hadn't been kidding. This man, de Valois clearly had been a personal friend of Pope Gregory. Not only that, but he'd also been a close political ally of the anti-Spada group within the Vatican. Just the sort of chap he needed on his side when the run-up to the papal election began in a few days time. Maybe there really was a God after all.

Pouring out his coffee, Foscari checked his luggage and saw to his satisfaction that his chaplain had already packed his suitcase which was now lying open for inspection on a low table by the sofa. He counted up the number of socks. Good. There were enough for a week if he needed that long. On the desk lay his Bible, a bound copy of the *Universi Dominici*

Gregis, the rules for electing a new Pope, and a much thicker file prepared for him by Father Donnelly which contained the intimate details of every cardinal who was eligible to vote, along with their photographs and any other information that might prove useful should there be any doubt about a candidate's suitability to fill the office of Supreme Pontiff. All of this he would need on his return to Rome when the preparation for the Conclave would begin. Then he, along with over one hundred or more other cardinals would all be locked up together in a secure building for however long it took to elect the new Pope, and God help anyone who tried to get out of it by feigning anything other than a *grand mal* seizure or a heart attack. Foscari's word would be final. No one would be allowed out of the building until the business of the election was complete and the column of white smoke finally emerged from the chimney to signify that a decision had been reached.

Picking up the file, Foscari allowed his laptop to go into sleep-mode. The mere thought of the Conclave filled him with dread. He'd never felt himself completely adequate for the role the Church expected him to fulfill. And yet now it fell to him of all people to guide his fellow cardinals in choosing the man who would hold the Keys of St Peter.

'Pff—' but were the others any better, he thought, idly flicking his way through Donnelly's folder. More to the point, how could he establish a united front against Cardinal Spada and his supporters with any hope of electing a Pope that was suitable for holding office? One glance at the section of the folder detailing the South American cardinals was enough to convince anyone that the likelihood of establishing a common front from that part of the world was extremely remote. Likewise, their North American counterparts were completely divided in their views over the running of the Church, some of the more conservative ones supporting the Spada camp while the others remained uncertain as to which way they would go regarding the ordination of women and issues governing the right to abortion in the USA. Clearly the forthcoming election was going to be a difficult and protracted one.

From the Far East came no fewer than thirteen cardinal electors and from Africa another thirteen. That made a total of twenty-six in all, but it still wasn't enough to counter Spada's influence within the all-important European block. The Africans would most likely vote with the Nigerian group headed by Cardinal Jacob Ibekwe, but to win an overall majority, Ibekwe would have to pick up support from beyond Africa, and that would be difficult. It was still the cardinals of Europe – fifty-six in total – who dominated the Conclave. It wasn't that Spada was any less conservative in his views than Ibekwe, but he'd always been cunning enough to keep them solely within the confines of scholarly debate, and, unlike his African colleagues, he didn't have the problem of witchcraft to queer his pitch.

Witchcraft. No, Foscari didn't have to take that one on board in his assessment of the situation, but he did have something as equally bizarre and medieval to contend with, and that *something* was the issue of vampires.

Vampires… What on earth had Donnelly been thinking about with all that talk about the Undead? As if the situation wasn't bad enough already with likelihood of organized crime taking over the Vatican, Foscari now had to do battle with the legions of the damned as well. Not only that, but in less than a day's time he had to travel to London to rescue a young English lady called Rachel Morrison who apparently was going to be sacrificed to Satan by a man called Jimmy Silver, himself reported to be a vampire, and who was equally determined to install his partner in crime Lorenzo Spada as the next Pope.

Well that much was nonsense of course, but even so, it was beginning to look as if the European vote was going to be determined by criminal interests and that the all important Italian majority of cardinals would be swayed by the Camorra who had just poisoned Pope Gregory. The link with vampires was something he wasn't prepared to countenance, but it just might lead to something more concrete and rational if he looked hard enough. Now, who were all those people Father Donnelly had told him about? He knew who Cardinal de Valois was, but what about all the rest? What about Jimmy Silver?

Sinking deeper into his thoughts, the Dean considered his position. There was still quite a lot he didn't know about Jimmy Silver and his associates. Just how much power and influence did this mysterious Englishman have in the Italian underworld, and how far did it extend? Evidently far enough for him to have compromised Cardinal Spada by all accounts. Perhaps if he did a bit of digging around on the internet he might come up with something. After all, what harm could it do? He might even discover some clues as to Silver's whereabouts and the precise nature of his business interests in Italy while he was at it.

Laying aside the folder, Foscari reached over to his laptop and began searching. Ten minutes later and he still hadn't found anything resembling the name Jimmy Silver. It was then that he recalled what Father Donnelly had told him about Silver having been a British aristocrat called Sir James Blackthorne, and that the name Jimmy Silver was most likely a pseudonym he'd adopted to cover his tracks. With this in mind, Foscari began sifting his way through several lists of existing British and European aristocrats but once again came up with nothing except an oblique reference to a Sir James Blackthorne having once been associated with the family name of Westvale and a note referring him to yet another website that required him to pay a regular annual subscription of two hundred Euros to access.

Despairing of the situation, Foscari got up from his chair and went over to the window once again. Down in the square he spied two cardinals alighting from a taxi – the first of many who would arrive over the next few days to attend the Conclave. One of the men he recognized as Archbishop Emeritus, Massimo Puzo, twice investigated for money - laundering but never prosecuted, while on Puzo's right he saw the eminent theologian, Archbishop Modesta from Spain, once rumoured to have been a close friend of the dictator General Franco and just about as right-wing in his religious beliefs. There were still quite a few like that, thought Foscari with a sigh, but there were also some good men too, if only he could convince them all to agree on electing a suitable candidate to fill the pope's chair other than Cardinal Spada.

Returning to his laptop, he began searching once more. Too his surprise, something caught his eye. It was a freeview website specializing in aristocratic names dating from the year

1700 to the present day. Without hesitation, he clicked on the text line and began scrolling down the page. Pretty soon he came up with a reference to the name of Westvale. It was dated 1807 and mentioned a character called Lord Bartholemew Westvale and there were some biographical details to go with it.

Apparently, Bartholemew Westvale had been born in the year 1739 and had married a certain Mary Anne Montague of the county of Dorset in 1763. Together they produced two children – a boy and a girl. The male child was christened Percival Augustus Westvale and the girl was named Caroline Elizabeth Westvale. Percival was later killed in the Napoleonic War and when Lord Bartholemew Westvale finally died a widower in 1807, the family line of Westvale became extinct.

'So, what happened to the daughter?' muttered Foscari scrolling further down the page. There wasn't very much apart from a brief footnote stating that Caroline Westvale had scandalized society by her elopement with a certain Sir James Blackthorne in the 1790s and that she was dismissed by her family and never heard of again. It was later believed by some, that both she and Sir James had fled to Venice in 1797, but after that the historical records appeared to have fallen silent.

Well that was strange. There really had been a member of the British aristocracy called Sir James Blackthorne, only he'd belonged to the eighteenth century and wasn't contemporary. So what was Donnelly talking about when he'd said that Jimmy Silver used to be a member of the English nobility called "Blackthorne." Not only that, but there was also a picture of the Blackthorne coat-of-arms pictured in the article showing three wolf heads on a shield. Surely it couldn't be the same person, could it? Impossible.

Shrugging his shoulders, Foscari considered another individual that Donnelly had mentioned. Again it was an aristocrat, but this time the person in question came from Italian nobility and his name was Count Francesco Grimaldi who Donnelly referred to as being in charge of an organization known as the Bene Noctu which had some connection or other with vampires just like Jimmy Silver, only they weren't quite as hostile to the Vatican as Silver appeared to be for some reason. Maybe they were all good Catholics, mused Foscari grinning at the irony of it.

Continuing to scroll through the website, he failed to locate any contemporary Grimaldi's, but he did find plenty of dead ones, including a certain "Count Francesco Grimaldi" who had apparently expired around the year 1789. After that, the historical records fell silent and the Grimaldi line died out, all their lands and property being bequeathed to the Church for reasons which appeared somewhat obscure, but which had something to do with financing the upkeep of their family tomb situated somewhere on the outskirts of Rome.

Foscari let out a groan of despair and sat back in his chair. He was getting nowhere. So far, all the people he'd investigated appeared to be dead. Not only that, but they'd all died a long time ago. So long ago in fact that their family lines had become completely extinct; the Grimaldi's having lapsed in 1789 and Sir James Blackthorne – alias Jimmy Silver – being last reported alive in 1797 along with his partner Caroline Westvale, both of them rumoured to have fled to Venice in the year Napoleon Bonaparte had conquered the city and declared it a peoples republic. Tapping his fingers in frustration, the Dean was about to give up and close down his laptop when he had a thought.

Venice... Here at least there was a connection. Lorenzo Spada had been patriarch of Venice and he still had business interests there, whatever those interests might be. Spada was Jimmy Silver's creature and the main candidate to succeed Pope Gregory should the vote go in his favour. The Pope had also mentioned the Lion of St Mark on his deathbed, which was the symbol of that city. For some reason, Venice was important in the outcome of things, but how? There was clearly a link between that ancient republic in the north of Italy and events currently unfolding in Rome if only he could find out what. But so far, all he'd managed to discover was the fact that most of the main protagonists in this drama were all clearly dead, or if they weren't then they bloody well should be.

Pulling open the drawer of his desk, Foscari drew out his rosary. Running its beads through his fingers, he began thinking. Father Donnelly had mentioned someone else. Her name was Sterling, though he hadn't elaborated much further on the precise role she played or the type of people she associated with. He knew there was some connection between this woman and Cardinal de Valois, but other than that he didn't have much to go on. Perhaps the internet might throw up some clues about her?

A few minutes later and his question was answered with a short paragraph detailing the exploits of a notorious female criminal of that name who had once dominated the London crime scene for much of the 1980s until her mysterious disappearance in 2003 along with the fact that someone answering to her description had been found shot dead by the Camorra on the streets of Naples around about the same time. After that, her trail ran cold and she vanished from the pages of history never to be heard of again.

More dead people, thought Foscari fingering the silver crucifix on the end of his rosary. And there was a connection with Naples and the Camorra too. What did it all mean?

Cursing his arthritic leg, the Dean stood up and walked over to the votive image of Christ the Savior which hung on the wall of his room. Kneeling before it, he clasped both hands together in prayer. Normally when he prayed, a deep sense of peace and inner calm would come over him, making him feel as if God were actually listening to him and that all would be well in the end. This time however, no such feeling of peace and inner serenity was forthcoming. Instead, in its place, there lurked a shadow of dark foreboding and fear, together with the growing realization that everything he thought he knew about the history of civilization and humanity was one big fat lie.

Who the hell was Sterling, he thought? What was her part in all of this?

8

The Suffolk Marshes
England

Sterling lay crouched down low in the reed beds. She was playing a waiting game.

The Suffolk marshes could be one of the bleakest places in the world and even more so when the weather was bad. It was still only September but there had been no warm days. The sky was grey with clouds for as far as the eye could see. Even so, she had begun to appreciate the beauty of its remoteness and isolation. They were ideal conditions to hold a kidnap victim in preparation for their extraction by sea.

She found it hard to believe that such isolated places still existed within a hundred miles of London. Barely nine hours ago she'd been standing outside a pub in Hackney when she'd received a phone call from her handler telling her to drive to Suffolk and await further instructions. According to Cardinal de Valois, her target had taken out a short-term lease on the cottage she was watching, and was using it as a safe-house from which to plan his operations. That he was working for Jimmy Silver was a foregone conclusion. Just how much he actually knew remained to be seen.

The night had been a long one, though she'd managed to snatch a few hours sleep beside her motorcycle, using its bulk to shield her from the cold north wind that blew in from the sea. Hands folded neatly across her chest, her pulse had slowed itself down as she entered the sleep of the Undead. But she was denied the luxury of dreams. Vampires cannot dream. They can only remember.

She did not remember *being* Julie Kent.

She was able to recall names, dates and events from the time before, but they were not real memories. They were simply facts recycled from an impersonal database. Pale sketches from someone else's life. *The person she used to be.*

She could remember Julie's last hours quite vividly even though it was all a long time ago. Way back in 1977 in fact. Julie had been out for a night in London with some friends from university when she'd been lured to a private party at some swanky rich mansion house in the fashionable district of Knightsbridge. Her friends had sensed danger and declined the invitation, but not Julie.

Julie had splurged herself sick on champagne. No society child is a stranger to alcohol, but Julie had yet to master it. She was naive. And careless. And stupid!

She did not remember the precise moment she became a vampire, though she knew it had something to do with a woman she'd met at the party and the fact that this woman had bitten deeply into the side of Julie's neck. After that everything went blank and she woke up in the back of a limousine traveling south. She wasn't Julie anymore, but neither had she become Sterling yet. Julie had ceased to exist the moment those long canine teeth had punctured her body. Now she was simply too weak to resist and could only remember the face of a man glancing over her shoulder at her from the front passenger seat of the car. It was Jimmy Silver and he was traveling to the south coast to dump her body out at sea.

I guess I was lucky. I survived. Thousands don't, and the ones that do are usually too brain-damaged to function properly. But I was different. Somehow the immersion in cold sea water woke me up and I made it back to the beach alive but without any immediate memory of who I was or what had happened. After that, I adopted the name of Sterling and survived as a petty thief on the streets of London until I hit the big time and morphed into an alpha vampire just like Jimmy Silver had done way back in the eighteenth century when he'd been Sir James Blackthorne.

Vampires don't age. My real age would be sixty-five by now but I look no older than twenty. The same age Julie was when she died. I wonder where Julie's soul is now?

Movement.

Someone was driving down the narrow dirt-track towards the cottage. Maybe the pick-up had been arranged for today? If that were the case, then she'd made it only just in time. No one was going to transport Rachel Morrison out of the country on her watch.

Keeping her attention focused on the silver hatchback, she reached for her mobile and dialed a number. A man's voice answered.

'That you, Sterling?'

'Yes, Joe. I'm at the cottage now. Where the hell are you and the boys? Things are beginning to hot up around here.'

'Sorry kid, but we got called in at short notice. Then we hit some roadworks north of Harlow which slowed us up a bit and Gordon's motorcycle broke down again. We'll be another two hours at least.'

'Then you'll be too late. I'm going in on my own.'

'I wouldn't, Sterl. You don't know what's inside that place. There could be anything in there.'

'Yeah, like Rachel Morrison for example! Two men have just arrived in a silver hatchback. I think they're transporters. They must be taking her down to the beach. There's a motor launch tied up by the jetty and a larger vessel anchored out at sea. It looks like de Valois was right. They're taking her out of the country.'

'What for?'

'I don't know precisely. The cardinal wouldn't give me the full details, but if Silver's involved in it then I guess it won't be anything good. Apparently, young Rachel is pregnant. That ring any bells with you, Joe?'

'Oh, Christ! Hang in there Sterl. We'll be as quick as we can—'

With that, the man called Joe rang off, leaving Sterling alone in the marshes with only her motorcycle for company. Turning her attention towards the silver hatchback parked outside the cottage, she squinted through a pair of binoculars. What were the two men up to she wondered? Were they going to the cottage to collect Rachel or... No, wait. They weren't collecting. They were delivering.

She looked on as the men opened the rear door of the hatchback and pulled out a long bundle wrapped in what appeared to be an old duvet cover secured with rope. Whatever was inside the duvet was about the length of a small adult human body.

They must have drugged her, thought Sterling maintaining her vigil in the reed beds. *They've drugged her and brought her up from London in preparation for transportation to the boat. Looks like de Valois was right.*

The two men easily withdrew the body from the rear of the car and carried it over to the cottage. Halting at the front door, one of them pressed the bell. Presently, the door was opened and the two men went inside, hefting the bundle with them as they went. A few long minutes elapsed and then the men left the house, returning to their vehicle with a third individual – presumably the same person who had opened the door to them. Then they drove off down the road.

Satisfied she wasn't being watched, Sterling stood up in the reed beds and considered the situation. It looked like they'd left Rachel in the house, tied up and drugged. What should she do? Joe had warned her not to venture into the cottage alone, but how much time did she have before the men came back? It was now or never. She had to rescue Rachel before it was too late.

As she approached the cottage, she could see that it more resembled a small farmhouse with a yard outside. The yard was overgrown with coarse grass, while to the left were fertile green fields rolling down to the banks of a shallow river that ran down to the sea. Nearby was an old barn with one of its doors hanging off. Clearly the place hadn't been worked as a farm for quite some time.

She crept forward, crouching low in the long grass. The farm was in total darkness, not a single light shining in any of its windows. There was no one standing guard either. It looked like the building was completely deserted.

As she drew closer, she could see the front door of the house more clearly. To her surprise it was standing open by a couple of inches. In their haste to leave, the men must have forgotten to close the door. She couldn't believe her luck.

Cautiously, she pushed the heavy wooden door further open and tiptoed into the hallway. The hinges were in need of oil and creaked loud enough to wake the dead. Damn!

She waited and listened. Nothing. No sign that anyone had heard her. Only the empty silence of a long-abandoned farmhouse and the distant roll of thunder coming from somewhere over to the west.

Relieved but still cautious, she wandered down the hallway checking each room with her Beretta 9mm pistol held out in front of her in both hands. Judging by the light angled through the ground floor windows, it was around mid-morning. Maybe Joe and the boys would turn up soon. She certainly hoped so.

The cottage looked deceptively small from the outside but was possessed of much grander internal dimensions. Stepping forward, she walked over into what she took to be the living room. Here things weren't so good. There were pieces of what looked like the joints and broken arm-sockets of a child's doll scattered across the floor. The stench of rotting flesh was appalling but it wasn't the only smell in the building.

Stepping closer, she could see that the pieces of broken doll were in fact the body parts of a small infant which appeared to have been torn apart in a violent feeding frenzy. As she carefully skirted the remains, there was a sudden noise. It seemed like it came from upstairs. Gripping her handgun tighter, she made her way back to the hall and approached the staircase. Here she could make out in the gloom the remains of another small child propped up against the banister rail and yet a further half-eaten cadaver nearby. At the bend in the stairs was a gnawed femur bone with some flesh still remaining on it, together with a litter of empty wine bottles and a pool of urine and vomit. Clearly someone was a messy eater.

She continued on up the stairs. Reaching the landing, she sniffed the air. The scent of rotting flesh was still strong, but it was overlaid with another smell. There was something else in the building with her.

Catching sight of a fleeting shadow reflected in a full-length looking glass on the landing, she fired a couple of shots then gave a groan of despair as the mirror dissolved in a shower of broken glass. She'd wasted two of her precious bullets.

'For fuck sake get a grip,' she murmured to herself, traversing the landing in the direction of what she took to be the door of the main bedroom. The door was locked, indicating the need to keep whatever was inside the room secure.

That must be where they're holding Rachel, she thought. Loathe to waste yet another bullet to shoot the lock, Sterling kicked the door, causing it to fly open with a sharp crack and a flurry of splintered wood. Entering the room in one lithe movement, she backed herself up against the wall and checked the place out.

The room was surprisingly clean in comparison to the scene of carnage on the staircase. On the bed lay the cloth bundle she'd witnessed the two men bring into the cottage. Walking over to it, she laid her pistol to one side and pulled a switchblade out of her jacket pocket, cutting the ropes securing the bundle. Pulling aside the cloth, her heart skipped a beat. There inside the old brown duvet cover lay the sweetest little girl child she'd ever seen.

But it wasn't Rachel.

For one thing, Rachel had been much older than the small child wrapped up in the bundle who couldn't have been more than twelve years of age. And for another, Rachel had brown hair and not the flowing blond curls possessed by the sleeping child on the bed. Checking her mobile, Sterling scrolled down the images she'd been given by de Valois. Nope, the girl on the bed definitely wasn't Rachel Morrison. In fact, she wasn't even human at all.

The first sign Sterling knew something was wrong, was when the old-fashioned bulb of the ceiling light suddenly surged into life, burning at ten times its normal brilliance before bursting with a pop.

'Shit—!'

Sterling dropped her mobile and tottered backwards on her heels. The thing on the bed was suddenly on top of her, its fingers closing around her neck with a grip as strong as steel. She could see its eyes glowing like red hot coals as the vampire-child sank its fangs deep into her shoulder. Putting aside whatever maternal feelings she may have had for the girl, Sterling wrenched the snarling creature from her neck and reached for her gun, firing three shots into its chest at point-blank range. The vampire-child began shrieking and flailing its arms and legs out wildly on the bed in its death panic. Then everything went still. The infant vampire was dead.

Sterling knew what was coming next. At first nothing happened, then a thin column of smoke began to rise up from the child's body followed by three jets of blue flame which issued from the bullet holes in its torso. Soon, the body was ablaze with holy fire, consuming the child in less time than it took to butter a slice of toast.

She'd never got used to it – the way the flesh, bones and sinew burned while leaving everything else in the room, including the bedclothes, completely untouched by the flames. Spontaneous human combustion it was called, but Sterling knew it only as "The Fire from Heaven". It was what happened to all vampires who found themselves on the wrong side of a Vatican bullet, but she'd never shot a child before. Jimmy Silver must be one hell of a sick bastard to have planted an Undead child on her like that. Maybe he was just softening her up in time for the final battle when it came? Whatever the case, it was a salutary reminder of the terrible fate that lay in store for her if Silver ever caught her off her guard. She was just about to leave the room and phone de Valois when she heard a noise. There was someone coming up the staircase. No, not *someone;* it was several people in fact, and she recognized one of the voices. It was Joe Rackham and he'd brought some friends with him.

'You took your time,' was all she said when the grizzled old Hell's Angels biker poked his head round the door and entered the room.

'Sorry, Sterl. We came as fast as we could.'

'Make it faster next time, okay.'

Joe nodded then pointed at the charred and blackened corpse on the bed. 'Anyone you know, Sterling?'

'Not funny, Joe! It could easily have been me!'

Another man entered the bedroom and glanced round sniffing the air. 'Christ, it fucking stinks in here,' he exclaimed wafting a broad hand in front of his nose.

Sterling frowned. 'Yes, it's the smell of Hell in case you hadn't noticed, Gordon; but I dare say someone like yourself would probably recognize it well enough. Where's Jerry Skinner?'

'Back in London. We've got a job on tomorrow. He's going to need the taxi and he had to get it cleaned out.'

'Oh really. Well he didn't tell me about it. I am of course assuming he got his orders from de Valois, because if he's moonlighting on me again then he's going to regret it.'

'Relax, Sterling. Everything's sweet. We've just got a pick-up job, that's all. Now let's get out of here before the police arrive. You never know. Silver may have given them a tip-off to set us up.'

9

She was late.

Detective Superintendent Sally Reid was filled with a growing sense of foreboding as she walked towards her car for the morning drive to work. She'd always been grateful for the peace and tranquility of her home, situated as it was in the heart of the Surrey countryside, but for some reason this particular morning felt different. There was no birdsong.

Normally an early riser, Sally was used to the sound of the dawn chorus greeting her ears almost as soon as she opened the front door, but today there was nothing but an eerie silence. She put this down to the series of bad dreams she'd had the night before which had so disrupted her sleep as to cause her to wake up a full hour later than she usually did. Even so, she found the complete absence of any birdsong somewhat unsettling.

Stranger still had been the events of the previous day. It wasn't so much the briefing in the incident room that was causing her to feel uneasy as the later discussion she'd had with Inspector Lefarge in the police canteen and all that he had said. Anyone else would have laughed it off as being nothing more than the crazy ramblings of an old London copper way past his sell-by date. But somewhere deep within her soul, Sally knew that Lefarge had been telling the truth.

Even more disturbing was what Lefarge had to say about the serial killer known as Charles Martel. In this respect, it hadn't been so much *what* the inspector had revealed to her as *where* he'd actually got his information from. Lefarge obviously had some involvement with the British intelligence services, and whatever that involvement was, it clearly went all the way to the top. There was something big going off in the world and she had a feeling it was in some way connected with another briefing she'd attended only a few days ago regarding the theft of forty kilos of plastic explosive from a Ministry of Defense supply depot on the outskirts of Leamington Spa. This, coupled with the fact that police and anti-terrorism units were reporting a sudden uptake in radio-chatter from several known Islamic terrorist cells had put everyone involved at senior-command level on a state of high-alert, including herself.

And there was an Italian connection too.

According to a source inside Interpol, the C-4 plastic explosive that had disappeared from the MOD building had last been reported traveling via Suffolk to somewhere in Europe, heading roughly in the direction of Venice. This same Interpol source had also confirmed that the transportation had been arranged by the Camorra and financed with some dark money that had its origins from a bank located in central Italy. To Sally's mind, everything that Lefarge had told her, including some of the more loony stuff, was all beginning to fit into place. But who was the target of the impending attack?

Putting the matter out of her mind, Sally walked towards her car and smiled with satisfaction. The vehicle had been a present to herself when she'd been promoted to the rank of Superintendent and it was her pride and joy. A vintage 1970s British sports car, it was more of a status symbol than a means of getting to work and it also had a cute little key to open the driver's door with and start the engine.

Rummaging in her shoulder bag, Sally felt for the key fob and was just about to insert the key in the door lock when she experienced a sudden gust of air coming from somewhere just behind where she was standing. Normally this wouldn't have been anything out of the ordinary, were it not for the fact that the air had been unusually still that morning without so much as a hint of a breeze in the trees. She also had the feeling she was being watched.

Turning round, she looked down the drive. 'Who's there?' she exclaimed. 'Show yourself!'

Nothing. There was no one there. Apart from a small grey squirrel that stared up at her from beneath the foliage of a low-spreading mulberry bush, the driveway was completely deserted.

Shrugging her shoulders, Sally made to open the car door but found the path of her key blocked. Try as she might, she couldn't fit the key into the lock. Someone had jammed what looked like a piece of matchstick into the key slot and it wouldn't budge.

'Damn!'

Kneeling down, she tried to pick the fragment of wood out of the lock with some tweezers she kept in her bag but it was no good. The lock was jammed solid.

It was then that she heard the sound of footsteps on the gravel path. Again the sound came, this time accompanied by another gust of air just like before. Hardly daring to breathe, she stood up slowly and turned to face her attacker.

She knew she was dead almost as soon as she gazed into those narrow, piercing eyes. The same eyes she'd seen in the police mugshots. The eyes of Charles Martel, the so-called Executioner of Paris. It was just like he'd appeared out of nowhere, complete with his unsheathed Japanese sword and a grin on his face as wide as the crescent moon.

Her head came off with a swish of the sword before falling to the ground and coming to rest beside the rear offside wheel of her car. So this was death she thought, gazing with her rapidly diminishing vision at her headless body lying on the driveway. *As easy as that.*

For a moment she panicked, then, realizing the absurdity of the situation, she surrendered herself to death. It was kind of warm and peaceful, and not at all as bad as she thought it would be.

'Adieu mademoiselle,' were the last words she heard before she closed her eyes and died. Evidently her killer was a gentleman.

* * *

It was almost lunchtime and the little coffee shop near Trafalgar Square was beginning to fill up with customers. Hardly anyone noticed the young woman with the ruined face as she walked in off the street; and if they did, they simply averted their gaze and carried on scrolling down their mobile phones or chatting to friends. Nobody wanted to know Jenny Hancock. She was bad news.

Scanning the room, she quickly spotted the person she'd come to meet. Over by the alcove near the front window sat a young lady with blond hair, cut in the ska-style of the previous century, cropped short on top with long side wings hanging down in front of the ears. Her name was Debbie Stephenson, one of London's most notorious shoplifters and the scourge of Oxford Street. Soon, both women were engaged in intimate conversation at their table. Their mood was quiet. The meeting had an air of privacy.

'How's business Debbie?'

'Not good,' the woman with the ska hairstyle replied. 'Shoplifting's getting more difficult these days, what with the security cameras an' all.'

'I know. It's the same in my line of work. People ain't carrying money on them like they used to. I can still lift their cards and smart-phones but I have to sell the phones on cos' I don't know how to access their bank accounts and pin numbers.'

'That what you're here for, Jenny?'

'No. I've got something you might be interested in, that's all.'

'Such as what?'

Glancing round, Jenny reached into her jacket pocket and pulled out a small rectangular object before sliding it across the table towards her friend.

'What's that?'

'It's a book, Debbie. Take a look inside and tell me what you think.'

Opening the book's black leather cover, Debbie began fluttering her way through its pages. On the front flyleaf, someone had drawn a coat of arms in blue biro depicting three wolf heads on a shield with the single word "Blackthorne" written underneath. On the reverse of the flyleaf was a list of numbers and letters all mixed up together with the names of two cities – Zurich and Lugano. The rest of the book – its main text – was printed in black Gothic lettering and contained some rather strange diagrams together with what looked like the traditional northwest European image of the Devil complete with cloven hooves and horns.

'Hmm... Looks like an antique volume to me,' exclaimed Debbie without passing the book back to her friend. 'Unfortunately, someone's scribbled on it so it's probably not worth very much I'll give you fifty quid for it. It's just the sort of thing Sterling might be interested in.'

'One hundred—'

'Seventy quid and that's my final offer, Jenny. Take it or leave it.'

'Okay then, Debbie. Seventy quid it is. The book is yours. I'm pleased to be rid of it anyway. The damn thing was giving me the creeps, along with the bloke I nicked it from. He looked too much like Sterling's old enemy Jimmy Silver for my liking. And talking of creeps; where's Skinner? You told me he might be coming.'

'He's been working on his taxi, Jen. Say's he's picking up some important Italian geezer at the airport tomorrow. A bloke called Foscari I think his name was, but he wouldn't tell me any more than that.'

'Oh… I see. You mean it's got something to do with Sterling then?'

'Can't really say. It's more than my life's worth to meddle in her affairs. You know what I mean.'

'Yeah, well I'd best be on my way then. The afternoon shopping crowds should be building up in Oxford Street by now. Ta-ta, luv.'

'Bye, Jenny. Look after yourself.'

10

Late afternoon. Paolo Foscari looked again at the package he'd found posted through his letter box.
He knew Father Donnelly had been as good as his word. The package contained one outbound ticket to London together with a sealed envelope containing five hundred pounds in British currency – his expenses for the two or three days he would most likely have to stay in England while he waited to collect Rachel Morrison and deliver her to the relative safety of the Vatican City. But what would happen after that?
From the moment he'd received the news of the death of Pope Gregory, he'd known his days as a Vatican bureaucrat were over. The hands that held the airline ticket and money were trembling now, not so much with the anticipation of his trip to London, but also with the imminence of the election of the new Pope and all it might imply. The art of politics had never been his greatest strength. He'd always left such things to others more worldly than himself. But now…?
Something was bothering him. Only a few minutes ago he'd been resting on his bed. Not sleeping, just resting in preparation for his flight in the morning. Getting up, he'd walked across the room and glanced in the mirror. He was wearing his black cassock and red skullcap. An early start the next day meant he would have to rise promptly, say his prayers and make for the airport in a Vatican car as quickly as possible.
Picking up the package containing his airline tickets and money, a single thought entered his mind. He'd done all the research he could, looking up Cardinal de Valois, Jimmy Silver, Sterling and the enigmatic Count Grimaldi, but he'd completely neglected searching for the one individual responsible for bringing them to his attention in the first place – Father Michael Donnelly! Now why hadn't he thought of that before?
Three quarters of an hour later and his methodical sifting through the register of active catholic priests had yielded nothing. There was no mention of the name Michael Donnelly

belonging to any clergyman currently in the service of the Church – not even in Ireland let alone the Vatican City. According to the register of practicing clergymen, Michael Donnelly did not exist.

Cardinal Foscari was about to bring his hand down on the shiny metal button of the Vatican's internal telephone and call for security when something stopped him. The phone had rung itself, prompting him to reach for the receiver and inquire as to who it was that wished to speak with him. To his surprise, it was Father Donnelly.

'Foscari – is that you?' came the voice in a broad Irish accent.

'It is,' answered the Dean, wondering why on earth he was being so accommodating towards Donnelly when all he wanted to do was have the priest apprehended and brought in for questioning.

'Did you get the package I sent you?' Donnelly continued, 'the one containing your expenses and flight details. Sister Bernadette should have delivered them by now.'

'She has,' replied Foscari. 'I've got them right here.' He was about to add something about his misgivings regarding Donnelly's true identity, but the priest got in first with his reply: 'Right. Good. You'll be met by our people in London, Foscari. A taxi will pick you up outside Terminal 2 of Heathrow airport and take you to where you'll be staying for the duration of your time in England. Once you've met your contact and picked up Rachel Morrison, you will return immediately to Rome on the Vatican jet. Is that understood?'

Foscari nodded, before adding, 'and who exactly is my contact may I ask?'

'You don't need to know that, Dean. Just concentrate on the papal election when you get back. That's where you'll be needed the most in the weeks to come. Until then, it would serve all our interests if you just keep a low profile. Don't take your full cardinal's regalia with you on your trip. Wear a plain cassock at all times and ditch the red skullcap. Just make like you're an ordinary priest.'

'Why?'

'Just do it, Your Eminence, that's all I'm saying. It might just save your life.'

'What—'

There was no reply. Father Donnelly had hung up and put the phone down on him. He was on his own.

11

It was early morning and Sterling was back in London now.

A fine mist has descended on the city by the time she reached the gentleman's club in St James's, which was where she wanted to be. The club was jokingly referred to as "The Bishop's Palace" owing to the fact that it catered mainly for certain high-ranking members of the Roman Catholic and Anglican clergy whenever they were in town. Pressing the intercom button at the side of the front door, she waited.

'Yes. Who is it?' came a voice from the intercom.

'My name is Sterling,' she answered, 'and I have a meeting with Cardinal de Valois.'

The voice paused: 'Just a moment.'

There was a short interval of about ten seconds before she heard an electronic buzz followed by a click which told her the door was open.

'You may enter now,' came a different voice. 'Cardinal de Valois is upstairs in the library room. It's the third door along the end of the corridor.'

She was not aware of the presence of many people in the building. It just wasn't that sort of a place. Climbing the stairs, she reached the first floor landing and turned left down a wide passageway until she came to a set of double doors at the far end of the corridor. Here, the familiar scent of cigar smoke told her that someone was present and that this someone was most likely the person she had come to see.

The rear of a brown leather armchair framed by an antique marble fireplace greeted Sterling as she entered the library. Seated in the chair was a middle-aged gentleman, cigar in hand, hunched over a large chessboard, totally absorbed in one of those complicated endgames to which certain types of intellect can become all too easily addicted to. It wasn't like the Edward she knew for him to be seated like that with his back to the door of a public room. All too easy for a potential assassin to slip a garrotte smoothly round his neck and then exit the building without so much as a whisper of suspicion. But she was wrong:

'You're late,' said de Valois turning round in his chair. 'Is there any particular reason for that?'

'I walked,' she replied, regarding the man with a mixture of fear and respect. The news she was about to tell him was bad and she was reluctant to give it.

'Sit yourself down,' gestured the cardinal pointing to a chair. 'I was just finishing off this interesting little endgame before you arrived. It's really rather elegant, don't you think?'

'If you say so, Edward. I'm not much of a chess player myself.'

'But you used to be a fine musician,' continued de Valois, placing a black King firmly in check.

'That was a long time ago... Before the change.'

'I know, I know – before you became one of the Undead. It must be such a sad business to lose one's soul.'

'Are you joking with me Edward, because if you are, it's in very bad taste.'

'Merely an observation, that's all. It's what people like me are here for Sterling – keeping creatures like you under control.'

'Since when have I ever been a threat to the Church, cardinal?'

'Never, as far as I am aware. Your feud with Jimmy Silver has always been enough to keep you on the right side of the Vatican. If it hadn't, you'd be dead by now.'

'Killed by one of your assassin priest's no doubt?'

'Precisely my dear. It's nothing personal you understand – just the way we do business. Oh, and talking of *business*, how did your little trip to Suffolk go?'

The expression on the cardinal's face and the manner in which he'd phrased the question put her immediately on her guard. She'd seen it all before. The way he smiled at the end of his sentence and lifted his cigar to his lips.

'Edward,' she said. 'I didn't find the girl. I was unable to rescue Rachel Morrison.'

'I know.'

'You do...?'

'Yes, Sterling. I received an intelligence report only this afternoon. Rachel's been taken out of the country and was last heard of heading in the direction of northern Italy. You missed her by about nine hours apparently.'

'It was a set-up, Edward. I barely escaped with my life.'

'How so?' replied the cardinal, raising an eyebrow.

'Someone planted a revenant on me. The thing was alive. Jimmy Silver's work more than likely. Two of his henchmen placed an undead revenant in one of the upstairs bedrooms of the cottage. The revenant – a demon child – was tied up in a cloth bundle. I thought it was Rachel, but when I opened the bundle the damn thing had me by the throat.'

'And…?'

'I blasted it with a 9mm bullet, but I was lucky. Where were your priests Edward? Where was my backup?'

'Unavailable my dear. We simply don't have enough exorcists to spare. They've all been pulled back to Italy until further notice.'

'Why?'

'Because with the death of Pope Gregory, Jimmy Silver's attention has now moved to Rome, or so we've been led to believe.'

'By who?'

'By higher powers than myself, Sterling. In any case, I've told you not to ask me questions like that before. You know they can't be answered.'

Sterling looked down at the chessboard on the table in front of the cardinal. The black King was no longer in check. Both sides in the game were now evenly matched. It was going to be a close thing. Looking up, she spoke:

'How long will it be before you have to return to Rome for the election, Edward?'

'Not long. I received my orders this afternoon. I'm due to fly back tomorrow morning all being well.'

'What about me? What do I do?'

The cardinal glanced up from the board. 'Stay in London until further notice. I'll keep you informed should you be required elsewhere.'

'But what about you, cardinal? What will you do?'

'Oh, I'll be safe enough for the time being. As for yourself, it would be best if you kept as low a profile as possible.'

'Why? What's going to happen?'

Narrowing his eyes to slits, the cardinal poured her out a large glass of brandy and pushed the glass across the table. 'We are under attack, Sterling. The Church is at war. Pope Gregory did not die of natural causes. It seems likely he was poisoned by one of Silver's agents.'

'Who?'

'We're not sure. My contact in Rome informed me it may well have been Cardinal Lomellini the head of the Vatican Library but there were others involved, including agents of the Camorra, hence the connection with Jimmy Silver.'

'It would make sense, Edward; but why poison Gregory? What would he have to gain from such an act?'

'Gain?' echoed de Valois, somewhat taken aback by the young vampire's naivety. 'He would have everything to gain and we would have everything to lose. The Church would be nothing more than a puppet in the hands of whoever Silver managed to put in charge of the Vatican as the new Pope. As for yourself and others like you, only those vampire clans loyal to Silver would prosper. The rest would all be hunted down and exterminated.'

'Including Grimaldi and the Bene Noctu?'

'Count Grimaldi would be the first on Silver's hit list. His feud with Grimaldi goes back centuries – even longer than his feud with your good self. In any case, that will be the very least of your problems given certain other matters which have recently been brought to my attention.'

'Such as?'

'It's Charles Martel— He's killed again.'

'Holy fuck—!! Where?'

'Right in your own back yard, Sterling. His latest victim was a high-ranking police officer called Sally Reid. She was decapitated while leaving her home in Surrey early this morning.'

'How did you know it was Charlie?'

'Because he left his calling card. Sally's body was mutilated just like all the rest and that's not our only problem.'

'It's bad enough, Edward. What if he comes after me? He used to be Europe's *numero uno* vampire slayer after all. What the hell am I going to do?'

'That's why I'm telling you to keep as low a profile as possible until further notice.'

Sterling took a swig of brandy and banged her glass down on the table. 'And the other problem? You said there was something else—'

'Oh yes – several things in fact. Vatican intel suggests that young Rachel Morrison is to be sacrificed to the infernal powers in return for their support in getting Silver's man elected as the new Pope.'

'Why should that surprise me Edward? He's done things like that before.'

'Indeed he has my dear, but that's not the only thing going on. According to news received from one of my contacts, a significant quantity of C-4 plastic explosive was recently transported to Venice, the precise reason for which has yet to be ascertained.'

'Why should that be a problem?'

'The transportation was carried out by the Camorra who have connections with Jimmy Silver. Venice is also the personal fiefdom of Cardinal Lorenzo Spada who is topped to be one of the main contenders in the forthcoming papal election.'

'And you think there might be a connection?'

'It's a possibility. There's an awful lot hanging in the balance at the moment and the stakes are quite high; though I can't think for the life of me where the plastic explosive fits in. Still, we don't want to get caught napping do we?'

'No, I suppose we don't, Edward. Is there anything else I should be aware of while we're at it?'

'Yes, there is as a matter of fact. You'd best lay in an extra place at you're dinner table for the next couple of days.'

'Why?'

'Because you'll be entertaining a distinguished visitor, that's why. If in the meantime you should need to get in contact with me, use the Vatican landline wherever possible and try not to use the Internet. My email address may already have been compromised. Now, if there's nothing further you wish to discuss with me, I shall bid you farewell,' continued de Valois gesturing her with a dismissive wave of his hand. 'Oh, and Sterling…'

'Yes, Your Eminence?'
'Just one more thing.'
'What's that?'
'Good luck—'

12

As his aircraft dropped through the clouds, Foscari caught his first glimpse of England. He was surprised how green everything was. Back in Italy the land could appear parched and dry this time of the year, but here in Britain everything was as fresh and verdant as the first day of spring.

What was he doing here? That he had to collect someone called Rachel Morrison and escort her back to the Vatican for the duration of the papal election was certain. But what about everything else Father Donnelly had told him, and why had he agreed to travel to London in the first place? It wasn't as if he didn't have any choice in the matter, was it?

Choice...

Why had he chosen to enter the priesthood all those years ago back in his little home town high up in the Dolomite mountains? He'd been certain back then that a life in the service of God was the life for him. Now he wasn't so sure.

"Because you're such a good manager, Foscari," he remembered Pope Gregory having said when the Holy Father had promoted him to the office of Dean of the College of Cardinals. A *manager...* Was that all he was in the eyes of his peers? Just someone who kept the machinery of the Vatican running while others more worthy than himself aspired to higher things? Foscari was no mystic that much was certain, but neither was he a Holy Fool. He knew the world for what it was and accepted it as such. Maybe that was why he'd been given the task of bringing Rachel to the Vatican, and maybe – just maybe – that was why he was here right now, suspended several thousand feet in the air above English soil about to rescue the soul of a young woman from the clutches of eternal damnation.

As the call to fasten his seatbelt came, he glanced once again out of the window. Down below, the distinctive shape of the buildings and city were beginning to appear along with the meandering outreaches of the river Thames. Then he heard the unmistakable sound of the plane's undercarriage being lowered, followed shortly after that by a sudden jolt as the aircraft touched down on the tarmac and slowed itself to a halt at the end of the runway. His journey was over. He'd arrived in England.

In the main terminal, everyone was in a mad hurry to get places. People with friends and family to meet. Relatives to visit. It all made him feel rather sad and alone in the world. But not for long.

Craning his neck, he could just about make out the figures of two men standing a little way to one side of the crowd. One of the men was holding up a piece of white card with his name written on it in black marker pen. He waved, and the man holding the white card waved back, beckoning him to come forward to where they were standing next to a small coffee counter wedged between two larger retail outlets.

'Cardinal Foscari?' inquired the taller man, folding the piece of white card in his two enormous hands and depositing it in a nearby litter bin. Foscari nodded and waited for the man to continue.

'My name's Joe Rackham and this here bloke is called Gordon. We're here to escort you to your destination, Your Eminence. Come on, look sharpish Gordon and pick up the cardinal's luggage. It's quite a walk to the taxi rank.'

They weren't what he was expecting of an ecclesiastical reception committee. For one thing they weren't priests, and for another they both appeared to be wearing leather motorcycle jackets complete with blue Levi jeans tucked into biker boots below the knee. When the man called Gordon bent over to pick up his suitcase, Foscari noticed that the back of his jacket was emblazoned with the distinctive flying death's head of the Hell's Angels motorcycle club – a one-time notorious gang of renegade bikers who had last had their heyday in the UK and America back in the 1970s and 80s. How ironic thought Foscari that a man like himself should have been placed under the protection of two Angels from Hell. But they weren't the only ones…

As the cardinal was ushered out through the front entrance of the terminal building, he could see at least four other gang members standing idly beside their motorcycles waiting for him near the taxi rank. That they were clearly blocking the road for other driver's didn't seem to bother them in the slightest, and it was only when a traffic cop came over and had a word with them that they grudgingly straddled their machines and moved to one side to allow other vehicles to pass.

'This is your taxi,' said the man called Joe as they walked towards a rather grubby black London cab. The cab seemed terribly old-fashioned and out of place among all the other cars lined up in the rank. Indeed, the same could be said for the driver of the ancient taxi who by now had emerged from his cabin and was helping Foscari into the back seat along with his suitcase. He appeared to be a man well into his fifties just like Joe, and he was wearing the same type of leather jacket and blue denim jeans, only in his case, the motorcycle boots had been replaced with a pair of more practical white trainers.

'Exactly where is it that you're taking me-?' inquired Foscari as the man sat back in his driver's seat and closed the door with a clunk. '- Only I was told I would be staying at a religious establishment for the duration of my visit to London.'

'There's been a change of plan,' replied the driver turning round in his seat. 'According to Sterling, I'm to take you to a warehouse on the south side of the river. It's for your own protection apparently.'

Before he could reply, the driver slammed the old taxi into first gear and floored the accelerator pedal, causing the vehicle to pull away from the kerb and merge with all the other traffic in the road. As it moved away, Foscari heard the sound of six motorcycle engines revving up to follow on behind. It looked as if Joe and his gang of bikers were going to be providing the escort security for the journey to wherever it was that he was being taken.

'My name's Jerry Skinner by the way,' said the taxi driver glancing from side to side as he negotiated the busy London streets. 'I'm a friend of Sterling's in case you didn't already know.'

Sterling... There was that name again. The same one Donnelly had mentioned in passing, but neglected to furnish him with all the details of exactly who she was or her place in the overall scheme of things. According to his own research, she was a one-time notorious British criminal who'd been shot dead on the streets of Naples back in 2003, but clearly this wasn't the case, and the mere fact that he was now in the company of her associates filled him full of horror.

'This is all highly irregular,' exclaimed Foscari starting to panic. 'I was distinctly told I was to be taken to a place called St Jude's and not some derelict warehouse beside the Thames.'

'Sorry padre, but I've got my orders. I'm to take you to Sterling's place without delay.'

'Sterling's place—?' But I can't possibly be seen there. I have to organize the papal election in a few days time! I demand you let me out of this vehicle at once—'

'No can do. The orders came directly from Cardinal de Valois so it's not as if I've got much choice in the matter.'

'De Valois? But I outrank de Valois. I'm Dean of the College. He's just a bloody exorcist!'

The man called Skinner drove on, quietly oblivious to the Dean's request to be released from the taxi. When the cab stopped at a set of traffic lights, Foscari tried the door handle but found it was locked from the inside. He was effectively being held prisoner inside the vehicle until it reached its destination.

'Are you an exorcist, padre?' inquired the driver ending his short silence at last.

'What?' replied Foscari distractedly.

'Are you an exorcist?' repeated Skinner leaning into a turn and beckoning one of the motorcyclists to move up level with the taxi to guard its flank.

'Er, no I'm not,' answered the Dean. 'Few members of the Curia actually carry out exorcisms. It's not our job.'

'Too bad,' Skinner replied gesturing the outrider to reposition his bike. 'I only asked because we're two priests down at the moment.'

'Two priests down…?'

'Yeah. Sterling reckons they got ambushed by some revenants. Both were killed of course. One of them had the blood sucked out through his eyes. Nasty business it was.'

'Ah, then in that case I'm definitely not an exorcist,' Foscari answered, wondering what on earth Skinner had meant by his use of the term *revenant*. 'I mean, I've had a little training in it, but I'm not a real exorcist.'

'Don't worry about it,' continued Skinner taking another turn in the road. 'For what it's worth, I'm not a real taxi driver either! Enjoy your stay at Sterling's place. We're almost there.'

13

It wasn't what he expected.

Access to the five-storey red brick building was via a narrow street situated in a district of London almost untouched by the hand of time. As the metal roller-shutter door slowly opened, Foscari found himself being led through a small loading bay and then up through several flights of dusty concrete steps until he reached what he took to be the second or third floor of an old Victorian warehouse.

'We're one of the best equipped outfits in the south of England,' remarked Joe, leading him through yet another door and down a short corridor towards what he took to be the nerve centre of the building. 'This place used to be a tea warehouse back in the nineteenth century, but now it's mostly used for storing contraband goods, if you know what I mean.'

'Drugs?'

'Yeah, and a few other things when Sterling lets us. It's antiques mostly, plus a bit of knock-off designer gear we move through the street markets. Debbie usually handles that end of things.'

'Debbie?'

'Yes – Debbie Stephenson. She's one of London's top grafters. Does a bit of shoplifting on the side as well.'

'So, you're a criminal organization then?'

'Good heavens no. We're what you might call "Sterling's Irregulars." The business end of things is just a sideline. It's how we finance the operation. Let's face it, the CIA did pretty much the same kind of stuff for years until things got so bad that the American government had to step in and actually pay them.'

'And what precisely is the nature of this *operation* might I ask?'

'Exterminating vampires, that's what. Time was when the Hell's Angels were just a motorcycle club that dabbled in organized crime. Then we got ourselves busted by the Feds back in 2003 and much of the global network was taken down.

The British chapters of the HA didn't suffer much, but we still had to keep a low profile. Other biker-gangs have largely taken our place now and the names have changed. Any more questions?'

Foscari shook his head. He'd heard enough.

'Good. I'll take you through then,' responded Joe, leading the Dean under a low sandstone archway set into a whitewashed brick wall. 'Don't worry. Her ladyship will be down in a moment so you won't be on your own for long. Me and the boys have got another job on. It looks like there's a killer on the loose. Priests are going down like nine pins. Sterling reckons the war's kicked off ahead of schedule so you'll probably be a lot safer locked up in this old warehouse for a few day until we see how things are shaping up. Bye for now—'

There were to be no introductions then thought the Dean as the sound of Joe's footsteps receded into silence leaving him all alone in his new surroundings. It was a huge room with a high ceiling lost in shadow and from which hung an ancient chandelier suspended from the rafters by a single length of chain. Other than this, the only other source of illumination came from a number of plain wax candles that shone through the gloom like the yellow eyes of wolves.

As his vision adjusted to the dimness, Foscari could just about make out the looming shapes of what he took to be several items of quality antique furniture that would have been more in keeping with one of the best houses in Rome or Paris rather than stored here in a derelict South London warehouse. Clearly someone was using the place to fence stolen property.

'Cardinal Foscari—?'

It was a woman's voice that he heard. Cold and austere, it seemed to fill the limitless void of the chamber with an eerie chill as its owner stepped out into the light and stood with both feet planted slightly apart on the carpet. The woman had an athletic appearance and wore a black leotard beneath a red, tabard-style dress.

'I am Paolo Foscari,' replied the Dean with a mixture of fascination and dread. 'You would be Sterling I take it?'

'Yes, cardinal. At least that's what I call myself these days,' said the woman, motioning him to be seated on a nearby sofa. 'I expect you must be tired after your journey from Rome. Here, let me take your suitcase and I'll make us some coffee. Do you take milk and sugar?'

'Er, I think I'll have mine black with lots of sugar,' answered the Dean, clearing away a pile of magazines and newspapers from one side of the sofa to the other so as to make a space for himself to sit down.

As she went to fetch the coffee, Foscari repressed a shudder. He'd never before seen such hard features on a woman. She was like a piece of granite stone, the way she'd just stood there staring at him from behind those dark sunglasses of hers. He guessed her age to be around twenty-five at most, but there was a surly confidence in her expression that could quite easily have belonged to a mature forty-year old.

Once he was seated and waiting for his host to reappear from the kitchen, he whiled away his time idly flicking through a few of the magazines and papers which lay in a heap to one side of him. They proved to be the usual collection of contemporary journals and weekend glossies that litter the living rooms of most suburban houses, except for one or two items which turned out to be photocopies and press cuttings from old newspaper articles dating back twenty years or more. Then Foscari noticed one magazine in particular which had a picture of the former president of the United States, Jimmy Carter on the front cover and realized that some of the material he was reading was as much as forty years out of date.

Presently, Sterling returned with two steaming mugs of coffee on a small tray and placed them on the floor near Foscari's feet. Then, picking up her own mug from the tray, she walked over to an adjacent table and seated herself down on a high-backed antique chair. Pulling open a drawer beneath the table, she drew out a small wooden box. Opening the lid of the box, she pinched a small quantity of white powder between her thumb and forefinger before sniffing it sharply up her nose. Then, placing both her elbows squarely on the table, she cupped her chin in her hands and gazed at Foscari intently: 'I take it Joe has filled you in on the precise nature of this place and everything that goes on inside here,' she said at length.

'Indeed he did,' replied the Dean, taking a sip of coffee and nibbling on a digestive biscuit, 'though I must say it came as quite a shock. I wasn't expecting it.'

'I suppose not. There was a last minute change of plan owing to unforeseen circumstances.'

Looking at the woman again, Foscari wondered what colour her eyes were behind those dark glasses of hers.

'My eyes are not what you would consider as being exactly normal, Your Eminence. You really don't want to see them, you really don't...'

Foscari stiffened and gripped the arms of the sofa in surprise. Had she just read his mind he wondered? The woman merely smiled, registering his discomfort with something approaching mild amusement. She'd recently washed her hair and a single strand of it hung down over her brow like a thin black pencil line. Flicking it aside with a movement of her index finger, she quickly got to the point.

'Who sent you here, cardinal?'

Foscari cleared his throat nervously. 'It was an Irish priest called Michael Donnelly if you must know.'

'Ah, *Father Donnelly.* That high up, huh?'

'Yes... Well, I mean he lives upstairs from the Pope so I suppose he must have some influence in the Vatican.'

'That's not what I meant,' answered the woman quietly but without elaboration. That she perhaps knew a whole lot more than she was letting on quickly became apparent when the Dean asked his next question:

'You know Michael Donnelly then?'

'Indeed I do, Cardinal Foscari. We met the last time I was in Rome with Cardinal de Valois having an audience with Pope Gregory. I've heard the news by the way. It's so sad.'

'Yes - He was poisoned.'

'I know.'

'You do—? How?'

'De Valois told me. I had a meeting with him shortly before he left for Rome.'

'The papal election...?'

'That among other things. The situation is quite dangerous Your Eminence. I expect Donnelly briefed you on all the details otherwise you wouldn't be here.'

'He did,' replied Foscari going on the defensive. How much this woman actually knew was open to question, but he was becoming increasingly anxious about the extent of her knowledge of Vatican politics given the fact that she was an outsider and most probably not even a Roman Catholic.

'Julie Kent's parents were catholics, Cardinal Foscari, though I myself am most definitely not moving in that direction I can assure you.'

Dammit. She'd done it again. She'd read his mind just like Father Donnelly. Were they both related he wondered, and who the hell was Julie Kent?

'Before we go on, Sterling, there's one question I would like to ask you.'

'And what is that, cardinal?'

'Who exactly is Michael Donnelly?'

'Father Donnelly is what is commonly referred to as a Seraphim, Your grace.'

'He's a *what?*'

'A Seraphim. It's one of the highest orders of Angels and closest to God. He was put in charge of looking after Pope Gregory while he was still alive and assisting Cardinal de Valois to run the Order of Exorcists. Do you want me to spell it out for you or would you prefer me to write it down in ancient Hebrew. I can do that as well…'

The conversation fell silent. For a moment, Foscari could have sworn he heard the sound of laughter in the air, but dismissed the thought from his mind almost as quickly as it had arisen. Then, taking her up on her sarcastic response, he continued with his line of questioning.

'And you… What exactly are *you*, Sterling? Donnelly never told me.'

'Goodness me, what a question,' the woman replied feigning embarrassment. 'Perhaps you would like something else to drink, Your Eminence. Something a little stronger perhaps?'

A brief interval elapsed after which Foscari found himself still seated on the sofa, only this time he was sipping the darkest of claret wines from a tall, long-stemmed crystal goblet. The wine tasted excellent and was from an estate he wasn't altogether familiar with.

'It's from Burgundy, cardinal. It was part of a consignment of vintage wines Joe and the boys bought in last month. Like it?'

'Mmm, yes I do. It's one of the finest I've ever tasted.'

'Good. I'm pleased,' she replied, watching intently as Foscari's long gaze drifted over to the pile of faded magazines and old newspapers on the sofa. She continued watching as his age-freckled hand reached out to one of the ancient press-cuttings and he began reading:

'Julie Kent...' he said at length. 'This article is dated July 1977 and is about a young English woman called Julie Kent. It says she went missing in London back in July 1977 and her body was never found...'

'So?'

'Well you mentioned her name earlier on, and the young woman in the press photograph looks a bit like yourself except that she's got ginger hair and this newspaper cutting is well over forty years old. She's not wearing dark glasses either.'

'I didn't have them back then, cardinal. Didn't need to.'

'What do you mean? The woman in this newspaper can't be much older than nineteen years of age. If you were her, then you'd most likely be well into your sixties by now. And why are you still wearing those sunglasses? It's not particularly bright in this room. Do you have a problem with your eyes?'

'No, Your Eminence. I do not have a problem with my eyes, but other people might.'

'Oh – I'm sorry,' replied Foscari realizing he'd gone too far. 'You are disfigured in some way perhaps?'

'No, it's not that, cardinal...'

'Then what ? What is the problem with your eyes?'

Sterling kept on looking at the Dean, never taking her gaze off him for a second. *He's got to learn sometime,* she thought. *Best do it now while he's still in a receptive mood. That claret wine I gave him should calm him down a bit.*

Satisfied she had Foscari's full attention, Sterling leaned forward in her chair with both hands resting on her knees:

'Do you believe in vampires, Cardinal Foscari?'

'Well I don't disbelieve... I mean, I wouldn't be in the Catholic Church if I didn't have some belief in the possibility of demonic forces at work in the world.'

'Do you believe in vampires?' Sterling repeated slowly, gazing directly into Foscari's eyes.

Foscari blinked, taken aback by the sudden change in the subject matter of their conversation. 'If you mean, do I believe in the sort of vampires you see in the movies, then no I don't. Why do you ask?'

Sterling took off her sunglasses and looked at him, channeling her gaze into his mind. He remembered seeing two piercing orbs of crimson light where there should have been eyes, then fear took hold of him and he began trembling violently in his seat.

At first he thought he was having an epileptic fit. There was a sudden flash like an electric shock surging through him, then the room disappeared and Foscari found himself in a very strange place.

The smell of blood and fear was strong. He knew he was witnessing everything Sterling had ever seen and done over a lifetime. He saw scenes of violence that would have shocked even the most hardened forensic pathologist, so intense were the images that now paraded before his mind's eye. In some, the hapless victims were seen trying to make a run for it before Sterling closed for the kill.The screaming was the worst part, but it usually didn't last very long before each individual was very quickly dispatched and drained of their blood with fiendish mechanical precision. Exactly what manner of creature he was dealing with, Foscari did not know, but all these acts of carnage he was now witnessing certainly weren't the work of a young 1970s teenager called Julie Kent. No, the person who carried out these attacks was clearly something else; a homicidal maniac, an escaped lunatic, or someone who was demonically possessed, he couldn't say. All he could do was tear himself away from Sterling's gaze and try to run.But he couldn't...

'Not yet, cardinal!' came a voice out of the darkness. 'There's more…'

The scene now shifted to the interior of a fashionable London apartment where a party was in full swing. It was 1977 and a young woman with ginger hair had just entered the room. Foscari guessed the girl was Julie Kent and that this would be the last time she would ever be seen alive. The next series of images saw Julie as the victim of a frenzied vampire attack by a well-to-do patrician lady called Virginia Cavendish, followed by an interval of time that concluded with Julie's body being washed up on a beach after Jimmy Silver had arranged to have it dumped somewhere out at sea. She survived the attack but wasn't the same person she'd been before. The change was subtle at first, but when it was complete there was no sign in those long pale features and jet black hair of Sterling's that Julie Kent had ever existed at all. As the days passed into years, Julie assumed the name of Sterling and developed an alarming drug habit. Now it was the 1980s and her desire for human blood and random acts of violence had increased to such an extent that she was barely able to control it. A short while after this, her reputation as an underworld enforcer was established in one sickening act of carnage that would have made the Kray twins green with envy and she was now known to the police simply as "Sterling" – one of the most notorious villains on the streets of London. By the late 1990s when by rights she should have been well into her forties, instead she had the fresh and unblemished appearance of someone in their early twenties. She was now running a crime gang from an old Victorian warehouse near Tower Bridge where everything was going smoothly for her until she decided to seek revenge on the woman called Virginia Cavendish for what she'd done to her. This was too much for those individuals who held power in the land, and Sterling was forced to flee the country and seek refuge in America before traveling to Naples in 2003 where she was gunned down in the street by two Camorra hitmen operating under the instructions of Jimmy Silver…

'They used special bullets, cardinal. You know what I'm saying?'

'They did what?' murmured Foscari coming out of his trance.

'They used special bullets,' repeated Sterling, putting her dark sunglasses back on. 'The bullets were made of silver. Does that mean anything to you...?'

'No... Should it?' he answered, creasing his brow in thought. 'I know you need silver bullets to kill werewolves and the undead, but...'

'Good,' said Sterling. You're getting warmer. Anything else...?'

Foscari was silent for a moment as he considered the matter. Running a series of B-movie images through his head, he utterly failed to make the necessary connections. Then he thought about what Father Donnelly had told him about Jimmy Silver and still couldn't believe it, at which point Sterling chose to intervene:

'I trust Donnelly briefed you about what manner of creature Jimmy Silver is and all that he's up to?'

'Yes he did, and a great deal more besides. I didn't believe a word of it though. I thought he was having a joke – especially about Silver.'

'Well he wasn't. Why do you think I was born in 1957 as Julie Kent but only look about twenty years of age?'

'You've had plastic surgery?'

Sterling shook her head.

'Good genes?'

'Quite the opposite, Cardinal Foscari. There's nothing good about my genes now – or Jimmy Silver's for that matter.'

'I'm still not following you.'

'It's really quite simple, cardinal. It's because we're both vampires... And we're not the only ones either.'

'How many?' inquired Foscari, leaning forward almost as if he were engaged in the act of hearing confession.

'Thousands, Your Eminence. There are thousands of us scattered across the face of the planet. The bulk of the population is centered in Europe and its numbers are growing rapidly. That's half the problem... We've been too successful'

It was now that the Dean recalled his conversation with Father Donnelly and what the priest had told him. Together with his own research into Jimmy Silver and the mysterious Francesco Grimaldi, everything was beginning to make sense.

'We're divided up into clans,' Sterling continued, 'though I myself belong to no clan other than Joe Rackham and his gang of bikers, and they're all mortal humans like yourself and Jerry Skinner.'

'The taxi driver?'

'Yes. Him. We've been together for a long time have me and Skinner. All the way back to the 1980s in fact.'

'So how come you work for the Church if you're, erm... one of the Undead?'

'I was compromised, Your Eminence. The Vatican gave me a choice. Either I cooperate with them or I get a silver bullet in my chest. Cardinal de Valois is my handler.'

'I see...' replied Foscari, his voice tailing off as he noticed the unmistakable shape of a pistol sticking out from under the pile of magazines on the sofa.

'Careless of me,' exclaimed the woman, snatching it away and placing it on the small octagonal table beside her chair.

'You carry a firearm, Sterling?'

'Yes, cardinal. It's a Beretta. I use it for close encounters with the Undead. It's standard Vatican issue in case you didn't know.'

'The Vatican gave you a gun!?'

'The weapon was issued by Cardinal de Valois in his capacity as head of the Order of Exorcist. The only other people licensed to use one are the assassin priests who belong to the Order.'

'Assassin priests...?' muttered Foscari in surprise. 'I had no idea.'

'Well you should have. In the Middle Ages it was crossbows and silver daggers. Now they use guns. The Vatican weapon of choice is the Beretta.'

'And the other gun...?'

'What other...? Oh, I see,' replied Sterling following the cardinal's gaze. 'That's a Noguchi Magnum revolver. One of Joe's men must have left it there. It most likely belongs to Spike or Gordon. Damn fine weapon. You could kill a bear with one of those things.'

'And what exactly do they use it for, may I inquire?'

'Dunno. Intimidation value I guess. As well as helping de Valois out, they also do a bit of business on the side. Drugs I expect. I've learned not to ask.'

Disturbed by her answer, Cardinal Foscari allowed his gaze to wander once again. When it eventually returned, it came with a simple question:

'Where's Rachel Morrison? I have a busy schedule ahead of me tomorrow, escorting young Rachel to Rome.'

'Yes, I do believe Cardinal de Valois briefed me on the matter,' replied Sterling looking evasive. 'I'm afraid there's been a bit of a problem on that score, Dean.'

'A problem? What sort of a problem? The Vatican jet will be arriving tomorrow at Heathrow and I've got to get back to Rome in time for the election.'

'Don't worry, Your Eminence. Cardinal de Valois will be handling that end of things for the time being.'

'He's what!?'

'De Valois has taken over the administration of the Conclave in your absence. He thought it prudent in the circumstances.'

'Why?'

'Because Rachel Morrison has been kidnapped, that's why?'

'Kidnapped— But how?' He was about to add words to the effect that Rachel was to have been kept under the watchful eye of the Vatican to prevent her being sacrificed to the infernal powers but he guessed Sterling already knew.

Settling into her chair, she fixed the Dean with a stare. Foscari flinched, but then relaxed when he realized there wasn't going to be a repeat performance with those eyes of hers.

'I'm afraid we were set up, Your Grace. It was a trap. A few days ago we received intelligence that someone working for Jimmy Silver had rented a cottage in the Suffolk marshes. Naturally we assumed the place was going to be used to hold Rachel until she could be shipped out of the country. When I entered the cottage I was attacked by a demon revenant. I barely escaped with my life.'

'And Rachel…?'

'She's gone. According to de Valois, she was last reported heading in the direction of northern Italy, most likely bound for Venice. Presumably that's where Jimmy Silver has his current base of operations.'

'Or Lorenzo Spada…'

'Pardon me?'

'Oh, I'm sorry. I was just thinking aloud, that's all. According to Father Donnelly, Cardinal Spada is Jimmy Silver's creature, and the city of Venice was once his personal fiefdom. Spada is the main contender for the office of Pope, assuming the election goes his way. Silver means to install Lorenzo Spada in the Vatican.'

'Yes, I've heard his name before. De Valois told me. So you think Venice is the key then? That's where we should go looking for Rachel?'

'Well, judging from what you've just told me, I can't see it being otherwise, unless of course Silver's already moved on with his plans and carried out the human sacrifice.'

'I certainly hope not.'

'Why do you say that, Sterling?'

'Because if Silver gets his man elected as the Holy Father, then it's the end of the road for all those vampire clans who refuse to pledge allegiance to him, and that includes myself and Count Grimaldi. We'd all be as good as dead; and with Grimaldi gone, the balance of power would shift in Silver's favour. Control of the Bene Noctu and the papacy combined would effectively render Jimmy Silver immune from prosecution by the Order of Exorcist and the vampire council. He'd be able to do whatever he liked and there'd be no one to stop him.'

'Count Grimaldi is the secretary of the Bene Noctu, isn't he. What's his part in all of this? Donnelly didn't fully explain the situation to me.'

'Donnelly briefed you well enough, cardinal. Francesco Grimaldi is the only representative of the Undead allowed to negotiate with the papacy on our behalf. It is Grimaldi who helps maintain the balance of power between the Undead and the rest of humanity. Without the council of the Bene Noctu acting as referees, all forms of negotiation between human kind and those vampires loyal to Silver will break down. There'd be a bloodbath.

'So the Bene Noctu function a bit like the United Nations then,' exclaimed Foscari with a chuckle.

'Not funny!' snapped Sterling with a frown. 'Grimaldi and the Bene Noctu have been keeping a lid on things for the last three hundred years. Once they're gone then everything you understand as civilization will crumble into dust along with that cosy little dreamworld you've all built for yourselves in Rome. Humanity would become nothing more than a herd of beef cattle waiting for the slaughterhouse. Now do you appreciate the gravity of the situation, Your Eminence?'

Lost for words, Foscari put aside his wine glass and said vaguely: 'The Lord will find a way. I shall pray for guidance...'

'The time for prayer ran out when Pope Gregory died, cardinal. In any case, I somehow doubt it would do any good with Charles Martel on the loose.'

'Charles Martel...? Isn't he the one responsible for killing that English vicar... er, oh, I forget his name...'

'David Saunders?'

'Yes, that's the man. Father Donnelly told me all about it. Apparently he was decapitated with a Japanese sword. Nasty business it was.'

'Hmm, well you'd better get used to it, Paolo, because you're going to be seeing more evidence of his handiwork tomorrow when we visit the autopsy room.'

'When we *what*...?'

'We've been invited to attend a police autopsy. There are a few questions the authorities would like to ask you about the nature of the killing.'

'Ask me...? What the hell have I got to do with it for Christ sake?'

'Don't worry. They don't suspect you, Your Eminence. They just need your assistance with a few theological details, that's all.'

'What kind of details? I never knew David Saunders and I'm not even an Anglican priest.'

'Oh, I shouldn't let that concern you, cardinal. After all, it's not the Reverend Saunders' body we're going to be looking at.'

14

Foscari's shoes squeaked on the floor as he walked down the corridor towards the mortuary. A mortuary assistant led the way, pushing open the fire doors as they went, Sterling following silently behind.

'The examination room isn't far,' explained the man as they turned into yet another passageway and headed off in the direction of a short flight of stairs. As they reached the bottom of the stairs, the cold, filtered air of the morgue caused Foscari to rub some warmth into his arms and draw up the collar of his thin coat. Sterling didn't feel the chill, and the mortuary assistant seemed accustomed to it as he moved to open the door of the examination room and ushered them both inside.

The first surprise was the presence of a uniformed police officer standing in the room next to the examination table the assistant had directed them to. Beside the table stood another man in full surgical scrubs and wellington boots. He was leaning over a body laid out on the table and glanced up when they entered.

'Cardinal Foscari has arrived, Dr Grainger. Is it alright for him to view the body now?'

'Yes, yes of course,' replied the man straightening up. 'I'm almost finished here.'

Foscari was shocked by the sight of him. Pale faced, unshaven and with dark shadows beneath his eyes, he looked like he hadn't slept for days. The police officer by contrast seemed more relaxed and in charge of himself. He appeared to be a man well into his fifties and most likely very close to retirement age.

'Hello inspector,' exclaimed Sterling walking over to where the policeman was standing. 'This is Cardinal Foscari. He's come to help you with your inquiries. Cardinal Foscari, this is Inspector Lefarge. He's an old friend of mine.'

The inspector raised a closed fist to his mouth and gave a nervous cough. 'Sterling,' he replied with a curt nod of his head before extending his other hand to Foscari in greeting.

Shaking the inspector's hand, Foscari made to greet the medical examiner also, but quickly realized his mistake. Dr Grainger was wearing surgical gloves and they were smeared in blood.

'Sorry about the gloves, cardinal. I was just stitching her up when you both arrived. She's quite a mess I'm afraid. I've never seen one this bad before.'

Inspector Lefarge pursed his lips as if suppressing a bitter taste in his mouth, or maybe trying to choose his words more carefully before he spoke. 'Sally Reid was one of my colleagues, Dr Grainger.'

'Oh, I am sorry. I didn't know that.'

Foscari looked down at the woman's body. She was laid out on the metal gurney like a piece of freshly butchered meat. That she'd been decapitated was more than obvious from the marks around her neck.

'I had to stitch her head back on,' continued Dr Grainger admiring his handiwork. 'The cut was clean and most likely carried out with a sword. She was found in the driveway of her home next to her car. She must have been on her way to work when it happened.'

'I see,' replied Foscari, 'and you think the killing may have had some sort of religious significance?'

'We're not sure,' put in Lefarge. 'Sally wasn't done like all the rest of them. We've had a number of killings over the past few weeks and in all cases the victims had certain parts of their body removed.'

'Such as?'

'The liver and sexual organs mostly.'

'Just like the Reverend Hitchins in Regent's Park and Sister Mary Kelly…'

'Yes,' the inspector replied, flickering a glance in Sterling's direction. 'I see you've been well briefed on the matter, cardinal.'

Sterling looked away. She was standing a few paces behind where the three men were gathered around the body. Dressed in her black leather jacket, jeans and biker boots, she remained silent and non-committal. She alone knew what had happened to Sally Reid and why. The woman had simply known too much, and that fact alone had sealed her fate. It was the way Charles Martel worked even if his more regular victims happened to be vampires like herself.

Bending over the metal gurney, Cardinal Foscari took a closer look at the victim's remains. The body of Detective Superintendent Sally Reid looked quite peaceful as it lay there beneath the cool white beam of the autopsy light. Indeed, were it not for the stitch marks around her neck, a person could have been excused for thinking she was merely taking a short nap before returning to her duties at West End Central police station. But she wasn't. She was dead.

'Well, apart from the obvious decapitation, I can't see anything particularly out of the ordinary with Sally Reid's body,' observed the Dean. 'I mean, nothing of a satanic or ritual nature at any rate.'

Lefarge gestured to the medical examiner with a discreet movement of his hand, and Dr Grainger obliged by pulling back the sheet covering Sally's torso. Foscari drew in a breath, held it for a brief moment and then exhaled with a long *'Pfffff...'*

'What in God's name is that!?' he exclaimed pointing at two raised marks that were clearly visible on the top left section of Sally's torso just below the collar bone.

'We were rather hoping you could help us out with that one, cardinal,' remarked the inspector dryly.

'Yes,' nodded Dr Grainger. I've never seen anything quite like them before. They weren't present when she was brought in and seem to have appeared later of their own accord.'

'Bruises?'

'That's what I thought at first, but on closer inspection, I found they more resembled two raised patches of pigmented skin close together. They were present on all the other bodies we examined – at least, all the ones brought in here, including the body of the Reverend Hitchins found in Regent's Park. He had his liver removed as well by the way, which we took to be a clear sign of ritual activity.'

'Let's not be too hasty, doctor,' said Foscari taking on the persona of a rationalist. 'I mean, they might just be birthmarks in Sally's case.'

'They're not birthmarks,' cut in Sterling, drawing an immediate glance from Lefarge.

'No they're not,' exclaimed the medical examiner. 'Birth marks don't just suddenly appear overnight.'

'But *burn marks* do,' added the inspector throwing his comment into the arena.

Foscari peered closer at the two marks on Sally's upper torso. 'A branding iron perhaps?'

'More like frostbite,' countered Dr Grainger. 'I've only ever witnessed it a couple of times before when I worked in Canada, but those two skin lesions are a dead-ringer for frost damage. I'd stake my reputation on it.'

'Since when does a person get frostbite on their chest?' argued Lefarge. 'Frostbite usually sets in on the fingers and toes surely.'

'Well that's what it looks like to me, inspector. I took a tissue sample from the area and examined it under a microscope. Those two marks were caused by a sudden blast of intense cold.'

'*Or the breath of Hell,*' exclaimed Sterling walking up to the gurney and standing close behind the cardinal. 'The infernal realm normally burns by cold, not by heat.'

'She's right,' added Lefarge. 'Those two marks on Sally's chest weren't caused by heat. They were the result of something very cold in the shape of a hoof print. A cloven hoof. The sign of the Devil.'

Foscari laughed nervously. 'Oh, come now inspector. It would take an entire council of expert theologians several months to decide if satanic forces had been involved with…'

A sudden chill ran up Foscari's spine as he felt Sterling's ice-cold breath on the back of his neck. He turned. She was staring at him with a mischievous grin on her face. 'You got that book I gave you, Hooky' she exclaimed addressing Lefarge.

'Yes I have,' the inspector grunted, patting his breast pocket with the palm of his hand. 'I've got it right here.'

'Good. Let's go and have coffee while Dr Grainger gets on with his work. Perhaps the cardinal will be able to make something of its contents when he sees it.'

* * *

They were seated together outside a café several street blocks away from the morgue. 'It's safer this way,' said Lefarge glancing about. 'You never know who might be watching.'

Removing a plastic evidence bag from his tunic pocket, he opened it and placed the small black book on the table in front of Sterling and the cardinal.

'Well, what's the verdict?' inquired Sterling, regarding the book with some degree of familiarity. 'Is it a code?'

Lefarge shrugged. 'Apart from the names of two cities in Switzerland, the police cipher unit couldn't make head nor tail of the message scribbled on the reverse side of the flyleaf. These days, cipher isn't used very much for encoded information. Hasn't been since the 1940s. The chaps in SIS couldn't crack it either so they sent a copy of it up to some professor at Oxford University. Only then were we able to glean some sort of insight into the true nature of its contents.'

'Which were?'

'Hard to say really. It appears to be a rare form of cipher more commonly used in eighteenth century Italy. Specifically during the Napoleonic War.'

'Hmm... Jimmy Silver was around then and he was in Italy too. Given the description Jenny Hancock gave to Debbie about the bloke she stole the book from, it sounds an awful lot like Silver.'

'Oh, Christ! I'd better give Debbie a ring now and warn her. Once Silver finds out who nicked his book, he's going to go bat-shit crazy and come looking for it—'

'Or send Charles Martel in his stead. 'Yes, inspector; give Debbie a ring and tell her to watch her back. Jenny as well!'

Foscari was only half-listening. He was far more interested in the image of the two crossed keys that were embossed into the fresh leather of the book's cover than anything else.

'How did this book come into your possession?' he inquired with a frown. 'It belongs to the Vatican Library – the Secret Archive to be precise. What is it doing here?'

'One of my associates brought it to me,' answered Sterling. 'Is that a problem?'

'It certainly is,' Foscari exclaimed reaching across the table to pick up the book. 'This volume is quite rare. It's an Incunabulum – a book printed before the year 1501.'

'I know,' Sterling confided. 'The last member of the Curia to have it in their possession was Cardinal de Valois and he returned it to the library in Rome.'

'When?'

'About two years ago. It kind of came in handy when we were dealing with certain matters of an infernal nature.'

'Black magic you mean! This little volume happens to be a grimoire.'

'You don't say, cardinal – I'd never have guessed.'

'For the love of God, what on earth was de Valois doing with a grimoire? He's supposed to be a bloody exorcist!'

'Fighting fire with fire if I remember correctly. Anyway, it still doesn't explain what it was doing in Jimmy Silver's possession, assuming it actually was Silver who had the book when Jenny blagged it off him.'

'Oh, but it was… It most definitely was…'

There was a pause. Sterling gave a sharp intake of breath and looked at Foscari. 'How do you know?'

'How do I know…? Because I know that Jimmy Silver was once called Sir James Blackthorne and because he scribbled his former surname together with his ancestral coat of arms here in the front flyleaf of this damn book, that's how I know!'

'Uh… Oh, I hadn't noticed,' exclaimed Sterling, following Foscari's pointing finger. 'You're right— Three wolves heads emblazoned on a shield. How did you make the connection, cardinal?'

'Father Donnelly told me about Jimmy having once been a minor British aristocrat called James Blackthorne back in the eighteenth century. The rest I got from ancestral records off the internet. The name of Westvale was also mentioned. Apparently, Jimmy Silver – alias Sir James Blackthorne – eloped with Caroline Westvale and they were last reported living in Venice in 1797. Of course, I didn't believe a word of what Donnelly told me about Silver having been a vampire, but I do now.'

'*And you'll believe a damn sight more in a few days time, Paolo...*'

'Pardon me? I didn't quite catch that—'

'Uh...oh, it was nothing cardinal. I was just thinking aloud that's all.'

Foscari gave a cursory nod. Satisfied with her explanation, he resumed his examination of the grimoire.

'This book has recently been rebound,' he announced, stroking the shiny black leather of its cover with his thumb. 'I seem to recall Cardinal Lomellini putting in a request a few months ago to have several old volumes provided with new covers and bindings, and this must have been done then. I wonder why...?'

'Who's Cardinal Lomellini?' inquired Lefarge, dunking a large digestive biscuit in his tea and taking a bite.

'Umberto Lomellini is head of the Vatican Library,' Foscari replied. 'He's one of Lorenzo Spada's associates.'

'Spada is in Jimmy Silver's pocket,' confided Sterling, explaining the situation to the inspector. 'De Valois reckons Jimmy is backing Spada to be the next Pope so he can get the Vatican under his control and destroy the Order of Exorcist.'

Lefarge nodded sagely and continued dunking his biscuit. Privately, Sterling wondered how on earth his wife put up with him – assuming he had a wife of course.

'These inscriptions on the reverse of the flyleaf are interesting,' continued Foscari, opening the book and turning over the first page. 'Although most of it is written in code, there are two words that stand out.'

'You mean the names of two cities, Zurich and Lugano,' the inspector observed. 'You think they might be significant?'

'I certainly do,' replied the cardinal, wincing a little as Lefarge soaked the remains of his soggy digestive into his tea. 'Zurich and Lugano are the two main cities of Switzerland that feature heavily in the international banking industry.'

'Another Vatican banking scandal?' exclaimed the inspector, quick off the mark. 'I'm old enough to remember the first one back in the 1970s.'

'I'm not sure,' replied Foscari, ruminating on the inscription scribbled on the flyleaf. 'Two cities in Switzerland aren't enough to go on. I need more information.'

'Like a master grid to decipher the coded message,' added Sterling. 'This is Jimmy Silver's handwriting in the book, I'm certain of it. I've seen his scrawl before.'

'You have?'

'Yep. The bastard sends me little handwritten letters occasionally just to remind me he's still alive and thirsting for revenge. It's all quite flattering really.'

'He does?'

'But of course, Paolo. Vendettas are what all alpha-vampires do. It's an aristocratic thing apparently, and the feelings are mutual. We both hate each others guts.'

'Oh... Right— I was forgetting. But where could we lay our hands on a master grid for decoding such an obscure cipher?'

'How about asking Lomellini,' suggested Lefarge, almost immediately realizing his mistake and retracting it with some embarrassment.

'I somehow doubt he would be forthcoming,' answered Foscari wryly. 'In any case, the position of Vatican Librarian is largely an honorary title. Cardinal Lomellini is no academic...'

Foscari's words tailed off as his thoughts began to focus on the events of a few days before. Soon he was thinking: *Lomellini was in the Pope's bedroom when we were kneeling in prayer... I saw him with my own eyes. He was looking for something. The coffee cup? The cafetiere? The empty poison vial perhaps? No, there was something else. Something near the Pope's bed...*

'Sterling—' he exclaimed with a sense of urgency, 'get on the phone to de Valois and tell him to double the guard on the papal apartment. The doors have already been sealed and no one is to enter or leave without my express permission, is that understood—'

'Why? What's the problem?'

'Don't ask questions— Just do as I say and tell him to keep an eye on the secret staircase as well. I dare say he knows where it is.'

'No need,' replied Sterling reaching for her mobile; 'Donnelly is watching that.'

'But Father Donnelly is an old man.'

'Yes, and Cardinal de Valois is no spring chicken either. Don't worry, Paolo. Father Donnelly is more than capable of guarding a narrow staircase, I can assure you of that.'

Feeling a bit left out of things, Lefarge dunked a second biscuit into his tea and interrupted. 'But it still doesn't solve the problem of how we get our hands on a master grid though, does it?'

Oh, it just might,' replied Foscari thoughtfully. It just might...'

Sterling made a gesture for silence and brought her mobile up to her right ear. 'It's de Valois,' she said. 'I've got through to the Vatican.'

'Thank Christ for that,' muttered Foscari. 'Tell him to check the seals I had put on the doors of the papal apartment. Ask him if they've been tampered with.'

'*Ssh...*' hissed Sterling, swearing under her breath. 'He's trying to tell me something.'

There was a pause of several minutes as the conversation with Rome progressed. Evidently, a good deal of information was being downloaded and Foscari strained his ears in an effort to make out what it was that de Valois was saying. When Sterling finally ended the call, he could restrain himself no longer.

'How's the situation in Rome, Sterling? Have all the cardinals arrived for the election yet? I really should be getting back you know.'

The vampire shrugged and put her mobile back in her pocket. 'According to Edward, upwards of two-thirds of the electors have turned up so far. He reckons it will be another five days before the Conclave can be assembled for the vote. We've got plenty of time.'

'Good. Did he mention anything else?'

'Yes he did, your Eminence.'

'Such as what?'

'He said he had an absolutely spiffing game of chess with Father Donnelly. Quite spectacular in fact—'

'No, I mean how does he think the vote will go?'

'Well, from what he said, it looks like Lorenzo Spada is still firm favourite for the post along with Alfredo Riboldi the Archbishop of Palermo who is running a close second. Of the remaining four contenders, only Cardinal Ibekwe from Nigeria stands any chance of attracting a block vote from Africa, but he'll be neutralized by the European group on account of his ultra orthodox views.'

'Ah… It looks like it's going to be the Italians then. That figures…'

'Yes it does rather, which makes it all the more vital to ensure that Spada is knocked out of the contest before the final vote is cast. If Spada gets in, then Jimmy Silver has control of the Vatican, and the Camorra gain control of the Vatican Bank.'

'Money laundering! I thought as much,' put in Foscari banging his fist down on the café table much to the surprise of the other customers.

'Yes,' replied Sterling, 'and on a scale far larger than anything that's ever gone on before, not to mention Silver being able to disband the Order of Exorcist and establish globalised control of the Undead. If he manages to pull it off, then every vampire in Europe will be forced to follow him – myself included. We wouldn't have any choice.'

'But who would be a suitable candidate to run against Spada? Who would be willing to take on the role of Supreme Pontiff?'

'Who indeed, cardinal,' replied Sterling, airily. *'Who indeed…'*

Foscari looked away, nodding an apology to one of the customers sitting close by before engaging with his friend once again.

'What else did de Valois have to say?' he inquired anxiously.

'Not much other than what I already know. He confirmed the delivery of a significant quantity of plastic explosive to the Italian mainland with Camorra involvement thereby implicating Jimmy Silver and Lorenzo Spada in the transportation. The consignment was held in Venice for a short while, but was then moved south for some reason.'

'Rome?'

'We're not sure, but de Valois thinks Silver may be using the Camorra to stage some kind of atrocity in the capital to deflect attention from the coup he's planning with the papal election. The matter has since been handed over to the anti-terrorist units who are monitoring the situation.'

'And what about Rachel Morrison? She's the main reason why I'm here after all.'

Sterling watched Foscari's eyes, tracking his thoughts. 'Sorry, cardinal. We've got no intel on Rachel. She's most likely being held somewhere in Venice being prepared for whatever fate awaits her.'

'Well, according the Father Donnelly, it was human sacrifice, and given all that I've witnessed over the past few days I no longer doubt it. How much time have we got?'

'Difficult to say, Your Eminence; besides which we've got another problem. It looks like Charles Martel has struck again.'

'Where?'

'Venice— Same pattern as before, only this time the victim wasn't connected with the Church.'

'Who was it?'

'A young Romanian woman called Daniela Albescu. The circumstances of her death and the wounds inflicted on her body all bear a striking similarity to those victims we witnessed in the UK.'

Foscari looked shocked. 'But why should it be Martel? I mean, it could just as well have been anyone else. I'm sure Italy has just as many lunatics of its own without the need to import them from England.'

Sterling shook her head. 'All the signs point to the fact it was Martel who carried out the killing – signs which we shall probably have confirmed when we talk to the Venetian authorities.'

'De Valois has contacted the carabinieri I take it…?'

'He has. We're leaving on the Vatican jet tomorrow.'

'Oh good. I'm pleased to hear it. I need to be getting back to Rome for the Conclave.'

'We're not going to Rome, cardinal. The jet has been diverted to Venice as a matter of urgency. You're being kept out of the loop for a while.'

'Pardon me?'

'We're going to take a look at Daniela's body, Your Eminence. Cardinal de Valois has a few suspicions about her death he needs investigating. It has also become necessary to postpone the papal election for a few more days until the security situation can be sorted out – and that includes keeping you away from Rome. As leader of the Conclave, your life may well be in danger.'

'I see... And where exactly will we be staying in Venice when we arrive?'

'Somewhere Jimmy Silver would least expect, cardinal.'

'Where?'

'Never mind that for now,' replied Sterling getting up from her seat and bidding Lefarge goodbye; 'Oh, and bring that book with you as well. I've a feeling we're going to need it before the week is out. Now come along Your Eminence – we mustn't keep Lady Westvale waiting. *I dare say she's been waiting long enough already...*'

15

Dipping through thin clouds on a crisp, clear morning, the Vatican jet made a slight course correction affording Sterling and Foscari a breathtaking view of the Adriatic coastline below. Next came the long road and rail causeway that links the city of Venice with mainland Italy followed by the distinctive outline of the Campanile di San Marco together with the meandering course of the Grand Canal. The approach to Marco Polo airport isn't the easiest one for airline pilots to negotiate and there were cheers of relief from the other passengers when the plane finally bumped down on the tarmac and juddered to a halt. As they made their exit from the side door of the jet, Foscari was able to catch a brief glimpse of the interior of the plane's cockpit. The pilot lay slumped across his control panel in an attitude of relief. Evidently, the landing had been a traumatic one for him and not one he cared to perform too often. A bad omen...

'So where did you say we'd be staying when we arrived in Venice.'

'I didn't, cardinal; but if it makes you feel any better, we'll be checking into the hotel *Principe* for one night until we get our bearings. After that, de Valois has arranged for us both to stay at a private house for the duration of our visit. It's an old palazzo dating back to the eighteenth century in a nice quiet part of town where we won't be disturbed.'

'Will we be long? I mean... the election...'

'I shouldn't worry, Paolo. Just long enough to get the information we need.'

As they walked out of the terminal building, Sterling sniffed the air. 'Good,' she declared; 'No trace of another vampire in the vicinity. That's not unusual for a city like Venice. Too much water.'

'What's water got to do with it?'

'Most vampires have a problem crossing water, cardinal. Even walking across a bridge can freak some of us out. As for myself, I'm okay with it in small amounts. Likewise sunlight, but I wouldn't care to stay too long in the tropics though. It might prove bad for my skin.'

* * *

A couple of hours and a bus ride later, Sterling and Foscari found themselves walking through the Piazza San Marco. They'd checked into the hotel *Principe* and decided to take a walk before their meeting with the Venetian police. Soon the smell of freshly roasted coffee drew them towards Florins café where they ordered two cappuccinos and a toasted sandwich apiece before settling down to take in the late-season tourist chatter. Close by to where they were sitting, a middle-aged Dutch guy was explaining to his English girlfriend about how, several centuries ago, the place had functioned as a high-class brothel for the wealthy elite of the city and curious visitors from Europe.

'Sounds like we arrived a couple of centuries too late,' Sterling whispered across to Foscari with a gleam. The cardinal wasn't paying attention. He was too preoccupied in wafting away a hungry flock of pigeons intent on gorging themselves stupid on his toasted bread sandwich and the delicious strips of bacon concealed within it.

Satisfied with his efforts at fending off the pigeons, Foscari took a sip of coffee. 'This private house where we'll be staying… Is it far?'

Sterling brushed a fall of black hair from her face. 'Not far,' she replied. 'It's in the Dorsoduro district – an area largely populated by students, but its streets are quite secluded with lots of narrow alleyways and canals crisscrossed with ancient bridges. It's almost completely surrounded by water.'

'Oh, so you've been there before then?'

'Not me. It's the description Cardinal de Valois supplied me with. He always likes to brief me well before any mission.'

Forgetting herself, Sterling leaned forward to spoon the froth from her coffee. As she did so, Foscari caught sight of the handle of a gun protruding from the inside pocket of her jacket.

'You didn't tell me you were packing,' he exclaimed in surprise.

'But of course, Paolo. It's my Beretta 9mm. What did you expect?'

'Sterling, we've got a meeting with the police this afternoon. You can't go in there with that on you.'

'Relax. They already know about it.'

'They do?'

'Yeah... De Valois told them. Why do you think we flew in on the Vatican jet. We've got diplomatic clearance!'

'Ahh, I see-e-e-e... So this was all planned from the beginning then?'

'I expect so, cardinal; though de Valois doesn't always fill me in on all the details. He usually takes his orders directly from the Pope or Father Donnelly if the Pope isn't around. Er, which he currently isn't.'

'Uh-huh,' Foscari nodded, still with his eyes fixed on the handle of Sterling's Beretta pistol. 'And the other gun – where is that may I ask?'

'What other gun?'

'The Japanese weapon...'

'Oh, the Noguchi magnum you mean. Like I told you, it belongs to Joe Rackham. He picked it up shortly before we left for Venice but I could sure do with it now. I shouldn't have left it in England. That was a mistake.'

'Why do you say that?'

'Well, it's just this gut-feeling I've got, cardinal. The Noguchi has a lot more stopping - power that's all.'

'Christ Almighty! How much stopping –power do you need Sterling!? Isn't your 9mm stopping-power enough?'

'I hope so,' she replied, anxiously scanning the crowded square. I certainly hope so.'

* * *

Sterling remained silent as the blue-and-white police boat made its way towards the mortuary at the Ospedale San Lazzaro. Behind them, the water frothed a warm muddy brown as the twin outboard motors churned their way down the canals, reminding her of the milky foam on top of the cappuccino she'd drunk barely three hours before. For some reason she glanced upward, swinging her gaze around in search of movement in the buildings that towered above the narrow waterway. She'd sensed an evil presence lurking somewhere in the city but couldn't work out exactly what it was.

Together they disembarked at the city hospital alongside a fleet of water ambulances rocking gently at their moorings. Overhead the sky was still porous after a short rainstorm, allowing the light of a silvery sun to emerge from behind thin veils of aqueous cloud. Again, Sterling caught the psychic flash of the same presence she'd sensed before. It was closer this time, almost taunting her with its imminence. What the hell was it, she thought – an ogre perhaps, or maybe some other fey creature Jimmy had decided to put on her case? He'd already pulled that stunt before in the Suffolk marshes and she didn't want a repeat performance. Whatever this new thing was, it sure liked to play with its food.

'This way!' The shout came from a young carabinieri officer who'd just appeared on the landing stage in front of the hospital. His eyes were shaded with a peaked cap and he wore a white-holstered pistol at his side. Helping the cardinal out of the boat, the young man directed them both to the reception area of the hospital where they were introduced to someone in higher authority.

'This is Major Balzano,' said the young man deferentially. 'He's dealing with the case of the girl found in the canal.'

The major greeted Cardinal Foscari warmly but did not shake his hand. He was clearly ignorant of the protocols involved in dealing with a senior representative of the Vatican and didn't want to appear awkward in his presence. As for Sterling, he raked her with a suspicious stare. It was obvious to the cardinal that Balzano had taken an immediate dislike to her, and who could blame him. She was a hardened criminal after all and it was perfectly natural for him to be on his guard.

'The victim's name was Daniela Albescu,' said the major leading them towards the block at the rear of the hospital marked Anatomia Patalogica. 'She was a young Romanian student studying art history at the city university. Her body was found in a side-canal in the Dorsoduro district about thirty-six hours ago.'

'And her estimated time of death?' inquired Foscari, breathtakingly trying to keep up with Balzano's brisk walking pace.

'Hard to say,' replied the major nodding politely as he passed someone he recognised. 'What's left of the body is in a remarkable state of preservation. Oddly enough, submersion in water has a tendency to slow down the rate of decomposition so we haven't got that marker to go on.'

'What about her liver? I saw a documentary on TV once where a pathologist was able to estimate the approximate time of death from the temperature of the victim's liver.'

'Ah, yes – *the liver*... Well there was bit of a problem there, cardinal.'

'Oh really. What?'

'She didn't have one—'

Before Foscari could respond, Major Balzano halted in the corridor to talk with another police officer who'd just emerged from what he took to be the entrance to the path-lab.

'Did forensics get anything, Gustavo?'

'Not yet, major. She's a bit of a mess.'

'What about the divers?'

'The divers found nothing boss. Short of draining the canal there's nothing more we can do.'

'Surely *something* must have been found lieutenant?'

'Only a pair of fake designer sunglasses, most likely from one of the stalls near the Rialto. We also found a nine-inch dagger.'

'A weapon-?'

'Yes boss. A fifteenth-century medieval blade according to the experts. They get quite a lot of them in Venice.'

Major Balzano shook his head. 'Check out those shades then, Gustavo. You never know, we might get lucky.'

* * *

The light was bright and the air much colder as Sterling and Foscari were ushered into the morgue. Major Balzano walked them towards an older man wearing surgical fatigues and with a set of stereo-binocular magnifiers perched on the dome of his forehead.

'This is Professor Alessandro Rossi our chief medical examiner. Professor, these two people are Cardinal Paolo Foscari and his associate, Miss… er, *scusi signorina* but what did you say your name was?'

'Sterling,' the woman answered quietly. Just *Sterling.*'

'*Si, signorina* – Miss Sterling… She is from England I believe'

'Then I am both pleased and honoured to make your acquaintance,' replied the medical examiner nodding respectfully, his surgical magnifiers slipping forward and ending up on the tip of his nose. 'Come with me to the autopsy room. We've got her on the table.'

'*Dominus Satanus,*' were the first words that came to Foscari's lips when he saw the corpse. Sterling flashed him with a glance. She knew what he was thinking.

The seventeen-year-old victim had been laid out on the steel gurney, her young body chalk white beneath the overhead lighting. Sterling was unfazed, but Foscari could scarcely believe what he was hearing as Professor Alessandro began his discourse.

'We got to her pretty quickly before decomposition could set in. The victim's name is Daniela Albescu and she's from Romania. A CT-scan at the hospital gave us precise data on her wounds, including the strange incision around her navel…' At a nod from Balzano, the medical examiner moved closer to the body and continued with his report. 'But the wound that killed her was to the carotid artery in her neck. She died reasonably swiftly and without putting up much of a fight.'

Foscari waved a hand over the other wounds. 'So, all these other cut marks – there was no need for them?'

'No need at all, but she wasn't killed immediately.'

'What do you mean?'

'A blood test revealed clear signs that Daniela had been tranquilized before the killer carried out his work. She would have been alive and dimly aware of what was being done to her.'

'The removal of her liver, I presume?'

'That most likely happened after the killer cut her throat, but we were wondering if the removal of her liver had any religious significance?'

'Satanic ritual, you mean?'

'*Si—*' Alessandro glanced at the major then back to Foscari. 'Centuries ago, the liver was regarded as being more important than the heart in many cultures – and also among medical practitioners as well.'

Foscari picked up his cue to continue. 'Well I suppose the liver has long held a tradition of supernatural value among certain cultures, so I suppose in Daniela's case Satanic involvement can't be ruled out.'

There was silence in the room. The only sound came from the muffled hum of the morgue's refrigeration system and the occasional human voice from the corridor outside. Foscari knew he would have to be more specific.

'Satanists usually fixate on those parts of the body that have symbolic importance. Traditionally, the liver was regarded as the area of the body where the soul was located. Taking a young soul is the ultimate insult to God. It is also what the Church calls a Primary Evil – an act initiated by the will of Satan or some other demonic entity rather than by the hand of man. If a human being is involved, then they are simply carrying out the instructions of their infernal master, which in Daniela's case would be the Devil.'

Sterling wasn't listening. She was starting to feel an eerie chill creeping up her spine, together with the distinct sensation of being watched. The creature that had done this terrible thing to Daniela was somehow in the building and intent on making its presence felt – but only to her. What the hell was it she wondered?

'You say Daniela was tranquilized,' said the cardinal trying to change the subject. 'Why?'

Almost to himself, Alessandro replied; 'because the killer wanted Daniela alive and conscious when he extracted her unborn child from her womb.'

'Daniela was pregnant?'

'*Si*— All the signs are there, Your Eminence. Her womb was left intact though.'

'Then how did he remove the body?'

'We're not really sure, cardinal. There are of course several pharmaceutical methods on securing the termination of a pregnancy, but in Daniela's case none were in evidence. However, when we made a closer inspection of the victim's naval area, we found something rather strange.'

'And what was that?'

'See here,' the professor continued, drawing Foscari's attention to the woman's stomach. 'There are clear signs of something having broken the skin of Daniela's navel and penetrated through into her womb beneath.'

Foscari looked. It was difficult to make out at first, but sure enough there was a definite redness and disruption of the skin in the area of the woman's navel that was unmistakable.

'A surgical instrument perhaps?' said Foscari glancing up.

'No. Not a surgical instrument, Your Eminence, but something that was used very much like a surgical blade.'

'Then what made the incision?'

'A tongue! The killer used his tongue to pierce Daniela's naval then inserted it into her womb and stomach.'

'Impossible—'

'I agree, cardinal. Quite impossible – unless of course you happen to have a particularly long tongue with a serrated edge to it, but that wasn't all...'

'You mean there's more to this abomination then?'

'Yes. It would seem that the killer regurgitated a large quantity of pre-chewed Valerian into the woman's stomach in order to administer the tranquilizer. In case you didn't know, Valerian is the herbal form of the drug Valium in its non-titrated state.'

'Mother of God!' exclaimed Foscari standing back from the body. 'What in the name of all that's Holy are we dealing with here?'

Sterling creased her brow. She looked perplexed. 'I've seen some pretty weird shit in my time, cardinal, but this is a new one on me. What's your take on it professor?'

Alessandro turned to the major, briefly making eye contact with him before addressing the cardinal: 'Cardinal Foscari,' he said. 'Have you ever heard tell of a creature known as the Aswang?'

Standing back from the body on the gurney, Foscari shook his head. 'No, I haven't.' he replied noticing Sterling's growing interest.

'Well neither had I until yesterday,' the professor went on. 'You see, we have a young Filipino nurse working with us here in the hospital. She overheard me talking to a colleague about this case the other day and interrupted us. Anyway, to cut a long story short, she sat herself down and began telling us a very strange tale.'

'Uh-huh. Go on professor; I'm listening.'

'Apparently, there is a legendary creature that haunts the Philippines know to the locals as the *Aswang*. The name, Aswang is an umbrella term for several varieties of evil shape-shifting creatures in Filipino folklore, such as vampires, ghouls and werewolves. Spanish colonists noted that the Aswang were the most feared among the mythological creatures of the Philippines, even in the sixteenth century.

'They can assume human shape, though in their natural form they are more ghoul-like with a pale grey skin and a bat-like nose. Their featureless silver eyes glow faintly in the dark while the vertebrae along their backs form a noticeable ridge, and they possess needle-like fangs and claws.

'Aswangs are also noted for their black, forked proboscis tongue which is able to stretch several times the length of their bodies. The tongue is designed to pierce flesh and move solids in both directions through its long tube. After chewing on Valerian root, Aswangs use their tongue to pierce the naval of a pregnant woman and inject the valerian juice into the body, thereby tranquilizing her. From there, the Aswang will employ the tongue to suck the unborn infant out of the womb along with a large amount of amniotic fluid—'

Foscari waved a hand to signify he'd heard enough. 'But why, professor? What is the purpose of such an act?'

'Simple—Aswangs always consume the firstborn as a means of living a prolonged and healthy life. It's how they survive to a great age and perpetuate their kind.'

'But in your victim's case, the liver was missing as well,' observed the cardinal. 'Clearly the Aswang was looking for something else.'

'The hoof marks, you mean…?' queried Alessandro peering over Foscari's shoulder.

'Yes, professor. There have been similar killings in England and in most of the cases there was a raised patch of scorched flesh in the shape of a cloven hoof just below the victim's collar bone. I don't see one on young Daniela here.'

'That's where you're wrong, Your Eminence. She had such a mark when she was brought in, but it seems to have faded overnight. At least, it wasn't there this morning when I looked.'

'That's because the sacrifice has been accepted,' whispered Sterling to the cardinal. *'We've got here too late…'*

Foscari smiled thinly at the medical examiner and took his companion aside for a moment. *'What do you mean, Sterling? It's Rachel Morrison we're after. She was pregnant as well if you remember.'*

'Did you say Rachel Morrison?' Balzano exclaimed in surprise.

'Yes I did major. Is there a problem?'

'There might be. One of my officers found a young English woman of that name wandering around outside the carabinieri HQ only the other day. She appeared to be in some distress and complained of having been drugged and kidnapped. Apparently her captors let her go and dumped her close by our headquarters where they knew she would be noticed.'

'Where is she now?'

'We had her transported to a secure psychiatric unit. Apart from the bit about being kidnapped, she wasn't making very much sense.'

'That figures,' muttered Sterling to herself. The already low temperature in the room had dropped even more now and she could hear the distinct sound of mocking laughter inside her head. That it came from one of her own kind she could tell. But who…?

'I must see Rachel immediately,' Foscari demanded. 'I have orders to place her under the protection of the Vatican without delay.'

Balzano was about to say something when Sterling cut in. 'I shouldn't bother, cardinal. Young Rachel is safe enough for the time being. It was Daniela they were after.'

Foscari looked incredulous. 'What do you mean?'

'We've been set up, Paolo. Jimmy Silver's played us.'

'I'm not following you.'

'Isn't it obvious. He's used Rachel to lure us away from Rome and draw us both into his killing ground. He wants us both dead and out of the picture. It's a trap.'

'What are we going to do?'

'Do? Well I don't know about you, but I'm going to buy myself a nice strong coffee, score some top-end dope and then make a couple of phonecalls. We've just been shafted royally—'

Foscari watched his companion leave the room before turning to Alessandro and Major Balzano: 'Professor, Major, *molte grazie.*' Then he took a final glance at the corpse and made the sign of the cross in the air with his hand. *'Grazie, Daniela... In nomine Patris et Filii et Spiritus Sancti... Amen.'*

16

'Did you sleep well?'

It was Sterling who asked the question. She was sitting in the lobby of their hotel near the Grand Canal waiting to check out. The cardinal had just emerged from the elevator. He'd breakfasted in his room, not wishing to be seen with a woman who had no obvious connections with the Church.

'No,' said Foscari resting his meager suitcase on the thickly carpeted floor. 'There was too much noise coming from the room next door.'

'What sort of noise?' inquired his companion with a smirk.

'You know full well what I mean,' Foscari snapped back irritably, palming out the creases in his cassock with the flat of his hands.

'Oh-h-h-h, *that* sort of a noise. Well I'm sure you'll find the atmosphere at Lady Westvale's palazzo far more appropriate for a man of the cloth, Your Eminence. It's usually as quiet as the grave from what I've been told.'

Half an hour and a gondola ride later, Sterling and the cardinal found themselves standing outside the stuccoed façade of a five-storied stone palazzo that had undoubtedly seen better days. The house was situated at the end of a narrow winding lane, and unlike many of the other grander houses of Venice, its front entrance did not open out onto a canal but instead graced the shadow side of a quieter square inhabited solely by a couple of stray cats and a public well. There were also a pair of tall, wrought iron gates which guarded a narrow passageway leading to the rear of the house. The gates were security padlocked and topped with razor wire. Evidently, whoever lived inside the house was not encouraging of visitors.

'Who did you say it was that lived here?' asked Foscari as they viewed the building.

'Lady Caroline Westvale,' Sterling replied checking her mobile for incoming calls and texts. 'She's a former British aristocrat who's lived in Venice for quite some time. Locals refer to her as "the English lady" and tend to avoid her for reasons which will shortly become apparent.

For a moment, Foscari was reminded of the piece of research he'd done before traveling to London. The name, Caroline Westvale was familiar to him. It belonged to the former partner of Sir James Blackthorne – aka Jimmy Silver – who had scandalized English society back in the eighteenth century when they'd eloped and the couple had fled to Venice some time around the year 1797. But that had been well over two hundred years ago. It couldn't possibly be the same person.

Walking up to the plain wooden door that formed the main entrance to the building, Sterling rang the bell. It wasn't long before Foscari heard an electronic crackle followed by the sound of someone speaking: 'Yes. Who is it?' came a dark, Tuscan voice over the intercom. The voice seemed to belong to a woman but he couldn't say for certain.

'My name is Sterling,' his companion replied. 'I have an appointment to see Lady Westvale. I've brought Cardinal Foscari with me.'

'Just a moment,' came the voice once more. Yes, it was a woman's voice alright, only coarse and dry like cheap whisky.

There was an interval of silence that lasted for a few seconds. Then: 'Lady Westvale will see you both now. Take the stairs to the first-floor landing and knock.'

An electronic click told Foscari that the door-lock opened automatically. Sterling pushed the door gently with the palm of her hand and ventured inside. The entrance hall was quite spacious with an eerie baroque staircase that ascended in successive flights of stairs up the central spine of the building. Reaching the first-floor landing, they paused. Though tidy and well-kept, the place had an air of melancholy about it like so many of the older Venetian palazzos. Set into a classical portico of solid marble was a double door with two brass doorknobs in the shape of lions heads. Sterling knocked three times and waited.

'Come in,' came a feminine voice that sounded surprisingly English. Sterling stood aside allowing the cardinal to open the doors and pass through first. Entering the room, Foscari was astonished by what he saw. The room was exquisitely furnished and decorated in contrast to the plain stairwell outside. Paintings in antique frames hung on the walls, neo-classical landscapes, views of Venice and several eighteenth-century female portraits, most of them bearing an uncanny resemblance to the woman he now glimpsed sitting on a sofa next to the fireplace. Some remote ancestors perhaps?

The woman got up from the sofa and walked towards Cardinal Foscari. Of an indeterminate age, she wore her auburn hair high off her forehead and tied in a chignon at the back of her neck, just like some of the women in the portraits on the wall. A grey knee-length skirt and a white cotton blouse brought her firmly into the twenty-first century however, even though Foscari somehow got the impression that she didn't quite belong there. A pair of dark sunglasses completed the picture, giving her the appearance of someone who did not reveal their secrets gladly.

'Ah, you must be Paolo Foscari,' she said brightly. 'I am Caroline Westvale – Lady Caroline Westvale – though some people call me *the countess.* Cardinal de Valois told me you were coming.'

'And my name is Sterling,' his companion put in, clearly irritated at having been cut out of the proceedings.

'I know who *you* are madam,' Lady Westvale replied sharply before turning once again to Foscari. 'Please remove your coat, Your Eminence. I will have my maid fetch us all a drink. What would you like?'

'A coffee would be fine thanks.'

Foscari watched as the woman walked over to the fireplace and gently pulled on a length of red tasseled rope. A servant's bell rang somewhere deep inside the house, followed by the sound of approaching footsteps. Presently, a smaller, much younger looking woman entered the room. With her black, geometric hairstyle and dark Italian eyes, she couldn't have been much more than twenty years of age and spoke in the same rich, dry tones that Foscari had heard over the intercom.

'Yes, Lady Westvale?' she inquired, barely able to suppress a giggle. From the expression on her face, Foscari guessed that her relationship with her mistress most likely approached the lesbian end of the spectrum with a smattering of bondage thrown in for good measure.

'A coffee for our honoured guest, Nicoletta,' said the countess, glancing briefly at Sterling. 'And the same for this woman here.'

'Very good, your ladyship. And will you be having one too?'

'Yes. Make it the French way. Black with no sugar—'

As Nicoletta went off to prepare the coffee, Foscari and Lady Westvale exchanged smalltalk.

'And how was your hotel, Cardinal Foscari? I trust you spent a pleasant evening.'

'We stayed at the *Principe,* Lady Westvale. Just off the Grand Canal. The evening was pleasant enough.'

'Ah yes, the *Principe.* A first-class establishment.'

A picture of structured elegance in her patrician hairstyle and bright red lipstick, Caroline Westvale resumed her seat on the sofa. Yes, she did indeed bear a striking resemblance to the women in the portraits, thought Foscari. Her family must have been resident in Venice for quite some time.

The coffee arrived just as Lady Westvale was about to put another handful of wood pellets on the fire. 'I don't feel the cold that much myself, but these old houses have a tendency to get a bit chilly the closer you get to autumn. Isn't that right, Nicoletta?'

'Yes, m' lady,' the maid replied with a mischievous grin before putting her tray down on the low coffee table that separated her mistress from the new guests. 'Will that be all?'

Westvale nodded and watched as Nicoletta left the room. The two women were obviously having a private joke between themselves. One that was lost on Foscari, but not on his companion who had not once taken her eyes off the countess ever since they'd entered the room. He waited until Nicoletta had disappeared through an adjoining door before continuing with his conversation.

'How long have you lived in Venice, Lady Westvale?' He did not think it too personal a question but was surprised by her response.

'Why do you ask?' she answered coldly. Her gaze was steady and it made him feel uncomfortable.

'No particular reason,' he responded quickly, 'only I noticed that some of the portraits in this room seem to have a close resemblance to yourself and I was wondering if they might be your ancestors.'

There was a pause as Lady Westvale allowed her gaze to wander slowly around the walls. Her cold expression was gone, replaced by an almost wistful look as she studied each portrait in turn. It was almost as if she were reminiscing.

'You would do well to ask your friend over there for her opinion on the matter,' Lady Westvale replied. 'I'm sure she could offer you a more satisfactory explanation than I, isn't that right Sterling?'

Sterling said nothing in response but just kept on staring at the countess. It was almost like a stand-off encounter between two apex-predators on the African savannah the way they just kept staring at each other like that. Then Foscari made the connection: *'They're both vampires,* he thought; *'and they both hate each others guts. Why…?'*

The countess smiled and offered him a biscuit with his coffee. 'De Valois mentioned something about a book you wished to show me, cardinal. Do you happen to have it with you?'

At this, Sterling shifted in her chair and gently patted the left side of her jacket where her Beretta pistol was concealed beneath. Clearly she was taking no chances and wanted Lady Westvale to know as much. Foscari noticed this too, but chose to ignore it, instead reaching down to open up the small suitcase he'd brought with him for his overnight stay. 'Here,' he said, taking out a small plastic zipper bag containing the newly rebound volume. 'We were wondering if you could cast some light on the inscription written down on the flyleaf, your ladyship.'

The countess reached over and took the book from Foscari's hand, removing it from the bag. Then she inserted an expertly polished fingernail beneath the cover and opened it at the first page. A slight lifting of her eyebrows told him she'd recognized something.

'It's Jimmy, isn't it?' observed Sterling dryly. 'That's his coat of arms on the flyleaf. Three wolves heads on a shield with the name Blackthorne written underneath. It's your former partner… The man who betrayed you and then dumped you here in Venice all those years ago. Let me see now… That would have been some time around the year 1797, wouldn't it Caroline?'

'*How…dare…you…*' hissed the countess, almost spitting out her words as she regarded Sterling with all the scorn and venom that a person of her rank might have employed way back in the eighteenth-century when titles such as her own still carried some weight in the world. '*How…dare…you.*'

Foscari glanced at the portraits on the wall once again. That Lady Westvale was a vampire just like Sterling was now more than apparent, but she was a vampire already a good deal older and of a much higher status than his companion, outranking her both in years and in whatever arcane pecking order that happened to exist among the shadowy elite of the Undead.

'Where did you get this?' inquired Westvale, barely able to suppress her emotions.

'One of my associates brought it to me in London,' Sterling replied gamely. 'The book was stolen by a pickpocket and sold on to a friend of mine. Turn the flyleaf over and take a look at what's written on the other side.'

Swiftly turning the page, the countess gave an immediate verdict.

'It's a Vatican cipher code—'

'Oh good,' chimed Sterling. 'What does it say?'

'I don't know.'

'What do you mean you don't know?'

'Just that. I mean, I really don't know. It's been customized by a private individual to the extent that it's practically undecipherable.'

'Try, Lady Westvale. You're the only person I know who might have used a code like that back in the 1790s when you and Silver were spying against Napoleon. That was the main reason you were both in Venice, wasn't it?'

'Yes it was, but I can't read these things anymore. It was way too long ago.'

'But it's in Jimmy Silver's handwriting, Caroline. That's his coat of arms on the front – Sir James Blackthorne, your former partner – the same man who abandoned you here in Venice surrounded by water so you couldn't leave. It's time to get your revenge Lady Westvale. Break this code and maybe we can help you escape from here. Cardinal de Valois could even grant you immunity from prosecution by the Vatican exorcists to keep them off your tail when you finally leave. It might even be possible to get the Heavenly Powers to review your case.'

'Fat chance of that, Sterling... Not after what I've done to Nicoletta...'

'Oh... I see. You've turned her then?'

'Yes. It happened three nights ago. I didn't want her to age you see. I wanted her to stay young forever.'

'Forever? There's no *forever,* Caroline. Not for any of us. You know that.'

'I know, but I've grown so fond of her in the short time she's been with me that I couldn't bear to be parted from her. She's my friend.'

Sterling shook her head. She understood. She'd loved and lost as well, and knew how lonely life could be.

'Please try, Caroline. You're our only hope...'

The room became silent as the countess began focusing her attention on the encoded message scribbled on the reverse of the flyleaf. Not all of it was in code and some of the numbers ran in sequence along the line only to be followed by yet another mad jumble of letters and symbols that made very little sense.

'It's Silver's handwriting alright,' the countess said at length, 'and these are the names of two cities in Switzerland – Zurich and Lugano.'

'Yes,' said Sterling sitting forward in her chair. 'The cardinal here thinks the encoded sections may refer to some of the main lending banks in the Swiss banking industry and that they may also contain coded references to certain members of the Roman clergy.'

'The College of Cardinals you mean?'

'Yes, Lady Westvale,' put in Foscari; 'Most likely Lorenzo Spada and those members of the college who support him. As you know, the Pope died recently and now Spada is the main contender for the role of Supreme Pontiff.'

'I see. And you want me to break the code and discredit him and his co-conspirators by uncovering a banking scandal within the Church?'

'Got it in one!' exclaimed Sterling. 'We think Jimmy Silver is backing Spada to be the next Pope. That book you're holding in your hand could well be the key to unraveling the whole plot. If Spada gets elected as Pope then he can disband the Order of Exorcist thereby giving Silver power and influence over the Bene Noctu. If Silver gains control of the vampire council, then both you and me are as good as dead and the whole world goes to hell. I can't put it any plainer than that.'

'I won't do it! I can't risk getting on the wrong side of Jimmy…He's…he's *way too powerful.*'

'What choice do you have?' Sterling replied, her voice growing darker. 'If you refuse to co-operate, then de Valois will have no alternative but to sanction you. He'll put an assassin priest on your tail and then it's the end for you and your pretty little girlfriend.'

Caroline Westvale's eyes narrowed behind her shades. *'You bitch. You've set me up…'*

'You're damned if you do and damned if you don't,' grinned Sterling, mildly amused by the irony of her words.

Taking a more conciliatory tone, Cardinal Foscari regarded the undead countess with a look of pity and said in a small voice: 'Please try, Lady Westvale. We haven't got much time.'

Silence fell on the proceedings, broken only by the somnolent tick-tocking of a large antique clock that hung on the far wall. A protracted sigh told him that his words had taken effect and that the countess was now prepared to divulge whatever information she possessed.

'Vatican ciphers took many years to evolve, cardinal. I won't bore you with all the details except to provide you with an explanation of the magnitude of the problem which now faces us.'

'Go on, your ladyship,' Foscari said gently. 'Please tell us everything you know. My apologies for my friend here. She can be a bit blunt at times.'

Sterling grimaced and sat back in her chair waiting for the countess to begin.

'Originally, the ciphers used by the Vatican were simple letter-substitution codes and relatively easy to crack, but as time went on they became more sophisticated.'

'How sophisticated, Lady Westvale?'

'Well, the cipher used in this book is probably from the Vatican library. It was used for papal communications throughout Europe between 1538 and 1787. Although it is a substitution code, it underwent several modifications over the years until it became more difficult to crack.'

'I see,' observed Foscari, furrowing his brow. 'So what happened then?'

'These early ciphers were replaced by polyalphabetical codes. Most of which were still easy to break until a special template was introduced to further confuse the code-breaker. The code you have here is a polyalphabetical substitution code – a basic pen and paper cipher, but one for which you need a special grid or template to perform the decryption.'

'And where might we obtain such a template, your ladyship?'

'I'm not altogether certain, cardinal. In fact the master grid may not even be written on paper at all. It could be a machine.'

'A machine?'

'Yes. An early form of computer, constructed from a series of interlocking dials and wheels. Cipher machines were known to have been in use from as early as the seventeenth century.'

'But what about the sequenced numbers, Lady Westvale? Surely these must represent something to do with the Swiss banks.'

'Perhaps cardinal, but they could also be Nulls.'

'Nulls?'

'Yes. Nulls in a code don't necessarily mean anything. They are false encryptions designed to confuse any potential code-breaker, who first needs to recognize the nulls for what they are and discard them. For example, the number 777 written here on the line above the encoded information in the book could very well mean something, but the longer sequences of letters mixed with numbers could contain nulls, and vice versa. There's simply no way of telling without the use of a template. Nulls are almost invariably numbers, which naturally makes your work all the more difficult if you are dealing with bank accounts or even the name of the bank itself.'

Foscari glanced down at the encoded message then looked back at Lady Westvale. 'But what can we do? There's so little time…'

Taking the book from Foscari once again, the countess studied the encryption. 'You will definitely need a template to decode this information, cardinal. From what I can see, it's most likely been derived from a Code Eleven – an old Vatican cipher dating back to the eighteenth century. I recall Jimmy having used one to communicate with London when we were spying against the French back in the 1790s.'

LUGANO – 777
COSOLS32 XXX
COSOIT31 – OIRDNOS
45798653Z 5457X056791
ZURICH – RXPGP
COSOZU33 XXX
44678965Z6160X097892

'And do you still possess such a template, your ladyship?'

'No, I'm afraid I don't. It must have got thrown out the last time I redecorated this place. That was back in 1965 so I guess it's long gone by now. Gone, just like everything else that was good in this world…'

'Good!?' exclaimed Sterling. 'If you're referring to Jimmy Silver then I don't think there was anything particularly *good* about him. Look what he did to us!'

'I didn't mean Jimmy himself,' snapped the countess. I was referring to the glittering world we once inhabited. The palaces, the music, the parties, the soft glow of candlelight…'

'The naked power more like!' snarled Sterling. 'You didn't want to give up the power you both enjoyed as aristocrats. None of your kind ever did. That's why you took up spying against Napoleon and the French revolutionaries, wasn't it?'

The countess shook her head. 'You simply don't understand what it's like to lose an entire age, young lady. This world we now inhabit is so shabby in comparison to what we once enjoyed. The world has grown smaller. Small and mean…'

'It's not the world that's become smaller, Lady Westvale; it's just the people in it!'

Foscari sensed an argument was beginning to develop between the two vampires, prompting him to intervene before things turned nasty.

'How else might we come by such a template, your ladyship?' he inquired politely.

'I'm not sure,' Westvale replied glancing sharply at Sterling. 'You might try the Vatican library or maybe ask Francesco Grimaldi the current secretary of the Bene Noctu. Grimaldi might even be able to decipher the entire code for you if you ask him nicely.'

'And where might I find Francesco Grimaldi, countess?'

'In his crypt!' answered Sterling butting in. 'He lives in the catacombs beneath an abandoned eighteenth century villa on the outskirts of Rome along with most of the city's dead from that era. You can't miss it—'

'How do you know?'

'Because I've been there, cardinal. It's not a place to linger either. Might I suggest you begin your investigations in the reference section of the Vatican library. It's a damn sight more welcoming.'

Lady Westvale got up from where she was sitting. 'I'm just going to have a word with Nicoletta about dinner tonight. She's preparing us a small banquet to mark this occasion. In the meantime, pray amuse yourselves as best you can. There are plenty of books and magazines to read.'

'Thank you, your ladyship,' replied Foscari. 'Would it also be possible to access the internet while we're here? Perhaps researching a few Swiss banks might yield some clues.'

'Be my guest, Eminence. There's a computer in my study and the password is "gondola." I doubt if you'll have very much joy though. Switzerland is practically overflowing with banks. Far too many of them if you ask me.'

*

The countess was right. Foscari had never seen so many banks in one country before. Where could he possibly begin? Eventually, both he and Sterling gave up their internet search and wandered into the dining room summoned by the countess who led them both towards a long table where a sumptuous meal was waiting for them. Nicoletta had been invited too, and stood near the head of the table beaming a smile of culinary triumph before taking her seat next to Lady Westvale as they all sat down.

'How did you get on with your research?' inquired their host as she poured the wine. The first course was minestrone soup followed by a series of one-bite starters that included partridge on roasted Tuscan bread with hibiscus sauce.

'Not very well,' replied Foscari taking mouthful of partridge. 'Too many banks.'

'Hah! Like I said, the Swiss do go in for banking in a big way – and please call me Caroline. I do so hate formalities at the dinner table. You are our honoured guest here, cardinal.'

'Thank you, Caroline; and you may call me Paolo. I must say I found your autobiography fascinating reading. I happened to notice it when I accidentally opened one of your files. I hope you don't mind.'

'Not at all, Paolo. So now you're a believer in the Undead I take it?'

'I suppose I must be, though my friend Sterling here has more than convinced me of it by her activities over the past few days.'

'I'm sure she has, Paolo. And did she also mention how we vampires happen to sort out our disputes among ourselves?'

'Yes. A bloody business I hear.'

'Indeed it is,' replied the countess. 'Our feuds can be quite deadly, which is why I prefer to live here in the relative safety of this little island city of ours. Being surrounded by water has its compensations… and of course, its *distractions,*' she added, glancing in the direction of her youthful partner.

Foscari looked away, too embarrassed to comment, while Sterling took a gulp of red wine before crunching down on her Tuscan bread with a single angry bite. He could tell that the corruption of the young seemed to irritate his companion almost as much as it did himself, and he was more than relieved when Nicoletta finally got up from the table to serve the next course.

'I thought Tortelli with parmesan and lavender would go down well as the first proper dish, though there's roast leg and rack of goat with artichokes if you prefer, Paolo.'

'No, the Tortelli will be fine, Caroline, and might I just say that your taste in wine is excellent.'

'Thank you, cardinal. You are a connoisseur then?'

'Not as such, your ladyship, but my nose tells me this is a particularly fine vintage. What say you, Sterling?'

'Yeah. Fucking great… *Just fucking great…*'

Something was bothering her. Tugging at his sleeve she whispered into Paolo's ear: *'There's something not quite right here, cardinal.'*

'Yes. It's definitely getting a bit on the chilly side if you ask me.'

'That's not what I meant. Look at Nicoletta. She senses it too.'

'Senses what exactly? I don't sense anything.'

'You wouldn't cardinal because you're not one of us. It's the same sensation I experienced earlier on today. There's something stalking us. It's fairly close to the house, and, what is more, it's not afraid of water.'

Foscari glanced at Nicoletta. Her normally cheerful expression had vanished. She was tense and on her guard.

'Is everything alright, Paolo?' asked the countess offering more wine. Evidently she hadn't sensed anything yet, but the cardinal couldn't help noticing that the temperature in the room had dropped even further, causing him to rub his forearms vigorously with his hands.

'Ah! You are cold,' she observed, putting down the bottle. 'I shall put some more pellets on the fire while Nicoletta fetches you something to drape over your shoulders. These old Venetian houses have a tendency to get a bit draughty this time of year.'

'*It's Charles Martel, I know it is.*' whispered Sterling as their hosts left the room. '*Silver's put the Executioner on my tail. He means to end it here.*'

'Stuff and nonsense! It's just got a bit cold, that's all. You heard what the countess said. It's the time of the year.'

'No it isn't, Paolo. I've been feeling this thing coming on all day. At first I thought I'd picked up the presence of another vampire in the city, but when I saw what happened to Daniela, I wasn't so sure.'

'But that was caused by an Aswang, whatever they are.'

'Yes, but that's what's so strange about it, cardinal. I keep picking up the presence of Charles Martel on my psychic radar. It was Martel who killed Daniela and did all those things to her. He performed the sacrifice of the unborn child inside her womb – the ultimate insult to the Church and all that it holds as sacred. Don't think Daniela's surname was a coincidence, Paolo, because it wasn't.'

'Albescu?'

'Yes – Daniela the White. In Romanian, the word Albescu means white – the colour of purity and innocence. Daniela was chosen because of her name!'

'*Scusi,*' said Nicoletta coming back into the room and draping a padded leather jacket over Foscari's thin shoulders. 'It's my winter coat so it will help keep out the chill. Have some more wine. That should help as well.'

'*Grazie,*' replied Foscari, pulling the coat around his shoulders like a shroud. He watched as Nicoletta left the room again before turning to Sterling: 'But Charles Martel is a mortal man is he not?'

'No, I don't think so. In fact, I sometimes doubt if Martel has ever been truly human.'

'What makes you think that, Sterling?'

'Aswangs are *shapeshifters.* It's possible Charles Martel is a creature capable of taking on human form. In North America, shapeshifters are called Skinwalkers, while in the Philippines they are known as Aswangs – it's a general term for creatures who seem to live out their existence somewhere between the physical realm and the more fluid planes of reality.'

'Like angels and demons you mean?'

'Yes – something like that. They can dematerialize at will and reappear in another form – usually human or any other animal they happen to be hunting down at the time.'

'But Martel worked for the Church—'

'I work for the fucking Church, cardinal, but it still doesn't make me any better than Charlie, does it? For that matter, Lady Westvale and her sweet little poppet Nicoletta aren't exactly smiling angels are they?'

'I suppose not, Sterling… Oh, and look! Here she comes now with the dessert.'

'— Macarpone mousse with yoghurt sorbet and cherry sauce – it was the best I could do at such short notice, Your Eminence. There was some left over in the fridge from last week.'

'It's more than welcome, Nicoletta,' beamed the cardinal as Lady Westvale returned to the table. Before long, they were all seated again enjoying the dessert. After a while coffee was served, and the conversation became more relaxed and convivial.

'And how do you see the election going, Paolo? I'd hate to see it passing to the Germans. Not after the last time.'

'There's no fear of that, Caroline. It looks like an Italian contest from what I can gather. I only hope it doesn't go to Lorenzo Spada.'

'You think he stands a chance then?'

'I can't really discuss the matter over dinner, Caroline. We are almost at the point of going into Conclave and I am the Dean of the Electoral College. All I can say is that it's going to be a close-run thing.'

'I quite understand, cardinal. But tell me – how would it feel if you yourself were in the running for the top job, hmmm?'

Laughter played around the corners of the woman's mouth. She was teasing him, he knew, but all the same, the thought of himself seated in the Pope's chair appalled him. *God forbid,* he thought clutching Nicoletta's jacket around him like a security blanket. The room was still getting colder in spite of all the wood pellets heaped on the fire. Any further drop in the temperature and he stood a good chance of going down with influenza.

'What happened to the other girl?' asked the countess, noting Foscari's reaction and changing the subject.

'What other girl?'

'The young English woman – the one they found wandering around outside the carabinieri headquarters. I heard it on the news.'

'Oh, Rachel Morrison you mean... She's being held in a secure unit for the time being. The police are keeping a watch on her as well. Apart from that I can't really say any more.'

'I quite understand, cardinal... And Sterling - What is your opinion on Lorenzo Spada? Do you think he stands a chance of becoming the next Pope?'

Before his friend could answer, Foscari heard the beep-beeping sound of an electronic device coming from somewhere deep inside the house.

'That's the intruder alarm, Nicoletta,' said the countess. 'You'd best go and take a look at the CCTV screen. It's probably just a stray cat, but you'd better check.'

A couple of minutes elapsed before Nicoletta came back into the room with a puzzled expression on her face. 'You'd better come and take a look at this, Caroline,' she said. 'There's something lurking outside the gates. I don't know what it is.'

'What do you mean you don't know what it is?' replied the countess somewhat dismayed.

'Just that!' snapped her partner. 'It's like nothing I've ever seen before. Come and see for yourself.'

Throwing her napkin down, Lady Westvale excused herself from the table and followed Nicoletta out of the room to examine the monitor screen. Meanwhile, Sterling glanced at Foscari: *'It's Martel,'* she said knowingly.

'Let's not jump to conclusions, Sterling. Like the countess said, it's probably just a stray cat. There's loads of them in Venice.'

'It's not a fucking cat, Paolo. It's the Executioner. I know it is.'

Foscari was about to counter her suggestion when his companion drew out her Beretta and thumbed the safety mechanism.

'Steady on Sterling. There's no need for that—'

'Want a bet, cardinal! Martel's a killer. He's going to do for us all—Yourself included!'

In a matter of seconds, they were all standing in the kitchen looking at the CCTV monitor. The screen was quite small but the image was clear enough. It showed the tall wrought iron gates that secured the narrow channel leading to the rear of the house.

'What's that?' exclaimed Foscari pointing to what appeared to be a large dog squatting on its haunches just beyond the gates.

'I'm not altogether sure,' replied his friend sliding her Beretta pistol back inside her jacket. At this, Nicoletta expanded the screen so they could take a closer look.

It wasn't a dog. In fact it didn't resemble any living animal know to science. More like a gigantic crawling bat than anything else, the creature was moving. But only just.

'What the—' Sterling's words died on her lips when she realized exactly what it was they were looking at.

'It's dematerializing , cardinal. It's beginning its transformation…'

'It's what?'

'That thing down there – it's shapeshifting.'

Foscari looked on in horror as the creature slowly dissolved into a column of thin grey smoke before passing easily between the vertical iron bars of the gate. As it did so, it began to reappear on the other side of the gate in the alleyway of the house, slowly forming itself into the shape of a man that became steadily more solid before it began walking with long, languid strides down the narrow channel towards the rear courtyard of the palazzo.

'Shut the back door!' ordered the countess. 'It's making for the back door—'

Nicoletta jerked a nod at her mistress then ran across the kitchen, making her way down a spiral staircase with Sterling in hot pursuit. To their relief, they found the back door locked and secure, but their relief quickly turned to fear when they saw a vaporous trail of smoke slowly begin seeping its way through the paper-thin gap between the door frame and the wall.

'What the hell is it?' exclaimed Nicoletta clutching at Sterling's arm as the steadily encroaching tendrils of smoke continued to filter their way into the small basement room before reforming themselves once again into a familiar human shape. A shape that had a voice:

'What is the matter, *mademoiselle?* Do you not recognize your old friend perhaps?'

The voice had a thick Parisian accent and was addressing Sterling who was now standing with Nicoletta at the foot of the spiral staircase. It was a horrible sound, all strangled and broken as if its owner were inhaling broken glass. Sterling didn't hesitate, nor did she answer Nicoletta's question, but quickly drew out her Beretta and began firing wildly at the terrible apparition standing in the centre of the room.

'Nicoletta— Get upstairs now!' she yelled. 'Tell the others to get out of the building. It's Charles Martel! He's the Aswang—!'

All Nicoletta saw before she turned to leave were the muzzle flashes from Sterling's gun as they lit up the room. It was then that she caught a glimpse of what it was that had caused the English vampire to panic. Charles Martel was thin almost to the point of emaciation, but his slim, cadaverous body belied the hideous strength that dwelt beneath its skin. She could also make out the deep crimson lambency of his aura as it glowed in the darkness between each muzzle flash, black tendrils of energy reaching out and crackling in the void. It was all too much for Sterling who now began to back off towards the staircase firing as she went.

'Get up the fucking stairs Nicoletta! He's lethal—'

For a moment, they were both together in that terrible little room, Sterling and Martel each facing the other down in a desperate contest of wills that could only have one outcome. Then Martel spoke again:

'Why the hostile reception, *mademoiselle?* Your bullets have no effect on me. In any case, it is the cardinal I have come for, not yourself.'

He was lying of course. He'd been sent by Silver to settle the score with her, that much she knew; but the death of Foscari would only have cleared the way for Spada to become Pope, and that had to be avoided at all costs.

'Shove it, Martel! The cardinal is under my protection. You're out of your jurisdiction – *and you haven't got your sword...*'

She crouched low and fired into the darkness. A flash answered her back, several of them, and the bullets hit the walls spilling stone dust into her hair. The bastard was armed, but where had he got his gun from?'

'I can manipulate things at will now, Sterling. Didn't Jimmy tell you that? Ahh, too bad *mon cheri* – I will have to kill you as well. The bullets are special by the way – just like your own.'

Sterling backed up the stairs, a useless 9mm in her hand. She'd exhausted all her ammunition and had nothing left to load it with. Reaching the kitchen, she ran down the hallway to warn the others. When she entered the dining room, she found Foscari kneeling on the floor. He was praying.

'This is no time for prayer, Paolo! We've got to leave.'

'I'm calling in the big guns, Sterling. Please don't interrupt me.'

'You're what?'

Foscari didn't reply. From the crease of his brow she could tell he wasn't joking, but what did he think was going to happen? Was he hoping for Jesus to intervene? Fat chance of that.

A fine haze of smoke began rising through the floor, prompting the countess to ring for the fire brigade until Sterling gestured her to put the phone down. She knew what the smoke was. Martel hadn't even bothered to use the staircase. Aswangs usually didn't.

The temperature in the room plummeted even further until it was well below freezing. Foscari felt the chill but kept on praying all the same as if his very life depended on it. As Martel began to materialize back into his regular human form, Lady Westvale glared at Sterling.

'What have you brought into this house you crazy bitch!? What manner of creature is this?'

'It's an Aswang, your ladyship. I don't know how Silver did it, but somehow Charles Martel is an Aswang now and there's not a damn thing we can do about it. Our only hope is to leave this house and cross over some water using the canal system. That might slow him down a bit.'

'But I can't cross water like you, Sterling. Neither can Nicoletta. We're both trapped!'

Foscari was acting like a man possessed, tumbling out his prayers and clutching his rosary to his lips as if it were the very last thing on earth. 'Bless us and save us Saint Michael – you're our only hope.'

By now, the smoke rising from the floor had morphed back into the shape of Charles Martel, his thin face and piercing eyes giving him an altogether otherworldly and demonic appearance. Sterling noticed that he was still armed, only this time it wasn't a gun he was carrying but a long Japanese sword which had manifested in his hands – the same weapon he'd used to execute all his other victims, including the Reverend Saunders.

Nicoletta screamed and backed off. She was new to the ways of the Undead and didn't know how to defend herself. Lady Westvale also backed away; too genteel and cultured to withstand such a creature as Martel. Only Sterling and Foscari stood their ground.

Martel's fractured voice boomed out, filling the room with his presence.

'*Ma foi!* But aren't you a sight, priest; kneeling there on the floor with your rosary beads. All your prayers can't save you now, Foscari. Prepare to meet your God!'

In that terrible moment, Foscari felt all of time since the beginning of the universe open up to receive him. Somehow he could see the night sky extending itself into infinite space, hurling a myriad of stars across the empty void, and it was all cold and endless and he was less than a speck of dust in it. The memory of something not worth remembering.

Now he recited the Lord's Prayer and the Twenty-Third Psalm before returning once more to implore the archangel Michael for help. All the while, Sterling circled the room pointing her empty handgun at Martel and screaming blue murder at him to back off, but all to no avail. Charles Martel – or the creature he had become – advanced slowly on the kneeling cardinal with his sword raised and ready to strike. And then…

Almonds— There was the distinct smell of almonds in the air. The same aroma Foscari had noticed when he was in the Pope's bedroom several days before. Martel noticed it too and hesitated in mid-step, lowering his sword momentarily to his waist. Sterling also stopped her circling and lowered her weapon before turning to the countess who had begun to shake uncontrollably where she stood. Nicoletta too, was trembling with shock.

'Sterling. What's wrong? What is it?'

The English vampire shook her head. She too was beginning to shake. 'I don't know, Nicoletta. I really don't know…'

All at once, the whole dining room lit up with an overwhelming blaze of light, drenching the walls and furniture with its savage brilliance. The light was so intense that it seemed to penetrate the skin of everyone present in the chamber, causing them to see the bones beneath their flesh. In spite of the fact Sterling was wearing dark sunglasses, the light was so strong that she was forced to shield her eyes with her forearm and cower on her haunches beneath the shadow of the dining table.

'What's going on?' said Nicoletta, crouching under the table with Sterling and the countess. 'What's happening? It's like the whole room is on fire.'

And so it was. From everywhere emerged searing tongues of flame, each with a single all-seeing eye at its centre, and all the while Cardinal Foscari just kept on praying, seemingly oblivious to the holy fire that continued to blaze all around him.

'Paolo! Get out of there! You'll be killed,' bellowed Sterling. She was about to add something else but the words died on her lips when she saw what it was that had suddenly appeared in the middle of the room.

'Holy fucking shite!' she whispered to herself, hardly daring to say it out loud. 'It's the fucking Seraphim. Foscari's called in the Seraphim—!'

Now she knew she was in trouble. For any vampire like herself, the mere presence of an archangel usually meant certain death – and yet, oddly enough, she was still very much alive. By rights, she should have been combusted into a pile of ash by now, but for some reason she hadn't, and neither had Lady Westvale or Nicoletta for that matter. The same could not be said for Charles Martel, however; for, as his sword slowly dropped from his grasp, another sword came crashing down on his shoulders, wielded by the towering figure of a mighty archangel with outstretched wings and a face that blazed with Holy light.

For a moment, Martel stood open-mouthed in shock before uttering a strangled cry as he collapsed to the floor, his body shriveling up into the ghoul-like creature he truly was – a deathly thing that reeked of sour and poisonous putrefaction. But it wasn't over yet; for even as the Aswang resumed its natural form on the dining room carpet, billowing clouds of smoke and vapour began rising from its monstrous hide, filling the room with a toxic stench that defied description. Then, all at once, a steady sequence of tiny blue flames began to issue from the corpse before coalescing into a swirling vortex of fire that consumed the Aswang in a matter of seconds, leaving nothing but a shallow mound of pale grey ash on the floor, together with an all-pervading sense of evil and malevolence that hung in the air like a shroud.

'I've only just had that carpet cleaned,' was all Lady Westvale could say as they emerged from their hiding place beneath the table. Nicoletta was weeping softly – not so much because of what she'd just witnessed, but because she now realized how her own life might end one day at the hands of the Church. Sterling too was shaken. She'd seen the Holy Fire once before and knew what it meant for all vampires if they got on the wrong side of Heaven.

As the smoke and haze slowly dispersed, Sterling could make out the figure of a small, elderly man standing exactly where the archangel had been standing only a few moments before. The man was a Catholic priest and it was someone she recognized only too well.

'Father Donnelly... How...?'

'That, I think would be a *confidential matter,*' replied the old priest with a sly grin.

'But where's the Archangel Michael?' protested Foscari, somewhat disappointed that the miracle he'd just produced was over.

'I AM the Archangel Michael!' roared the old man in a thick Irish accent. 'Who the feck did you think I was?'

'But you're just an old priest...'

'My name's Michael in case you hadn't noticed – *Michael* Donnelly; and I was sent to the Vatican in disguise by *you know who* to keep an eye on Pope Gregory while he was still alive. When Jimmy Silver had him put out of the way, I had no alternative but to improvise as best I could – which is where you and those three abominations standing over there by the table come in – one of whom has overstayed her welcome in this world by over three centuries I believe.'

Lady Westvale shrank back. She knew it was to herself that the angelic priest was referring and didn't want to suffer his wrath.

'Don't worry countess. If I'd wanted you dead, you'd be lying on the floor with that other pile of shite by now. Sorry about your carpet by the way.'

The countess didn't move. She was terrified to the point of distraction. Sterling was nervous as well and took a gulp of claret to calm her nerves; then another, and another...

'There's no need for that,' said the faux priest, 'you're working for us now.'

'I guess so Michael, but it still doesn't make it any easier, does it? I mean, here we are in Venice and we're still no further on in preventing Lorenzo Spada becoming the next Pope.'

'She's right,' said Foscari. 'I can't delay the Conclave any longer. The press are starting to get suspicious and there's still the problem of deciphering the codes. The countess here has drawn a blank. We need an expert to help us out.'

'I'm afraid I can't help you with that one,' replied the archangel. 'My heavenly authority only extended to protecting Pope Gregory while he was still alive. It was already stretching matters when I contacted you about Rachel Morrison and I'm strictly forbidden to interfere in the election of a new Pope once the Conclave is in session. The matter is out of my hands now.'

'But what can I do?' Foscari protested. 'There's so little time...'

Donnelly placed a comforting hand on the cardinal's shoulder: 'You need to find the power within yourself Dean Foscari; and, above all, you must have faith. As for me, I shall now return to my Father's realm, for my work here is done. It's up to you and Cardinal de Valois now – oh, and your infernal companion Sterling of course—'

And with that, the angel simply vanished from the scene without so much as a word of farewell, leaving all those present in the room stunned into silence. Lady Westvale was the first to speak:

'Well,' she exclaimed to Sterling, 'there's nothing else to be done here. You'd best get yourselves off to Rome and attend to matters there. I've a feeling that's where the final showdown will be. If you happen to see Jimmy Silver, do give him my regards – then put a bullet in his brain with my compliments. I've been stuck here in Venice far too long on his account.'

Nicoletta escorted Sterling and the cardinal downstairs to the front door and let them out. As the door closed behind them, they turned into the square and were immediately surprised to see someone they both recognized. It was Joe Rackham and he looked concerned.

'Joe—! What are you doing here?'

'I came as fast as I could, Sterl. De Valois gave me a call from Rome. Said I had to get here pronto. He even sent the Vatican jet to pick me up at Heathrow. Spike's here too, and Gordon. They're back at the hotel. It looks like things are kicking off.'

'What's happened?'

'I'm not altogether sure. All I know is that upwards of thirty to forty kilos of plastic explosive have been transported to Rome and the Italian secret services are doing their nut trying to find it. They reckon someone's going to set it off during the election so they're treating it as a major terrorist threat. Oh, and Cardinal de Valois said I had to give you this…'

Reaching into the inside pocket of his jacket, Joe retrieved a black, metallic object and handed it to Sterling: 'It's the Noguchi Magnum I usually carry. De Valois said I had to give it to you. There's a silencer with it in case you need to keep things quiet.'

Sterling took the gun and examined it carefully. It was black and very compact – the very height of Japanese craftsmanship. 'Thanks Joe, it's the fucken business! You packing as well?'

'The chief said he could get me a Glock from Vatican security once we arrive in Rome. Best chuck that Beretta of yours in the nearest canal when we leave. You won't be needing it anymore. That Noguchi's like a cannon. You could stop an elephant with one of those.'

'How about ogres?'

'Yeah – them too. Come on, we'd best get a move on. The plane's waiting on the tarmac at Marco Polo airport. We've got an emergency flight window scheduled for midnight. It's got diplomatic clearance an' all so you won't have to worry about the gun. Just keep it concealed, that's all. We don't want to frighten the nuns—'

'Nuns?'

'Yes. Benedictines. Twelve of them apparently. Now let's go!'

17

Joe was right.

Boarding the jet at Marco Polo airport, they found some of the passenger seats already occupied by twelve nuns of the Order of St Benedict, all clad in dark habits and vests that covered their bodies from head to foot like black Islamic burkas. Shortly before take-off, they were joined by a thirteenth nun wearing a blue cloak and vest – a breathless late arrival who'd only just managed to grab a seat before the specially chartered Alitalia aircraft taxied off down the runway and leapt into the night.

The seating arrangements on the plane were those of any conventional airliner, only more spread out with a double aisle, forcing Joe and Sterling to remain separated from Foscari, Spike and Gordon but within speaking distance of the blue-clad latecomer who had chosen to sit some distance away from the other nuns who were further down the aisle in the mid-section of coach class. About twenty minutes into the flight, the woman clad in blue began making eye contact with Joe and Sterling before passing them a small note cupped secretly in her left hand. Reaching out across the aisle, Joe took the note and passed it over to Sterling who read it, then crossed over the aisle to speak with the enigmatic nun in blue.

'You're *one of us,* I take it,' said Sterling laconically, realizing the nun wasn't all she appeared to be. 'What's your business here?'

'The name's Sister Elizabeth,' replied the woman in hushed tones. 'I'm a member of the Celestine Order. Our convent is situated just outside Venice and I work for Cardinal de Valois.'

'Oh really? He never told me.'

'He wouldn't. Our association with the Order of Exorcist is strictly classified.'

'I see. So what's the score, Sister? Is there anything I should know?'

The nun glanced down the aisle then back to Sterling. 'It's those Benedictine's. One of their number is working for Jimmy Silver.'

'How do you know?'

'I don't. I received a call from de Valois telling me to keep them under surveillance. They're bound for Rome. Originally there were eleven of them, but they were joined by a twelfth member when the plane touched down briefly in Paris en route to Venice.'

'So-?'

'So we don't know who she is. Usually, de Valois gets to know the names of everyone traveling on a Vatican chartered flight, but this twelfth nun is a bit of a mystery. I was ordered to follow her and if necessary make an intercept.'

'An *intercept...?*'

'You know what I mean.'

'Oh, I see. So why not just bushwhack her up here in the clouds at twenty thousand feet? We've got diplomatic immunity.'

'No. I have to follow her once she gets off the plane and see where she goes. De Valois wants her tracked. He reckons it's got something to do with the Conclave.'

'Is there anything else I should know?'

'Not for the moment, Sterling. I'll keep you in the loop if there are any further developments. In the meantime, de Valois wants you to maintain a low profile. If he needs you and the boys to kick the doors in, then he'll tell you when and where to strike. Until then, just act naturally as if this conversation never took place. Now where the hell is Cardinal Foscari? I need to have a word with him.'

'He's sitting up in the front of the plane in business class with Spike and Gordon.'

'How ironic. That's usually where the Pope would be sitting if he were traveling on this flight.'

'What do you mean?'

'Oh, nothing. Just an observation, that's all. Anyway, we'd best split up when we get off the plane in Rome. We don't want that spare nun getting suspicious. Bye for now. See you later.'

And with that, Sister Elizabeth wandered off to the front of the aircraft for her meeting with Foscari. Whatever it was she had to discuss with him, Sterling didn't know or care. She had far more pressing matters on her mind; such as deciphering the code in that damn book for one thing, plus whatever else lay in store for them once they landed in Rome.

As the plane began its descent, she checked the handle of the Noguchi revolver in her jacket pocket. Its cold metallic presence was somehow reassuring, even if she preferred using her more familiar Beretta pistol. Still, she'd heard some good reports about the weapon, and if Joe liked it then that was good enough for her. Joe didn't fuck about in a firefight.

18

'She's given us the slip,' exclaimed Sister Elizabeth.

They were all standing in the concourse of the main Terminal building of Rome's Ciampino airport. Elizabeth had been late coming out of bag-check and now they knew why.

'Did you see where she went?' asked Sterling absently. She'd been conferring with Joe and Foscari about something and wasn't paying very much attention.

'No. I only let her out of my sight for a second and then she was gone. Someone came up to me and asked me for the time. It must have been a distraction.'

'What do you think she's up to?'

'Hell knows. I've informed de Valois and he says she's got to be found at all costs. We're only eight miles from the centre of Rome. She could be up to anything. Oh, and he also said he wants to see you as soon as possible. He says it's urgent.'

'Can't it wait? I've got to visit the Vatican library.'

'Why? You got a book overdue or something? He wants to see you now, Sterling and that's an order! He also wants to see Paolo as well.'

Cardinal Foscari glared at the woman: 'I'm not responsible to de Valois. As Dean of the electoral college I outrank him in all matters. He takes his orders from me now—'

'I rather think de Valois takes his orders from a higher power than you, cardinal,' murmured Sterling, checking her phone and prodding in a number. Presently her call was answered and she spoke:

'De Valois— What the fuck's going on!? I've got this nun here called Sister Elizabeth who says I've got to see you right away, but I've got to go to the— Oh, I see – it's like that is it? Right… Yes… *Ahh*, that's not good. Fuck's sake! Shit! That's bad… The bastards… What about Grimaldi – can we get him on our side? Oh good… What? – The other nun's name-? Just a moment…'

'Hey, Elizabeth; you don't happen to know the name of that suspect nun do you?'

'Yes I do. One of the regular Benedictine nuns said she'd given her name as Sister Theresa but it was more likely an alias. Listen; I've got to go now Sterling. God knows what damage she could do if we can't take her down.'

With that, Sister Elizabeth hurried out of the Terminal building hot on the trail of the faux Benedictine nun who called herself Theresa. As she disappeared from view, Joe looked at Sterling: 'You reckon it's got something to do with the bomb?'

'Christ knows Joe. Let's go and hear what de Valois has to say. In the meantime, you can take a look at the code in this book. See if you can make any sense of it.'

*

Foscari was more than a little surprised by the grandiose scale and opulence of the rooms which formed the inner sanctum of the Minor Order of Exorcist. Expecting to be taken to a much smaller suite of offices located somewhere in the vicinity of the Vatican City, nothing prepared him for the baroque splendour of de Valois' headquarters – nor did he anticipate that it would be so heavily guarded. There were Swiss Guards everywhere; all of them carrying police carbines and wearing dark grey combat fatigues instead their more familiar parade uniforms.

'A necessary precaution in the circumstances, Dean,' said de Valois as they were ushered into the main office. 'I trust you had a pleasant flight?'

'I did, thank you,' replied Foscari greeting his colleague with the traditional masculine embrace practiced by all members of the Roman clergy.

Now he recognized him. Above average height and sporting a neatly trimmed mustache with chin whiskers, Edward de Valois more resembled the wily Cardinal Richelieu of the history books than any modern churchman Foscari was familiar with. He was even more surprised by Sterling's attitude towards the Chief Exorcist as she promptly dropped to one knee and kissed the sapphire ring he'd extended towards her on his right hand.

'Bless me Father for I have sinned' she said half-jokingly.'

'Get up you little monster,' exclaimed de Valois with some humour in his voice. 'You know full well you don't mean it!'

Like a naughty schoolgirl, Sterling grinned and sat herself down directly in front of the Chief Exorcist's desk. Joe sat down beside her, but Foscari remained standing, not wishing to appear in any way subordinate to Sterling's boss. Spike and Gordon remained outside the room seated on a bench under the watchful eye of a Swiss Guard. Evidently, Vatican security weren't taking any chances.

'And how is young Rachel Morrison?' inquired de Valois sitting himself down at his desk. 'You said she was found wandering around in Venice.'

'She's fine, Edward. Like I said on the phone, she was being used as bait to lure Foscari and myself into a trap. Charles Martel attacked us in Lady Westvale's house, but the Seraphim intervened and settled the fucker's hash big time.'

'Good,' remarked the chief exorcist relaxing back in his chair; 'now all we need to do is deal with Spada.'

'What about the C4, Your Eminence?' put in Joe. 'There's still upwards of forty kilos of plastic explosive somewhere in the city and nobody knows where the fuck it is.'

Foscari was appalled by the use of so much foul language, but guessed it was normal in the circumstances. Leastways, de Valois didn't appear to mind as he calmly answered Joe's question:

'I'm aware of that fact, Joe. That's why I put Sister Elizabeth on the case. I've also alerted the Italian security services to have NOCS units placed on standby in the event of trouble.'

'NOCS-?'

'Italian counter-terrorism police, Joe. They're a shock-and-awe group usually called in as a last resort.'

'Do we want them?'

'Maybe not. That's where you and the boys might come in handy if Sister Elizabeth fails to make her intercept. In the meantime, Cardinal Foscari here will have to postpone the election for a little while longer.'

'I can't,' replied Foscari. 'It's already been delayed long enough. The election of the new Pope has to go ahead. People are growing suspicious.'

'Very well, Dean; I take your point, but it will be difficult for me to convince the police. There are limits to Vatican authority in matters such as these.'

'Then for God's sake try, Edward— I think I have a plan.'

Sterling raised her eyebrows in despair: 'He's got a plan, Joe – We're saved...'

'Just humour him,' replied the old biker quietly before turning to de Valois. 'Hey, Edward; how about fixing me up with that shooter you promised me.'

Reaching into a drawer, de Valois pulled out the gun Joe had requested and slid it across the desk towards him. 'It's a Glock 17 standard Vatican issue pistol. Just don't get too trigger happy with it, that's all.'

Foscari grew alarmed. 'Whoa— Wait a minute! You can't have a gun-battle in the Vatican. Not in the middle of a Conclave.'

'Might never 'appen,' replied Joe checking the weapon. 'If it does, just stay out of my way. This here Glock is the business.'

'I can't allow it! Not in a house of God—'

'We may have no choice,' confided Sterling, checking her own pistol. The Glock is an excellent weapon but this Noguchi is just plain awesome. Anyway, Paolo – what's your plan?'

'The codes, that's what. I think the answer may lie in the codes.'

'Codes?' exclaimed Joe. I wasn't told about no codes.'

De Valois coughed slightly and cleared his throat: 'Sterling found some codes in a book she was given. She thinks they might be old Vatican cipher codes.'

'So...?'

'So they were lifted off Silver by Jenny Hancock in London,' replied Sterling, removing the slim volume from her inside pocket. 'They've got Jimmy's old coat-of-arms scribbled in the front. Here, see for yourself.'

Joe took the book he was offered and opened it at the flyleaf. Then he went into a focused study while the others talked among themselves. From the furrow of knots in his brow, Foscari could tell that the academic process was alien territory to his mind.

As Joe studied the book, Sterling glanced up at Foscari who was standing close by her chair. 'So what's your plan, Paolo? You said you had a plan...'

Foscari looked at de Valois then back to Sterling. 'Well, first we've got to decipher the code, so I suggest we begin our investigations at the Vatican palace. There's most likely someone there who can help us interpret old cipher documents dating back to Silver's time.'

'And how do you propose to do that?' put in de Valois. 'Access to the Secret Archive is denied to all but the most senior academics, and then only if they have specific letters of introduction from respected academic institutions. I have enough problems getting in there myself and I'm the Chief Exorcist!'

'Yes, but I'm Dean of the College, remember. I can say I'm visiting the archives on matters of State. I can't be denied access on that account.'

'Mmm... What if Lomellini tries to block you? He's Spada's man and also the senior librarian.'

'He doesn't need to know. In fact, I somehow doubt if he actually reads any of the applications for historical research. He has very little interest in academic matters and probably leaves all that sort of thing to his underlings.'

'Very well then. I shall give them a call and say you're coming over.'

'He's not going on his own,' exclaimed Sterling. 'He needs someone to watch his back, and I don't mean Vatican security. Silver's most likely infiltrated the place with his own agents by now. We can't afford to take any chances.'

'Point taken, but it's not going to be easy getting you in there. The custodians of the Vatican library don't take too kindly to vampires as a rule.'

'So tell them I'm on a mission from God! It should be enough leverage in the circumstances—'

Heaving a sigh, the exorcist picked up his phone and dialed a number. A tense conversation followed and the matter was settled. Putting down his phone, de Valois looked at Sterling: 'I told them there was an urgent matter of protocol that the Dean had to consult and that you're his palaeographer.'

'I'm his what—?'

'Palaeographer... It's an expert in ancient texts. You're his translator, Sterling. I take it you can read old documents with those *special powers* of yours. Most vampires have the ability, I believe.'

'Well, I suppose...'

'Good— Then off you go and don't be long. The person you'll be meeting is a Jesuit priest called Tommaso Ancelotti – he's one of the archivists. Just don't try to flannel him, that's all. He's got a PhD in medieval studies and knows what he's talking about. If he can't decipher your code then no one can.'

'What about Joe?'

'What about him?'

'Can he come too?'

'Absolutely not. I'm pushing my luck in getting you in there, never mind a member of the Hell's Angels motorcycle club. No offence, Joe, but you'd most likely be stopped at the front door.'

'None taken, boss,' replied the biker, handing Sterling the book. 'I can't make head nor tail of it anyway – assuming it is a code, of course. In the meantime, is there anywhere me and the boys can get a bite to eat around this place? I bet the grub in here fair makes yer bollocks tingle.'

*

Sterling was not surprised that Foscari had suggested a trip to the Vatican archives. What did surprise her however, was the fact that de Valois had allowed her to accompany him in the first place. Even more surprising, was that she'd actually managed to gain admittance to the building without so much as a questioning glance from the Swiss Guards who manned the front gate.

And so, Sterling found herself heading off with Foscari towards the entrance of the Secret Archive through the Porta di S. Anna and in via the Porta Angelica. Stepping out of the warm Roman sunlight, she was relieved when she entered the cool darkness of the building's interior. She was even more relieved to discover that Foscari was no stranger to the endless miles of passageways and rooms, or indeed to some of the staff who actually worked there.

'As Dean of the College,' Foscari explained as they walked, 'I sometimes come here to research historical documents concerning Vatican procedures. It's part of my job.'

'Oh...*Good,*' replied Sterling, increasingly overwhelmed at the sheer size of the place. There seemed no end to the darkened, hushed passageways within, and, when at last they reached the point of no return, she began to focus once more on the problem that faced them. It was something that Joe had said about the cipher code contained within the book: *"assuming it is a code, of course"* was the phrase that he'd used, and for some reason she just couldn't get it out of her mind.

Now they came to a long room with a high, ornate ceiling. A series of scholarly tables and chairs ran down the central aisle of the room, all of them unoccupied. Evidently, it was a slow day in the reference section.

Clutching a notebook and pencil, Foscari approached the reception desk and introduced himself to the young man seated behind the computer screen. At first, the man barely lifted his head to acknowledge the cardinal's presence, but his mood quickly changed when Foscari introduced himself:

'I am Cardinal Paolo Foscari, Dean of the Electoral College and I have a meeting with Father Ancelotti. There are some important documents I need to view.'

Awestruck was the only way to describe the expression on the young man's face when he realized who it was that was standing there in front of his desk. Still fairly new to the job, he was used to dealing with research academics and polite scholarly priests, but he'd never locked horns with a cardinal before – at least, not one so high-ranking as Foscari.

'Just a moment, Your Eminence... I... I think he's down in the stacks. I... I will give him a call. Is there... erm, do you have a reference number for any particular document? You're allowed three out at any one time.'

'He already knows. We rang ahead on his extension earlier.'

'Ah... Right... One moment while I call him.'

The receptionist was so flustered that he'd not even noticed Sterling as she stood there studying him intently. In less than six months time the young man would be dead from the undetected cancer that was slowly eating its way into his brain. Pity...

'He'll be up right away, Your Eminence. Please take a seat at... er, well, anywhere you like really. Things are running a bit slow today.'

Going over to one of the research desks, Foscari pulled out a chair and sat down, bidding his companion do the same. The legs of the chair made a hollow, woody noise as they were moved, causing the receptionist to wince a little. Clearly such intrusive sounds were alien to his nature as a librarian.

Presently, footsteps were heard approaching the central aisle where they sat. It was Father Ancelotti the Jesuit archivist and he had a look on his face like thunder.

'Where did you get the book from!?' he exclaimed without introduction.

'What— The Incunabulum?' replied Sterling innocently.

'Yes. It's a Vatican document. I have no record of it having been removed from the Archives. How did you come by it?'

'Jenny Hancock—'

'Who?'

'Jenny Hancock... Oh, you wouldn't have heard of her, Father Ancelotti. She's a London pickpocket.'

At this point, Foscari thought it best to intervene before the archivist called security and had them both arrested.

'Cardinal Lomellini authorized its removal and passed it on to a man called Jimmy Silver who is an international master criminal, or so I am led to believe. Apparently this woman called Jenny Hancock stole it from his breast pocket on a London street a few days ago and handed it over to my associate here via a professional fence called Debbie Stephenson. Isn't that right, Sterling...'

'Yes Paolo. That's about the long and short of it. And here we are today wanting some answers as to what it was precisely that Jimmy scribbled down in the flyleaf of this book.'

Removing the book from her own pocket, she placed the thin volume on the table in front of the archivist and waited for his reaction.

'This is all highly irregular,' replied Ancelotti with a frown.

'So sue me,' cut in Sterling. 'In any case, Lomellini is your boss, is he not? Why don't you bring the matter up with him and see how far you get!'

'I could sign for it,' suggested Foscari trying to calm the situation. 'I dare say we shall require it for a little while longer in the circumstances.'

'What for?'

'Ah! I'm glad you asked me that, Father Ancelotti. There is an encrypted message written down in the flyleaf of the book and we were wondering if you could perhaps enlighten us as to its precise meaning. I'm assuming you have access to old Vatican ciphers in your library stacks?'

'We do,' replied the archivist placing the document wallet he was carrying on the desk. Pulling on a pair of white gloves, he sat down and began scrutinizing the contents of the book, taking occasional glances at the material contained in his file. As the seconds ticked by, Foscari leaned over to his companion and whispered in her ear: 'Why don't you go and get yourself a bite to eat, Sterling. I've a feeling this may take some time.'

'I'll stay,' she replied firmly. 'Jenny may have risked her life getting this book to me so I reckon I owe her that much.'

Slow time lapsed into several minutes, at the end of which Father Ancelotti looked up from the book: 'I can't make much sense of it I'm afraid. The long series of numbers in the code may very well be a nomenclater.'

'A *what?*' ventured Foscari, utterly baffled.

'- A nomenclater. It's a series of low numbers used to represent letters and high numbers for words; but without the inclusion of actual letters in the text and their respective locations, it just doesn't make any sense. I'm using a Code Eleven Vatican cipher here but it's not working. The name's

Zurich and Lugano obviously refer to cities in Switzerland, but apart from that I can't help you.'

'A Code Eleven...' observed Sterling; Lady Westvale mentioned that.'

'Who?'

'Caroline Westvale – she's someone we contacted in Venice about the code, but she wasn't very forthcoming about it either. It was herself who suggested we contact the archives here; oh, and Count Francesco Grimaldi as well.'

'Who's he?' inquired the archivist, his interest suddenly aroused.

'Count Grimaldi is the Secretary of the Bene Noctu.'

'And what kind of organization is that might I ask? I don't recall it being on my list of recognized academic institutions.'

'You wouldn't,' Sterling replied, ignoring Foscari's cautionary tugging at her sleeve; 'It's the vampire council of Europe, and Grimaldi is the presiding council member. He's been dead for well over three hundred years you know. Isn't that simply amazing!'

*

Once more, Foscari and his companion found themselves standing outside in the warm Roman sunshine having been escorted out of the building by five members of the Vatican security police, one of whom was brandishing an automatic pistol.

'What did I say!?' exclaimed Sterling angrily. 'What the fuck did I say?'

'Erm, I think it was the bit about the vampire council and Count Grimaldi,' replied Foscari meekly. 'Jesuit priests don't have much patience with that sort of thing as a rule... especially academics like Father Ancelotti.'

'Humph! Oh well, we weren't getting anywhere with him anyway. Let's go and talk to Grimaldi. Maybe he can sort things out with this bastard code. If he can't then nobody can.'

19

Sterling and Foscari were seated at a sidewalk café on the outskirts of Rome when the messenger arrived. He was a young man, thin and unwashed with the sallow complexion and mannerisms of a long-term drug addict. The colour of his aura suggested to Sterling that he was no longer human but somehow the result of a vampire transformation that had gone horribly wrong, leaving him brain damaged and fit only for taking orders from other vampires more powerful than himself.

The smell of death was strong, causing Foscari to recoil a little until Sterling caught his arm. 'Steady,' she whispered. 'This doesn't happen to all of us.'

'What do you mean?' Foscari replied, almost on the point of throwing up. 'I thought you were taking me to see Count Grimaldi?'

'I am,' admonished his friend continuing to stare at the pale youth standing in front of them. 'This is Grimaldi's manservant. He's come to take me to see the Count. You should feel honoured, cardinal. After all, it's not often an ordinary mortal like yourself gets to see a senior clan master like Francesco.'

'I don't understand.'

'You will Paolo. You will. Anyway, I think the young man wants us to follow him. Come along. We haven't got all day.'

*

The messenger led them through a series of twisting backstreets until they came to a crumbling old Italian villa with an overgrown garden. Long deserted on the outskirts of Rome, the villa was uninhabited except for a family of stray cats that endlessly patrolled its grounds. Other than that, there was no one about apart from Sterling, Foscari and their feral guide who approached the building warily.

Following the messenger through the garden, they came to a door. The door was half open enabling them to gain access to the house. The ground floor was entirely devoid of furniture, but the interior door to its cellar also stood open, and their messenger-guide hurried downstairs without even bothering to check if Sterling and Foscari were following him.

The basement had a stone floor and smelled strongly of mildew. The only light came from the steady flame of a candle perched atop of an antique silver holder set on an old table. This table was situated against the far wall to the left of a small timber door with rusty hinges of an old-fashioned design. This door too was partially open and unguarded.

'That's strange,' said Sterling entering the door with the guide, and bidding Foscari to follow them. 'Grimaldi usually has someone guarding the entrance to his realm. I hope nothing's happened.'

*

They found themselves in a low, sloping passageway lit by a series of low-wattage bulbs set in the ceiling of the tunnel. 'This villa serves to conceal one of the entrances to the Roman catacombs,' explained Sterling. 'They're where the citizens of Rome used to bury their dead – *and not-so-dead,* if you know what I mean.'

'Thanks for the warning,' said Foscari glancing round with increasing trepidation at the narrow shelf-graves cut into the walls of the corridor. The dead, some of them still dressed in the clothes they'd worn in life, watched with empty eye sockets as the trio traveled ever deeper into their realm. Then, after they'd walked for what Foscari estimated must have been over half an hour and descending three levels, they came to one of the larger, more elaborate burial chambers reserved solely for the ancient dead.

'This is the main council chamber,' his companion remarked. 'It's where Grimaldi hosts all his meetings of the Bene Noctu – the Vampire Council of Europe.'

'Oh, really Sterling – I'd never have guessed.'

Together, they stepped into a vaulted chamber, staring round at its grisly décor. The room had been turned into a shrine, and clearly served the function of a meeting place. Its red ochre walls were inset from floor to ceiling with human skulls, all neatly embedded into its ancient mortar. The skulls surrounded a narrow vertical alcove containing the mummified remains of an adult male clad in the costume of an eighteenth century gentleman, complete with a three-cornered hat perched at a jaunty angle on his head. Elsewhere, equally mummified cadavers of men and women dressed in the clothes of their time hung suspended in a standing position from hooks set into the walls, interspersed with the skeletal forms of long-dead monks and holy men clutching strands of rosary beads in their bony fingers. Most of the dead still possessed enough skin to cover their bones, even though it was as stiff and as yellow as parchment. Then one of the dead stepped out of the shadows, causing Sterling to draw her weapon. It was the corpse of an adult male dressed in eighteenth century clothes, its skeletal face grinning with rakish mirth beneath the brim of its three-cornered hat.

'Delighted to meet your acquaintance once again, Sterling. And I see you've brought Cardinal Foscari along with you this time. It's not often we get so distinguished a visitor down here. I am truly honoured I am. Truly honoured.'

Sterling gave a wry smile and put away her weapon, gesturing to Foscari that all was well. 'It's alright, Paolo; he won't bite. This corpse here knew we were coming.'

'What the hell—?'

'Don't look so surprised, cardinal,' said the skeletal wraith in the eighteenth century costume. Your visit to my realm has been long anticipated.'

'I don't understand…'

'Should you tell him or should I, Sterling?' continued Grimaldi beckoning to the messenger who was cowering in the corner of the room. Her vision wavered as the walking corpse slowly fleshed itself out and became Count Francesco Grimaldi, former Lord of Milan and now acting secretary of the vampire council.

'He knew we were coming, Paolo,' confessed Sterling. 'Ancient vampires like Francesco here have a certain degree of precognition. They somehow know what's going to happen before it actually does.'

'Don't be too hasty to judge your friend, Cardinal Foscari,' put in Grimaldi, filling a clay tobacco pipe and putting it to his mouth before lighting it on a nearby candle flame and puffing it into life. 'You are very lucky to have met such an illustrious person as Miss Sterling here, you really are.'

The cowering messenger now emerged from the shadows and blurted out something in Italian to Grimaldi, prompting him to reach into his waistcoat pocket and bring out a small plastic sachet of white powder. The messenger snatched the packet from Grimaldi's hand and scurried out of the room.

'Poor boy,' apologized the count. 'He's a heroin addict and depends solely on me to provide him with the necessary medication to get him through the day.'

'How considerate of you,' replied Sterling with a sarcastic grin. Grimaldi merely arched an eyebrow and puffed on his clay pipe: 'Thank you for that. It's not often I receive any praise these days. My fellows tend to see me as a bit of a dilettante... a decadent fop left over from a more genteel age, but I prefer to think of myself as something of a philanthropist, wouldn't you agree?'

Sterling said nothing. She knew most vampires of Grimaldi's generation had a tendency to treat human beings as their pets and servants until such time as they decided to do away with them. Jimmy Silver was the same.

Failing to get a response, Grimaldi sat himself down on the edge of a stone sarcophagus. 'These tombs,' he said with a sweeping gesture of his hand, 'were forgotten by humanity well over two hundred years ago when they became full up and no longer available for burials. We vampires however, never forget. You need not fear any violence from me while we are here, and I trust I may expect the same from you?'

Sterling nodded. Even though Count Grimaldi was much higher up the Undead hierarchy than herself, she had no reason to doubt his sincerity. He simply had too much to lose if Jimmy Silver gained the upper hand and had Spada elected as the new Pope.

'Pray be seated, Cardinal Foscari,' said the count, pointing to an empty chair that had once accommodated a fully dressed corpse. 'Your companion and I have some important matters to discuss and they are not for the eyes and ears of mortal men like yourself.'

Foscari reluctantly took his seat. Much of what was being discussed he could not make out from his vantage point at the far end of the room. He also found the way the vampire lord kept turning round at intervals to look in his direction somewhat unnerving, and guessed that part of the discussion was mostly about the political crisis that was rapidly developing within the Vatican together with its potential threat to the vampire power structure throughout Europe as a whole.

'But pray tell me, my dear,' said Grimaldi to Sterling after they'd been talking a while; 'how exactly are we going to deal with the problem of Jimmy Silver? He already has control of the greater part of Italy as far as the region of Naples. It's only a question of time before he allies with the Calabrians. What possible good would my permitting you to join the vampire council actually do? Your association with the Church hasn't entirely gone unnoticed among our ranks.'

'That's not the point, Your Excellency. We've got the future to think about after Silver's been defeated. It may well have escaped your attention, but my dealings with Cardinal de Valois are one of the few things protecting your ass at the moment and preventing the Church from ordering a mass culling of all vampires across the face of the planet!'

'Just like the old days you mean?'

'Yeah. Just like the old days.'

Grimaldi rose to his feet and heaved a sigh. 'You drive a hard bargain young lady.I will put the matter to the committee and see what they say, but beyond that I'm afraid my hands are tied. Now, what's all this about a book? I understand you wish to ask my advice about some code or other.'

Sterling beckoned to Foscari, indicating that it was okay to come over and join them while she showed Grimaldi the book. Almost as soon as she pulled the slim volume out of her pocket, Count Grimaldi's crimson eyes began to glow brighter. 'Ohhhh...' he exclaimed softly; 'it's the Incunabulum. Where did you get it?'

'A mate of mine called Jenny Hancock nicked it from Jimmy Silver in London.'

'But how?'

'Don't ask me. The bitch got lucky I guess. It's got Silver's coat of arms written in the flyleaf, but it's the inscription on the reverse of the page I'm interested in. See—'

LUGANO – 777
COSOLS32 XXX
COSOIT31 – OIRDNOS
45798653Z5457X056791
ZURICH – RXPGP
COSOZU33XXX
44678965Z6160X097892

Sterling and Foscari gathered round the count, peering over his shoulder as he examined the coded message with focused concentration. His pipe was drawing well now, and the smoke was sweet in the otherwise stagnant air.

'Well, Grimaldi— Do we have an answer yet?' exclaimed Sterling growing increasingly impatient.

'Hmm, well not so much an answer, but I think I can make out part of it.'

'Which part?'

'The top line… The part with the numbers 777 and also the letters RXPGP at the end of the fifth line.'

'Is that all?'

'I'm afraid so. Much of the rest is just numbers and letters all mixed up.'

'Nomenclators and nulls, huh?'

'Yes, yes, Sterling! I didn't realize you had some knowledge of cipher.'

'I don't. A Vatican archivist told me… Oh, and Lady Westvale as well.'

'Ah – I see…'

Sterling sensed some reluctance on Grimaldi's part to continue and was relieved when he finally spoke.

'The number 777 may not be a code at all but a reference to the Angel of Abundance.'

'I don't understand, Grimaldi. What does that imply exactly?'

'You mean you don't know?' exclaimed the count, genuinely surprised.

'No – Should I?'

'Mmm, well maybe not, Sterling. You haven't been around that long – as a member of the Undead I mean. You wouldn't necessarily know about these things. Most people don't, with the exception of a few elder vampires like myself.'

'Does that include Jimmy Silver as well?'

'Precisely my dear – and Jimmy Silver; which probably means it's him that we're dealing with here along with the reference to the city of Lugano. Have you any idea what that might mean?'

'Yes, Francesco. Me and the cardinal here think it's got something to do with the Swiss banking industry along with the city of Zurich, but we can't work out which particular bank it's referring to and don't know what the rest of the code means. That's why we came to you.'

'Hmmm…' pondered the count, taking a draw on his pipe. 'Well, if the number 777 is a reference to Abundance, then the first line is Silver's way of indicating that the information encoded in the text is, as you suggest, a clear reference to the Swiss Banking system and the city of Lugano. It would seem to indicate that Jimmy holds his main assets in a bank in Lugano, which by the way just so happens to border directly with Italian territory in the region of Lombardy.'

'You mean it's a reference to his criminal activity?'

'Oh, it's a great deal more than that, dear heart. The information encoded here could very well be a detailed description of his entire financial empire together with the means of unlocking it, if only I could crack all the nulls and nomenclators in the code; er, which I'm afraid I can't.'

'Try, Francesco – Please try. You're our only hope.'

Count Grimaldi furrowed his brow. Tapping out his pipe on the stone sarcophagus, he replied: 'It's a bit of a long shot but I think I may be able to decipher one section of the text that reads "RXPGP" after the word "Zurich". Just a moment—'

Walking over to an old wooden chest, he produced an ancient key from his waistcoat pocket and inserted it into the rusty lock of the box, opening the lid of the chest with a creak.

Then he began rummaging through its contents, all the while muttering to himself in an archaic Italian dialect long since dead to the world. At length, the count came trotting back clutching a scrap of parchment in his hand.

'This,' he announced proudly, is a Code Nine. I remember using one of these back in the year 1760 when I was in my early twenties. I was still human then and very much in love with a pretty young lady from Tuscany who's family weren't too keen on me. We had to communicate in coded messages smuggled into her family villa in old wine casks.'

'How incredibly gallant of you,' remarked Sterling, growing increasingly impatient with the count's reminiscence. 'What the fuck does the code say for Christ's sake!?'

Ignoring her reply, Grimaldi straightened his back and grimaced with pleasure as his spine crackled. Then he regarded her strangely: 'This piece of parchment here is another Vatican cipher grid. Long ago, my brother Onofrio served as the chief cipher clerk to Pope Pius VI. That chest over there is full of his papers, and some of them contain valuable information pertaining to the type of substitution codes commonly used in the eighteenth century, which would be the time when Silver was using them.'

'So, what does "RXPGP" mean then, Francesco?'

'Just give me a moment and I'll tell you...'

Count Grimaldi sat down once more on the edge of the sarcophagus. He was humming a little tune to himself as he studied the book, taking occasional glances at the parchment for guidance. Sterling sat down beside him and waited for the verdict while Foscari stood expectantly to one side, shivering in the cold air of the crypt. Suddenly, Grimaldi drew in a breath and exclaimed: 'Ah-hah!'

'Well—'said Sterling. 'Have you got it yet?'

'Indeed I have,' answered the count looking up with a triumphant grin. 'The letters RXPGP are a substitution code and I know what it means.'

'You do...? Tell me—'

' "SPADA," – that's what it means.'

'You sure?'

'Of course I'm sure. See here,' he said pointing to the parchment. On its pristine white surface inscribed in oxidized brown ink were a set of horizontal and vertical lines forming a grid of square boxes, each containing a single random letter. Above this, on the top line, were written the more familiar twenty-six letters of the alphabet set out in perfect order.

Both Sterling and Foscari looked on in fascination as Grimaldi traced his finger down from the regular ABC alphabet on the top line to the more irrational sequence of letters laid out below. Directly beneath the alphabet letters S, P, A, D, A on the top line were the corresponding code letters R, X, P, G and P, spelling out the name of Spada.

'Simple when you know how,' beamed Grimaldi wiping the tomb dust off his fingers. 'Quite simple…'

'Yes, but how does it relate to everything else?' demanded Sterling. 'So the line in the book now reads as: "ZURICH – SPADA." So what—?'

'Presumably it's a reference to Lorenzo Spada's banking concerns in Zurich, my dear. It would seem that Jimmy Silver's financial interests in Lugano are directly linked with those of Cardinal Spada's in Zurich.'

'Ha! Money laundering,' boomed Foscari; 'I knew it. The two are working together.'

'Yes, but it still doesn't explain the rest of the text in the code though, does it?' Sterling cut in; 'and we still don't know where all the dark money is coming from or which banks are being used to move it around. Without that knowledge we've no real proof.'

'You've got a point, Sterling. The last time anything like this happened, the dark money largely came from the proceeds of raw heroin refined in Sicily by two Mafia families and then shipped by their colleagues in America to New York via their infiltration of the Italian civil airlines.'

'But that's the Sicilians, Paolo. Jimmy Silver only deals with the Camorra.'

Foscari sighed. 'The world has moved on since the 1970s. We could be dealing with anything here from computer chips to refined cocaine. Who knows? The only thing that should concern us now are the names of the banks being used and how we can establish proof of Spada's involvement. Do that, and we can knock him out of the papal election.'

'Yes, but we need to establish how the money is being transported out of Italy in the first place. They must be using an Italian bank somewhere on the mainland to initiate the flow of capital. I somehow doubt if they're using goods or commodities like diamonds and antiques the way some organizations do.'

'The Vatican Bank is out of the question, Sterling. The Italian security services have been keeping a close eye on the place ever since all that trouble with Roberto Calvi back in the 1980s. Only a fool would consider using it now.'

'Well how about the Venetian banks then?'

'Too obvious. The Banco Veneto is too high-profile, and in any case, it's subject to the powers of the Italian banking inspectors like any other mainland bank in the country. No, Sterling – what we're looking for is a much smaller financial institution. Something like an ordinary provincial bank that wouldn't attract much attention from the authorities.'

'I agree,' added Grimaldi lifting his eyes up from the book. 'Pope Gregory himself was about to launch an investigation into Spada's financial dealings shortly before he was assassinated.'

'Oh-,' exclaimed Foscari in surprise. 'Why didn't you tell me that before?'

'Because I thought you already knew.'

'No, I didn't; and how on earth did a creature like yourself get to know may I ask?'

'De Valois told me. He usually sends one of his agents down here from time to time just to keep me in the loop, so to speak.'

He kept that one dark, thought Foscari glancing at Sterling who simply returned his gaze with a shrug. Then his thoughts turned backwards in time to the incident with Cardinal Lomellini in the Pope's bedroom: *Ahhh yes, I see it all now. Gregory was no fool. The cunning old fox knew his life was in danger. He must have baited a trap for the conspirators in the event of him being poisoned...*

His train of thought was suddenly broken by the count who had resumed his examination of the book. 'The key to the whole thing,' he declared. 'is to know the names of all the banks being used in the operation. Without that information, I'm afraid there's not much hope.'

'Can you do it?' implored Sterling hopefully.

'Well I have a feeling the letters "OIRDNOS" at the end of the third line in the text may be the clincher, but I'm damned if my Code Nine here can decipher it, and as for the coded expression "COSOIT31," I'm afraid that I am at a complete loss to know what it means.'

'Then in that case, can we at least count on your support and that of all the other vampire clans in the event of Spada being elected as the next Pope? That's when all hell will break lose… You know that.'

Grimaldi shuffled nervously on his feet, the hard leather of his eighteenth century boots scuffing the dusty flagstones of his tiny domain. 'I shall put the matter to the representatives of the Bene Noctu and they can take a vote on it. Other than that, I can't promise you anything.'

At this, Sterling turned on the count with venom. 'You know what, Francesco – screw the vampire council! I'll sort this out my own way like I've always done; just me, Joe and the boys. If it comes to a fight then we're more than a match for Jimmy Silver. Always have been. Always will be—!'

Then she stormed out of the crypt, kicking a pile of old bones as she went. Foscari apologized to the count and followed her up to the world above, only too pleased to remove himself from the stagnant air of Grimaldi's kingdom.

'That could have been better,' he said as they stood outside in the garden of the abandoned villa. The shadows were already beginning to lengthen as the sun declined in the western sky. Evening had arrived.

'Uh-?' exclaimed Sterling.

'I said, you could have handled that a bit more diplomatically. Now you've lost the support of the Bene Noctu.'

The young vampire glanced around the garden, half-expecting an attack at any moment. 'I somehow doubt if that matters anymore, cardinal. Come on, let's get out of here. We've got to get back to base. De Valois will be waiting for the verdict.'

20

In the office of the Chief Confessor the mood was sombre. Cardinal Martinelli looked at de Valois: 'Is she to be trusted?'

'Sterling is one of our best field-agents,' the exorcist replied.

'Then why isn't she here?'

'She was sent on a mission with Foscari. I'm expecting her return at any moment. It is imperative that we have all our pieces in place before the Conclave sits. We're getting close to the endgame now and I need to tie up a few loose ends. Once we're all locked up inside the Sistine Chapel for the vote it will be too late. Silver will be able to stage whatever it is he's got planned and we won't be able to stop him.'

Martinelli glanced wistfully out of the window. It was already becoming dark outside. As the sun dipped below the dome of St Peter's basilica, the air suddenly chilled.

'And how about you, Sister Elizabeth?' he said turning in the direction of the blue-costumed nun seated next to de Valois. 'Any news about the plastic explosive and the Benedictine woman you were tailing?'

'I'm afraid not, Your Eminence. I have been unable to intercept the agent thought to be responsible for its transportation. As yet, we don't know where it's going to be detonated. Somewhere in the Holy City I expect. Vatican security are on the case and the Italian authorities have brought in sniffer-dogs sensitized to C4. Other than that I've heard nothing.'

With a troubled heart, Martinelli looked inwardly for a moment weighing up the options. On impulse, de Valois said: 'How is the work progressing on the Sistine Chapel, Ottavio?'

Ottavio Martinelli hesitated. Perplexed. 'The carpenter's have almost finished raising the floor of the chapel for the cardinal electors to meet. According to the Secretary of the College, it will be ready in a couple of days at most.'

'Forty-eight hours… It's barely enough time.'

'It's all I can give you, Edward. The election has been delayed long enough. We can't hold it off any longer. The press office is running out of excuses.'

There was a soft knock on the door and another blue-clad nun entered carrying a tray. Placing a large thermos jug of coffee on the confessor's desk, she bowed slightly and then departed almost as invisibly as she'd arrived.

'I'd have preferred a brandy at this hour of the day,' observed de Valois, 'but I dare say none of us will be getting very much sleep tonight anyway.'

'No, Your Eminence,' remarked Sister Elizabeth meekly. 'I guess we won't.'

Reaching across the table, Cardinal Martinelli poured out the coffee and handed a cup to de Valois and Elizabeth respectively before settling back in his chair with his own cup, blowing air across its rim to cool it down before drinking.

'How many cardinals have yet to arrive?' inquired de Valois playing for time.

Martinelli paused. 'All told, a total of 113 electors have checked in at the Casa Santa Marta and have been allocated their rooms. That leaves us with three who have yet to make an appearance – Cardinal Kumara of Sri Lanka; Cardinal Shilongo of Burundi, and lastly but by no means leastly, Duncan McKenzie for South Africa.'

'You think they'll make it?'

'I don't see why not, Edward. They don't have any significant medical problems that would preclude them from attending the Conclave.'

'What about McKenzie? He's on our side and a strong opponent of Spada. Both he and Shilongo could tip the African vote in our favour. They're not conservative hardliners like some of the rest. Neither for that matter is Kumara.'

'Maybe so, but there is some question about McKenzie's age. He's nearly eighty and very close to becoming ineligible to vote. You don't happen to know his date of birth by any chance?'

'No I don't, Ottavio. I'll have to get Dean Foscari to look into it. He's got the records.'

There was another knock on the door, louder this time and most likely delivered by a man. Martinelli's suspicion was confirmed when a member of Vatican security entered the room followed by Sterling and Foscari hard on his heels.

'*Scusi,* Your Eminence, but there is a Cardinal Foscari who wishes to speak with you, and he's brought someone with him…'

'It's okay, Jovanni. We were expecting them. You can let them in.'

Now there were five people gathered together in the Confessor's office and not enough chairs to go round. Politely, Foscari remained standing while another chair could be fetched for him. Rather ironically, it proved to be an antique throne that was delivered, last reported to have been used by a Borgia pope back in the fifteenth century. In spite of it having a well-cushioned seat, Foscari felt distinctly uncomfortable in it. Evidently, the Pope's chair didn't suit him; a fact that had not gone unnoticed by Cardinal Martinelli who sat behind his desk observing Foscari's discomfort with amused interest.

'Well - what's the verdict?' asked de Valois sliding the thermos jug in Sterling's direction. 'What did Grimaldi say about the code?'

'No luck I'm afraid. He wasn't able to make any sense of it,' replied Sterling declining the offer of coffee while taking the book out of her pocket and handing it to de Valois. 'You may as well have this back. It's overdue for return to the Vatican archives I believe.'

'Yes, we don't want to get fined for an overdue library book do we,' remarked Foscari wriggling in his seat. Just what was it about the Roman Catholic Church that denied even senior prelates like himself the simple joys of comfort in their old age.

'What's the problem?' said Elizabeth who had remained silent up until this point.

'It's this seat,' replied the Dean. 'I can't seem to get comfortable in it…'

'No, I mean the book. What's the issue with the book?'

'We think there may be a coded message on the front flyleaf,' explained de Valois; 'only no one's been able to crack it yet. Here – You have a try.'

Passing the slim volume over to the nun, Cardinal de Valois waited patiently for her verdict while Foscari offered a few comments of his own concerning all they knew about the code so far.

'We think the coded message may refer to a money laundering exercise being operated between Lorenzo Spada and Jimmy Silver using the Swiss banking system, but as yet we can't establish which banks in Zurich and Lugano are being used, or how all the dark money is being transferred out of Italy. Naturally, we've ruled out the Vatican Bank given all that trouble a few decades ago.'

'That's hardly surprising…' murmured Sister Elizabeth tapping a shrewd finger to her lips as she examined the encrypted text. 'What exquisite handwriting by the way. Eighteenth century freehand by the look of it. Quite exquisite…'

De Valois raised his eyebrows in despair as Elizabeth maundered on, muttering all the while to herself with occasional intervals of tongue-clicking as if she were truly enjoying the process of her investigation.

'We know the number 777 on the first line is a reference to Jimmy Silver,' continued Foscari, 'and that the Swiss bank where he holds all his assets in based in Lugano. According to Count Grimaldi, the expression "RXPGP" on the fifth line is a substitution code for the name "Spada" and clearly refers to Lorenzo Spada's holdings in Zurich, but apart from that, Grimaldi couldn't make any headway with the rest of the encrypted information. We also took the book to the Vatican Library and asked an expert there if he could help, but unfortunately he drew a blank.'

'Hmmm, that doesn't surprise me either,' replied Elizabeth crooking her finger to her chin. 'You see, what we have here is not really a code at all – at least not in the usual sense of the word, and it's most definitely got nothing to do with the Vatican.'

'How do you mean, Sister?'

'What I mean is that you've all been barking up the wrong tree. Oh, it's a code of sorts, but it's not an old Vatican cipher. And you're not dealing with a Swiss bank either.'

'Eh-?' queried Sterling with a sharp London accent. 'Of course it's a Swiss bank! Zurich and Lugano – They're both in Switzerland, aren't they?'

Elizabeth smiled thinly. 'Well, they are my dear, but Lugano *is* rather close to the Italian border, don't you think?'

'What's that supposed to mean?'

'Everything. Let me explain…'

Just as the nun prepared to give her spiel, there came a tapping sound at the window.

Tap, tap, tap…!

Sterling went for her gun and turned to the window ready for anything. She knew from bitter experience that Jimmy Silver was capable of springing surprises on her and she wasn't taking any chances.

No worries. It was only a crow.

She relaxed a little and managed a small, shaken smile. Just a crow, that was all. It sat on the outer sill in the cool, dripping rain, its glossy black feathers plastered together in a comic way and its little eyes looking in at her through the window with what amounted to a grin on its face. Sterling relaxed all the way and grinned back at the bird: *That's okay my friend. The joke's on me...* But after a couple of weeks dealing with a major international incident, she felt she had a perfect right to be jumpy.

Tap, tap, tap…!

Sterling's grin faltered. There was something in the way the crow was looking at her that she didn't like. And it occurred to her that the crow was somehow connected with her old enemy, Jimmy, or maybe one of his agents checking up on her. It certainly felt that way.

Then the crow grinned at her in the way a human might grin, and its beady little eyes seemed to grow larger, rimmed with red in a darkly rich crimson much like her own.

It's trying to get inside my mind That's the sort of thing Jimmy Silver would do if he were here. Maybe it is Silver… Maybe he's changed again or somehow evolved. He must be well over two hundred years old – almost as old as Count Grimaldi. Perhaps he's turned into an Ancient? I know he can dematerialize at will. Maybe he can shapeshift as well... Turn himself into a crow, or a wolf, or anything... Just like... Just like Charles Martel—

With a sudden movement, Sterling rose up out of her chair, bringing Joe's Noguchi Magnum into a firing position in one quick, fluid motion. Almost immediately, the others dived for cover, expecting her to open up on the bird there and then, but she didn't.

A kind of terror seized the crow. Its eyes widened with fear as its rain-drenched wings fluttered, scattering water before it let out a strangled *caw!* A moment later and the window was empty except for the night.

Sterling lowered the Noguchi to her side, feeling dull and stupid. She told herself it was just a crow after all. If she'd blown out the window with her gun it wouldn't have made any difference. They still weren't any nearer preventing Jimmy Silver from putting his man in the Vatican and changing the course of history forever.

But a crow appearing at a window after dark...? Weren't crows supposed to roost early? What had it been doing there looking in at them like that? Sterling shook her head and sat down, much to the relief of everyone present.

'As I was saying,' ventured Sister Elizabeth once everyone had settled down, 'we aren't dealing with a Vatican cipher code or a Swiss bank at all.'

'Then what exactly *are* we dealing with?' inquired de Valois, locking eyes with his agent.

'Can't you guess?' she answered quietly without dropping her gaze.

'No. We've had the better part of two weeks to guess. Tell me—'

Elizabeth took a sip of coffee and replaced the cup on its saucer. 'What we are dealing with here is an Italian bank with branches in Switzerland.'

'How do you know?'

'Simple. If you reverse the letters "OIRDNOS" on the third line of the code where it says: "COSOIT31 – OIRDNOS", you get the word, SONDRIO which is the name of an Italian town situated close to the Swiss border.'

'So—'

Elizabeth smiled. 'So, the town of Sondrio is the headquarters of the Banca Deposito di Sondrio – a relatively insignificant Italian deposit bank in northern Lombardy which also has branches in Zurich and Lugano!'

Now everyone was paying attention. The news of Sister Elizabeth's revelation sent a shock wave around the room. The crow was forgotten.

'I have to admit it's a possibility,' said Foscari, 'but how can you be sure it's the Banca di Sondrio and what do the other letters and numbers mean? Take the expression COSOIT31 – What exactly does that refer to?'

'Oh, now that's an easy one, cardinal. It's the Swift code used for making large transfers of capital between banks, which is what Jimmy Silver and Lorenzo Spada must have been doing rather a lot of. So for that matter is the so-called cipher, COSOLS32XXX and COSOZU33XXX which just so happens to be the Swift code for the Lugano and Zurich branches of the Banca Sondrio in Switzerland.'

'But how do you know all this?' queried Martinelli with growing suspicion.

Elizabeth feigned a coy expression. 'I have a confession to make, Your Eminence. You are the Chief Confessor after all, so I guess it's okay. Before I became a nun, I used to work in the banking industry. I simply recognized the Swift code of the Banca Sondrio. It's quite well known in Italy. Child's play really.'

'Bravo!' exclaimed de Valois clapping his hands. 'A significant breakthrough indeed, but without any other bank information such as PIN numbers and account details we are still no further forward in exposing Spada's illicit dealing with Jimmy Silver or the full extent of Silver's criminal empire. How can we do that?'

Again the nun smiled. 'Not a problem, cardinal. Just take a look at the rest of the code – the numbers in particular. Do they look somehow familiar to you?'

De Valois read the text, knotting his brow in concentration. He had a fine mind but the full significance of the numbers was lost on him and he passed the book back to Sister Elizabeth.

'No, I'm afraid I don't.'

'Ah, then let me explain, Cardinal de Valois. Take the long number, 45798653Z5457X056791. If you count along the line you find that the number is separated in two places by the letters Z and X. These are not arbitrary separations or nulls in the code.'

'They aren't?'

'No. They break up the line of numbers into three separate sections, 45798653 followed by 5457 and 056791. The first eight digit number is the account number. The four digit number is the PIN number for the account and the six digit number is the bank's sort code.'

'You mean...'

Elizabeth nodded. 'Yes, Your Eminence. It means we've got all the information we need to access all of the accounts – the Banca Sondrio in Lombardy and all of its branches in Switzerland. If we hand these over to the authorities then it's only a question of time before Spada's involvement becomes evident and his bid for the papacy collapses.'

Martinelli considered the nun's words carefully. 'Yes, but we've only got forty-eight hours before the election takes place. Such an investigation by the authorities could take months or even years. We simply haven't got the time.'

'I say we just torch the accounts and transfer them all into the Vatican bank,' exclaimed Sterling. 'I mean, we've got all the PIN numbers and the Swift codes. What more do we need?'

'Hmm, maybe we keep that idea in reserve for the time being,' observed de Valois. 'If we simply empty the accounts then we risk alerting Silver as to what we're up to, giving him time to cover his tracks and allowing Spada to win the election.'

'I agree,' added Martinelli. 'We don't even know where all the dark money originated from or how it was being channeled before it reached the bank. That would have been Silver's end of the operation and we've got next to nothing on him. If we had, then we could just leak it all to the press and be done.'

'Oh, I think I might just happen to know where such information might be found,' said Foscari interrupting.

'You do?' replied de Valois, surprised.

'I think so, but I'm going to need a bit of muscle from Joe and the boys. We need to force a door.'

* * *

Somewhere to the east of Rome in the cold spine of the Apennine mountains a crow came to rest, perching itself in the branches of a dead tree. An hour later and a campfire glowed in that dark wilderness. Jimmy Silver sat beside it moodily cooking the carcass of a small rabbit. Turning it slowly over the flames by means of the crude rotisserie he'd made, he watched it sizzle and drip grease into the fire. There was a light breeze blowing the savory smell into the night and a pack of wolves had come to join him. They sat about thirty metres away from the fire, howling at the full moon while secretly coveting the aroma of the roasting meat. A red Ferrari sports car was parked nearby.

Silver ignored the wolf pack.

He wore an expensive coat, handmade leather boots and a smart pair of trousers. The night wind tugged fitfully at his collar. There were dark portents in that wind.

He didn't like the way things were going.

The assassination of Pope Gregory had worked like a charm, paving the way for his creature, Lorenzo Spada to assume the role of Supreme Pontiff. The killing of David Saunders had been a smart move as well. It must have seriously rattled de Valois, removing one of his most experienced exorcists while hitting him on his home turf. Then there was the planting of that revenant on Sterling in the Suffolk marshes. He hoped she'd appreciated the joke but somehow knew she wouldn't. The slaughter of those other members of the clergy was an afterthought. Just something to lay a false trail and buy him some time. Pity about Sally Reid though. She'd just got in the way.

It was then that things had started to go wrong, wasn't it— Yes. That was the moment his plans had definitely begun to take a swerve. He hadn't noticed it at first. The plastic explosive had been well on its way to Rome for the big event he'd got planned for the sitting of the Conclave. Sister Theresa and the Camorra had seen to that, and he had no doubt that it would work well enough if everything went according to schedule.

If...

No. There was something wrong. He sensed it with every fibre of his infernal being.

Sterling should have been killed in Venice along with Foscari and that bitch of a whore Caroline Westvale. But for some reason the Aswang had failed.

Why?

The trip he'd made to the Philippines to persuade the Aswang skinwalker to take on the form of Charles Martel had been a brilliant idea. Foolproof in fact. But it had failed. At least, the Aswang hadn't reported back to him up here in his mountain lair. What had happened to it, he wondered?

Many years ago, he had evolved a form of psychic ability. Most vampires do if they live long enough. It was a thing which he accepted in himself but which he still didn't fully understand. In recent months, he'd also evolved the ability to shapeshift and transform himself into the shape of an animal. In his case, a big black crow that could fly vast distances in the blink of an eye and see things that were happening hundreds of miles away. But just recently this skill of his had failed him. He had been able to look into the room where Sterling, Foscari, de Valois and the Chief Confessor were holding their meeting, but he hadn't been able to hear anything of their conversation. At least, not all of it. Then Sterling had made the connection and pulled her gun on him. Now that had never happened before.

Somehow she had known. God damn it! *She had known.*

Then the meeting had faded and he found himself transported back to the lonely mountain, wrapped in his black overcoat, looking up and seeing nothing but the stars in the night sky. And then there had been a voice inside him that said: *They're on to you. They know something...*

Now he knew who it was that had stolen the book from his pocket. Her name was Jenny Hancock and she was a friend of

Debbie Stephenson who happened to be one of Sterling's sidekicks. She must have passed it on to Sterling.

But who was the nun? The nun in the blue uniform. He'd never seen her before. One of the Vatican's special agents more than likely. Well, no matter; he had his own nuns on the case, hadn't he. There had been Sister Veronica who had played her part in the assassination of Pope Gregory and now he had Sister Theresa to put the finishing touches to his plans. If she couldn't accomplish the task he'd set her then nobody could.

But the book...

He cast a sudden furious stare at the wolves and almost immediately they backed away, fighting and snarling among themselves.

How had the girl managed to lift the book from his pocket? No one had ever done that before. Got so close without him detecting her intentions. In the past, he would have taken her life without a moment's hesitation. What had happened that had put him off his guard? What had changed?

His thoughts chased each other like wild animals. He didn't like it and made a mental note to track down Jenny Hancock and kill her once he'd got Spada safely installed in the Vatican.

Then there was Sterling to consider. Oh yes, there was always Sterling.

A vampire like himself, she'd been a thorn in his side for the better part of forty years. He still felt a burst of anger when he thought about her. The upstart! The dumb little cunt from the gutters of London. He should have made a better job of finishing her off back in 1977 when he had the chance, but how was he to know she would survive and come back to haunt his every step...

But she had, and now it was high time to take her down too. Soon he would have the Vatican under his control, and, when he did, Sterling would lose all her protection. *Her sanctuary.* Then he could send out a team of assassin priests to deal with her. Now that would be an irony if ever there was one.

The rabbit was almost done. He turned it a few more times on the spit then transferred it to his plate. As he did so, he experienced a fleeting sensation of déjà vu, recalling a time over two hundred years ago when he'd last sat out in the Italian mountains waiting for Napoleon to pass by with his army on the way north to Austria. He'd been that close to the young French general he could have put a pistol shot clean through his brain. But he hadn't. Why...? What was it that had stopped him?

In a sudden rage, he almost slung the freshly cooked meat into the fire. He should have been able to remember a thing like that, goddammit!

'Napoleon Bonaparte,' he whispered, but this time there was only a shadow of a memory. He was losing himself. Once, he'd been able to look back over the centuries like a man reading a photograph album. Now he could barely recall the events of the last few months. Beyond that, there was nothing but a haze that would sometimes clear a bit, just enough to afford him a glimpse of some enigmatic object or a face caught in the warm glow of candlelight, but little else.

The earliest memory he could be certain of was when he realized his book had been stolen by that little shit Jenny Hancock. Apart from that, nothing else mattered to him now he was no longer truly a human being. A vampire was more like an onion; slowly peeling away one layer at a time everything that was once human – organized thought, memory, and feelings...

He began to eat the rabbit, slowly chewing on the tender meat, piece by piece. Mulling things over in his mind.

Sterling had gotten out of control and had the colossal effrontery to challenge him over his leadership of the other vampire clans. Not only that, but she'd now got his precious book. He'd made a copy of some of the spells written down inside it, but not nearly enough. Then there were his bank details. Why had he been so stupid as to write them down in the flyleaf of the book? Was he losing his touch perhaps?

He looked up at the moon and smiled.

But she was too late. His plans were already in an advanced stage. The venue was underground in the vast necropolis beneath St Peter's basilica. That was where he would strike at the heart of the Vatican. His human associate Lorenzo Spada was expendable. Once Sister Theresa had planted her bomb beneath the Sistine Chapel, the ensuing explosion would kill most of the cardinal electors trapped inside, along with Spada, Foscari and that dangerous clown, Cardinal de Valois. Then new cardinals would be chosen from among the bishops who would no doubt fall into line and elect another Pope who would be so ineffectual that it made no difference. It was a win, win, win situation. No contest.

He might even go there himself. As a crow perhaps or possibly even a wolf. Catch Sterling off her guard in some quiet corner of the Vatican and finish her there. No fuck-ups this time. This time his plans were going to succeed.

Chewing on his last few morsels of rabbit, he slung the bones out into the night and watched as the wolves fought over them. Then he stood up with his hands on his hips and roared out laughter at the moon.

His hour of glory had come at last.

21

Foscari watched as Cardinal McKenzie made his way up the hill towards the Casa Santa Marta. He walked with the aid of two aluminium sticks and waved one of them at Foscari as he ambled forward. A Swiss Guard carried his suitcase.

'Good morning, Dean. I bet you never thought you'd see me again.'

He was the oldest member of the Conclave. In another two years he would be eighty and unable to vote. He also had severe arthritis and there had been some concern as to whether he would turn up at all. Well, thought Foscari with some relief, McKenzie had made it, so he could at least count on his vote against Spada if nothing else. Duncan McKenzie hated the Italians.

'On the contrary, replied Foscari. We wouldn't have dared hold the election without you. I've arranged for you to have a room on the ground floor of the Santa Marta. I fixed the ballot for you when the rooms were being allocated.'

'Ha!' McKenzie jabbed one of his sticks against the cobblestones. 'I wouldn't put it past you Italians to fix the election too!'

He hobbled off towards the entrance of the Casa Santa Marta, the Swiss Guard following in his wake. Behind him came Cardinal Kumala of Sri Lanka and Cardinal Shilongo of Burundi.

'Same old Duncan, I'm afraid,' confided Shilongo softly. 'It will be his last election, so I guess we'll have to humour him.'

'Oh, it's not a problem. He's been baiting me for years. This will be our third Conclave election and most likely our last—'

Foscari stopped at his own words, realizing what he'd just said. Shilongo wrinkled his brow. Perplexed. Then he and Kumala went into the building, swallowed up by the small crowd gathered in the reception area.

Good. The Conclave was almost assembled. One hundred and sixteen cardinals all gathered together under the same roof. Here they would stay until the following morning when the voting would begin in the Sistine Chapel where they would all be locked in with a single key until they had elected a new Pope, whoever that might be.

And who would he be voting for wondered Foscari? McKenzie was out of the question. He was way too old and it was doubtful he would get on with the largely Italian bureaucracy who ran the Vatican. De Valois would have made a superb candidate if only he didn't have more pressing matters to occupy his time. Dealing with Hell for one thing.

So who did that leave?

The Americans—

There were five of them coming up the hill right now. As they drew closer, Foscari recognized the Archbishop of Chicago, Mark Kominski, and quietly ran the man's credentials through his mind: *aged 69, a liberal reformer who was suitably media-savvy and a good communicator. Now he might make a possible candidate for Pope.*

Then Cardinal Willard, the Archbishop of Boston came into view. Like Kominski, he was good with the press and a moderate reformer. He was also popular with the Vatican too. The North Americans and Canadians could yield nineteen votes in total and it was assumed that Cardinal Canaro of Houston would pick up most of them, which would be okay assuming they all voted in a block, but Foscari sensed division among their ranks – a suspicion that was soon confirmed when he saw who it was that was following on behind. It was Lorenzo Spada and his sidekick Cardinal Lomellini walking together with Archbishop Philipe Champney of Quebec. Had they been conferring with the Americans he wondered? What had they said? Was the election a done deal already?

There was no time to lose. Foscari would have to bring his plans forward now or everything would be lost. Spada smiled thinly as he passed by but did not exchange words. It was obvious from his body language that he was reluctant to speak at such a late stage of the game. Did he know something about the book? Had Silver somehow told him?

Summoning up his courage, the Dean made an excuse to leave and hurried off towards the papal apartments. It would have to be now or never.

* * *

Sterling glanced up. A crow had just perched itself on the head of one of the statues that topped the main façade of Saint Peter's Basilica.

'It's the statue of Christ the Redeemer,' whispered Sister Elizabeth following her gaze; 'the others are the Twelve Apostles.'

'Uh-huh,' replied Sterling absently. She had other things on her mind.

'So, what do we do now, Elizabeth?'

'We wait. The election doesn't start until tomorrow morning which gives us plenty of time to hide ourselves beneath the Sistine Chapel and intercept Sister Theresa or whoever it is that's going to plant the bomb.'

'That easy, huh?'

'I never said it would be, Sterling. At least we've got security clearance and a pass to get us down there. De Valois does have his uses sometimes.'

'And you think that's where the bomb will go off?'

'It's the most logical place to put it in the circumstances. Blow up the cardinals while they're all sitting in the Chapel. It kind of fits in with Silver's plans.'

'Yes, but I don't see how it would work, assuming—'

The crow had moved again. This time it had flown off across the square and perched atop one of the colonnades close to where they were both standing, cocking its little head to one side as if it were listening in to their conversation.

'Assuming what?' asked Sister Elizabeth noting Sterling's distraction.

'I don't know,' she replied. 'I mean, what about Spada? Surely he would be killed in the explosion too.'

Elizabeth pursed her lips, thinking. 'I expect Silver's got something else planned then. We've got to find Theresa before it's too late. Once she's planted the bomb we'll have a devil of a job trying to find it.'

'What about using sniffer-dogs?'

'Oh, she's way too clever for that, Sterling. She's most likely masked the scent. There are ways you know.'

'She's around here somewhere,' Sterling ruminated, 'and she's got the explosives with her. She's got her mobile too. That's how she's going to detonate the bomb.'

'What? You mean plant it first and then dial in the detonation from outside the Basilica?'

'I don't think so... She's a suicide bomber. She's going to set it off in close proximity.'

'But she's a nun, Sterling! Suicide is a mortal sin among us Catholics. We don't... I mean, it's strictly forbidden.'

'Yes, but she's under Silver's control. He is a vampire, remember.'

'Uh...? Oh yes. I was forgetting. He can control minds.'

Walking close to the Basilica, they noticed a line of black-clad nuns making their way slowly towards the building.

'What if she's got herself in among that lot,' exclaimed Elizabeth pointing at the nuns who by now had merged with the last crowd of tourists allowed into St Peter's for the day. 'It won't be long before the Sistine Chapel is closed for the election. Come on. Let's mingle—'

* * *

It was just before 2 a.m. when Foscari roused himself from his bed. Slipping his arms into his cassock, he carefully fastened each of its thirty-three buttons before tying his red silk sash around his waist. Finally, he put on his elbow-length, nine-buttoned scarlet cape that told the world exactly who he was: Cardinal Paolo Foscari – Dean of the Electoral College of the Roman Catholic Church.

Picking up his pectoral cross from the nightstand, he kissed it gently. The cross had been a gift from Pope Gregory who had presented it to him when he'd been made Dean. Murmuring the prayer of protection, he hung the cross around his neck so that it lay next to his heart. Then he sat on the edge of the bed and worked his feet into his shoes before tying up the laces. Only one thing now remained – his biretta of scarlet silk which he placed reverentially over his skullcap.

There was a soft, cryptic knock on the door. That would be Joe.

'I came as quickly as I could, Your Eminence. I had difficulty getting in. The place is so well guarded.'

'So it should be, Joe. Now follow me. This shouldn't take long, assuming everything goes according to plan.

'Where exactly is it that we're going, padre?'

'To the Pope's bedroom. That's where.'

'Oh…Right. Only that.'

* * *

Satisfied the place was deserted, Foscari walked quietly toward the landing, beckoning Joe to follow him. The last time he'd been here, the landing had been thronged with a crowd of worried looking people, all anxious to know about the condition of Pope Gregory. Now there was no one about.

In front of them lay the doors of the Pope's private chambers which Foscari himself had ordered to be locked and secured until further notice. The red wax seals and scarlet ribbons were still in place where the security staff had put them, and it was evident that they hadn't been tampered with.

Breathing a sigh of relief, Foscari looked at Joe. 'This is the main entrance to the papal bedroom but we're not going in through here.'

'We're not?'

'No. We can't afford to break the wax seals. It would attract too much attention and alert Spada as to what we're up to. We need to use the secret way.'

Joe shrugged and followed Foscari toward the next flight of stairs that led up into the gloom of a narrow attic corridor. At the end of that corridor lay what looked like the door of a small apartment.

'This is the door I need opening,' said Foscari. 'See if you can shoulder it, and try not to make too much noise.'

Examining the door briefly, Joe turned to the cardinal.

'Door's open, boss.'

'Pardon me?'

'I said, the door's open. Look—'

Foscari contemplated the door. Joe was right. It had been left open by approximately one inch, but it seemed there was no one around. At least, there was no indication that anyone was there.

Joe pulled out his gun, but Foscari bid him put it away. 'I don't think that will be necessary, Joe. This door has been left open deliberately.'

'By who?'

'By Father Donnelly I expect.'

'Who's he?'

'He's our guardian angel, Joe, that's who he is. He knew we would be coming eventually and left it open for us.'

The interior of the flat was very much as Foscari remembered it from his meeting with Donnelly several days before. Nothing had been touched and there was no sign of a forced entry. Good. That meant no one had broken in with the intention of locating the secret way down to the Pope's bedroom. And yet, something in Donnelly's flat was different. The picture on the wall. That was new. An ancient lithograph depicting the fourteen Stages of the Cross – all the stages of Christ's final journey to his crucifixion. What was Father Donnelly trying to tell him he wondered? Had the picture been deliberately put there for him to find and interpret as he may? Angels were such mysterious creatures.

It didn't take Joe long to push the hinged bookshelves aside and reveal the secret staircase leading down to the papal bedchamber. The place smelled stale and airless. Foscari felt around for a light switch and turned it on. The room looked exactly as it had done on the night Pope Gregory had died. The huge Renaissance bed; the curtains tightly drawn, and the desk with the Pope's ancient briefcase propped up beside it.

No. Lomellini couldn't have hoped to find anything here. He wouldn't have had the time. Still, there was no harm in trying...

Pulling open the briefcase, Foscari rummaged inside. There was nothing. The case had been emptied, most likely by Pope

Gregory's ever-vigilant private secretary. But what if Lomellini had come back after the bedroom had been sealed off? Father Donnelly's small flat hadn't been the only entrance to the secret way. There were others.

Cursing softly, he closed the briefcase and tried the middle desk drawer, much to the amusement of Joe who found the spectacle of a senior member of the clergy engaged in an act of burglary highly entertaining.

To his relief, Foscari found the drawer was unlocked and quickly pulled it out, swiftly examining its contents: A single box of paracetamols; an old photograph of the Pope and his relatives enjoying a holiday somewhere by the sea; a five-hundred lira banknote in the old currency and a Vatican directory listing the names of all the cardinals in the Church. Sliding open the other four drawers, he found a similar assortment of miscellaneous objects and personal memorabilia but nothing of any major significance.

Foscari stood up and walked around the room under the ever-watchful gaze of Joe. If the Pope had hidden something in his bedroom then it must be in here somewhere. Returning to the desk, he got down on his knees and began feeling underneath. At first his hand encountered nothing. But then:

A secret drawer. And there was something inside. A small red folder containing a number of documents. Rising to his feet, Foscari spread the documents out on the desk and began reading. Bank statements. Swift codes. Money transfers and the names and addresses of all the cardinal electors currently holding official appointments in the city of Rome, including several others from abroad. Many of the papers bore neatly penciled notations in the Pope's own handwriting: *Spada. Transferred 40.000 euros to Lomellini via the Vatican Bank!!*

So, Lomellini was receiving money from Spada. Presumably for his assistance in the poisoning of Pope Gregory. The entry was dated three weeks before the Holy Father's death so there was a connection. But there was more. Much more. Turning over the page, Foscari glimpsed another of the Pope's marginal notations: *Spada. Received 70.000 euros paid into COSOZU33 – Zurich from COSOIT31 – Sondrio – Jimmy Silver.*

Sondrio! There was that name again. The one Sister Elizabeth had worked out. The name of the small Italian town on the Swiss border where Jimmy Silver's own bank was located, and they had all the account details and PIN numbers as well. It was too good to be true.

But even so, all the evidence Foscari now had were a couple of bank transactions. He was going to need an awful lot more than this if he was ever going to sink Spada's chances of being elected Pope.

It didn't take him long to find out. Attached to the list of bank transfers was another document:

Most Holy Father

In answer to your question, it has been ascertained that Lorenzo Spada has a sum total of 3.5 million euros on deposit in the Vatican Bank. It would appear that the greater part of his income is not being properly registered.

I remain your obedient servant,
   F. Lamattino (Commissioner)

Well that was interesting. But it was when Foscari turned over the page that he really got a shock. To his astonishment, he found a list of names. It was a summary of the bank records of every senior member of the electoral college including his own. The Holy Father had secretly used his authority to access all his colleagues personal financial details from the Vatican Bank!

It felt dirty reading them. *Dirty but nice.* Most of the figures made sense. It was normal for some cardinals to have a tidy little nest-egg of money squirreled away in a bank. Martinelli for example was worth 87.679 euros, which was a perfectly legitimate sum given his age and the fact he came from a wealthy family. But it was to the others that Pope Gregory had circled in red biro that drew his attention the most. The group of cardinals from Africa, South America and Asia who had banked significant amounts over the past six months, and of these the majority of the accounts were associated with the all-too familiar Swift codes belonging to Jimmy Silver.

Evidently, these foreign cardinals were by now fully under Silver's control and likely to vote for Spada in the forthcoming election. Foscari would have to act fast.

Carrying on with his reading, the Dean found even more information revealing the full extent of the Pope's investigation. As well as clear evidence that Silver was using his money to influence the election, there was also some indication of the nature of the old vampire's criminal empire together with the involvement of certain members of the Church. Indeed, some names even came up associated with Mafia families and the Camorra centered around the drugs trade. The evidence had been damning enough to have attracted the attention of the CIA and Interpol as another letter from Commissioner Lamattino clearly showed:

Most Holy Father

We have received information from Interpol and the CIA that the following individuals have been involved in the illicit transportation of depressant, stimulant and hallucinogenic drugs between the United States, Italy, and possibly other European countries...

Leading off the list of names was Umberto Lomellini and Lorenzo Spada followed by a police file detailing how the Mafia moved their refined heroin across the Atlantic. There was enough information concealed in the letter to finish off Spada's plans for good if only Foscari could get it leaked to the press on time.

'Found what you were looking for, Your Eminence?'

It was Joe who spoke. He'd been admiring the Pope's bed, all the while pricing it up for the London antique market.

'What's that, Joe?' answered Foscari tucking the documents under his arm.

'I said, have you found what you were looking for? Anything interesting?'

'Yes, yes; I have as a matter of fact. Something very interesting indeed.'

'Oh good. Only I was just thinking; this here bed would fetch a hefty price in London. I mean, just look at all the decoration on it.'

'I wouldn't be too hasty, Joe. There may very well be a need for leaving that bed right where it is for now given what I've just found out.'

The biker went silent for a moment and took a step back. It was evident something was preying on his mind.

'You reckon we get out of this in one piece, boss?'

'It's too early to say, Joe. But I've got a feeling the contents of this folder may contain the answer to your question. Now come along. Let's get out of here. This place is giving me the creeps.'

* * *

It was getting on for three in the morning when two solitary figures picked their way along the narrow path that formed the central axis of the vast necropolis beneath St Peter's Basilica. Over eleven hours had passed since they'd entered the building and descended the ornate staircase to the ancient catacombs below. Now, on either side of them, laid out like a row of houses on a Roman street were a line of brick mausoleums of the type any latter-day tourist might encounter among the ruins of Pompeii or Herculaneum.

But these houses were not ruins. This was a city of the dead, and had been for the past two thousand years, the oldest district dating back to the second century AD. In some places, the vaulted sepulchers were no more than simple tombs and shelf-graves, but others were clearly intended for the wealthiest elite of the city together with frescoed walls and richly decorated mosaic floors. All the funerary opulence that money could buy.

'Where are we, Elizabeth? We must be under the Sistine Chapel by now surely?'

'I don't know, Sterling. I've never been down here before. A compass and a map would have helped. This place is like a maze.'

'How long have we got?'

'About twelve hours. The cardinals will be assembling early this afternoon to take their first ballot.'

'And their last if we don't find this frigging bomb.'

'Shhh— De Valois ordered me to do a recce, that's all. If Silver's agent is going to plant her bomb, then this is most likely where it will be. Sister Theresa is bound to show up sooner or later.'

'Or something else...'

'Pardon me?'

'I said, *or something else*... Look – down there on the path. Just in front of you.'

Gazing down to where Sterling was pointing, Sister Elizabeth saw what she took to be a sequence of human footprints outlined in the dust of the catacomb floor. The bare footprints veered off to one side of the path where they suddenly changed into the unmistakable paw marks of a large dog-like creature; first one foot, then another, all leading down an alleyway that ran off at right-angles to the lane they were walking along. Slowly, Elizabeth turned her gaze back to Sterling who answered her unspoken question for her: 'Yes, Elizabeth. It is what you think it is.'

'Oh... Shit! I hadn't counted on this...'

'Stay calm, Lizzy. Werewolves only attack in packs. It looks like this one is a solitary.'

'Yes, but the size of the thing... I mean, look at the dimensions of the paw prints. What's a beast like that doing here in a house of God?'

'Search me. Looks like Jimmy's been dabbling in magic again. Either that, or he's evolved the ability to transform himself into a werewolf at will. Whatever the case, it doesn't bode well for either of us.'

Just then, they heard a low, feral howl that steadily increased in intensity until it filled the cavernous chamber with its strange melancholy sound. After a small interval, the howl was answered by another wolf call followed by several more; first one at a time, then altogether in chorus.

'Looks like we're not alone, Liz. Silver's brought some friend to the party.'

The howls were hideous beyond imagination, causing Sister Elizabeth to shield both her ears with her hands in order to block out the sound. Then the noise suddenly stopped, leaving both women standing in an eerie silence as the temperature around them quickly began to drop.

'What do we do when we find the bomb?' inquired Sterling drawing out her gun in case they were set upon by the wolfpack.

Elizabeth was starting to shiver. 'We attempt to disarm it, don't we. Don't worry. I'm good with bombs I am.'

'Oh, great. So now I'm sharing my space with a bomb disposal expert. What if you fuck up?'

'I won't. Now come on; let's carry on down the path. I've a feeling it's leading us in the direction of the Sistine Chapel.'

* * *

Foscari walked down the corridor and knocked softly on the door of Martinelli's apartment. He was expecting a slow response, but to his amazement the door opened almost immediately and there was Martinelli, fully awake and dressed in his cassock.

'Can I come in? I've got some important information.'

Foscari followed the Chief Confessor into his apartment and wasn't at all surprised to see Cardinal de Valois similarly attired in his official robes, reclining on the sofa. He was in the middle of making a phone call and raised the outstretched palm of his hand briefly in greeting.

Taking Foscari over to an armchair, the Confessor bid him make himself comfortable. 'Can I get you anything, Dean? A coffee perhaps?'

'That would be more than welcome, thank you.'

As Martinelli went into the kitchen, de Valois ended his call and focused his attention on the Dean.

'Well, Paolo – What did you find in the Pope's bedroom?'
'Enough.'
'What's *enough?* I need details. Please be more specific.'
'Here,' replied Foscari, handing the red folder over to the exorcist. 'Read it for yourself.' He placed the folder on the

coffee table and pushed it over to de Valois. 'It's a file of bank transactions and statements linking Lorenzo Spada and Umberto Lomellini with Jimmy Silver – a major international criminal mastermind and senior member of the Undead! More specifically, the timing of one of the transactions clearly implicates Spada and Lomellini with the poisoning of Pope Gregory.'

De Valois picked up the folder and frowned at the pages as Foscari guided him through the details. 'Not only that, but there is also evidence to show that a significant number of cardinals from Africa, Asia and South America have received money directly from Silver to swing the election in Spada's favour. It's bribery, de Valois. Bribery pure and simple—'

The exorcist was still reading. 'I am aware of the implication that bribery may have taken place, but we're too close to the election to make it stick. As for the link with the assassination of Gregory, we need more proof than a single transfer of money from one bank to another. I need hard evidence of serious crime having been involved. Facts, Paolo! I need facts—'

Martinelli came back into the room with the coffee and offered a cup to Foscari who accepted it with a nod before turning his attention back to de Valois. 'If it's facts you want, Edward, then I have more than enough of them to sink both Spada and Lomellini's chances for good, together with a number of other cardinals. The only problem is how we go about it and what it is exactly that we reveal to the public.'

'Oh... And why is that might I ask?'

'Because the information I have in my possession also concerns the involvement of senior members of the Church in the international drugs trade, that's why. Commissioner Lamattino has evidence from the CIA that Spada and his associates have been involved with the transportation of narcotics between Italy and the USA. Here... See for yourself—'

Picking out a swatch of papers from the folder, Foscari handed the selected documents back to de Valois and waited patiently for the exorcist's response.

'It's worse than I thought,' de Valois said. 'The contents of Lamattino's report would certainly finish Spada and his circle for good, but the damage to the Church would be irreparable if we leaked it to the press. We can't afford to take the risk.'

'We're damned if we do and damned if we don't,' replied Foscari handing the papers over to Martinelli who began sifting through them with even greater concern than de Valois. 'I say we take that risk and deal with the political fall-out later. What do you say, Martinelli?'

The Chief Confessor raised his head. 'Foscari's right, Edward. I say we get this material over to the press office right away. It's going to be bad, but not nearly as bad as the prospect of Jimmy Silver and Spada gaining control of the papacy. That scenario we must avoid at all costs.'

'Good. It's agreed then,' responded the Dean with some relief. 'We make the matter public just before the cardinals gather for the election. If I can delay the ballot for a couple of hours, then it should gain us enough time for the shit to hit the fan. After that, it's all in the hands of God.'

'- And Sterling,' added de Valois reaching for his phone once more.'

'What...? Oh, yes. I'd forgotten about that. How are Sterling and Sister Elizabeth doing? Have they located the bomb yet?'

'I don't know. I've been trying to call them for the last thirty minutes. I can't seem to get a signal through for some reason. I hope they're both alright...'

* * *

'What is this place, Sterling?'

'I don't rightly know, Liz. It looks like an ancient theatre or something.'

Sterling and Sister Elizabeth were standing in the middle of a circular mosaic floor several metres in diameter that was almost entirely surrounded by a four-foot high wall of red-painted brick. The wall was tumbled down in places and there were a series of passageways leading off at intervals into the darkness beyond.

'I know what this place reminds me of,' said the nun looking round. 'It's like an ancient Roman arena the way it's been constructed. Especially with all those passageways leading off it.'

'Okay, so where are all the gladiators then, Elizabeth?'

'You're standing on one.'

'I'm what—?'

The vampire glanced down. There in the centre of the mosaic floor was the image of a Roman gladiator, complete with sword and shield, neatly outlined in black tessera stones on an otherwise pristine white background.

'It's someone's tomb, Sterling. We're standing in the middle of a gladiator's tomb. Looks like whoever was buried here made a fortune in the Roman arena and lived to retire a wealthy man.'

'Wealthy enough to be buried in this place? It must have cost a fortune.'

'Yes, well Roman gladiators were the movie stars of their time. Look over there. That marble plinth must have been the base for his memorial statue.'

Out of pure curiosity, Sterling walked over to the plinth and examined the inscription chiseled into its near side. The inscription was in Latin and there was the image of a gladiator shown together with his name.

'Publius Lupercus,' declared Elizabeth reading the inscription. 'He survived twenty fights and was awarded the laurel crown together with a considerable sum of money before he retired. There's an image of a wolf carved beneath the inscription. The name "Lupercus" means *"the slayer of wolves."* Most likely it was his adoptive name for the fight game. Who knows…'

Sterling stood up from where she'd been crouching at the base of the plinth. She paused. 'There,' she said. 'You hear it?'

'Hear what?'

'That fluttering sound. It must be a bird or something.'

The nun listened for a few seconds. 'No. I didn't hear anything.'

At that precise moment, a huge bird flew just inches above their heads and came to rest, perching on one of the top-most stone benches that surrounded the faux arena. It was a large black crow with the same beady little eyes Sterling had witnessed looking in at her through the window of the Chief Confessor's office, only this time the eyes were deep crimson like the fires of Hell. It was almost as if the crow were sitting up there like a spectator at the Roman games, eager to view the carnage that was about to take place below.

'What's a crow doing here, Sterling? How did it get in?'

'I don't rightly know. Maybe it's not a crow at all. Maybe it's…'

The sound of howling wolves came on again. They were still some way off but seemed to have drawn closer this time.

'You still packing?' hissed Elizabeth, drawing out her gun and holding it out in front of her with both hands in the firing position.

'Naturally,' replied her companion, producing her Noguchi pistol together with the silencer Joe had given her. 'This here Magnum revolver should hold them off for a while.'

Back-to-back, the two unlikely protagonists braced themselves for the attack, ready to blast away at anything remotely canine that emerged from the passageways leading into the funerary arena. But nothing came. At least, not immediately. There was a lull of several seconds – the usual case before wolves attack. Then all hell broke loose.

'ON ME—!!' shrieked Sterling, taking aim at the first beast that emerged from the passageway immediately to their left. It was a massive grey werewolf and he looked mean and pissed off, his lambent eyes glowing putrid yellow in the half-light.

The vampire fired off four rounds of silver bullets from her silenced weapon then watched as the creature staggered on its feet before collapsing to the ground in a mass of blue flames that quickly consumed its body until there was nothing left but a thin mist of grey ash outlined on the cold mosaic floor.

Next it was Sister Elizabeth's turn to shoot as three more of the creatures emerged from the passageway, bearing down on them as they stood shoulder-to-shoulder in the middle of the arena. A fusillade of shots from the nun's 9mm Beretta downed the trio before they could do any damage, followed by several more just to make sure. Again, the bodies of these phantom wolves burst into flame and then collapsed into ashes, little more than three shallow mounds of carbonized flesh and bone that gave off a strange, sickly-sweet odour reminiscent of a slaughterhouse on a warm summer day. Then everything went silent. The attack was over. At least for now.

'How many rounds have you got left, Lizzy?'

'A few. Not many. How about you?'

'Same. I reckon we're going to have to think of something else.'

Much to her friend's surprise, Sterling reached into her pocket and took out the book she'd been carrying.

'The Incunabulum? What the hell do you want that thing for!?'

'Close encounters, Elizabeth. That's what this book is for. It's our insurance policy.'

'Uh-huh. No way. I'm not getting involved in Magic. I'm a good catholic and—'

'- Don't worry, Liz. The only magic you're going to witness down here is the look on Jimmy Silver's face when he realizes what we've done.'

'And what's that, Sterling?'

'Torched his entire financial empire, that's what! You didn't think I was going to wait until de Valois got his act together, did you? Edward may have his good points, but he does have a nasty habit of erring on the side of caution at times. In any case, I have all of the Swift codes and account numbers, plus all the other information I need to access the money.'

'What information?'

'Personal details. I guessed Silver would have used his mother's maiden name as security for his bank account. Most banks ask for that sort of thing when you first set up business with them. You see, in all the years that I've know him, I've been able to do a bit of research into his ancestry. It wasn't easy, but I managed to trace his family tree way back to the eighteenth century and worked out his lineage from there. It only remained for me to get Joe to send one of his men up to Silver's main bank in Lombardy and arrange to transfer all his assets straight into the Vatican Bank. Since it was said to be *"all in a good cause"*, nobody thought to question it, and so the transfer went straight through. It only remained for me to tip-off Interpol and the Italian authorities as to what had happened and why, and the matter was settled. Quite simple really when you think about it.'

Elizabeth smiled. 'Impressive, Sterling. But what about the bomb? We haven't found the bomb yet.'

'No we haven't, but I somehow doubt if we'll have far to look. HEY— WATCH OUT!!'

Elizabeth ducked as the huge crow suddenly dived at her, screeching like a banshee before it flew off, disappearing into the darkness in a flurry of smoke and feathers.

'What the hell was that!?'

'*That*, Lizzy? That was Jimmy Silver making an exit. Now let's find that fucking bomb before those wolves come back. Next time I have a feeling we won't be so lucky.'

* * *

It was around 3.30 p.m. when the cardinals finally began boarding the fleet of white minibuses that would take them to the Sistine Chapel for the election. Foscari had managed to delay the sitting of the Conclave for an hour. It had barely been enough time to allow for the press-release to take effect and he was concerned that the ballot would now be taken before the news about Spada's involvement in drug-trafficking became common knowledge.

Monsignor Brevet stood in the centre of the lobby with his clipboard calling out the names of the respective cardinals as they filed out of the building in silence. The atmosphere in the Casa Santa Marta had turned more somber since lunchtime. Only Lorenzo Spada seemed unconcerned by it all. He was leaning against the wall with his arms folded, smiling at everyone as they passed by. Privately, the Dean wondered what had happened to improve his mood. Perhaps he was just doing it to discomfort the opposition.

Foscari, as leader of the Conclave, was the last to leave, immediately behind Cardinal de Valois and Martinelli. They made eye contact briefly as they walked towards the minibus, only speaking when they felt they wouldn't be overheard.

'You think we can do it?' whispered Foscari to de Valois as they prepared to board the bus.

'I dare say.' replied the exorcist glancing round, 'but it's going to be a close run thing.'

'What about Sterling and Elizabeth? Have you heard from them yet?'

'No, no I haven't. There was still no way I could get a phone call through, but I notice Spada's just climbed into the bus and doesn't seem too concerned about the bomb. Maybe he knows more than we do.'

Foscari was able to ask Martinelli for his opinion on the press release, but could tell that his mind was now set on higher things. When eventually the Chief Confessor spoke, it was almost as if he were replying to a telepathic suggestion. 'Just thank God for the internet,' he said before hoisting the skirt of his cassock to climb aboard the bus. Following him up the steps, it felt to the Dean as if he were herding a flock of doomed sheep onto a farmyard truck. *Like lambs to the slaughter,* he thought. *I hope Sister Elizabeth finds that bomb.*

Taking a seat halfway down the aisle, Foscari removed his cardinal's hat and placed it on his lap. Monsignor Brevet sat beside the driver, turning briefly to check that everyone was on board. Then the doors closed and the coach pulled away, its tyres rumbling softly over the cobbled piazza as it began the short journey to the Sistine Chapel where the election was due to start. *How would the voting go? Would Spada's supporters just sit tight and ride out the storm of popular protest, relying on bribery and intimidation to secure them the ballot? Who could tell. It was all in the hands of God now… God and that abomination in the mirrored sunglasses. What on earth had Pope Gregory been thinking of doing business with a creature like Sterling?*

* * *

'What are you doing?'

'Drawing a circle, Elizabeth. What does it look like I'm doing?'

Mystified, the nun looked on as Sterling edged her way around the mosaic floor in a crouching position, drawing a large white circle with a piece of chalk as she went, all the while muttering some strange incantations from the book she was clutching in her left hand. When she arrived back at the place where she'd started, she took a small black candle from her pocket and lit the wick with her lighter, taking care to melt the blunt end of the candle before pressing it firmly into the floor in the middle of the circle so it stood in an upright position illuminating the otherwise gloomy surroundings with its steady glow.

'There. That should just about do it,' she exclaimed. 'Jimmy won't get through that in a million years. Well, not without a lot of help at any rate.'

'Sterling... What have you just done?'

'Black Magic, Lizzy; that's what I've done. It's the only thing that'll stop those wolves and that bastard crow. I've a feeling Jimmy's learned how to shapeshift and I don't want us getting on the wrong side of it.'

'But it's Black Magic...'

'So?'

'So, this is the Vatican in case you hadn't noticed, and I'm a fucking nun for God's sake! Jesus Christ, I can't believe it—!!'

'Don't worry, Liz. It's all in a good cause. This here book is full of the stuff.'

'What about de Valois? He's the Chief Exorcist. He'll blow his stack.'

'It was him who suggested it.'

'Oh... I see. Well, if de Valois sanctioned it then I suppose it's alright, but it still doesn't mean that I approve of it.'

'Shh—!' hissed Sterling, tilting her head to one side. 'What's that noise? It sounds like chanting.'

Elizabeth focused her attention on the sound for a couple of seconds then delivered her verdict: 'It's the Vatican choir. They're intoning the names of all the saints of the Catholic Church. The ceremony takes place in the Pauline Chapel just prior to the election. The Pauline Chapel is situated immediately next to the Sistine Chapel. It's the private chapel of the Holy Father, which means the Conclave has already begun.'

'What? Right above our heads...?'

'Yes. In a few minutes, the cardinals will pass through into the Sistine Chapel where the doors will be locked behind them until such time as the first ballot has been taken. If they fail to elect a Pope on the first ballot with a significant majority, then a second ballot will have to be held, and so on until a suitable candidate is found. It's all quite tedious really.

'It won't be tedious if that bomb goes off, Lizzy. I reckon there's enough plastic explosive down here to blow them all the way to Hell.'

* * *

Was this the reason why he'd been born, wondered the Dean? Was this what his life had been leading up to? It all felt so hollow and mechanical.

By the time Foscari arrived in the Pauline Chapel, the cardinals were already waiting for him seated in their pews. Monsignor Brevet met him at the door and together they walked towards the altar to begin the opening ceremony. At the microphone, he turned to face his audience and made the sign of the cross:

'*In nomine Patris et Filii et Spiritus Sancti.. Amen*'

He then implored God and the Virgin Mary for their guidance in the choice of the new Pope and prayed that the cardinals would all vote in such a way that was pleasing to Heaven.

It was a short address, and when he'd finished reading it from the book held out in front of him by the Monsignor, Foscari felt completely drained, as if all the life had been sucked out of him. Was it his age, or had something else made its presence felt, trying to siphon off his energy and break his resolve before the ballot could be taken?

Brevet closed the book and put it away. The ceremonial crucifix by the door was lifted by one of the functionaries while two others held aloft lighted candles, solemnly leading the choir out of the chapel singing as they went. Foscari remained standing at the altar with his head bowed in silent contemplation:

Silver has drawn us all into his killing ground. If Sterling can't stop him, then we're all dead. Best they don't know. It would only lead to a mass panic. It's the choristers I feel sorry for. Most of them are quite young... And I'm so old. So very, very old...

The chanting grew fainter as the choir proceeded towards the Sistine via the Sala Regia with the cardinals following on silently behind them down the central aisle. After a while, Brevet whispered in Foscari's ear: 'Eminence, we should be going now.'

* * *

The choir was singing the Veni Creator Spiritus by the time the cardinals took their places standing behind rows of desks in the Sistine Chapel. When the choir had finished the hymn, Foscari advanced towards the Sistine altar and began to administer the oath of the Apostolic Constitution before taking his seat at the end of the long desk nearest the altar. He could do nothing now but wait as each individual cardinal queued quietly in the central aisle then stepped forward one at a time to swear their own version of the oath before returning to their seats.

Who would it be? wondered the Dean, sitting within spitting distance of Michelangelo's famous painting of The Last Judgement. *Maybe Spada would croak at the first hurdle without any assistance from either de Valois or himself. After all, it was obvious the election wasn't a done deal, or why would Jimmy Silver have considered using explosives. Now that was the crux of the matter. Why did he feel the need to blow up the entire electoral college when all he had to do was get rid of Gregory? More to the point, what on earth was that big black crow doing fluttering way up there in the upper clerestory windows—!?'*

Rubbing his eyes in disbelief, Foscari watched as the crow hopped from one side of the precipitous window ledge to the other before finally settling down to observe the proceedings below with fixed intent. In another moment, the crow had vanished, transforming itself into a shimmering orb of blue light that seemed to hover in the stillness of the ceiling void for a few seconds before floating downwards until it reached a point immediately between the shoulders of two of the African cardinals where it came to a stop and lingered for a while, apparently satisfied with its grandstand view of the Conclave.

No one present seemed to have noticed the strange ball of light other than the Dean, and when Foscari nudged the Archbishop of Toledo seated on his left, the partially deaf cardinal merely glanced up and shook his head. He hadn't seen anything either.

It took about three quarters of an hour for the entire college to swear their oaths. Then, when Archbishop Manstein, the Master of Celebrations was certain everyone was back in their seats, he stepped up to the microphone and gave the order to close the doors of the Sistine Chapel. It was 5.35 p.m. precisely and the first ballot was now officially in session.

From the moment Manstein closed the doors, Foscari knew something was wrong.

The task of delivering the first speech had fallen to Cardinal Alberto Corelli, the ninety-two year old veteran of seven previous Conclaves. Assured of his neutrality, Foscari had permitted him a voice in the proceedings, if only to read the preliminary meditation before the voting began. Now he wished he hadn't.

'That could have been better, Paolo,' whispered de Valois into the Dean's ear. The exorcist was sitting to the right of Foscari and didn't like the way things were going. Corelli's speech had been blatantly in favour of Spada as well as being a veiled criticism of Foscari and the previous Pope.

'How was I to know he was in Spada's camp,' replied the Dean. 'The old devil's been in a care home for the better part of five year's. Up until three days ago I actually thought he was dead—!'

'Nonetheless, you should have checked him out. It could cost us the vote.'

'Not if I've got anything to do with it,' Foscari replied before rising out of his chair and making his way toward the microphone. Corelli's attack on him had been quite a shock, but what concerned him the most was the effect it must have had on the other electors. He could see that it had amused Cardinal Spada who was seated almost immediately opposite him across the aisle next to Lomellini. And he could also see, if no one else could, the brilliant blue orb of energy that had now drifted along the rows of seated electors until it came to hover like a saintly nimbus of light directly above Spada's head.

Had the Almighty chosen Spada? Foscari wondered. *Surely not...*

Deep in thought, he continued walking towards the microphone, desperately trying to figure out a way of limiting the damage done by Corelli's speech. He sensed the need to slow things down in order to give the electors time to focus on the issues at stake. Turning to face the Conclave, he grasped the microphone. Just as he was about to speak, the great bell of St Peter's began tolling six o'clock, drowning out any chance of him being heard above the din. He paused and waited for the noise to subside before beginning his delivery to the assembled college:

'Cardinal electors, we may now proceed to the first ballot. Since it is quite late and some of us are not in the best of health, should any of you wish to postpone the ballot until tomorrow, then please feel free to express your wishes to the college and I will call for a recess.'

There was a pause, and then Spada suddenly rose to his feet: 'Cardinal Foscari, the people are anxious to hear our verdict. I myself have recently been diagnosed with a heart condition, but in my view it would be inconsiderate of us if we decided to adjourn for the night. I say we proceed with the vote.'

Foscari glanced at de Valois. The exorcist's face remained impassive. Someone in the audience coughed. Spada sat back down in his seat.

'Very well,' exclaimed Foscari holding up his own ballot paper. 'It is decided then. We shall vote. This is the ballot paper which you will find in the red folder in front of you. Please ensure that you put down one name only and that your handwriting is legible otherwise your ballot will be rendered null and void. Now, will the scrutineers please take their positions and we can begin.'

The three cardinals who'd been chosen to count the ballots, now rose from their separate places and made their way toward the altar. Foscari wandered back to his seat to collect the pen he'd been provided with to register his vote. Shielding his ballot paper with his free hand, he wrote in capital letters the name of his choice of candidate: *MARTINELLI*. Then he folded the paper and walked back to the altar, solemnly placing the paper onto a silver chalice that covered a large ornate urn. Observed by the scrutineers, Foscari then lifted the chalice in his hands and tipped his vote into the urn. Then he replaced the chalice, bowed to the altar and resumed his seat, relieved that it was all over.

One by one, the cardinals came forward to cast their vote. Too tense for prayer, Foscari simply watched as each member of the college passed by on their way to the altar. Martinelli seemed uncharacteristically nervous. His wrists trembled as he dropped his vote into the urn before returning to his place and slumping down in his chair with his left hand cupped around his forehead in an attitude of despair. *Was he worried about the outcome of the election or the potential detonation of the bomb beneath the Sistine Chapel?* Even de Valois appeared to be growing more anxious, his right hand nervously fingering his pectoral cross as he leaned over and whispered once more into Foscari's ear: 'I hope to God, Sterling and Elizabeth have managed to disarm that bomb. They've been down there an awfully long time…' Foscari nodded but made no reply. He was too busy observing the activities at the altar to pay the exorcist very much attention.

Now it was Spada's turn to vote. The Dean leaned forward in his chair, watching intently as the former Patriarch of Venice walked up the aisle to cast his ballot. The next couple of minutes would reveal an awful lot about Lorenzo Spada and his intentions for the papacy if he ever became elected Pope.

And what a performance it was. Like a seasoned actor, the Venetian approached the altar with all the reverence of a saint. Raising his eyes toward heaven, he made an almost theatrical sign of the cross before intoning the sacred oath and dropping his vote in the urn with a flourish. Then he turned and walked back to his seat with a triumphant gleam, giving Foscari a wry look as if to say: "There. That's how a future Pope would have done it!!"

Yes, it was true. Cardinal Spada was possessed of all those qualities it took to fill the role of Supreme Pontiff – confidence, charm, charisma, and above all, the ability to work a crowd. Indeed, he seemed to have everything a human being needed to appear before the eyes of the world as God's representative on earth, were it not for the fact that he was lacking in one important thing, and that thing was a *Soul...*

Foscari could sense it in much the same way as a gifted clairvoyant might have glimpsed it – an empty, shrieking void where Spada's soul should have been, almost like those darkest of nights when the moon is void and blackness reigns in the shoulders of the sky.

The man simply had no soul. Or if he had, then it was a dark one, completely devoid of anything remotely warm or human. And it was then with a sharp intake of breath that Foscari suddenly realized what it was that they were dealing with…

'Cardinal Spada is the Antichrist—!'

'I was wondering when the penny would finally drop,' murmured de Valois without taking his eyes off the ballot.

'How long have you known?' replied the Dean, more than a little relieved that the Archbishop of Toledo sitting immediately to his left was so hard of hearing that he couldn't possibly make out a word of what they were saying.

'Pope Gregory and myself were informed of the fact by Father Donnelly about three months ago. It was around the time Donnelly revealed to us that he was the Archangel Michael.'

'And the Pope was aware of this?'

'Of course he was. He is the Vicar of Christ after all. It was only fitting that he should be informed.'

'Why wasn't I told?'

'There was simply no need. Your involvement was only required once the Pope had been assassinated and everything started going wrong. After that, there was simply no way you could have been kept out of the loop. You had to be let in on it, given everything else the archangel told us.'

'And what was that?'

'*That* my dear Paolo is strictly classified for now, but I dare say you'll find out in due course. Just keep your mind on the outcome of the election and everything will become clear.'

'Yes, but if Lorenzo Spada is truly what we think he is, then what on earth can we do about it? According to Holy Scripture, the Antichrist always wins the first round.'

'But not the *second ballot,* Cardinal Foscari. It may be the case that Spada is the Antichrist, but where there is an Antichrist there is also an Ogmion.'

'What's an Ogmion? I've never heard that term before in theology.'

'You wouldn't. It's not commonly known in Christian teaching. The term was first mentioned by the ancient Greek writer Lucian of Samosata and belongs to the old Pagan tradition. Basically, an Ogmion is someone appointed by the gods to combat the forces of darkness and defeat them with a combination of eloquence and strength.'

The Dean gave a wry smile: 'And who might that be? I don't recall seeing anyone here remotely capable of attempting such a feat. At least, no one who comes to mind.'

'Ah, but that's where you're wrong, Foscari. He's a lot closer to you than you think. Closer than your jugular vein in fact.'

'What do you mean?'

'Oh, nothing. It's just that if everything goes according to plan, then the answer you seek will become immediately apparent to you. You'll see.'

The Dean was mystified. He didn't understand a word of what the exorcist had told him, and if the truth be known, there was a part of him that really didn't want to. More important was the fact that the first ballot was coming to an end and by the time the last man had voted, it only remained for Cardinal Weatherby to extract the voting papers from the urn and transfer them to another urn standing on the altar before announcing in his less than fluid Italian: 'One hundred and sixteen votes have been cast,' at which point he disappeared along with one of the other scrutineers into the sacristy room only to emerge seconds later with a small table which Cardinal Vosko, the third scrutineer covered with a white cloth before placing the urn containing the votes in the centre. Three chairs were then brought out and the counting of the ballot began.

Only now did Foscari fully wake from his reverie to focus once more on the Conclave. In the folder in front of him was an alphabetical list of cardinals eligible to vote. Opening the folder, he ran his finger down the column of names. Then he took up his pen and listened intently as the results came in.

Vosko removed the first ballot paper from the urn and made a note of the name before passing it to the second scrutineer who in turn passed it to Weatherby. The English cardinal then leaned into the microphone: 'The first vote is cast for Cardinal Spada.'

Had he not been so absorbed in the act of recording the votes, Foscari would have noticed the smile on Lorenzo Spada's face slowly broaden as the count progressed. Just then however, a sudden change in the atmosphere of the chapel caused the Dean to glance up, and when he did, he was more than a little surprised by what he saw. Spada was still sitting there behind his desk across the aisle, basking in the certainty of his election, but of the shining orb of blue light and the demonic black crow there was no sign. Together, they seemed to have vanished into the architecture almost as mysteriously as they'd arrived, strange ethereal messengers from another world who's precise meaning and purpose Foscari could only guess at.

As he returned to his list, the realization of what it was that he was involved in suddenly hit home. The eyes of God were upon him and everyone else assembled there in the chapel. It was to be here in this narrow chamber that the fate of humanity would be decided for better or worse. But what was his part in it all he wondered? What could he do about it? He was just a Vatican bureaucrat if the truth be told and most definitely not an *Ogmion,* whatever the hell that was.

* * *

Deep beneath the chapel something was stirring. The sound of chanting had long since ceased, but Elizabeth had not stopped listening. Instead, she was pointing at the ancient memorial plinth that was situated about ten paces from where Sterling and herself were standing, huddled together inside their magic chalk circle.

'There— Just now. Can't you hear it?'

'Hear what?' replied Sterling.

'The sound of crying. Listen…'

Sure enough, the faint whimper of someone crying could be heard filtering through the close air of the tomb. Grasping her pistol in the firing position, Elizabeth tip-toed her way over to the waist-high plinth before quickly swinging round to challenge whoever it was that had hidden themselves so ineptly behind the long-dead gladiator's monument.

'Vatican agents—Drop your weapon!!' she yelled, aiming her pistol at the intruder.

Satisfied her companion had done her work, Sterling walked over to see what the problem was. To her surprise, she found a young Benedictine nun cowering behind the plinth.

'I think we've found Silver's bomber,' observed Elizabeth kicking away the handgun Theresa had dropped to the floor. Pale-faced and on the edge of hysteria, the young nun lowered her head in despair.

'I reckon she's just about spent,' Sterling replied, pulling the woman to her feet.

'She's wearing a body belt,' exclaimed Elizabeth in alarm.

'So I've noticed, and I bet I know who gave it to her.'

The nun said nothing. Not even when Sterling began slapping her around: 'Hey bitch! Who gave you that bomb, huh? Was it Jimmy Silver? He give you the bomb, did he?'

Twice, thrice and five times over, Sterling continued with her interrogation until Elizabeth grabbed her by the wrist: 'That's enough! Can't you see she's terrified out of her wits. Here. Let me try.'

'Suit yourself, Lizzy, but we're fast running out of time. We need to deal with that bomb she's wearing before it blows us all to shit!'

The woman flinched as Sister Elizabeth took her gently by the arm. 'It doesn't have to be like this, Theresa. All you have to do is tell us how to disarm the bomb and you can walk away. We all can.'

Firmly clenched lips and an absence of eye contact was the only response forthcoming, so Elizabeth tried another line of inquiry.

'What convent do you belong to, Theresa? There were other Benedictine nuns with you on the plane. Are you all from the same convent?'

This time the young nun looked up. 'I'm not a real nun…'

'I thought not,' exclaimed Sterling. 'Let's scrag her now—'

'No. Wait! I think I'm getting somewhere,' Elizabeth replied with a frosty glance. Then, returning her gaze to the faux nun, she continued with her line of questioning:

'Who put you up to this, Theresa… Was it Jimmy Silver?'

Wrong move. The woman pursed her lips again and looked away. It was evident she was thinking of making a run for it. Then:

'He can change into a crow…'

'What!?'

'He can change into a crow… and a blue light.'

'Who can change into a crow? Tell me, Theresa—'

The woman became silent again, only this time it was Sterling prompting her with the muzzle of her gun that finally coaxed the truth out of her.

'Jimmy Silver can turn himself into a crow at will. He knows where we are. He can read our thoughts…'

Her voice was thin and ragged, lacking all trace of energy or emotion in it. Whatever sense of self she may once have possessed was now entirely consumed in that long blank stare of hers. It was the expression of someone who knew they were going to die and who no longer cared.

'I knew it!' hissed Sterling lowering her weapon. 'That crow outside the window of Martinelli's office in Rome… It was Silver spying on us. I was right all along.'

'Well, whupee for you,' exclaimed Elizabeth, ' but it still doesn't solve the problem of disarming that bomb Theresa's got strapped to her chest though, does it?'

'No, I guess not, but we could at least have a try. What do you make of it, Liz? You reckon you can handle it?'

'Perhaps, but I'm going to need a bit more light to work in. Fetch me that black candle you lit earlier – the one over there in the middle of the circle. It's not much, but it's a helluva lot better than the safety lights down here. They're worse than useless. I can't make out the colour of the wires on this thing.'

As Sterling wandered over to pick up the candle, Elizabeth motioned Theresa to remove her white shoulder blouse and black cowl so she could get a better look at the mechanism of the bomb. The young woman was reluctant at first, but after a while she relented and took off her outer garments to reveal the full extent of the problem. Twelve clear polythene bags of C4 plastic explosive secured with grey ducting tape had been carefully wrapped around her torso, together with a confusing array of wires, all linked to a small digital timepiece that was silently counting down the minutes and seconds to imminent detonation. Things didn't look good.

Now all three women sat huddled together in the gloom like some diabolical gathering of witches in a Goya etching, all pondering what to do next.

'What do you think?' asked Sterling. 'Can you do it?'

Sister Elizabeth ragged the tip of her tongue against her teeth: 'Nnnn, well from what I can see, whoever put this bomb together must have been a professional. It's been double-wired.'

'Is that bad?'

'About as bad as it could be. I think we can rule out snipping any of the wires. Any attempt to do so could set it off.' Then, looking at the young nun, she said: 'Theresa, do you happen to know who made this bomb?'

The woman shook her head. 'No. The bomb was delivered and strapped on me by two people when I arrived in Rome – a man and a woman. They didn't give their names and Silver wasn't with them. They both spoke with Italian accents.'

'Camorra?'

'I expect so,' Theresa replied before lapsing back into silence. Clearly she was resigned to her fate.

It was evident the young woman wasn't prepared to divulge any information about the Camorra, and Elizabeth was about to give up on her line of questioning when a thought suddenly occurred to her. 'Theresa—Listen to me. Twelve packs of C4 aren't enough to blow up the Sistine Chapel. Where's the rest of the explosive? How much have you got down here?'

The girl looked up. 'One hundred kilos. It's been rammed into one of the shelf tombs directly below the central aisle of the chapel. It's got a wireless link to the timer.'

'When does it go off?'

'I… I don't know. Pretty soon I think. The Conclave is still in session so it won't be long I expect.'

The Conclave is still in session… Theresa's words echoed around inside Elizabeth's mind like ripples in a pond. *The Conclave is still in session…*

'Sterling— What time is it?'

Since her vampire companion was one of the few people on earth who still wore a wristwatch, the answer came back almost immediately.

'It's almost half past six. Why do you ask?'

'Well, don't you think it's a bit late for the first ballot to still be in session. How long have we been down here…? I mean, it seems like an awfully long while.'

'I wouldn't know, Lizzy. I've never attended a Conclave before. Is it usual for things to drag on this late?'

'Can be, depending on the circumstances. But look what it says on the timing mechanism of the bomb. According to the digital clock, it's only 5.29 p.m. and the countdown monitor is reading at two minutes and seventeen seconds. Either your watch is running fast or…'

Elizabeth reached out towards the bomb. Nestled way down among the frantic tangle of wires was a tiny metal switch with a round top. Placing a finger directly beneath the switch, Elizabeth hesitated for a moment while Sterling drew in a sharp breath and Theresa screwed up her eyes.

CLICK—!

* * *

As the votes steadily came in, Foscari kept his head down, concentrating on the list of candidates. Each time a vote was announced, he carefully put a tick against the person's name. So far, the ballot was proceeding more or less as he'd anticipated. Spada had accumulated ten votes in the first ten minutes of the session. This had put him ahead by three votes, with Martinelli running a close second followed by Cardinal Kominski of Chicago and – oddly enough – Cardinal Weatherby, the only Englishman represented at the Conclave. Stranger still was when Foscari heard his own name read out and dutifully ticked himself off the list.

At first he thought nothing of it, but when it happened several more times and at such an early stage of the count, he began to grow alarmed. Whispers were already breaking out around the chapel and a number of cardinals were staring at him from across the aisle. Visions of himself sitting in the Pope's chair began to fill his mind until he could think of nothing else. In such a tight ballot even half a dozen votes could prove enough to swing the election in favour of a rank outsider like himself. Equally true was the fact that one of the early front runners might get three votes in a row and then receive none of the succeeding twenty, so bizarre could be the preliminary stages of a Conclave. Even when a hundred votes had been counted there was still nothing in it. But then something strange happened. Martinelli's vote faltered as the last few names came in and the ballot was closed. Spada was still in the lead but the distribution of the rest of the votes was equally alarming.

Spada 25
Champney 18
Martinelli 16
Foscari 9
Kominski 8
Others 40

The size of his own vote shocked him. It had clearly drawn support away from Martinelli, the only liberal candidate who stood any chance against Spada. The more he studied the figures, the more disappointing for Martinelli they looked. According to his own predictions, the Chief Confessor should have been well placed to be in the lead for the second round, yet Martinelli had come in third behind Champney the Archbishop of Quebec. What on earth was going wrong?

Then he remembered. It was when he'd seen Spada and Lomellini conferring with Champney as they'd walked up the hill towards the Casa Santa Marta a couple of days ago. Spada must have persuaded Champney to split the American block, which most likely explained why Kominski had only got eight votes when he should have scored at least twelve. Still, it wasn't all doom and gloom Foscari concluded. No candidate was anywhere near the two-thirds majority it would take to win the election, and there was always the prospect of the imminent press release concerning Spada's illegal financial dealings to tip the balance in favour of Martinelli when the news finally broke. It was all a question of getting the timing right and catching the Spada camp off-guard between ballots. As there could well be as many as three or four ballots in any one Conclave, that left plenty of time to drop the press release in the public arena and wait for the reaction. It would mean another Vatican banking scandal, but what was the alternative— Hell on earth?

Cardinal Weatherby had finished giving out the results. Holding up the red silk cord on which the ballot papers were threaded, he looked towards the Dean. Taking his cue, Foscari rose from his seat and took the microphone. From where he was standing at the altar step, he could see Martinelli studying the voting figures with a look of concern. Clearing his throat, he began his address to the Conclave:

'Brother cardinals. The first ballot has concluded with no candidate achieving the necessary majority. This being so, we shall now return to the hostel for the evening and resume voting in the morning. Might I also remind you that no written material may be removed from the chapel and that you are not to discuss this afternoon's vote with anyone other than among yourselves or put any information out via a laptop or mobile phone. Thank you for your patience and co-operation.'

Foscari stood and watched as the cardinals filed out of the chapel. Most did not leave the building immediately but gathered in the vestibule to witness their notes and ballot papers being burned in the stove by the doors – the source of the famous black smoke that would soon be rising up through the chimney of the Sistine to inform the world that a new Pope had not yet been elected. As he waited, Foscari caught sight of Martinelli emerging from the chapel and drew him aside. 'Did you speak to the press office?'

'Yes. Be telephone shortly before we assembled.'

'And?'

Martinelli put a finger to his lips to signal caution. Spada was passing by in the company of Champney and two cardinals from the United States. His usual vulpine expression was cheerful, but he did not look well. After they had strolled out into the Sala Regia, Martinelli continued: 'The press release is planned for nine o'clock this evening, and if everything goes according to plan it should hit the newspapers first thing in the morning. The only problem will be the lack of any senior members of the clergy to comment on it. We may have to rely on the bishops.'

Foscari nodded slowly. He had expected as much. 'Who?'

'I'm not altogether certain, but de Valois has access to the files of at least five hundred mid-ranking clerics. I'm sure he'll be able to come up with someone.'

Foscari stared at him. They'd clearly planned this all in advance, though exactly *how far* in advance he couldn't say. How had they known; and, more to the point, what was de Valois doing in possession of so many personal files?

'What's your agenda, Martinelli?'

'Agenda? Why, it's exactly the same as yours, Foscari. Putting the right man on the throne of St Peter's. That is our agenda surely.'

'And Father Donnelly... What was his part in the plan?'

Martinelli laughed. 'I only wish I knew! But I somehow sense that the only one with a plan for this election is God, and so far He seems unwilling to divulge its secrets.'

Foscari became silent considering this. It had been a long day and he was hungry. Suddenly he threw up his hands. 'Let's leave it there. I trust we can at least rely on the support of the Almighty if no one else.'

The Chief Confessor smiled as they walked out of the vestibule towards the waiting coaches. At 7.23 p.m. precisely, the metal chimney above the roof of the Sistine Chapel began to push out jet-black smoke into the evening twilight. Perhaps a new Pope would be elected tomorrow but it would not be today, that much was certain.

* * *

They were still there, all three of them, and they were still in one piece. The bomb hadn't gone off.

'What did you do?' asked Sterling.

Elizabeth grinned. 'This bomb was made by a master craftsman. Whoever put it together gave themselves a get-out switch in case they needed to change the timing of the detonation. All I had to do was switch it off.'

'You mean it's safe?'

'Yes. It's dead. And I somehow doubt if it's got an automatic restart. Jimmy's knowledge of technology is pretty rudimentary, so he wouldn't have known how the bomb was manufactured. In fact, I doubt if he even knows how to use an iphone. Most of the older vampires don't. I mean, if you've got the ability to shapeshift and walk though walls, then who needs an iphone. Face it Sterling, you'll have those powers one day, assuming the Vatican lets you live long enough.'

'You said it, Lizzy. I sure hope my case gets reviewed if I ever get out of this alive. The Vatican owes me big time.'

'Yes, well it's not over yet?'

'What do you mean?'

Elizabeth nodded her head in the direction of the wall that encircled them. 'Look,' she said; 'over there by the archway…'

Sterling looked. An eerie, billowing mist had begun to emerge from the darkness of one of the passageways. She could sense its power as it came on, eventually coalescing into a solitary orb of blue light that glowed like the spectrum of planet Neptune in the inky blackness that surrounded it.

'Jimmy's back—!!'

It was the young nun Theresa who screamed his name. She was cowering behind the marble plinth in a state of abject terror with both hands clamped firmly over her eyes. Now Sterling feared for the worse. It was obvious the girl was beginning to lose it. If she ran now and broke the magic circle of protection, then everything would be lost.

'Slowly, Theresa... You've got to stay calm... Take deep breaths. Nothing's going to happen...'

'THERESA— NO!!'

But it was too late. In one swift movement, the young woman got up and began running in the opposite direction to where the orb had emerged from the passageway. In an instant, she'd crossed the protective chalk circle and was now frantically trying to find an exit from the gladiator's burial chamber in spite of all the warnings from Sterling and Elizabeth to the contrary.

Round and round she sped, completely oblivious to the heavy bomb-load she was carrying. For a moment, Theresa's kinetic display of terror reminded Sterling of how some early Christians must have reacted when they finally came face-to-face with a pack of hungry lions in the Roman arena and decided to make a run for it. All to no avail of course.

'Get back inside the circle!' yelled Sterling. 'It's your only hope—'

The orb had stopped moving now and appeared to be growing in size, taking on the dimensions of a large weather balloon. Then, seemingly satisfied with its rapidly expanded girth, it began moving again in a counter-clockwise direction around the chamber, heading in the direction Theresa was coming from.

Sterling and Elizabeth could only look on in horror as the opalescent ball of blue light hovered above Theresa like some gigantic bird of prey, halting her in her tracks before beginning its slow descent towards the ground directly above where she stood.

'Theresa—Get out of the way! It's going to kill you!!'

But Theresa didn't move. She appeared to be in some kind of a trance, all the attention drawn out of her as the ball of energy continued its relentless descent, slowly crushing her beneath its terrible mass. Only at the last second did she let out a piercing scream as her body, plastic explosives and all, became a crimson smear on the cold mosaic floor, flattened beyond recognition into a bloody mash of rendered flesh and bone, vaguely reminiscent of a day-old piece of roadkill on a busy country road, her face pressed down into the mocking parody of a smile. Then, lingering for a moment as if to gloat over what it had done, the deadly ball of energy rose up from the floor to shoulder height before morphing into something resembling the shape of a man.

'Did that just happen?' exclaimed Elizabeth, her mouth wide open with shock.

'I rather think it did,' Sterling replied, swaying a little on her feet, 'and what's more. I'd hazard a guess and say it's Jimmy Silver who's responsible for it. The question is, what the hell is he going to change into next?'

They didn't have long to find out. As the blue orb continued to alter its shape, a strange transformation was taking place. Whereas before it had seemed to be changing into the form of a man, now it appeared to lengthen and increase in stature until it stood at least eight foot tall on its hind legs – a gigantic feral werewolf with a head to match, staring down at Sterling and Elizabeth from beyond their useless, broken circle of chalk.

'What the fuck—!!'

'It's Jimmy Silver, Elizabeth. I was right. Look at the eyes—'

Sure enough, as Sister Elizabeth gathered up the courage to gaze directly into the creatures face, she could see that its yellow lambent eyes were flecked with black crow feathers at the sides, together with a series of shorter quills that began in a narrow v-shaped ridge just above the browline before rising up to form a majestic avian crest on top of the beast's head.

'That's the clue. Don't you see. Jimmy can turn himself into a crow, and now he's turned himself into a werewolf as well just for our benefit. How many bullets have you got left in that automatic of yours, Lizzy?'

'Only three… How about you?'

'Not many. They're magnum rounds but I somehow doubt if they'll have any effect on that thing. We'll have to think of something else.'

'Such as—?'

Sterling didn't answer. She was too busy listening to another voice. It was the same dry, laconic voice she recognized from another time and it was one she was all-too familiar with. Jimmy was talking directly to her mind using telepathy – an arcane form of communication practiced only by vampires and a small percentage of human Sensitives with the mental stamina to control it. At first she tried to block it out, but experience had taught her that such attempts were at best mostly futile and at worse, just plain dangerous, so she just relaxed and let him come through: *'...It won't do you any good, my dear. This form of mine is way too powerful. I borrowed it from one of my feral friends out in the mountains and melded it with the body of a crow. The blue orb was merely a party trick, but quite effective, don't you think...?'*

'We've disabled your bomb, Jimmy—' She voiced her words but knew they would reach him anyway.

'I know... But it really doesn't matter. It was nothing more than a sideshow anyway. My creature, Lorenzo Spada is still firm-favourite to win the papal election, and Lomellini will be his second in command. Once I've dealt with de Valois and that clown, Foscari, control of the Vatican will be mine. What will you do then Sterling my dear, hmmm?'

She hadn't expected this. The bomb wasn't the main weapon he'd meant to use. It was a distraction, and both de Valois and Martinelli had fallen for it. If Foscari's attention was likewise diverted, then everything would crumble. Hopefully, he might somehow manage to manipulate the election in such a way as to swerve the attention away from Spada and place the vote firmly in the more liberal camp – the Americans perhaps, or maybe Martinelli. Also, there was always the possibility that Foscari might be able to find out more about Spada and Lomellini's involvement with money laundering. If not, then she still had one more card to play on that score, as well as another idea that was beginning to form in her mind...

Reaching into her pocket, she withdrew the slim leather-bound book she was carrying and began thumbing her way through its pages until she found what she was looking for. At the sight of the ancient grimoire, the werewolf twitched its head to one side and growled. Jimmy had recognized the book as his own but didn't fully understand the significance of what it was she was about to do. He was still hesitant to cross the chalk circle even though Theresa's panic-stricken flight had drained it of much of its power.

'What are you going to do?' said Elizabeth, still clutching her Beretta pistol like it was the last gun on earth. 'This is no time to be catching up on your reading.'

Sterling didn't answer, but simply motioned her companion to remain silent as she knelt down in front of the marble plinth and began memorizing the dead gladiator's epitaph before turning back to Elizabeth and removing a small, white cylindrical object out of the same pocket she'd taken the book from.

'What's that?'

'It's the right arm-bone of Saint Bartholemew of Sienna – a section of the ulna to be precise. It's a religious relic de Valois gave me. It also functions as a flute apparently.'

'A flute…? How's that going to save us?'

'Stand back and watch, Lizzy.'

Elizabeth looked on as her companion began muttering some words from the book she was holding. The words were strange and unfamiliar but she guessed they might be Etruscan in origin – she couldn't be sure. Then Sterling put the bone-flute to her lips and blew three clear notes before intoning what could only be taken as a command to the spirit world:

'…Publius Lupercus, gladiator and slayer of wolves – rise up from the dead and protect us from the man-wolf who has taken on a form that is most unclean. I request the Master of the Woods to grant this, my true desire and wish. So mote it be…!!'

Sister Elizabeth looked shocked: 'Sterling – You're calling up the dead. That's necromancy; you realize that!?'

'Well spotted, Lizzy.'

'But you called on the Master of the Woods... He's... I mean he's...'

'Yeah, I guess he is, Liz. You got any better ideas?'

'Well, no, but—'

Something was happening. The ground beneath their feet had begun trembling – ever so slightly at first, but growing in intensity until Elizabeth noticed a small section of the mosaic floor start to break apart to reveal what she took to be the outline of a bronze helmet enclosing the cadaverous head of a man long since dead. To her astonishment, this skeletal figure just kept on rising up out of its death-pit until it stood, legs apart in a fighting stance, a full six foot tall and clutching a small rectangular shield together with the most lethal curved sword she'd ever seen in her life.

'He's a Thrax! Publius Lupercus was a Thrax!!'

'A *what?*' Sterling answered, barely listening.

'Publius Lupercus was a Thracian gladiator. You can tell by the type of sword he's carrying. Sterling, you've brought a Thracian wolf-slayer back from the dead—'

'Course I have. What did you think I was going to do? We're down to our last six bullets and Silver's gone and morphed himself into a werewolf for fuck sake. If a Thracian wolf-killer can't deal with a werewolf then I don't know who can!'

The werewolf snarled, prompting Sterling to respond:

'BACK OFF SILVER!! I don't know how much power you've got, but it's not going to work, you hear me!'

There was no reply. The huge grey wolf just stood there on its hind legs, towering over everyone in the chamber, including the phantom gladiator. The only thing that was different was the colour of its eyes; for whereas before they had been a dull, lambent yellow, now they became a bright glowing orange, reminiscent of a newly risen dawn. From somewhere deep inside the belly of the beast came a low rumbling growl that steadily increased until it broke from the creature's jaws as a full-throated howl, causing everything in the chamber to vibrate with its resonance.

Sister Elizabeth clamped both hands over her ears to blot out the sound while the long-dead gladiator merely shifted his position to steel myself for the inevitable attack of the wolfman when it came. Sterling smiled. She knew Publius Lupercus would give a good account of himself if he had to.

Here goes... she thought as she drew out her Noguchi Magnum once more and aimed it squarely at the werewolf's torso.

'*An impressive weapon, my dear...*' came Silver's thought directly into her mind... '*But there's nothing you or your Thracian friend can do to stop me from killing you or your companion over there. I have decided that Sister Elizabeth shall suffer the same fate as Theresa. Call it a Catholic Martyrdom if you like. As for yourself, I might even decide to let you live, if only to see how long you can last on your own once I'm in charge of the Vatican and the Bene Noctu. Barely a few days I should expect. A week if you're lucky!*'

Silver had edged his way closer to the circle by now. His lupine hands, covered in fur, displayed long, six-inch claws, sharp enough to rip out a human heart in a matter of seconds. For a moment, Sterling caught a mental impression of herself being lifted off the ground in those powerful claws and lowered head-first into the creature's mouth. It was then that she thought she heard the gladiator mutter something in broken Latin. It sounded like a warding spell, but she couldn't be certain. Maybe he was buying her some time.

'Silver's going to attack,' exclaimed Elizabeth, her voice fractured with terror.

'Tell me something I don't already know,' Sterling snapped. 'Our friend, Lupercus over there is holding him off with a warding spell. It's likely some old wolf-charm he learned before the Roman's collared him and turned him into a circus attraction. Looks like I'm going to have to call in the marines as well. Silver's grown too damn powerful for me these days.'

'What are you going to do, Sterling?'

'Stand back Lizzy—This is going to be simply awesome!'

Elizabeth looked on as her friend retrieved the bone flute and put it too her lips, this time blowing gently on the mouthpiece to produce a single musical note. Then, opening the book at a different page, she read out a few words in Latin before completing the incantation in English with the words: 'In the name of Astaroth, master of the world, I command the spirit of Logan the machine-gunner to appear before me. Released from Hell, he shall respect and obey my every command. Appear! Appear! Appear!!'

At first nothing happened in the underground chamber apart from the steady hum of the air conditioning unit changing over into a different phase. Then, just as Elizabeth was about to exclaim that the spell hadn't worked, Sterling pointed to the floor a little way to the right of where they were standing.

Elizabeth looked on in horror as another section of the floor began to heave up and then give way to reveal the shape of a large man wearing combat fatigues and clutching what looked like a heavy, battlefield machine-gun in both hands. The man rose up slowly out of the ground and stood silently facing them as if he were waiting for instructions.

'But he's got no head, Sterling! That thing's got no fucking head—!!'

'He's called Logan the Headless Machine-Gunner, Elizabeth. He's something of an urban legend in certain part of the world. Logan was an American mercenary who got himself involved in a number of covert operations during the Vietnam War back in 1969. Guilty of numerous acts of genocide, he fast became an embarrassment to the Pentagon who decided to put CIA hitman on his tail to take him out. The hitman shot him at close range and blew his head off, hence the nickname "Logan the Headless Machine-Gunner." Time stands still for Logan now until he can even up the score and atone for all his sins. Because of the many crimes he committed while serving in Vietnam, he is fated to walk the earth forever, hunting down those as evil as himself until such time as he can reclaim his soul from Hell and find eternal rest with the Lord.'

'And he's on our side, right…?'

'Yes, Lizzy. He's bound to us for the duration, and will obey none other than ourselves.'

'Great. When do we start?'

'Just as soon as I invite our friend Jimmy Silver over there to discuss his bank account details with me. Stand back Lizzy. I've a feeling things are about to turn nasty.'

Elizabeth stood to one side as her companion held the book open at the front flyleaf. For a moment, the creature swayed on its hind legs then growled, prompting Sterling to unleash her attack: 'These *are* your bank details, aren't they, Jimmy...?'

The werewolf looked first at Sterling and then at the book with a dawning sense of realization. He'd seen the partially encoded information and knew what it might imply.

The wolf's lambent eyes seemed to grow larger. Now they were rimmed with red. A rich, dark ruby red that soon began to glow like the fires of Hell. Then the wolf leaned forward and, very deliberately, stared directly into her face.

He's trying to hypnotize me. And maybe he is a little. But maybe I'm too old for such things now...

Silver was inside her head in an instant, striking this way and that like a rattlesnake on amphetamines. She moaned as his will crashed into hers, ransacking her mind for any negative emotion it could latch onto. But she would not yield.

'*Why are you fighting, my dear? There's no denying me. I am your creator. I granted you eternal life. I made you what you are today. You should be grateful, really you should.*'

'Grateful for what, Jimmy? I didn't ask to be the way I am.'

'*Yes, but you reaped the benefit of it, didn't you? It's not many humans who possess the ability to manipulate the population in the same way that creatures like us do. One day you'll be a shapeshifter like myself. Imagine the power you could wield then, hmmm? And you would no longer have to slaughter the innocent and drink their blood.*'

'But I never killed the innocent—!!' She spoke these words out loud, but the thought died in her mind all the same. All those acts of carnage she'd committed over the past four decades just in order to feed – some of them must have been innocent victims. There was simply no way of telling.

'*How many?*' She heard Silver's mocking voice inside her head again. He was trying to undermine her will to fight by making her doubt herself. Well, two could play at that game.

'We've clashed like this before, Jimmy. It won't work!'

'*Ha! But you're running out of time, my dear. In case you hadn't noticed, I'm way too strong for you now.*'

'Oh really. Well you won't feel so damn superior once you've heard the bad news.'

'Bad news... What bad news?' Jimmy Silver's adoptive wolf-form shimmered and became slightly transparent. He was losing control. She knew she'd hit a raw nerve and immediately pressed home her advantage.

'Your bank accounts, Jimmy... And those of your associates...'

'What about them?' His voice seemed to tremble and waver in the psychic ether. It was almost as if he were trying to vocalize his thoughts through his wolf jaws but nature wouldn't allow him to. Quickly, Sterling threw him a sucker punch:

'I've torched the accounts, Jimmy. All of them...'

The werewolf stiffened and clenched its paws in disbelief as she continued:

'...And what's more, I've transferred all the money into the Vatican Bank. It should do more good in there than in your filthy paws. Maybe Foscari will put it to better use when he becomes the next Pope!'

'WHA-A-AT—!!'

'Yes, I thought that would surprise you, Jimmy. I had it all wired to the Vatican Bank. You see – all those codes in the book – well, they weren't really codes at all were they? As for Cardinal Foscari, I dare say the white smoke will soon be billowing out of the Sistine Chapel chimney before very long, don't you think?'

Sister Elizabeth never forgot what happened next for as long as she lived. The memory of it was permanently etched on her mind for the rest of her life. Everything went quiet for a moment as if to mirror that small interval of time before any great battle commences. Then:

A long resonant howl broke from the werewolf's mouth. From where she was situated, crouched down low behind the skeletal gladiator, Elizabeth could see what she took to be two smoky tendrils of vapour slowly emerge from the wolf's body and begin snaking their way over the broken circle of chalk to where her companion was standing.

'FU-U-U-UCK YOU-U-U—!!' bellowed Sterling as she opened up on the wolf with her magnum revolver, but it was too late. As the smoky black tendrils of ectoplasm reached her, Sterling could feel the icy chill of Silver's phantom hands penetrate her body and lock themselves around her lungs with an overwhelming grip. He was literally trying to squeeze the life out of her in a frenzied rage.

The werewolf grinned. She was quite sure it was grinning now, even though its features had now warped a little, morphing themselves into the vague suggestion of a crow. A crow with bright red eyes.

Strong as she was, Sterling was unable to break free from those terrible icy hands, and slowly she felt herself starting to black out as a constellation of stars began to dance in front of her eyes.

'Lizzy— Use your pistol on him! I'm starting to lose it.'

Fighting her terror, the nun stood up, bringing her Beretta into the firing position in a quick, sure motion more expertly than she could ever have dreamed.

'EAT THIS!' she thundered, and squeezed the trigger.

But the trigger would not move. Something was blocking it, and it wasn't the safety catch. The gun was jammed solid for some reason and the trigger wouldn't budge. Silver was stopping the firing mechanism with the power of his mind. What could she do?

It was then that she began to pray, and she prayed like she'd never prayed before:

'Holy Father, get me out of this shit right now!!'

As if on cue, the skeletal gladiator shifted his stance and clashed his curved Thracian sword against the rim of his shield. This had the effect of distracting the wolf long enough for Sterling to take a breath and yell out a command to the headless machine-gunner:

'Logan— Fire at the werewolf! That's an order—'

Heavy machine-guns of the Vietnam War era were truly awesome weapons for their time. They were the sort of artillery often seen poking out of the gun-doors of US military helicopters, strafing the shite out of innocent peasants working in the rice fields below. The sound they made was really quite unique:

THRRR – THRRRR – THRRRRR.....

The huge gun rattled out its tungsten-tipped ammo hitting the wolfman squarely in the chest. As he took the bullets, Silver staggered back, his body fragmenting into a myriad chunks of raw flesh and bone that were virtually unrecognizable as to the manner of creature he had been barely a few moment before.

It was then that the gladiator made his move, stepping forward and slicing through the wolf's neck with a single swordstroke almost to the point of decapitation. As the beast dropped to the floor, the gladiator stood back and became motionless once more as if awaiting further orders. Logan too became relaxed, cradling his machine-gun in both hands. His task was done and he was getting ready to descend back down into the infernal realms from whence he'd came.

Everything became silent now. Not a breath of air, nor the sound of a scampering rat disturbed the arid-stillness of the gladiator's tomb. Dawn was fast approaching and the witching hour had long since passed.

'Is he dead?' exclaimed Elizabeth, wiping the blood-mist from her face. It was a reasonable question to ask but she should have known better.

'Silver's been dead for years, Lizzy. What we really need to know is if he managed to turn himself into a *real* werewolf.'

'A *rougarou,* you mean?'

'Yes! That's what bothers me, Liz. And look— Here it comes now. Silver's spirit is starting to rise already. *'Oh Jimmy, you fucking, fucking bastard...'*

'This isn't finished,' came an all-too familiar voice from the steadily rising column of smoke that was emerging from the shattered body of the wolf. As the wolf's body began to burn, the column of smoke increased in density and turned into a blue sphere that floated upwards until it dissolved itself through the ceiling of the tomb. Bracing herself for the onslaught, Sterling prepared for the final battle, but it never came. Whatever damage Logan and the gladiator had done, it had succeeded in putting Silver out of action for a considerable period of time. His power was spent for the duration and it was now breaking dawn. Light was finally returning to the world and not a moment too soon.

'This ends here, Jimmy – Is that understood?' was all Sterling said in response. Then, with a gesture of her hand, she dismissed Logan and the gladiator who now began to sink back down beneath the earth from whence they'd sprung.

'Is that it then?' said Elizabeth, lowering her Beretta.

'Yes, for the time being, I dare say it is. We've busted Silver's criminal empire and given him a shock. I reckon we've put him back a hundred years or more.'

'So we can leave now…?'

'I don't see why not, though Christ knows what the Vatican cleaners are going to make of that floor when they open this place up in the morning. It fucking stinks in here.'

As they slowly made their way out of the catacombs, Elizabeth turned to her companion with a questioning look. 'There's something I've been meaning to ask you, Sterling.'

'Oh yeah… And what's that, Lizzy?'

'What exactly did you mean about Cardinal Foscari becoming the next Pope?'

Sterling smiled. 'Oh, it was nothing, Liz. Just don't forget to buy yourself a new frock when you're next in town, that's all. Now, come on you. Let's get going. I've a feeling the fireworks are about to start at the Conclave.'

22

The bell had already rung for Mass by the time Foscari dragged himself out of bed and headed for the shower. He was late, but the fact of the matter didn't seem to bother him. There were other things on his mind. The press release for one.

As he dressed himself, his hands trembled at the thought of what the day might bring. It was the morning of the second ballot and the future of the papacy was at stake – no, not only the future of the papacy but also the future of mankind itself, and he still hadn't heard anything about the press release. Had it somehow been intercepted he wondered?

He paused and told himself to remain calm. Surely everything was in order and Martinelli had arranged for the press release to go out around nine o'clock the night before. If everything went according to plan, the news concerning Spada's involvement with international drug trafficking and money laundering would become common knowledge and pretty soon every street café in Rome would be buzzing with it.

But there was a snag—

With every senior member of the clergy holed up in the Casa Santa Marta celebrating Mass before they were ferried off to the Sistine Chapel for the ballot, how could the news be brought to their attention in time to influence the second vote?

His only hope now lay with the bishops. If, as Martinelli had said, de Valois had enough influence among the bishops, then maybe – just maybe – one of them might be able to get the news through to the Conclave before it sat.

But how?

Foscari shook his head and glanced in the mirror. They'd seriously mistimed the press release, hadn't they. There he was, all kitted out in his cardinal's regalia – cassock, cincture, mozzetta and zucchetto – the Dean of the Conclave, ready to take Mass with his peers, including Lorenzo Spada. It all seemed so unreal.

* * *

The ground floor chapel was housed in an annex attached to the main building. As the cardinals all trooped in to celebrate Mass, Foscari became aware of a somber mood among them. At first he put this down to the modernist design of the chamber with its vaulted ceiling of wooden beams and glass, more reminiscent of a car dealer's showroom than any focus of religious devotion. But pretty soon he realized that their low spirits were more occasioned by thoughts of the outcome of the election than any effect of architecture.

It was Martinelli who gave the liturgy. A couple of days ago he'd offered to take charge of the morning Mass, and Foscari had been only too pleased to let him, given all the other business he had to attend to. Unfortunately, Martinelli wasn't quite up to the task. His singing voice, once the pride of the Vatican, had so altered over the years that it now more resembled a burst of bad radio-static than the clear diction required of a practiced celebrant. When Foscari finally stood in line to receive the Communion, the thought occurred to him that Martinelli's delivery of the liturgy had probably cost the Chief Confessor at least thirty votes in the forthcoming second ballot.

Spada, who was last to receive the host, skillfully avoided eye-contact with Foscari as he returned to his seat. In spite of his recently diagnosed heart condition, he seemed to be in a buoyant mood, confidant in the knowledge that by lunchtime he would most likely be the next Pope.

After Mass was over, some of the cardinals remained behind to pray, including Foscari who sat motionless in his seat staring blankly at the altar. But he wasn't praying. He was thinking…

Why was he still alive? Yes, that was it! The bomb hadn't gone off. It was almost as if a great shadow had been lifted from the world. At least that was how it felt, even if Spada was still a threat to the integrity of the papacy. But there was still the issue of the press release. Why, oh why had Martinelli left it so late? He badly needed some media exposure of Spada's involvement with dark money before the cardinals sat for the ballot. Once they were all locked up again in the Sistine

Chapel for the next vote, it would be too late. Nothing short of a miracle could stop Spada now.

'Help me, O Lord at my hour of need.' Foscari whispered as he rose from his seat and followed the last of the cardinals out of the chapel and into the dining hall for breakfast.

Philipe Champney was not at his usual place. Checking the room, Foscari noticed him seated opposite Spada and Lomellini, and they were deep in conversation. It was then that Foscari's suspicions were confirmed. Cardinal Champney was going to split the North American vote and allow Spada a clear run at the title, pulling the remaining votes he needed away from Kominski, the archbishop of Chicago. It was already a done deal.

Taking a seat between the archbishops of Cologne and Mainz, the Dean tried to make polite conversation, but his heart wasn't in it. As the silences became more prolonged, the two Germans politely excused themselves and went to the buffet to collect their food while Foscari remained where he was. He already had his toast and cereal but wasn't in the mood to eat it. His eyes were on Lorenzo Spada and Philipe Champney, the archbishop of Quebec.

Once more he ran the figures of the first ballot through his head. Yes, it made perfect sense for Spada to curry favour with Champney. If Kominski was neutralized, then the American block would collapse and the remaining 40 votes could well slide in Spada's favour. At least, they certainly wouldn't be voting for Martinelli after his less than satisfactory delivery of the Mass.

Raising his head, Foscari watched the nuns as they served coffee. Clad in their blue habits and headdresses, they moved between the tables in total silence, their downcast eyes and modest demeanor setting them apart from everything else going on in the dining hall. He presumed they were under strict orders not to speak with any members of the electorate, and when one nun in particular poured out coffee for Lorenzo Spada, he did not even turn to acknowledge her presence, merely carrying on his conversation with Cardinal Champney as she tilted the jug towards his cup, filling it up almost to the brim in an extraordinarily focused and precise manner. There was something peculiar in the way she lingered for a moment, passing her hand over the cup before moving on unnoticed to the next table as if her every movement and gesture had been designed to conceal her identity from all human memory. Indeed, he could not make out exactly who she was because she had not at any one time turned to look in his direction.

Choosing a suitable moment, Foscari rose to his feet and announced that it was high time to assemble in the Sistine Chapel. Following the cardinals out of the dining hall, he spotted Monsignor Brevet standing in the lobby with his clipboard. After a brief conversation, Brevet signaled one of the Swiss Guards to unlock the front door and allow the Dean to exit the building. Foscari had chosen to walk the short distance to the Sistine Chapel in order to clear his thoughts, and his decision to do so had not gone unnoticed among the rest of the assembly, not least Cardinal Spada, Lomellini and Philipe Champney who followed his progress with their eyes until he was out of sight.

Stepping outside into the daylight, he felt the breeze on his face. The cool morning air refreshed his spirits after the oppressive atmosphere of the Casa Santa Marta and he set off at a brisk pace across the piazza in the direction of the Vatican gardens, discreetly tailed by one of the security guards who had followed him out of the door.

Apart from the line of minibuses parked around the edge of the square, each with its own security guard, the area was remarkably free of traffic, having been cordoned off for the duration of the election. By the time Foscari reached the gardens, there were more security men present, lurking behind the trees in small groups or patrolling the grounds with dogs on the lookout for intruders.

Turning off the road, Foscari wandered past a fountain towards a gap in the trees. From where he was standing, he had a view across the city and the hills of Rome. The thought occurred to him that whoever was elected the next Pope would never again be able to wander the streets of that city or drink coffee with their friends at a sidewalk café, forever a prisoner inside the confines of the Vatican. The idea of it appalled him, and he secretly prayed that whoever became the next Vicar of Christ, it would not be him.

A sound of rustling leaves disturbed his meditations. Turning round, he caught sight of a security man stepping out from behind the cover of a laurel bush speaking into a walkie-talkie. The man was looking back down the road, and when Foscari followed his line of sight, he saw what the problem was. Several other cardinals had decided to follow him on his morning walk and were now hastening towards him at a pace that belied their years. Foscari promptly made to leave, trying to avoid them, but the frontrunner of the pack merely quickened his pace and caught him up. Immediately, Foscari knew who it was... *and it wasn't a cardinal.*

'Good morning, Bishop Gerritsen. And what can I do for you this fine morning?'

The man was out of breath and had an expression of urgency in his eyes, as did all the other churchmen who were with him. They at least were cardinals, though it was noticeable that both de Valois and Martinelli were absent from the delegation. Foscari sensed that something was amiss, but waited for Gerritsen to speak first as they carried on walking in the direction of the Apostolic Palace closely followed by the others. Eventually the bishop opened up and made the first move:

'Excuse me, Dean. I'm sorry to interrupt your morning walk but there's something I really must tell you. I hope you won't find it too alarming...'

'That would depend on what it is,' replied Foscari guardedly.

Ambrose Gerritsen pursed his lower lip and glanced at the others. One of the cardinals nodded, prompting him to reach into his thin leather briefcase and take out a newspaper: 'I don't suppose you've had much opportunity to read the morning papers, Dean, but you really must see this. It's all over the front page...'

Foscari regarded the flustered cleric with a degree of sympathy. He knew exactly what it was that was bothering Bishop Gerritsen and his little deputation, and suppressed a smile. Feigning ignorance, he took the partially scrolled newspaper from Gerritsen's hand and reached for his reading glasses. His close vision was still reasonably good but the print was quite small – except for the headlines of course...

VATICAN DRUG SCANDAL!!!
TWO CARDINALS IMPLICATED

That was well-timed, thought Foscari speed-reading the article. The story was spread across the first three pages of the newspaper and it was quite precise and detailed too, in spite of the lurid headlines. Cardinal de Valois had done a good job in getting the only available bishop in the vicinity to smuggle it through to the Conclave. 'Nice one, de Valois...'

'Pardon me?'

'Uh...? Oh, nothing. I was just thinking out loud, that's all,' Foscari replied glancing up at Gerritsen with feigned shock. 'This is terrible news. A Vatican banking scandal right in the middle of a papal election. Have the police been informed?'

'The anti-fraud units have already arrived, Your Eminence, but Vatican security have denied them access as yet.'

'Good—'

'What do you mean, *good?* The Guardia di Finanza are practically banging on our doors, Paolo!!! What are we going to do?'

'Do—? Carry on with the election, that's what we're going to do.'

'But the news... How are we going to elect a new Pope with all of this going on?'

'Because there's nothing to stop us, Ambrose... *and because we do the Lord's will.* At least, I haven't heard anything else to the contrary.'

'So we just go ahead and vote?' put in one of the cardinals incredulously.

'I don't see why not brothers. Are we not God's representatives on earth?'

'Well if you put it that way Dean, I suppose we are, though I must confess, I'd never thought of it quite like that before.'

Foscari regarded the bishop in surprise. 'But it is the crux of the matter surely.'

'Belief...?'

'Belief, yes. But also faith.'

The group of cardinals looked about themselves with a mixture of shame and realization. Some of them nodded in agreement and one of them spoke:

'The Dean is right. Above all, we must have faith. Faith in God and faith in ourselves. I trust that when this election is over, your wise words will be broadcast from the highest platform of the Church. *The very highest,*' he repeated with emphasis. 'And I trust you understand what it is that I am saying, Dean Foscari. Now, if we're all in agreement, I think it's high time we got a move on. We have a new Pope to elect.'

* * *

The cardinals assembled in the Sistine Chapel, each man taking the same seat they had occupied the day before. When the doors were finally closed, Foscari called for prayer and then opened the proceedings.

'My brothers. We shall now begin the second ballot. Will the scrutineers all take your positions please.'

Vosko, Weatherby and the other man stood up from behind their desks and made their way to the front of the chapel. All eyes were now on Foscari, but, strangely enough, they were not on Lorenzo Spada who remained seated on the other side of the aisle looking oddly distracted. He looked grey and agitated, like a man in the first stages of suffering a major stroke. 'Apparently, he has a heart condition,' whispered one of the cardinals sitting next to de Valois who promptly acknowledged this observation with a curt nod but said nothing in reply. Spada was no longer his main concern.

Leaving the altar and returning to his seat, Foscari picked up his ballot paper and once again wrote his nomination in big bold capital letters: **MARTINELLI.** Then he folded the ballot and went back to the altar, holding the paper high up in the air with the words, 'I call on Christ as my witness that my vote is given to the one who before God I believe should be elected.'

Placing his vote on the chalice, he tipped it ceremoniously into the urn and went back to his seat, lowering his head in solemn prayer. In the end, it took a full hour and forty minutes for all the votes to be cast, and when the last man had voted, Cardinal Vosko lifted the filled urn of ballots and showed it to the Conclave. Then the scrutineers followed the same procedure as before, Cardinal Weatherby transferring the folded ballots to the second urn, counting each one out loud until he reached 116. Following that, he and another cardinal set up a table and three chairs in front of the altar. Vosko then covered the table with a white cloth and set the urn upon it. Foscari took up his pen and awaited the announcements with nervous anticipation. He did not recognize the third member of the trio who had helped set up the table and did not recall his name. Come to think of it, he'd been unable to get a good look at the man's face which always seemed to be held out of his line of vision.

Weatherby took the vote that the nameless man had drawn out of the urn and pierced the ballot with his needle and thread before leaning into the microphone: 'The first vote cast in the second ballot is for Cardinal Foscari—'

For a brief moment, Foscari thought he was dreaming. He had about as much chance of becoming the next Pope as someone entering the State Lottery on a single ticket. But when the next name read out was also his own, then Martinelli's, then Foscari's again, he began to have second thoughts. Either his mind was playing tricks on him, or Bishop Gerritsen had done an absolutely brilliant job of smearing Spada's reputation within the Conclave. Then three votes came in for Champney and he began to relax. He could work with Champney if the man was elected Pope. At least Philipe Champney wasn't the Antichrist and he still had de Valois and Martinelli to back him up. Maybe Champney could be controlled in the same way. Maybe...

'The eighth vote cast in the second ballot is for Cardinal Foscari—'

'The ninth vote cast in the second ballot is for Cardinal Foscari—'

'The tenth vote cast in the second ballot is for Cardinal Foscari—'

No— It just wasn't possible! This couldn't be happening in the second ballot. The second ballot was only for eliminating all the Third World no-hopers; not for actually electing the Pope. There were only three people left in the running – Martinelli, Champney and himself. How come?

The next name read out was that of an African cardinal, then Martinelli's again, followed by an interval when Foscari's name wasn't mentioned at all. For a moment, he breathed a sigh of relief, but then all the votes started coming in thick and fast causing him to run his pen up and down the list of candidates, ticking off each name as it was announced. By the time Weatherby read out the final name, Foscari had gathered a grand total of 91 votes in favour of himself, more than enough to secure him an easy majority in the election.

Until this time, Foscari's position as Dean had made him feel detached from the Conclave – a mere overseer of the whole affair. Now he was its product, and even when he tried to accept the idea, his mind reeled at the thought of all it might imply. He'd just been elected as the new Pope and leader of millions of Catholics throughout the whole world.

The air suddenly became chilly. Through the upper windows came a strange murmuring noise, soft and strong. All the cardinals looked at one another. They couldn't think what it might be, but Foscari recognized it immediately. It was the sound of thousands of people assembling in St Peter's Square. The hour had finally arrived.

Then there came another sound, like the fluttering wings of a huge flock of birds. It was an outbreak of applause from the assembled cardinals, and none clapped more loudly than Martinelli. There were even a few cheers from the opposite side of the chamber, while close by, Cardinal de Valois sat in silent contemplation with both his hands clasped together beneath his chin. There was a smile on his face.

'You... *You* did this,' hissed Foscari angrily. He was not a proud man and the idea of him becoming God's representative on earth filled him with dread.

'I...? I did nothing, Paolo,' replied de Valois. 'It was all the Will of God. I merely handled some of the details. Bishop Gerritsen for one and Sterling for another. She's damn good in a fight.'

'But how did you know it was to be me?'

The exorcist didn't answer. Instead, he just stood up from his chair, an act that was taken as a signal for the entire Conclave to rise to its feet in a standing ovation. Foscari alone remained seated while all the other cardinals looked down on him applauding him, a tiny figure lost among a sea of scarlet vestments.

Normally it was the practice for the Dean to make the formal announcement of the outcome of the election, but since it was the Dean who had been elected, it now fell to the Cardinal-Deacon to summon the Secretary of the College and call for the doors of the chapel to be opened. Then he went up to the microphone and read from the constitution:

'In the name of the College of Cardinals, I ask you, Cardinal Foscari, do you accept your election as Supreme Pontiff?'

Foscari did not look up. Instead, he just sat quietly whispering the breath of a prayer: *'Lord I am not worthy... Holy Mary have mercy on me... Holy Mary have mercy on me...'*

'Do you accept?' came the Deacon's voice, only more insistent this time.

At last, Foscari raised his head. His eyes contained a glimmer of sadness. He stood up. 'I accept.'

The Cardinal-Deacon smiled and turned his head to the crowd in a gesture of relief. 'And by what name do you wish to be called as Pope?'

Foscari paused. He had no name to hand because he had not expected to be elected. Then he cleared his throat:

'GREGORY—! I shall be called Pope Gregory in honour of he who was so cruelly taken from us.' And as he said these words, he turned to look at Cardinal Spada in triumph only to find that Spada had already vacated his chair and was now hurrying down the aisle in the direction of the open doors clutching his chest. A few minutes later, he was found lying dead outside the Sistine Chapel, the victim of a massive heart seizure that had killed him instantly before anyone had a chance to intervene. An ambulance was quickly summoned to ferry him to hospital where he was pronounced dead on arrival and the last rites administered to him by a priest. Not long after this, white smoke billowed against a clear blue sky and the crowds all cheered in St Peter's Square. A new Pope had been elected.

EPILOGUE

They were sitting in the papal apartments drinking coffee; Cardinal de Valois, Sterling, Martinelli, Sister Elizabeth and the new Pope, all of them relieved it was over. Paolo Foscari no longer carried the name he'd been born with. He was now Pope Gregory, and it was a name he would take with him to the grave. He knew this to be true and had somehow come to accept it, albeit reluctantly.

'All's well that ends well, Paolo,' exclaimed Martinelli, before adding: 'or should I call you Holy Father…?'

'Gregory will be fine,' replied the Pope taking a sip from his cup. He was clad all in white, and the light seemed to emanate from his person like the steady glow of a candle flame. Now the administrator was a true believer and it showed. Sterling had to avert her eyes. She was a creature from a wholly different order of existence and knew she couldn't remain long in his presence. The power that shone from his body was simply too overwhelming.

Pope Gregory put down his coffee cup. 'You know,' he said; 'there's just one thing that I don't fully understand.'

'Mmm, and what is that?' inquired de Valois arching an eyebrow.

'Lorenzo Spada – How did he die? I mean, we knew he had a heart condition, but it was nothing very serious. I've just been reading his medical records and there's nothing to suggest any reason for concern.'

Sister Elizabeth glanced at de Valois then carried on serving the coffee without changing her expression. It was then that the Pope recalled sitting in the dining hall watching Cardinal Spada engaged in his conversation with Philipe Champney, and a glimmer of memory came into his mind. There was a nun – he hadn't seen her face. She had passed her hand deftly over Spada's cup while he was looking the other way. Could it have been her he wondered? 'Ah, this world; it is a wicked place,' he murmured gazing down at his pectoral crucifix.

'It's not the world that's wicked,' put in Sterling with a smile; 'It's the people in it.'

'Amen to that,' replied Martinelli clearing his throat before gently singing a Requiem. His voice was sweet and clear this time, quite unlike his previous performance during the Mass in the Casa Santa Marta chapel.

'You did it deliberately, didn't you,' said Pope Gregory once Martinelli had finished the Requiem.

The Chief Confessor blinked and lowered his head. Ashamed.

'You deliberately sang the liturgy at the Mass badly so it would lose you sufficient votes to secure my election as Pope. Am I correct?'

Martinelli could not refuse a question by the Holy Father and simply replied in the affirmative: 'Yes, Holy Father. It was the only way to ensure your victory if the poisoning of Cardinal Spada had failed to work. We simply had no other choice.'

'Thought so,' continued Gregory holding out his cup for a refill by Sister Elizabeth. 'I can't say that I approve of your actions, though in the circumstances I can perhaps absolve you of your sins. I hereby promote you to the office of Chamberlain in the absence of Lorenzo Spada. He won't be needing the position any more, so you may as well have it. As for you, de Valois, you may as well remain in your post as Chief Exorcist. You seem more than adequately qualified for the job, *especially with the sort of company you keep.'*

Sterling grinned, showing her teeth: 'You think of everything as being up there in heaven, don't you Paolo; but the fact of the matter is that the Universe doesn't work like that. If it did, then creatures like me and Jimmy Silver wouldn't exist, would we?'

'God is love, Sterling. At least, that is what I've always been taught to believe.'

'God is also sex, death and suicide, Paolo! If you'd had my life you'd have realized that by now.

The Pope considered the vampire's words. 'That was a good answer Sterling. Perhaps it is true that the Light cannot exist without darkness, but personally I choose the Light.'

'Some of us had no choice, Holy Father. I didn't choose to be the way I am.'

'*Neither did I,*' replied Paolo softly. There was a shadow of regret in his voice that spoke volumes. 'I didn't choose to be the Pope, nor did I choose to join the Church. It chose me. I'm only just coming to realize that now, though it's taken me an awfully long time to find out.'

'Amen to that,' exclaimed de Valois wryly. Turning to Sterling, he smiled. 'So what's the plan now, *mon ami?* Thinking of taking over Silver's empire now that he's gone?'

The vampire curled her lip and looked at him hard. 'Silver's not gone, de Valois. You know that.'

'Indeed I do my dear, but you gave him such a good kicking this time round that I doubt very much if he'll show his face again in a long while. As for Lomellini, he's holed up in a convent somewhere trying to avoid arrest by the anti-fraud unit. He's out of the picture too.'

'Then you'll have no further need of me…?'

'Yes, Sterling. You are correct. That will be all for now. You may depart to your own native land. Your services are no longer required here.'

The Pope gave Sterling a gentle wave as she made her exit from the room escorted by two members of the Swiss Guard dressed in their full ceremonial uniforms. She was clearly getting the VIP treatment and secretly reveled in it. What a tale she would have to tell when she finally arrived back in London. No one would ever believe her.

Turning to de Valois, the Pope had a quiet word. 'I do believe you're smitten by her, Edward. Surely you're not in love?'

Blushing slightly, Cardinal de Valois considered the Pope's observation carefully before delivering his answer:

'Ah…*mon Dieu,* Holy Father; but who could not fail to love her? She's so vicious!'

ABOUT THE AUTHOR

Ian Robert Bell was born in Newcastle-upon-Tyne, England in 1955. He studied for an MA degree at York University in 1979 before working as a picture restorer in a number of art galleries and museums in the north of England, including those of the city of Sheffield where he now lives. Though a restorer of paintings by profession, he took up creative writing as his main occupation in 2002 and works primarily in the mystery/thriller end of the literary spectrum. He is also the author of several other books, including: *London Underground, The Beauty and the Blood, Resurrection Blues* and *The Black Rose.*

Milton Keynes UK
Ingram Content Group UK Ltd.
UKHW020641310723
426074UK00019B/1392